Heaven and Other Zip Codes

A Novel

Mathieu Cailler

PRAISE FOR *Heaven and Other Zip Codes*

"Beautifully crafted with incredible range, *Heaven and Other Zip Codes* gives us an older and more soulful Holden Caulfield in protagonist Emerson Toffler. With lows "as deep as the Titanic's stemware...and ups Kilimanjaro-like", readers will fall in love with this page-turning, brilliant novel."

—Niles Reddick author of the
Pulitzer-nominated *Drifting too far from the Shore*

"*Heaven and Other Zip Codes* is a bittersweet love story crowded with all-too-human failings, and Cailler's easy and poised prose gives us complex yet knowable characters to care about. The final zip code may not be heaven, but it's still an endearing and heartfelt place."

—Kali White VanBaale,
author of *The Monsters We Make* and *The Good Divide*

"*Heaven and Other Zip Codes* will insist you love it... it will wrap and seduce you into its heart, with a story centering around love, art, intuition, and the messiness of it all."

—Susan Solomon, Editor of *Sleet Magazine*

"With clear and empathetic prose, *Heaven and Other Zip Codes* examines familial guilt and romantic passion. The secret lives of Cailler's characters reflect conflicts between what we want and what we owe the people we love. At times heartbreaking, at times bittersweet and even funny, Cailler searches the complexities of everyday affairs in this deeply moving novel."

—Donald Quist,
author of *Harbors* and *For Other Ghosts*

"Cailler mines the depths of the human heart."

—Cheryl Wright-Watkins, Essayist

"Mathieu Cailler draws his small cast of characters with such precision and soulfulness you immediately invest in them, then he sets them down in a world of unimaginable sorrow and unpredictable joy. Is it any wonder the results are unforgettable? Part love story, part mystery, part psychological thriller, *Heaven and Other Zip Codes* somehow feels both perfectly contemporary and deliciously old-fashioned. It's the kind of novel you want to curl up with for hours on a rainy afternoon. Or any afternoon."

—Margaret Evans,
Editor at *Lowcountry Weekly*

"*Heaven and Other Zip Codes* is peopled with flawed, confused, tender, angry, loving, hopeful humans struggling to navigate moral quandaries. More than love or lust, the need to create family drives this story of connections broken and mended, made and missed. Mathieu Cailler's most memorable creation is young Theo who must survive seventh grade as well as his parents' infidelities. Cailler's compassion for his characters shines, as does his uncanny ability to evoke the everyday details of life – how things look, smell and feel; the gestures people make; the things they witness out the window or under their feet as they go about their pained and joyous lives."

—Laurie Alberts, author of
A Well-Made Bed (with Abby Frucht)
and *Between Revolutions: an American Romance with Russia*

"Packed with raw emotion, *Heaven and Other Zip Codes* is a story about the tremendous bravery it takes to choose happiness and follow your heart."

—Racquel Henry, author of *Holiday on Park*

"*Heaven and Other Zip Codes* sits squarely at the intersection of rich, fully alive characters and masterful narration. Cailler is a deft craftsman who understands love and loss, humor and despair. In the end, the characters' frailties and triumphs leave us gratified, yet wishing the journey didn't have to end."

—Tim Antonides, author of *Rain*

Published by Open Books

Interior design by Siva Ram Maganti

Cover image © sirtravelalot shutterstock.com/g/mooddboard

ISBN-13: 978-1948598354

For my mother and father—
who showed me the beauty of surrendering to softness

"There are years that ask questions and years that answer."

—Zora Neale Hurston

SEPTEMBER

SEARCY WAITED IN THE foyer. It was ten minutes before Mr. Toffler and Theo's first session together. There wasn't homework—Theo had made sure to tell her this four times now—but Searcy had vetoed her boy's idea of canceling the tutoring session, thinking that there was always work that could be done, always something that could be previewed or reviewed. Even if it was just Mr. Toffler and Theo getting to know one another, that would be something.

She inspected herself in the reflection of a nearby grandfather clock. Her top was a tad low-cut, exposing a hint of cleavage, so she plucked a shawl from a hook near the front door and wrapped it around her neck. Hoit had purchased this stole for her in Milan on their honeymoon some three years ago, almost to the month.

Maybe it was best to wait outside for Mr. Toffler, where she could offer a wave and let him know he was on the right street, though she wasn't sure what to look for. She had found his flyer on the community board at church and had scrawled the info on her hand. His rate was fair, Theo's grades weren't strong, and she found it strained their relationship to complete homework with her boy.

As she sauntered along the brick walkway, she heard a leaf crunch behind her. Theo had been upstairs, soaking in as much computer time as possible. "Here we are," she said, scanning Theo from top to bottom. Each night, she prayed hard that her boy would find his way, become popular and happy, and flourish as a late bloomer. She had tried her best to make a nice life for him, a comfortable one. It wasn't fair that he'd lost his real dad at only three years old. "Theo, it's chilly and you're not wearing shoes. Go inside before you catch cold."

"I just want to see what kind of car he has."

He had always had an interest in cars, passed along from his dad,

Keith. "You can look from the window."

"Come on, Mom! I'll run inside as soon as he pulls up."

Just then, three minutes late, an old, orange car rumbled up the road. Searcy knew it was him. This was a cul-de-sac, and she would've remembered a car like this. She waved, and the car slowed down.

"What is that?" Theo said.

"No idea."

"Orange with a black top. The perfect Halloween car."

Searcy reminded Theo that he was supposed to get inside as soon as he got a look at the car but realized, after she'd done so, that he was already gone, his body blurring through the first-story windows.

"Sorry I'm late," Mr. Toffler said, getting out of the car, starting up the driveway. His voice was lower in person that it had been on the phone. "I'll be sure to make up the time. I left early. Made a wrong turn, and for some reason they're very 'anti-U-turn' around these parts."

"That's why I stood out here. I'm not a nut or anything." Searcy's eyes brushed over his body. He was probably about ten years her junior, maybe in his mid-to-late twenties, and he wore a white shirt, a gray tweed blazer, and black pants. His cropped beard wasn't the same shade as his dark hair, but a lighter brown, and his skin was tanned, probably from his convertible. A bag that looked like it belonged to a house-call doctor, with high-slanting tops, hung from his hand. He was another one of these L.A. hipsters. A man who looked like a boy, or maybe a boy that was trying to look like a man—she wasn't sure.

"Nice to meet you, Mr. Toffler," Searcy said.

"Call me Emerson," he said.

He extended his hand and they shook. His grip was hard, and his fingers were speckled with paint. They started up the brick path, side by side, and entered the warm house.

———

Emerson's heart steadied as they entered. Searcy didn't seem upset that he was late, and he was glad the line "I'll make up the time" had popped into his head, though it did seem like a pilot's phrase: "Uh, sorry, folks . . . I know we got out of O'Hare a little late, but we have a favorable wind today, so I'll be able to make up the time. Sit back. Enjoy the flight."

He took it all in: after the hardwood foyer, the room opened up on a brick kitchen with a cozy nook. To the right was a living room with a matching brick fireplace, and to the left, a formal dining room. Worn, copper pots and pans hung over the range stove, and something with aromas of tomato and thyme seemed to be boiling on the burner.

Searcy complemented this warmth, too. Her voice was soothing, and her mannerisms were gentle, yet at the same time, she was intense, like the very flames that blasted the pot. He let his eyes comb over her rosy skin and whiskey eyes. He wondered whether her hair, this auburn hue, was her natural tint, or whether it was dyed professionally. She wore yoga pants—like every woman in L.A., it seemed—and she was probably one of the many who wore the tight pants to everything *but* yoga.

"What a lovely home," he said, locating his manners. When he looked back at the formal dining room, he saw a boy sitting at the head of a table, a bit of evening light fluttering through the French doors behind him. "Hello," Emerson said.

"Hi, Mr. Toffler," the boy said.

"You can call me Emerson."

"No," Searcy said. "He'll call you Mr. Toffler."

"You must be Theo," Emerson said.

The boy nodded and Emerson studied the seventh-grader. Even though Theo was sitting, Emerson could discern chubbiness. There was never a good time to be husky, and even though Emerson was years removed from junior high, he still remembered that seventh grade was to torture what Paris was to romance. "Nice to meet you," Emerson said, heading over toward the boy, taking a seat on an uncomfortable chair.

"Looks like you've got things under control," Searcy said. "I'll let you guys be."

"Thank you, Searcy," Emerson said.

————————

Theo fished out his essay, laptop, planner, pencils, and pens. He wanted to ask Mr. Toffler if he was wearing cologne, because he picked up on a black-licorice smell that reminded him of a candy he sometimes ate with his mom, one that came in a purple box. He also could detect the odor of cigarettes, and he thought that Mr. Toffler had maybe used too much cologne to cover up the smoky smell.

That word returned to his brain—the word that no one ever called him, the word that seemed to occupy the air at school as much as oxygen. That word. *Cool.*

Here, with Mr. Toffler next to him, tall and older, with a beard and paint on his hands, he wanted to appear cool. He felt the same way in gym class when they played kickball and his classmates would be on base, screaming, "Bring me home!" or when he'd gaze at Sophie Carroll in the hallways, her eyelids glittery, and her braids dangling. "Do you want something to drink?" he asked. "Coffee?"

"No, I'm okay." Mr. Toffler said, smiling.

"Caffeine can be intense," Theo said.

"Let's see what you got here. Pass me your essay."

"Okay." Theo had started the essay on summer vacation in class. Mr. Toffler uncapped his purple pen, and Theo stared at Mr. Toffler's eyes. He'd made eye contact with him earlier, but for the first time, he was comfortable doing so. Theo had no clue what Mr. Toffler would call the color of his own eyes, but to Theo they looked like the sky after a long rain. They also looked a little sad, and the skin underneath was dark. *Where do you live? Where are you from? Do you have a dog? A girlfriend?* Theo wanted to ask all these questions, but he stayed quiet and watched Mr. Toffler go over the essay.

"This is solid," Mr. Toffler said. "A few grammar and spelling issues, but nothing major. Maybe add a little more here. *Why* did you like the restaurant? What did you eat?" He paused. "Is Hoit your brother?" he said, pointing to a part of the essay.

"My stepdad."

"Oh, yes. Your mom mentioned him on the phone. Away on business a lot, right?"

"Yeah," Theo said.

"Why was this restaurant special?" Mr. Toffler pointed to the paper.

"Okay," Theo said. His mom was right. If he had to do the work anyway, it was nice having someone around who could help. Theo wrote and wrote, filling the paper with words, sentences, and finally a paragraph. By the time he finished, his hand was sore.

"Watch your spelling here," Mr. Toffler said. "*Salmon* has an *L.*"

"Can you pass me that eraser?" Theo erased the word and started rewriting it. "One of those weird things."

"Exactly."

"Sometimes I feel that way, you know?"

"What way?"

"Like the *L* in *salmon*."

"How do you mean?"

"Like I'm there, but quiet. Like no one can see me."

"Really?"

Theo didn't think he should've said it, and he wondered if there was any way that he could take it back.

"I don't know about that," Mr. Toffler said. "Those are cool words, I think. They're sneaky and have all the power."

Theo didn't answer. He fixed the mistakes Mr. Toffler had circled and began typing up the assignment on his laptop. Time passed quickly, and he knew that Mr. Toffler was preparing to leave because he kept inspecting his watch. After the paragraphs were typed up, Mr. Toffler read it over on the computer and said the essay was ready. Theo was pleased. He hadn't received many good grades last year, which was why Mr. Toffler was now at the table. Theo showed Mr. Toffler, at his request, his daily planner and folders for different classes.

"I'm glad you go by Theo," Mr. Toffler said.

"What do you mean?"

"Your name's Theodore, right?"

"Yeah."

"Well, you could've gone by Ted."

"That's true. My mom just always called me Theo."

"I knew a Ted long ago. He was an asshole, so maybe I'm biased."

Theo waited for Mr. Toffler to excuse himself for accidentally swearing, but it never happened. "I like the name Mr. Toffler."

"You do? I think it sounds like a candy bar. I'll take a couple of Snickers, a Baby Ruth, and a Mr. Toffler."

"Candy's good, though." Theo saved his essay on the computer. "That's all for tonight."

"What are you gonna do now?"

"Probably play chess on the computer. Are you leaving?"

"Yes, but you'll see me a lot. Maybe one day you can teach me how to play chess."

"It's not too hard," Theo said.

"Good."

Theo walked Mr. Toffler out of the dining room, through the kitchen, and to the front door. He wanted to ask Mr. Toffler what kind of car he drove, but he knew that everything had gone well and that sometimes words could ruin that feeling. He remembered what Hoit always said about business: silence is your friend.

"Goodbye, Emerson," Searcy called from the top of the stairs. "I'll pay you at the end of each week if that's okay."

"Of course. See you all soon."

Theo held the door open, listening to Mr. Toffler's shoes on the brick. He waited until Mr. Toffler reached the driveway to bring the door carefully to its jamb. Then, from a window, he studied Mr. Toffler as he tucked inside his old, orange car.

Hoit wrapped up his meeting in Shanghai, seeing two gentlemen out the door of the hotel conference room. He caved into an office chair, scratched his forehead hard, and spun to face the wall-length windows that gave way to this galaxy of a city. Shanghai was unlike any other place even at ground level, so here, at thirty-three stories up, he took in the illumination. Every inch of this metropolis sparkled like Times Square, and yet, even with all these lights, he figured most people weren't home.

Soundbites from the meeting swirled: "Interesting, Mr. Hilbert . . . At this point, I think we need to look at other options as well . . . We will be in touch." It had been eight months since Hoit had left his cushy job at MYKA, a PR firm, to branch out and start a firm of his own. So far, the ups were Kilimanjaro-like, and the lows were as deep as the Titanic's stemware. In order to collect clients, he'd had to travel more than usual, flying wherever his colleague, Mason, thought they might be able to find work. Rejections had come in bunches lately, most clients preferring the expertise of bigger companies, and even though his small firm had produced a few successes, the rejections still made him feel lower than the triumphs made him feel high.

But he'd *looked* good. He'd *spoken* well. And for the first time in almost two hours, he totally relaxed, knowing that the clients could no longer see or hear him. The meeting had gone as planned, maybe not perfect, but he'd projected a vision of success, and sometimes,

Hoit wasn't sure what mattered more: others' perception or his own. He certainly believed the first was easier to craft.

Searcy had left two voicemails for him. "Hi, sweetie. It's me. Give me a call when you get a chance. I know with the time difference it's tough, but I'm tired of texting and would love to hear your voice." Hoit peeked at his watch. Eight o'clock at night meant four o'clock in the morning in L.A., so he would try her later. Multitasking had never been his forte—when he was on business, he was on business, and the rest of his life seemed to fade.

When he headed back to his hotel room, he found that the door was cracked with the housekeeping cart, and a maid was inside, turning down his duvet, placing a chocolate atop his pillow.

He entered. He didn't know the woman's name, but he had seen her this entire week, always in the morning when she was waiting at the far end of the hall for guests to begin filing out. Twice now, probably because Hoit always forgot to place his Privacy Please sign on the exterior door knob, she had entered and found him in bed, sprawled out. "So sorry," she'd say timidly.

"Knock, knock," he said, taking a few steps inside.

"So sorry. So sorry, sir."

"Are those the only English words you know?" Hoit asked.

"Oh," she said. She smiled. Her teeth were white, but crooked, producing a girlish grin. Hoit took a seat on the edge of the crisp bed.

"My name's Hoit," he said.

"Hi," she said. "Have a nice night." She folded her hands on her stomach and nodded.

"What's your name?" he asked.

"Biyu."

"Hi, Biyu." The temptation to make a joke regarding the Bayou came to him. After all, he'd grown up in Baton Rouge, not far from the muddy banks of the Mississippi. She was tall, thin, and her hair was cut at a flattering angle.

"Hello, Hoit," she said. Her eyes flirted with his gaze before fluttering down to the knot of his necktie. "Bye, Hoit." She grabbed hold of the cart and pushed it hard over the door's threshold and into the hall. The door shut with a thunk, and the room regained its quiet.

He kicked off his shoes, loosened his tie, and clicked on the TV. Room service, piled towels, turn-down service, plush robes, tiny bottles of shampoo—all of this had become home.

Even though it wasn't technically fall yet, the evening light weakened, and Emerson knew that it wouldn't be long before night was upon him, showing up like an uninvited houseguest. The nights were always the hardest. Maybe because the eyes could find fewer distractions.

Would it be more of the usual? Some booze? Some Internet porn? Maybe a couple of those pills he had left over from his back pain earlier in the year, when he'd fallen down some stairs at a mall?

Hopping onto his old sailboat in the marina, he descended the ladder into the small living quarters. Theo, Searcy, tutoring . . . this might be a good fit. Sure, he had some savings, but this was a good way to make some dough while protecting his painting time.

He didn't feel like a quiet night in. Maybe he would call Carly, the campaign manager he'd met at the bar last week. He'd gotten her number on a cocktail napkin, and it had been tacked to his corkboard above his bed. "Text me," she'd said, touching his forearm. But was it even worth it? Sometimes it was best just to have that initial moment, perfect and pure. He could see the future with Carly already. They would go out, laugh, smile, go back to his boat, have sex, see movies, and say things like "You like art! I *love* art!" Then, after a few months, discover that what they had was real, but not real enough. Gone were the days of epic romance like Marc Antony and Cleopatra, Romeo and Juliet, Chopin and George Sand. Hell, even his parents' story always delivered.

Tortillas, beans, and some left-over crab cakes from the other night stared back at him from the tiny fridge, and he put together some strange tacos before lolling on his bed. He thought about Theo being the *L* in *salmon* and his essay about his summer. In Emerson's high school days in Vermont, he taught sailing on Lake Champlain for a couple of summers and worked with all sorts of kids, and most of them were shits. It was nice to meet their opposite—a genuine boy. Searcy, too, came to mind. He found her attractive not only in her appearance but in the way she cared for her son—interviewing Emerson on the phone and waiting for him on the driveway.

He took a long draw of bourbon and stared at Carly's phone number. He wished morning would come sooner.

Jogging down Crest Road towards St. John the Baptist Church, Searcy listened to the rhythm of her breath. Inhale through the nose; exhale through the mouth, one laced-up sneaker in front of the other. Blood flowed through her body, warming her limbs and face as she picked up speed and finished strong, reaching the church.

On this Monday morning, the church's vast lot was empty, except for a few cars that most likely belonged to clergy. Just yesterday, at mass, spots were rare, but now, everyone was back at it, amassing sins for which they would undoubtedly ask forgiveness come Sunday.

She passed by a parked car that caught her eye. It was the old, orange car that she'd seen Emerson drive only days earlier. The vehicle was impeccable: black tires that appeared wet, wax-swirled paint, and chromed hubcaps in which she could see the reflection of her Nikes. The car was made by Volkswagen and called a Karmann Ghia. Why was he at church? She had never seen this car here before, though she gathered he'd been here at least once to staple his tutoring flyers to the community board.

Inside the church, light streamed through stained glass, casting blues, reds, and yellows among the pews, and a gentle fountain trickled into a large baptism pool.

She searched for Emerson, but didn't spot him. After sliding into a pew and lowering the kneeler, she folded her hands. By now, her heart paced at its normal clip, and she let her mind breathe. As always, she thanked God for allowing her to find Hoit three years ago. Her days as a single mother after Keith's passing were demanding, with her working multiple jobs—one as a bartender, another as a dentist's secretary—and Hoit had taken them in, both she and Theo, without hesitation, moving them miles away from smoggy North Hollywood into a rich enclave along the L.A. coast. She lived a quiet life now, pushing away her dream of fashion design, where instead of drawing the newest dresses, she now owned them. In fact, so much of what people desired, she had, so whenever she felt herself yearn for more, she stopped her prayers, and opened her eyes.

After muttering "Amen," she noticed Emerson exit the little chapel at the far end. She herself rarely entered the side chapel, believing that her words carried more weight when delivered directly at the altar and crucifix. She waved, but his face was angled towards the floor. Father Guffey hurried behind him and caught up to him near the church's exit. Emerson wiped his eyes. Father Guffey spoke to him, but she couldn't hear anything with the sound of the baptism fountain. Emerson nodded a lot, wrote something in the community prayer book, then he headed for the door and exited the church. Father Guffey waited for a few moments before returning to his office and shutting the door.

Searcy hurried to a nearby window. Why was he sad? Days ago he'd seemed so cheerful. She watched him head across the lot in his red bomber jacket and ripped jeans, then sink into his Karmann Ghia and light a cigarette.

Making sure no one was around, she worked her way to the prayer book, scanning all the lines, until she reached the last words. *The usual*, he had written in loopy cursive.

Mrs. Stanton called on a few students to come to the front of the class to read their essays. Theo slid lower in his chair, but he knew he would be called on. His bad luck was consistent. "Theo," Mrs. Stanton said. "Come on up."

"Okay," he said, remembering to breathe and be confident. He'd worked on the essay with Mr. Toffler, so he knew it was good. His underwear shifted as he strolled up to the front of the class, but he didn't pause to adjust it. At recess, he'd rearrange things behind the comfort of a locked stall door.

His heart thunked. His face warmed. He pushed through syllable after syllable, picking up his eyes every so often and trying to make eye contact with his peers. "After swimming all day in Maui's hot water, my mom and Hoit took me to this amazing restaurant for my birthday, which happens to be on the Fourth of July. The restaurant was called Mama's Fish House. It was cool because all of the fish on the menu were caught that day, and underneath each fish, they even wrote down the name of the person who caught it. They didn't have salmon because it's not local, so Hoit ordered something called ono for me. My taste buds went wild."

Sophie Carroll was off to his left, and he knew her freckles and braids would distract him, so he didn't swing his eyes that way. No, he focused on Mrs. Stanton. Her face was plain and consistent.

When he finished his paragraphs, there was light applause and Mrs.

Stanton gave him a thumbs-up. He returned to his desk, running the back of his hand over his forehead. Life, he thought, was staring at a clock, always wishing the hands would whip forward or backward, so he decided to pull his eyes away from the time and stare out a nearby window at a telephone wire on which a couple of crows rested.

The bell rang and Theo walked to his locker to get a snack for recess. His mom had cut out the salt and sugar, only giving him fruits and veggies. There were times when he was tempted to trade his apples and carrot sticks, but he knew they wouldn't go for it.

He plopped down with a few foreign-exchange students, most of them from Korea. They were his default friends. "Hi," he said. One of the boys said something that sounded like "*ann-yung.*" Theo extended his bag of carrots, and two of the boys reached over.

Hoit returned Searcy's calls.

"Hi," she said. "What time is it there?"

"Six in the morning," Hoit said.

"I can tell it's early," she said. "You sound groggy. How did the meetings go?"

He knew she would ask questions. "Pretty well."

"Did they say yes?"

"Not quite," he said.

"What then?"

Hoit ripped open the drapes, and the hard light made him squint. "They want to see more data first," he said, turning to fiddle with the tiny coffee machine.

"But you had the account before, when you were with MYKA," she said. "Remember what you did when the CFO was found with the prostitute? How you spun it? They owe you."

"I know." The pot started to hiss and gurgle, the water warming in the tank.

There was a long pause, and it sounded as though she had dropped a piece of silverware. "Oh," she finally said.

"How are you guys? What have you been up to?" Hoit asked.

"Good," Searcy said. "I hired a tutor to work with Theo."

"A tutor?" Hoit thought about asking how much that was going to cost him.

"Yeah. I saw a flyer at church and have been leaning in this direction for a while," she said. "The subjects are getting harder, and it's just better for him not to work with me."

He took a deep breath. "What's the tutor like?"

"Youngish. Kind. Thought it might be nice to have a man in his academic life. I feel like so many of his teachers are women, and then he spends a lot of time with me."

"Last I checked I was a man."

She laughed. "Of course. But you're gone quite a bit. Since you've started your own firm, it's been over two hundred days."

"You've counted?" He poured the coffee into a cup. It smelled better than it tasted.

"Anyhow, it was nice to be done with homework and be able to enjoy an episode of *I Love Lucy* before bed."

"I can't believe you two still watch that show."

"Theo loves Fred. He laughs every time he's in a scene. It's the high pants, I think."

"Tell him to come to China. All the men in this hotel have their pants up to their belly buttons. Especially anyone over the age of sixty." Hoit clicked on the TV.

"One day we should visit you," Searcy said.

"Yeah," he said. "See what it's like on this end of things." They spoke for a little longer and discussed the weather, the pool needing to be fixed, and the authentic food Hoit had been enjoying. Then they said their goodbyes.

These days, Hoit believed, it all came down to clarity. He needed to be clear in business, tell himself *exactly* what was going on, and when it came to Searcy, he tried to apply the same principle. Even though she was with him, living in his house, wearing his last name and the jewelry he bought for her—he sometimes thought he didn't love her enough. There was attraction, and he occasionally held tender thoughts. And he loved the *idea* of family, and a Thanksgiving dinner table, and Christmas stockings, but it wasn't his style to play catch in the yard, or to say "I love you," or to display his affection.

He looked to his parents, who were still in Louisiana, whom he hadn't visited in years. Hoit was the youngest of seven, and as a result he'd been raised by his sisters and brothers. He never once saw his parents kiss—something that he'd only thought about after he'd started dating. One photograph on a mantle, however, bore proof they had: his mother and father years before his birth, in New Orleans, kissing on their honeymoon. The photo seemed staged, with Hoit's mother in something of a dance pose, her back arched, and his father's hands wrapped around her waist, dipping his head to meet his new bride's lips.

A drizzle fell, pattering about the boat's hull, and Emerson slipped out of his bed, careful not to wake Carly. Yes, yes, he'd broken down after all.

He prepared some coffee. Sheets swaddled her lithe figure, reminding him of one of his favorite paintings, *In Bed* by Toulouse-Lautrec from the late 1800s.

He often chased his whiskey with bad decisions, and he'd possibly done so again. He had texted her the night he'd eyed her number on the corkboard, but she'd been busy, so they'd made plans for last night.

The black coffee rose in the pot, and Carly woke up. "Morning," she said. She wrapped herself in a blanket and crossed the stateroom to sit next to him on a small couch. Her makeup had faded, and her complexion seemed creamier than the night before. Her reddish hair rested loosely over her white shoulders.

"Here," Emerson said, passing her a cup of coffee.

"I've never seen a man besides Seinfeld own so many types of cereal." She counted. "Nine!"

"When you're a bachelor, cereal isn't just a breakfast food." He made himself a bowl.

"It's like a ten-year-old's dream in here," she said, turning her attention to the canvases that were stacked on the table. "I love how cute everything is in this boat. It reminds me of when I was a little girl, and my dad built me this playhouse in the backyard. Everything's small, like a pretend version of the real thing." Carly rose and got dressed, slithering into her jeans and turning her back to him as she fastened her bra. He found it amusing the way women were always shy the morning after. Six hours ago, she'd moaned, her breasts pressed against his chest, but now, with light sprouting through the portholes, she'd become modest.

He offered her some cereal, but she declined, stating that she needed to get home and wash up before she had to be at the mayor's office. He stared at the floating marshmallows in his Lucky Charms—a clover, a star, and a rainbow. Traces of food coloring seeped into the milk, leaving behind strands of blue and pink and yellow. His mom had always said, "Life's a bowl of Lucky Charms. Some days are marshmallows; some days are oats."

"When did you start painting?" Carly asked, buttoning her blouse.

"When I was about five."

"That's so cool. I like this one, the purple swirls and the two people kissing."

"Take it," Emerson said. "Didn't turn out the way I wanted."

"Really?" She wiggled her feet into her high heels.

"Yeah."

"Do you just paint all day here on your little boat."

"Pretty much. And some tutoring."

"Why the boat?"

"Short answer is that it's the cheapest way to live in LA. Boat was old. I fixed it up, and now I just have marina fees."

She planted a coffee-laced kiss on his lips, and he walked her to her car. "See you soon?" she asked when they arrived at her Honda.

"Yeah," he said. The evening had gone better than he'd anticipated. Maybe he'd been wrong. Carly was warm and smart, and he thought that his mother would use that word she always used when it came to good choices. "She's sensible, Emmy," he could hear her say. "Quite sensible." His mom—and his dad, for that matter—always had a way of sounding formal even when what they were saying was plain. He leaned against a banister that led to the dock and savored the arc of a seagull as it rose high into the morning light.

––––––––––

Searcy was teasing a strand of unruly hair when the doorbell rang. She descended the stairs, unfastened the lock, and pulled the door open. "Good afternoon, Emerson," she said as he ducked inside.

"Hi, Searcy," he said.

His smell was woodsy and suited, maybe too well, his red-and-black plaid shirt. "Theo's wrapping something up on the computer. He'll be down soon."

He smiled, causing his eyes to narrow.

Searcy walked him to the dining room where Theo's supplies were laid out.

"Look at that," Emerson said. "He's all set."

"I may have had something to do with it."

Emerson took a seat, and Searcy stood next to him.

"Let me ask you something, Emerson. I found your flyer at St. John the Baptist. Do you go there a lot?"

"Church is kind of a new thing for me. I moved out here from Vermont about a year ago. I used to go to church when I was a boy out there."

"Do you like it here in LA?"

"It's overwhelming, but the beach area is manageable for me. Are you from here?"

"Yes, all over LA. I grew up in North Hollywood, then went to the Fashion Institute downtown."

"You still work in fashion?"

He seemed to hide whatever it was he was dealing with at the church well, his eyes clear and his face open. So much of this world was pretending. "Not really," Searcy said. "I still sketch every now and then," she said, "but not as much. Just for me. I was a different person back then. It's almost like opening a time capsule, you know? I saw on your flyer that you attended art school in Boston, right? I bet that was something. And that you paint for a living. What are you interested in mostly? Oils, watercolors, acrylics?"

"Watercolors mostly, but every now and then, I try something new. Working with eye droppers right now instead of paint brushes, which has been fun. What's the word for the pose of a fashion sketch? I want to say 'croquet,' but I know that's wrong."

"Oh, to show off your design, a *croquis*." She laughed.

"That's it. What kind of clothes did you like to draw?"

"Gowns mostly. I love shoes, too, but could never seem to draw them well enough. Do you paint every day?" she said.

"Pretty much," he said, scratching the backs of his hands.

The only time his eye contact was interrupted was during the milliseconds he was forced to blink.

"How lovely," Searcy said. She heard the stairs creak and gathered Theo was on his way down. "Would you like something to drink? Some lemonade?" she said. "Let me get you some lemonade." She hurried into the kitchen, returning with a glass filled to the brim with pink sweetness.

"Thank you," Emerson said.

"Of course," she said. She retreated to the kitchen and closed the door, running her fingers through her hair. Her boy joined Emerson at the table, and she listened to their voices mix.

"Bad day at school?" Emerson said. The boy's mannerisms seemed heavy.

Theo put his head flat on the table. "I just realized it's going to be a long school year. It's only September, you know?"

Emerson noticed a red mark on his forehead, but didn't say anything. "You've done this before, though."

"I guess I always think it's gonna be different when the year starts out, and then it just turns into the same ole thing. Were you good in school?"

"I managed."

"I bet you were popular, though."

Emerson brought his bag up onto the table and reached deep inside. There was no reason that he brought this bag along other than to look professional. It was stuffed with painting supplies and old artwork that hadn't pleased him. "I made you something," Emerson said, his fingers scratching against dried oil. Knowing that one of the canvases was a semi-nude, he was relieved when he finally fished out a painting of a lemon tree—the trunk twisted, the limbs heavy with fruit.

"Whoa," Theo said, taking both of his hands and running them over the canvas, his nails picking at clumps of paint. "This is cool. Did you paint this just for me?"

"I did," Emerson said.

"Really?"

"Yeah."

"Thank you, Mr. Toffler." Theo held the painting out in front of him, his arms straight. Emerson studied the boy's eyes as they combed over the surface, inspecting the bright russet and saffron hues. With Theo's pupils steady on the art, Emerson called to mind his upstairs bedroom at his childhood home in Montpelier, where he would tuck away and scan pages of art books, trying his best to plunge into the paintings: caress the tender silk of Degas's ballet slippers, hop along the infinite dots of anything Signac, be still in the cold loneliness of *Nighthawks*. Emerson recognized the spell, so he let Theo sink into the painting, understanding the luxury a good fantasy could provide.

Finally, though, feeling guilty for not having started, he said, "All right. Let's get to work. What do you say, Theo?"

"Okay," he said, placing the painting on the seat next to him. "I have something on Columbus and his ships. The Piñata and the Maria or something."

"People are still studying Columbus?"

"I guess. The textbook is from 1992."

"So am I," Emerson said, popping his knuckles.

"Whoa," Theo said.

Hoit looked at himself in the reflection of the elevator doors as he pressed the Up arrow and waited. His burgundy tie popped against the gray of his suit, and he enjoyed the way his two-day stubble—something he'd seen celebrities doing recently—contrasted with the polish of his professional look. He knew that Mr. Wu and Mr. Suga could see him from the conference room at this particular moment, so he held back his smile, until he entered the elevator and the shiny doors shut behind him. A laugh flew from his mouth. *Yes.* He had heard it in both English and Mandarin, and in any tongue, it delighted. Bits of Mr. Suga's concluding speech surrounded Hoit in the elevator: "We love what you did for us when you were with MYKA, and we want you. Every time we had something, you came up with the perfect defense, the perfect strategy without rocking the boat. Is that the expression?" Hoit stood tall, pleased with himself.

The occasion certainly called for champagne at the lobby bar, but he didn't want to run into clients, so instead, he would celebrate in his room at this strange time, almost noon. He hadn't opened the mini bar before now, so he was curious what he would encounter. Almost all hard alcohol: vodka, gin, whiskey, tequila. Bottles of all shapes and colors. Greens, browns, blues, and yellows. He grabbed all the gins, threw a handful of ice into a tumbler, and slugged away, feeling the burn ride his throat and settle in his stomach. With nothing on the calendar tomorrow except for a conference call in the late afternoon, and the day after that, a flight to Tokyo, he could totally indulge.

He killed bottle after little bottle, flinging them atop the down comforter where they clinked together. On the TV, he found a station that only played American oldies music. Currently the Beach Boys' "In My Room" wrapped him, and it wasn't long before he joined in, sang along, and plugged in his own hums whenever he couldn't find the right lyric. Swaying at the foot of the bed, he spilled his glass of vodka onto his slacks. "Shit," he muttered. He hopped up, unfastening his belt, and sliding off his pants.

There was a sound that didn't seem as though it had come from the TV. Hoit fiddled with the remote and turned down the volume. "Hello?" he said. It had been a voice. And not Brian Wilson's.

"Hello?" a woman said. "Housekeeping."

Hoit's legs felt disconnected from his body, rubbery and worn. "Hold on," he said, working the locks, twisting the deadbolts over and over, before jerking the door open. "Biyu!" he shouted. "Come in!"

She put her finger over her lips and her eyes widened. "Hello, Mr. Hoit. You left your privacy sign up all morning, so I thought maybe you just forgot to take it down."

"Why are you whispering?" he said. "Come in! Come in! Big day for us, Biyu!" Her hair was shinier than it had been yesterday, maybe due to a product.

"Do you want the room cleaned?" she asked.

"Yes, yes! Sure!" he said, realizing he wasn't wearing pants. He ripped a robe down from the back of the door and fed his arms through the sleeves before tying the belt. Biyu wheeled in her cart. "Would you like a drink?" he asked, already pouring her one.

The lights from Shanghai's buildings burned through the window, melding into one strong beam, and he took a seat on the edge of the bed and felt the room shift.

"Thank you, Mr. Hoit," Biyu said. "Every day you are so kind. So good to me."

He inspected Biyu's marble eyes. "What do you mean?"

"Always leaving me twenty dollars for cleaning. Nobody else does that."

"Oh," he said, setting his glass on the bed. The tumbler toppled and a stream of cold liquid rushed against his thigh. "Not again! Damn!" He mopped up the mess with his robe.

Seconds later, as the room continued to spin—swirls of lights, bits of music, crunching ice, bottles clinking, eyelids fluttering—he felt hands, soft and delicate, on the nape of his neck. Biyu's hands. They were warm, almost hot, like she'd just washed them with scalding water. "You work so hard," she said. "You are so tight," she said. "You must relax," she said, her words coming in waves. Her fingers and palms kneaded and twisted at the knots on his neck, loosening his muscles and tendons with each push and curl. Biyu's hands then vanished, and she strolled over to the blinds, slowly pulling them shut, blacking out the polluted light.

Soon after, she clicked off each lamp, deepening the darkness. The TV silenced. The bottles pushed aside. And the last thing that stood out, the chain lock jingling against the door before being slid into place.

Searcy finished flossing and headed down the hall to tuck in Theo. Last night, too tired, she'd forgone their nightly prayers, but to-night she wanted to make sure they were delivered. She knew God admired consistency.

"Mom," Theo said, as she popped in. He sat at his desk. "Did I show you the painting Mr. Toffler made for me?"

"Yes," she said. "Twice."

He lifted it high above his head, like a Bible. "That's what he does when he's not tutoring. He paints. He was telling me about it. Sometimes he draws, too, before he paints, to make sure everything looks okay. He told me he drives to Java Bistro—you know the coffee place near the library—to sketch sometimes."

Searcy imagined Emerson painting this for her boy, and it didn't take long for her to recall Keith, singing to Theo every day, from womb to age three, always renditions of Bee Gee songs, in an enthusiastic fal-setto. Hoit, however, usually stuffed some Chinese toy or T-shirt with Mandarin characters in his pack and gave it to Theo while unpacking.

"I forgot to ask him if this was a special tree or something," Theo said.

It took time, but Searcy weaned Theo from his desk, strewn with doodles. Clearly, he had been trying to recreate Emerson's painting. Her boy's work was skilled, though every feature on the tree—the branches, the trunk, the greenery—seemed soft and droopy, like Dali's clocks.

As Theo tucked his arms under his quilt, Searcy sat at the foot of her boy's bed and bowed her head. Together, they whispered the Lord's Prayer in a powerful drone.

"Mom, what does 'thy will be done' mean?"

Searcy stayed seated. "It means there's a plan for you."

"Like God is controlling me?"

"More like helping you do things that are in your best interest."

"Oh," Theo said. There was a long pause. "Does God know me better than *I* know me?"

"Yes," she said.

Theo rolled over, fluffed his two pillows, then kicked out his flat sheet that he said was "hurting his ankles."

Searcy smelled his forehead and whispered goodnight into his ear. When she'd had Theo at twenty-two, a primal switch activated, something that told her, *You will care for this boy more than yourself.* The responsibility was preconditioned, physiological—as central as food and water. And while, in time, the baby grew, and weeks morphed into months and years, the instinct, the force, never dissipated.

Before she turned in, she headed over to her bottom dresser drawer, a place where she'd stuffed items that were too important to toss out, but too unnecessary to display. She located her old fashion sketches. Though she'd told Emerson that she still drew from time to time, it wasn't true. It had been years since she'd drawn a *croquis*, or a "croquet," according to Emerson. Those were the days of blithe freedom, at the downtown Fashion Institute, where she learned of fabrics and styles, and how to draw a balance line to position a model in a way that would best showcase a certain style. She had taken a class here and there, paying her way through school, working odd jobs. Then, one night, she met Keith. His hair was curly and his dimples were big enough to hold dimes. They'd married a year later and had Theo shortly thereafter.

She riffled through the heavy papers, checking out her soft lines and sculpted necks and tight waists. If things had gone differently, she wondered where she'd be. Maybe working for a new designer, drawing gowns for red-carpet events—rich, satin evening wear whose ruffles and pleats toyed with the pavement, but never touched it. But life was tradeoffs, and she had the most precious gift of all, her Theo. She dropped the papers back in the folder and the folder back in the drawer.

In bed, she propped herself upright with the help of some pillows and took out her laptop. She typed "Emerson Toffler" into a search engine and hit Enter. Not many results appeared, but the first was a link to his Facebook account. Since she didn't possess an account, she couldn't see all his photos, but she was allowed access to a few of his profile pictures. Most of them were of abstract, watercolor paintings, labeled with titles: *Ojai Spring, Dusty River,* and *Montpelier in July.* She found his paintings warm and happy, albeit a bit too modern for her taste.

A couple photos were of his face: one with an older woman at what had to be a gallery opening, and another a professional, black-and-white headshot in which his features were sharpened. His light eyes stared hard, and while he looked handsome, he seemed a touch timid, as if the idea of having a high-quality photoshoot embarrassed him. Searcy enlarged the photo, taking inventory of his features. There were mild, dark semi-circles under his light eyes, and his lips flirted with a smile. A buzz collected in Searcy's chest, a tightness, and she let a big breath stream from her lips. This warmth continued to build, strengthen even, before she shut her laptop and then her eyes.

Theo had, in his opinion, sustained a magical bloody nose—perfectly timed, right at the beginning of a science pop quiz that he wasn't sure he was ready to take, though Mr. Toffler had helped him.

As he sat on the crinkly paper, waiting in the nurse's office, he looked out the window that gave way to the road and trail that he used to walk home. He was glad he'd begged his mom to let him walk this year. It was only about a half a mile, and he didn't want other students making fun of him for being driven to school. He'd already been called a mama's boy last year, and it hurt him that he'd had to pretend not to like his mom, even if it was just for a minute or two.

At the park across the road, people jogged and walked their dogs. Some relaxed on benches and read. Others talked with friends. His eyes darted over the scene, finally settling on the parking lot by the jungle gym. There were a few children (lucky to still be too young for school) playing on the swing set.

The nurse entered and started working on his nose. "Keep your head back," she said.

"Okay, Dr. Avery."

"I'm not a doctor," she said. "You can call me Mrs. Avery."

"Okay, Mrs. Avery." His voice sounded strange. Mr. Toffler was like one of those kids on the swing set—he was free. He was probably somewhere cool right now with paint supplies: canvases, brushes, papers, and easels. No one was telling him what to do, and he didn't have to take Dr. Norvett's pop quiz on mitosis.

Mrs. Avery wedged a tissue inside his left nostril, then removed it. "All right, Mr. Theo. You're all set. And we didn't even have to operate." She snapped off her gloves.

She loved that operate joke. Theo had heard it almost once a month for the last few years, but now that he'd learned she wasn't a doctor, he found it even more ridiculous. He wondered if Mrs. Avery was married. His mom had told him that if a woman was married she should have two bands on her left ring finger: one usually with a diamond, the other plain, but Mrs. Avery just had a tattoo on her left ring finger—one of a little anchor—and Theo thought that was cool. The tattoo made him think of his dad. His mom had told him that one day he came home with one while she was pregnant. Theo liked when his mom told the story: "He just came home and lifted up the sleeve of his T-shirt. I couldn't believe it, but he'd gotten a tattoo of my name! There it was! *Searcy!*" Theo had seen pictures of it, the tail of the *Y* long and thin, underlining the rest of her name.

When Theo reentered the science room, he realized he was in the wrong class. The period had changed, and now an eighth grader sat in his seat, a tall, muscular guy. Dr. Norvett didn't stop. He just kept rambling. Theo wondered if he ever stopped talking, or if he just wandered around his home at night talking about cells.

Theo grabbed his stuff and rushed out of the room. He couldn't wait to be one of those people in the park, with dogs and coffee and books, with smiles and laughter. Or, even better, like Mr. Toffler, with peace and paintings. Older people were always talking about how great childhood was, but really, Theo thought, it was just adults wishing for another turn at youth in their full-grown bodies.

"Where have you been?" Mrs. Stanton asked as Theo entered her English class. All his classmates had their heads angled at their desks.

"Bloody nose."

"Do you have a note?"

"No."

Mrs. Stanton crinkled her nose. "Just sit down. We're writing essays about our weekends."

Are you serious? Theo thought, sliding in to his desk and dropping his bag to the floor. *Another essay on my weekend? What is this? Diary class? How many exciting weekends can a human have? Who does Mrs. Stanton think I am—James Bond?* With only fifty-two weekends in a year, Theo estimated that at least three were eliminated because of an illness. Six events you hated—marriages, baptisms, an uncle's birthday. Three, maybe four, for school crap. The list went on.

Theo's classmates wrote and wrote. Good time after good time, sports and friends and traveling and tae kwon do.

Mrs. Stanton's eyes locked onto Theo's, and he nodded, reaching for a clean sheet of paper and a pencil. *Fun weekend!!!* he scrawled, smiling at his sarcasm.

Hoit sloshed his razor in the hot water that rested in the sink's bowl and watched the minuscule hairs disperse.

The flash of pain returned to his temples, and he rubbed the thick skin on his forehead, abating the pain for a moment. As soon as his hand left his head, however, the ache returned, this time sharper than before.

It had been days since, but the memory loitered. The images had circled him on the plane from Shanghai to Tokyo, but he'd been able to chase them away with some smooth jazz from his phone. He hadn't *actually* cheated on Searcy. He hadn't gone to a whorehouse and sought out sex. The woman had come to him when he was weak with booze and happy with success. Miles and rivers and time zones apart, Biyu had touched him first, and he hadn't turned down her offer. They had kissed, and she had peeled off his shirt. Some of this was Searcy's fault, too. She had been the one who months ago, after a business trip, had chided him about how he should leave a tip every day for the housekeeping staff—at least ten percent of the room's worth, she'd said. He hadn't been sure how the subject had come up, and he'd thought her idea was ludicrous, but after listening to her logic, he came around. And, he had to admit, on the last couple of trips, everyone had been kinder to him—and when he needed more towels or another blanket, housekeeping was quick to deliver. But this—with Biyu—well, he hadn't expected her to see the money as an advance. If that was even the case. It had been a powerful day, though: one of those days that unfolded exactly how they were pictured early on, while drinking coffee, while sitting in the shower's stream. His hair had been in place, the words had come to him in the meeting—the perfect words—and the woman had entered and made him feel manly, delivered the lines as if reading from a teleprompter. He had been stressed. He had worked too hard. He *did* need to relax. She meant nothing to him. There were worse ways to cheat—to harbor someone inside your psyche and visit them whenever necessary. That was the most disgusting. Yes, that was real sin, even though those sorts of religious words fit more with Searcy's lexicon than his. He admired her commitment to God, but he couldn't get behind the idea of having faith in something that couldn't be seen.

He reapplied some shaving cream to his neck and brought the razor up, against the grain, enjoying the grating sound as the metal blade sliced the hairs.

He had only done two or three, maybe four, distasteful things in three years—strip clubs, porn at hotels, fondled a waitress, and slept with Biyu. And there was that time with Josie, too, the divorced neighbor, but that was just kissing in her garage, and he'd stopped it as soon as Theo had turned the corner on his bike. Hoit had understood that Searcy and Theo would be at a school bake sale until much later in the day, and he'd actually gone over to tell Josie that while it was fun when he'd been single, he was now married and that whatever they had, could not continue.

Nuptials weren't what everyone thought—they weren't about hand-holding and phone calls and feet atop feet in a warm bed. No, Hoit believed relationships were about inertia. From a percentage standpoint, he was a great husband. If he and Searcy had been married for an estimated 1000 days, and four were despicable, then he was still solid for 996 out of 1000. He did the math, figuring it to be roughly 99.6% good. Rounded up: one hundred percent.

He splashed some water on his face and patted his skin dry with a towel, inspecting his jawline. This world, much like his face, was about maintenance, and with that, he took to his room—which looked precisely like the one he'd stayed in over in Shanghai—and texted Searcy. *Thinking of you,* he wrote. He wrapped himself in a towel and waited for a reply.

OCTOBER

WHEN LOOKING AT SANDRINE Fournier's work, Emerson wished he'd been blessed with more than just two eyes. The pair wasn't enough to savor her expertise. She'd always been his favorite living artist, and her work was able to stabilize him in a way that pills or whiskey or women couldn't. Her work brought him back to his childhood home in Montpelier when his mom and dad would feed any interest of his. His mom had gone ahead and bought him a print of *Dripping with Malaise* for his twelfth birthday. Art wasn't just about paints and strokes for Emerson, but rather that a *certain* assemblage of colors, shapes, and lines could make him feel more connected to the planet.

Madame Fournier had moved out to LA from Nice some twenty years ago, after she'd married a Hollywood writer, and they were famous for their love story, having never married until they were both in their sixties. She'd been quoted as saying, "It takes six decades for a man to grow up."

After attending a gallery showing of some of Madame Fournier's lesser-known works, Emerson had learned she was no longer painting due to arthritis, and that she was living in a nursing home in nearby San Pedro. He treasured the idea of the two of them sharing the same coastline.

Thoughts of popping by entered his mind, but he always hated the "drop in" and trusted she might, too, so instead he'd written her a letter asking if he could buy her a cup of coffee sometime. It was all a pipe dream until today, when he checked his postbox and found a card.

Dear Emerson:

Apologies for not getting back to you sooner. Mail is delivered by sloth here.

Stop by anytime.
Sandrine

The post office's din hushed as Emerson read the sentences again. His parents would never believe it. From a print to a note. The very same tendons and bones that had splashed colors on so many of his favorite artworks had picked up a pen to write him.

He placed the card in his jeans, patting it every so often to make sure it was safe, then he texted Carly to see if she wanted to grab a bite.

Searcy had been unable to shake Emerson from her mind. It felt nice to have a man in her almost-daily life—three times a week, to be precise—and she'd seen a boost in Theo, too. Sure, the usual lethargy that came with school sometimes presented itself, but it was quicker to dissipate now that Emerson was around to buoy her boy. Was that a natural talent of his, or was he just used to prying his way toward silver linings?

Stride, stride, stride. Her knees loose, her gait long. She had been wanting to increase her mileage, mulling over a possible marathon, and Theo had mentioned that Emerson sometimes sketched at Java Bistro, so she thought she'd see if he was working there this late morning. If he was, she would pop in and say hi. If he wasn't, she would order a chai latte with coconut milk, sit on a bench, and take in the world.

At a crosswalk, she jogged in place, waiting for the light to change, inspecting a group of men unloading masses of pumpkins from a semitruck. Was it already that time of year? The 18-wheeler's air brake deployed, and the hiss startled her. Her life was so quiet these days that she was, in her opinion, "out of shape" when it came to commotion. Before it was jobs and rent and raising Theo and even homeschooling him for a few months when she couldn't find the proper school. Holt wanted her to stay home and be there, take it easy. He was tradition-al in that way, and she'd liked the break in the beginning, but now sometimes she pondered more—even missed worrying in some ways. In this rich bedroom community, most of the residents were older, even the parents at Theo's school, and she'd had a hard time making friends. There were a few from the League of Women Voters and a yoga class, but mostly her tranquility went uninterrupted.

Minutes later, she arrived outside Java Bistro. The shop was small, no bigger than her living room. She didn't care for coffee shops these days, with everyone putting their feet up on the furniture, their computers plugged into wall outlets, baristas barking out names: "Jim! Nonfat, decaf cappuccino! Jim!"

Emerson wasn't there, so she bought herself a latte and returned outside to sit on a bench. Warmth held her quads, calves, and hamstrings, and she wished she'd opted for something iced instead of piping hot. Maybe Emerson had worked outside today, where the light and beauty were more significant than here at the coffee shop. She turned her head and took in the smattering of cotton-candy clouds.

Strolling away from the Java Bistro, her gaze lined up with an orange flash in the nearby parking lot. There he was, leaning against the front fender of his car, chatting with a woman, a girl really. The girl was tall, with thick, red hair, and her laugh carried like a breeze. The girl brought her face toward Emerson's, and he inched closer.

Searcy darted behind a nearby lamppost.

They kissed once more, and her hands ran through Emerson's hair.

Searcy felt a twinge spread in her lower back as she watched the two of them tuck into the orange car and rattle off down the road. Passion of that kind seemed a lot like going to Mars—the idea was grand, but it made more sense to stay on Earth. She took a long breath, dropped her hands into her pockets, and started toward home.

––––––––––

This was Emerson's routine now: his drive on Whiffletree Lane, his parking spot under the jacaranda tree, and the steep driveway. Not long ago, Father Guffey had told him that most believed their lives were straight lines, their own divided lane on the highway, but that realistically, they were a grid of railroad tracks that bent, and intersected, and sliced into one another. Father Guffey reminded Emerson of his father—the shock of white hair and the gap between his teeth. His dad, though, didn't pick at it the way Father Guffey did.

He knocked at the door, and Theo answered.

"How's life?" Emerson said.

"Just beat this guy in chess. A guy from Sri Lanka. I don't even know where that is, but he was a lot better than I was. He wanted a rematch, but I didn't think I could beat him again, so I told him my computer was glitching and got out!"

The boy's white polo was stained near the buttons—presumably with ketchup.

"How'd you beat him?" Emerson asked.

"He moved his rook to the wrong place. It happens sometimes."

"Give yourself some credit."

"I did have a great move with my queen. You should've seen it. Just bam." Emerson wanted to be let in, but he didn't want to break the boy's excitement. It was the first time he'd seen him come to life in this way, his gestures large, his mouth unstoppable. He wormed his way inside, moving slowly so Theo wouldn't lose his train of thought, and then he shut the door. They walked over to the usual spot. Then Theo stopped and took a breath. "You see how good a move it was?"

"It does sound super impressive." Emerson sat down and folded his hands on the table. "Where's your mom?"

"Upstairs, I think. You ever read a book called *The Pearl*?" Theo asked. He was a little out of breath.

"Nope. Heard of it, though."

"The cover looks boring."

"I don't think we're supposed to do that."

"What?"

"Judge a book by its cover. But I agree, the cover is boring."

"Everyone judges everyone by their covers," Theo said. "Maybe you could paint something and send it to this . . ." He peered down. "This John Steinbeck guy."

"If he were alive."

"He's dead?"

"Yup. Schools love dead guys."

"Why?"

"Probably because they can't do something stupid that would make the school look bad." Emerson scooted closer to Theo. The faintest trace of sweat, most likely from P.E., made its way to his nose. Theo spoke about dodgeball and capture the flag. There was an innocence in Theo that he wanted to protect, one that he knew the world was eager to tear apart. Maybe Theo was an artist. Artists were always pressured to toughen up, but truthfully, Emerson believed it was tenderness that needed to be developed—and he hoped Theo would hold onto his.

Eventually, Theo cracked the spine of the book and smoothed out the pages. "Can we each read a page?" he said.

"Perfect," Emerson said.

Theo launched into the words. The boy's reading voice was serious and more polished than his normal speaking voice.

Most of the day, Emerson's mind was stuffed with thoughts about the past and future, but here with Theo, reading sentence after sentence, life seemed far away. He didn't care about the book's content; he just enjoyed the rhythm of Theo's voice. He remembered his mother, reading to him every night, the way she used to do the voices, clutching her weathered copy of *Stuart Little*. His mother's hair had always been wet, too, as she loved to shower just before bed, and sometimes, a bead or two would drop right onto the pages.

It was the first time in about a year that Emerson felt this fuzzy warmth take hold of his body. He didn't think about it, because he thought doing so might chase it away. Instead, he popped his knuckles and shut his eyes and hoped the paragraphs were dense with small type, forcing Theo to read forever.

Searcy listened from the kitchen. Her boy's voice was soft and he often pronounced words incorrectly, but Emerson rarely corrected him. "It's funny that the author calls the wife fat," Theo said. "I wasn't expecting that."

"What else is going on here?" Emerson asked.

"The boy was stung by a scorpion," Theo said.

Searcy could smell her garlic bread in the oven that was beginning to take form. Emerson now read, his low voice drifting about the house: "She looked up at him, her eyes as cold as the eyes of a lioness. This was Juana's first baby—this was nearly everything there was in Juana's world. And Kino saw her determination and the music of the family sounded in his mind with a steely tone."

She watched the bread swell through the oven window. This was what she imagined she'd have with Keith—reading, cooking, love in a two-bedroom apartment.

"One second they had it all," Emerson said.

"And now the boy is sick," Theo said.

"Life is fragile, right?"

"My world was like that. Perfect and everything. Then my dad died."

"I thought your dad was away on business," Emerson said.

Searcy neared the door to the formal dining room.

"My stepdad. My real dad died when I was really little." Searcy didn't like when Theo called Keith his "real dad," and she was happy Hoit wasn't around to hear it. "My dad died while jogging. He had a hole in his heart that nobody knew about."

"I'm sorry, Theo."

"It's okay. How about you. How are your parents?" Theo asked

"I was an only child like you. I had the best parents."

"What happened?"

Searcy heard Emerson rap his fingers on the glass table. "I don't want to talk about it."

"Oh, okay. I'm sorry, Mr. Toffler."

"Let's get back to it."

"Are you okay, Mr. Toffler?" Theo said. "Mr. Toffler, are you okay? You look . . ."

"Damnit, Theo! Get back to work. Read."

The room was flat for a moment. Searcy stood still, her feet planted firmly, not wanting to move an inch. Garlic perfumed the kitchen, and Searcy waited for Emerson to say more, maybe apologize to Theo, but he didn't.

Papers stacked, pens clicked, and snaps fired on Emerson's bag. Not a minute later, Emerson wrapped up the session, and Searcy swung her eyes to the digital clock on the stove. It was a few minutes early.

"Take care, Theo," Emerson said, composing himself. "We'll read more soon." His chair squeaked on the hardwood and Searcy heard their four footsteps take to the front door.

"Goodbye, Mr. Toffler. I'm sorry."

Searcy turned the corner just as the front door clicked open. Both of their backs were to her, but she spotted Emerson's hand atop Theo's head. He rubbed strands of her boy's straight hair, causing some to pop up in certain areas.

Theo was ready to go to the airport to pick up Hoit, but he waited on his mom. She was always doing something in the bathroom. Sometimes, he would go into her bathroom and see all the supplies she had in there—it was a city of bottles.

He paced in the living room, scanning photos of his grandparents, and all of Hoit's relatives. Hoit had so many siblings and cousins that

Theo didn't remember most of their names. One was Julia? Or maybe Rachel? Only one photo of Theo's real dad stood near the mantle. Theo knew that his mom had many others in an album by her bed but only one was in the living room. Why this one? She wasn't even in it. His dad was thin and young, leaning against a tree and holding a striped fish that he'd just caught. His smile was big, and his legs were hairy, and Theo found himself picking up the frame every few months, searching for something new, but he never did. He found it weird that he still even needed to look at it.

He knew his mom worried about him. He knew she worried about him because she said it, but she also looked it. She would give him a big stare in the morning, when he was eating his cereal, and smile. And she would kiss him hard before bed, too. Whenever he mentioned something about his feet hurting, they would go to Foot Locker, and she would buy him new basketball shoes. She was always quick with a solution: getting chubby—celery and water. Getting pimples—buy a white cream that burned. Getting iffy grades—hire a tutor. He knew she was concerned, but he was concerned about her, too. You didn't need to be older than someone to worry. You just needed to love them.

One more time, his eyes traced over his real dad. He wondered if he had made her happy, made her laugh and smile. She was almost too grown up. He wanted her to have some fun, some friends, stop going to church, stop jogging every morning. He wanted her to be like those adults he saw in the park—with dogs and stories and fun.

"Mom!" he shouted. "When are we leaving? I'm starving!"

"Ten minutes!" she said. "Have a banana!"

It was always ten minutes. It was always a banana, Theo thought, shuffling over to the kitchen and cracking the top of the fruit.

Hoit had heard it said by his colleagues that it took one day to adjust for every time zone you passed, and he didn't even want to think about how many days that would total.

With Theo at school, he suggested a walk. "Want to head down to the park?" he asked.

Searcy was rolling out homemade pasta—his favorite—and her hands were dusty with flour. "Yes," she said, a light smile on her face. "That sounds perfect. The dough will need to dry out a bit, so it might be nice to go for a stroll. Give me thirty minutes." Hoit translated Searcy time to human time, figuring it would be at least fifty minutes before she was ready to go. She smiled.

That smile always got him. The one he'd first seen in—of all places—Dr. Barmore's dentist office a few years ago. It had been Hoit's first trip to this particular D.D.S., and she'd worked there as a secretary. After filling out some forms, Hoit hadn't grabbed the magazine he'd wanted, *Sports Illustrated*. No, he'd selected *The New Yorker*, attempting to make himself seem cultured, poetic, and intelligent. Then, just as he'd fanned opened the magazine and crossed his legs, a shower of white "Please Subscribe" cards fluttered to the ground, and she'd suppressed a laugh.

"So much for trying to look smooth," he'd said. She'd laughed again, this time not having to hold it back, and he'd introduced himself.

"Give me a hand," Searcy said. "I'll be done faster if you help."

Hoit headed over to the kitchen island, watching her fasten the spaghetti-cutting attachment and begin feeding the mass of dough into the machine. The resulting pasta was light, covered with flecks of flour, and Searcy took the strands, like fine hair, and laid them out over tea towels to let them dry.

"Ready?" she said.

"Yes," Hoit said.

Searcy put on her socks and running shoes, and they headed out the door and down the driveway. The park where Hoit liked to walk was only about a mile away, and he imagined Searcy was happy to get in some exercise, as she had forgone her usual jog to spend time with him.

Whenever he wanted to be closer to her, he replayed the moments from Dr. Barmore's office. The courtship. The butterflies. The phone calls. When love was new, a person was always fifteen years old. Palms sweaty. Heart thumping.

He took her hand in his as they made their way down the road. The wind blew hard, but the sun burned brighter, their bodies oscillating between moments of chill and heat.

Cars zoomed by as they headed toward Crenshaw. The large cross on the façade of Saint John the Baptist beamed in the sunlight, and Hoit saw Searcy make the sign of the cross, and he felt compelled to do the same. He knew God would forgive him before Searcy would, and he wondered if he continued to live his life and be a good man from this point forward, would the stain of sin blur into the background and get lost in time? Would telling her force him to change, or would it just make her leave him?

At the park, they watched dogs dart up and down the lawn and chase tennis balls. "It's good to be home," Hoit said. Searcy wrapped her hand around Hoit's body as they took a seat on a nearby bench. Her fingers worked up his muscles and over his spine. The same patches of skin had been worked by Biyu, but Searcy's touch was softer, more loving, and Hoit breathed hard and shut his eyes.

"What's wrong?" she said. "You okay?"

Hoit stood and took a few steps forward. "Just had a back spasm when I sat down." He grimaced.

"Oh, God," Searcy said. She leaned forward and slid on her sunglasses. "Maybe all that time on the plane?"

"That has to be it."

"You've seemed odd," Searcy said. "Is it your back?"

Hoit paced in front of her. If only he had someone that he could bounce these things off of. He'd lost most of his close friends, and he figured a deep, out-of-the-blue call wouldn't be welcomed after he'd missed weddings and baptisms. His older brother, Jack. He could trust him. Though he liked that Jack believed he had the perfect life, and after telling his brother the truth, Hoit knew he'd never be able to get that status back. In business, he loved the word *aphorism*. It had been explained to him that to get to the bottom of anything in the business world, it was important to highlight *exactly* what wasn't going right. Maybe there wasn't a market for something, or the return on investment wasn't strong enough. Many times, these facts were too painful, so a person would work around them, trying his best to get lost in other details, but it did *always* come back to that pure statement. That *aphorism*. That concise declaration of truth.

As they started back toward the house, he pushed his hands into his pockets. With the quiet came the aphorisms: Maybe the fact that it was impossible for him to conceive children because of a botched hernia surgery long ago had made him feel like less of a man. Maybe this idea of an instant family at forty-four hadn't worked for him. Maybe he wanted a child of his own. With *his* DNA. With *his* last name.

He continued down the road, taking a gander at his arm, which he'd believed Searcy clung to. There had been some contact, he'd thought. But no, her arms were at her sides, sliding in stride with her gait.

The sex between Searcy and Hoit yesterday had been awkward at best. She'd made the first move when they'd returned from their walk, kissing him after her shower. He'd undone the towel around her chest, and after that, she'd stopped keeping score. Usually, Hoit talked during sex, telling her she was beautiful and that he was lucky. Most times, he paired these words with neck and earlobe kisses, but not yesterday. Yesterday, he'd seemed sad and distant, and the sex was over within a matter of minutes.

What bothered her most about last night was the way she thought of Emerson in her mind as she drifted off. Twice, she snapped open her eyes whenever the lull became too powerful. It wasn't profane or deserving of her flop sweat: the two of them had just been purposelessly strolling across a field, rich with wheat and this golden hue, bright, too bright, and she'd told him about her upbringing, and how her father was a drunk and beat her mother, and how she resented her mom, almost more than her father, for never moving out, for never making a move. She opened up about how Catholic school and God had always been comforting and her only sense of reliability, things she rarely, if ever, spoke about, and Emerson listened, nodded, touched her on the shoulder, his fingers barely detectable, and she'd enjoyed it.

Between this dreamlike scenario, looking at his photos online, and spying on him at Java Bistro, she was overtaken with lust. Maybe her domestic boredom had run its course, and now she was acting out. She wanted to find old Searcy—the one who was not only faithful in her actions but in her mind. Sinning was sinning—seen or unseen.

Downstairs, she spread seeded blackberry jam onto a slice of whole wheat toast. The house was quiet enough—with Hoit meeting with his business partner and Theo at school—to hear even the weakest of sounds: the buzz of electrical poles outside, the click of the analog clock on the wall, the sound of a fluttering hummingbird in the backyard.

She pulled her phone out from her purse. She located Emerson's contact information, but before allowing her thumb to press Call, she rehearsed her lines; she would be pleasant, but when it came time for the important part of the conversation, she would deliver her words with clarity: "Yes, it's sad," she would say, "but the school is now offering tutoring as part of the tuition, something called homework club"—she didn't know if she liked the sound of "homework club," but that could be revised—"and so Theo won't be needing your services any longer." She would stop there. She wouldn't stammer.

Taking a bite of toast and a sip of coffee, she rehearsed—this time not just in her mind but out loud. After running through it two times, the lines came easier, and she dropped her thumb to the screen.

The phone rang. And rang. And finally, she heard his message: "Hi, this is Emerson. Are you sure this couldn't be a text?" Then a beep. She hung up, not prepared for voicemail.

She decompressed, collected herself, and inspected her reflection in the window. Her bright blue, off-the-shoulder sweater had been a wise purchase, and she tossed her hair back to better see the lines.

Her phone rang. "Tutor" beamed on the screen. "Hi, Emerson," she said.

"Morning, Searcy," he said. He sounded groggy, like this was his first conversation after waking up. "Sorry I missed you."

"Oh," she said. "Just wanted to talk to you about something."

"Yes, of course."

She thought he sounded nervous. "I just—" Searcy started.

"I'm not sure if Theo told you," he said, "but I was rude to him the other day. He asked me something, and I kind of snapped. I've thought about it a lot, and I just want to say that I'm sorry for doing that. It was pretty awful to do that to such a wonderful kid."

"He mentioned it to me. He said he was sorry that he upset you, and that he hoped you would forgive him."

"He opened up to me, and I didn't do the same," he said. "I'm sorry, Searcy. These days, 'I'm sorry' is all I seem to say."

Searcy cleared her throat and took in the hummingbird that was now inches from the backyard window. The hummingbird lowered its head towards a glass, flower-shaped feeder that she filled with sugary water every week. She thought it to be the same bird as yesterday, recognizing its golden belly. "Don't worry, Emerson. It's fine." She paused. "*Are* you okay, though?"

"How's Theo doing?"

"He's well."

"I bought him something over the weekend, something I think he might like. A little art set. A wooden one, like my dad and mom bought me when I was his age. Well, maybe a little younger." His grogginess seemed to wean with each word.

Searcy switched the phone to her other ear. "The reason I'm calling is . . . well . . ." She stammered and took a breath. "I don't think we can have you at the house any longer because there's a homework club at school, and it is part of the tuition, and we think, Hoit and I, that it's best to have the boy work with his teachers—directly with the teachers that assign the work. Thank you for all you've done, though."

That's what she wanted to say.

That's what she needed to say.

But she didn't.

Instead, she pictured Emerson scanning the aisles of an art supply store, picking out items for her boy—brushes and paints and palettes.

"So what was it you wanted to say?" he asked. "I'm sorry I cut you off earlier."

Searcy wiped her brow. "I . . ." she said. "I . . . don't think. I don't think you should *only* work on academics with Theo." She took a sip of coffee. "Do you think you might have time to teach him art?" She exhaled and waited for Emerson's response, doing her best to relocate the hummingbird that had seemingly vanished.

———————

Emerson and Searcy hadn't discussed when exactly the painting lessons would begin, but he gathered that they would clear that up today. He wondered whether Searcy had told her boy yet, or whether he would get the chance.

He arrived earlier than usual, parked alongside the curb, and listened to Neil Young's "Down by the River." A neighbor, a woman he'd seen a few times, picked weeds in her front yard. She was fortyish and in good shape. She wore tight jeans and plucked dandelion balls, lifting one of her legs as she bent over. When she stood and faced Emerson, she appeared to be speaking. At first, he thought she was singing or talking to herself, or on some sort of hands-free device that he couldn't see—ones that made ordinary folks look schizophrenic, but then she motioned for him to roll down his window, twisting her hand about, laughing. He turned down the music and heeded her instruction.

"What are you doing here all the time?" The woman's voice was high. "I see your car, and then I see you walk into Searcy's home. Is everything all right? I'm Josie, by the way." She walked up to the car, sticking her hand in through the driver's-side window. Her vanilla scent packed a punch.

"Everything's good," Emerson said. "I work with Theo."

"Poor Theo," she said. "He's always had a hard go of things."

"He's fine," Emerson said.

"That's good to hear. And Hoit? Is he home yet? I thought I saw him the other day. The poor guy's been away for a long time."

Emerson couldn't believe he'd silenced Neil Young for this. "Well," he said, "I have to get going. Time for work."

"Have a nice day . . ." She seemed to want his name.

"Emerson."

"Emerson," she said. "Take care."

"Same to you, Josie." He shut off the car, made sure the emergency brake was up, and took to the driveway.

"Not fair that Searcy has *two* handsome men in her home, and I'm here all alone."

Emerson nodded and kept moving. When he reached the stoop, he knocked. He'd become accustomed to the same figures, and it startled him to see a large man open the door.

"You must be Emerson," the man said.

"Hoit, right?"

"Nice to meet you," Hoit said with a slight Southern accent. "Theo was just singing your praises."

"I pay him well," Emerson said, looking at Hoit's sharp green eyes that complemented his light-gray crew cut and two-day stubble. Black eyeglasses sat on his nose, and he kept his lips tight, never exposing his teeth.

"Come in," Hoit said.

"Smells good," Emerson said. "It *always* smells good in here."

"Doesn't it?" Hoit said. "Searcy's making chili, my favorite."

"That's my favorite, too," Emerson said.

"You've never had Searcy's. Takes it to a whole new level. Puts a cinnamon stick in there or something. She told me once, but I forgot." He let out a puff of air. Then, abruptly, he shouted for Theo. "Let's go! The tutor is here!" He looked back at Emerson. "I'll let you be. You guys meet over there?" He pointed to the dining room, and Emerson nodded. "Perfect. I'll be upstairs in my office. Searcy should be back in a bit. She had to run some errands."

Hoit took to the stairs, and Emerson strolled over to the pot of chili that cooked on the stove. The burner was turned to a low setting with flames stroking the base of the pot, discoloring the gun-metal hue. He pulled in a long draw, savoring the spices: maybe paprika, maybe cayenne, maybe some cardamom, too. Emerson could see his mom cooking, the kitchen far smaller than this one, sometimes still wearing her scrubs. She would almost always forget about some part of the meal until the smoke alarms chirped, and then his dad would sprint from room to room, flinging open every window, even in below-zero temperatures.

Hoit was taller than Emerson imagined, stronger, better looking, and overall cooler. He hadn't pictured Searcy with a guy who wore stubble and stylish frames, but then again she enjoyed fashion, so maybe she was the woman behind his look.

Hoit's vibe, though, didn't match Searcy's in an obvious way. At least what Emerson thought of Searcy's vibe. Maybe it was that Emerson thought hurt recognized hurt. And he thought of her as a woman that was doing everything she could to compartmentalize her pain, tuck it away in her brain, and forget about it. He wasn't sure whether this was because she spent a lot of time raising Theo on her own, or whether it was because her past had never been addressed. She carried herself as a woman, dressed the part, talked the part, but inside it seemed there was a fragile girl working all the levers.

"What's up?" Theo said.

"Not much, buddy. Just watching chili."

"You like chili?" Theo asked. He dragged his backpack behind him, like the carcass of a slain animal. "I hate it."

"It's my favorite," Emerson said.

"Yeah, it can be really good," Theo said.

"Gonna hurt yourself straddling both sides of the fence like that." Emerson laughed.

They got situated at the table. Theo's bottom lip looked fatter than his top one, and many of his long eyelashes were clumped together in large peaks. He was starting to enter puberty, too, signified by a cluster of pimples along his hairline. "You happy Hoit's home?" Emerson said.

"He bought me a samurai sword but told me he couldn't get it through customs, so he had it shipped. It should be here soon."

"Nice to have a guy around, too, I bet."

"You're here a lot, too, though."

"You sick of me?"

"No," Theo said, reaching up at the pimples. "What's that?" He pointed.

"Part of the cool news."

"Cool news?"

Emerson told him about the art lessons, and the boy's eyes widened. He passed him the art kit, and Theo flung open the top to discover the contents: oil pastels, pencils, watercolor cakes, paint brushes, sanding blocks, and kneaded erasers.

"Mr. Toffler," Theo said. He looked down at the table. "Can I ask you something?"

"Shoot."

"Are you my friend?" Theo said.

"Yes."

"But you're paid to be my friend." Theo said. He reached inside his backpack and pulled out *The Pearl*.

"I'm paid to be your tutor. I choose to be your friend."

"Would we have been friends if you were my age?"

"We both like art. We both hate school." Emerson saw Theo smile in the reflection of the glass table.

"I think I like it better this way, with you being older, 'cause you've seen it all, and you can help me out, you know? Are we gonna paint here at the house?"

"I'll talk to your mom about it, but it makes more sense for me to bring you someplace fun. Get you out of the house a little bit."

"So I'll get to ride in your orange car?"

Emerson hadn't thought about that. He wasn't sure if he wanted to be responsible for driving Theo. He knew he needed to move forward, though, and that this would help. He rubbed his eyes. "If it's all right with your mother."

"I always thought friends were overrated," Theo said. "One time,

I watched this show about lynx. They live alone. I always thought I was like them." Theo picked at an eraser in the art kit. "But it's nice to have a friend, too."

Emerson patted Theo on the back and tried to picture a lynx.

In time, they got to reading, ping-ponging back and forth, paragraph after paragraph. *The Pearl.* Coyotito, Juana, Kino. The beaches of California. The warm winds. The Santa Anas.

Theo sat down for dinner, and his mom served him a ladle of chili from the steaming bowl. He could tell that she had tried to make tonight special by eating in the formal dining room instead of in the kitchen nook, like usual. Hoit had been sleepy the last few days—jetlag—so this was the first time they were eating as a family.

Theo listened to Hoit tell story after story about China and Japan. "I think you'd really like these things called *yurts*," Hoit said. He kept saying the word, and by the end of it, all Theo kept hearing was *yurt, yurt, yurt*. As Hoit went on and on, Theo's eyes drifted to the candles in the center of the table, then to the bowl of fruit between the shiny candlesticks. Mrs. Stanton always talked about organization, and Theo always thought it just applied to students—keeping your backpack and folders clean, knowing your grade, heading your paper correctly. But no, it had to do with everything. He thought about how his mom did all these little things—candles and tablecloths and setting the table—and how it all just seemed to appear. She didn't make a big deal out of keeping the house warm and cozy. Things just happened. Someone had to wash these placemats, do these dishes, buy long matches to light the candles. Someone had to buy more candles when these ones would become tiny stumps, and the more Theo thought about it, the more he became tired.

"Did you miss us?" Searcy said.

"Did you guys miss me?" Hoit said.

"I asked you first," she said, smiling.

"Of course. Every time I saw something beautiful or interesting, I couldn't help but think of you guys and how much I wanted you there. It's funny, the world looks weird without someone to share it with." Hoit added some sour cream and shredded cheddar cheese to his bowl of chili. "How's school, Theo?"

It was always the same questions with Hoit. Theo referred to them as "the greatest hits": How's school? What's new? How's life? You hungry? How are the ladies treating you? It seemed like Hoit was asking questions out of duty, like it was something he had to do a couple of times a day, like brushing his teeth. "Okay," Theo said, taking a sip of milk. "I mean, I really love working with Mr. Toffler." He reached for a roll from the basket in the center of the table. Curls of steam escaped as he ripped the bread open. "He's cool and fun. And he really helps me with my work. He told me today that we're going to be doing some art."

"He *told* you?" Searcy said. "I was keeping it for a surprise."

"He probably thought you already told me," Theo said.

"You like the idea?" she asked.

"I love it."

"Good," Searcy said.

"Art lessons?" Hoit said. "Do you need those?"

Theo shrugged. "He's a good friend, too."

"A thirty-year-old man is your friend?" Hoit said.

Theo knew it sounded strange, and he didn't think Mr. Toffler was *that* old. Maybe Mr. Toffler was the first of many friends. Maybe he was a comfortable starting spot where he could learn about friendship.

"Why don't you just make friends at school? What about that Curtis kid from last year?" Hoit said.

"He moved," Theo answered.

"There are plenty of kids, Theo. Just get out there and meet people. Don't worry about being a little chubby or coming off as weird. Just be cool and nice. It's like business. If you go one-for-four, it's a success."

Silence hung in the air like a bad smell, and Theo took a bite of his roll. What did Hoit know about friendship? The only people Theo ever saw Hoit with were business people, and they always had these big white teeth and hairy forearms and reeked of cologne.

"Hoit," Searcy said. She narrowed her eyes.

"Mr. Toffler's just cooler than kids at my school. He likes me. I can tell," Theo said.

"You don't know him. Just because he has an old Volkswagen and a doctor's bag from the war, doesn't make him your friend," Hoit said.

Hoit was always trying to change him—make him smarter, hipper, cooler. Like Theo himself was a business that could be adjusted with a little effort. "You're the one who doesn't know him," Theo said in a whisper so only his spoonful of chili could hear him.

"I think it's nice," Searcy said. "Whatever makes you happy." She dragged her napkin over her lips.

Theo's cheeks flushed. He hoped no one could tell he was bothered. The room *was* dim, and the candles *did* make everyone look sort of rosy.

"Sorry I didn't make dessert," Searcy said. "I thought the home-made rolls were enough of a treat."

"I'm beat," Hoit said. "And a little stuffed. That was really nice."

"Go relax," she said. "Theo and I can do the dishes."

"I'll leave you two to it then." Hoit pushed himself up from the table, and the legs of the chair scraped against the floor.

Theo started collecting the empty dishes, piling in the spoons and butter knives. Mom blew hard on the candles, causing these doughnut-shaped clouds to swirl. Even though she'd only killed two flames, the room turned much darker than he expected.

Searcy watched her, and her father's, favorite movie, *The Bicycle Thief*—though he'd always called it a *picture*. It was one of the few positive memories she had of her dad—that and when he'd cube up stale bread and sop it in milk and sugar as a sort of bedtime treat. Other than that, he was a car without brakes, careening every which way and drinking himself to sleep. Ironically, it was her mother who'd passed first, years ago, of a sudden and serious cancer. Her father had moved to live with his brother in Iowa, and she had never visited.

Hoit let her know he was turning in early—his back pain still gripping—and planted pecks on both Searcy and Theo's cheeks before shuffling up the stairs.

"Feel better," Searcy said.

When the movie neared its finish, she noticed Theo had fallen asleep on her leg and she brushed his hair away from his forehead, feeling a couple of Braille-like zits that reminded her he was growing up.

The credits rolled, and Searcy thought of her father, sitting in his burgundy recliner, a glass of bourbon resting on his knee, passed out. Many times, her mother had told her they were leaving him, even packed bags and made reservations at nearby hotels, but when the time came, she couldn't follow through.

Searcy powered off the TV, woke Theo, and walked him to his bedroom. She fanned open his duvet and tucked him in. Her ears perked at the sound of wind and rain. "The clouds aren't holding back," Searcy said.

"Open the windows," Theo said.

The two of them listened to the rhythm of the droplets. The smell, that first rain smell—a combination of earth and water—washed into the room. There was a term for the smell, and her memory spun. If she could only grab a syllable, the first couple of letters, maybe she could decipher the rest.

On Theo's desk rested a photo of Keith, the one that she'd always kept downstairs, of him on a guys' trip, having just caught a fish. Why had Theo brought it here? Running her hand over her boy's bare arm, all the way from his wrist to his shoulder, listening to the downpour, she wondered how many more of these moments she'd have. Everything had an expiration date, and she was wise enough to know that hers was coming, too.

"Do you ever feel bad for little things?" Theo said.

"What do you mean *little things*?" she asked.

Theo sat up. "Like small things, things that aren't alive. They actually don't have to be small. Just feel bad for them?"

"Like what?"

"Like at school, there's this tetherball pole, but there's no ball on it. It's just a pole with a chain. And sometimes, I'll be in bed, and I'll think about that chain and the pole, just sitting there in the dark. Like right now, in the rain. Or I'll think of our roof, or the trees, or a book someone left at school on a bench, outside. All these things left alone, getting wet, they sometimes make me sad."

"They do?"

"Yeah. Like the table you have in the back yard, with the yellow pillows, just getting beaten up by the sun."

"Does it seem like everything is alive to you?"

"That's kinda what Mr. Toffler said."

"Did he?" She had purposely not been home for the last few tutoring sessions as a way of detoxing herself from Emerson, but it hadn't worked as well as she'd hoped. Emerson was the first man who'd reminded her of Keith. They shared charm, an interest in old cars, and most importantly affection for Theo.

"Something about the Native Americans," he said. "How they thought everything had a soul. He said it shows that I have a lot of love for life. I kind of wish I didn't, though. It's really tiring."

Searcy continued to stroke his arm. Eventually, the two of them whispered their prayers, and Searcy left, closing Theo's door halfway, before taking to her room. Hoit's gentle exhales soothed her as she slid into cold sheets. In the moments between Hoit's breaths, she listened to the tapping on the shingles above, thinking about how Theo had mentioned everything being alive in some capacity. Maybe the shingles were relieved to have rain? All that sun day after day—maybe a soak did them good? She wondered if there was a word for Theo's philosophy—a term for caring about *all* things. And, as soon as her mind focused on that thought, the word for the smell of first rain floated to the surface. Petrichor. "Petrichor," she whispered, wishing the word were as pretty sounding as the actual sensation.

Hoit sipped his iced tea and waited for his business manager, Mason, to show up to the restaurant. Mason was punctual, but Hoit was always early by at least ten minutes. He added a packet of sugar to his tea and stirred in the white powder.

Mason waved from across the room, and Hoit returned the gesture. Mason was a fast walker, moving quickly with everything: his speech, his mannerisms, his wit.

"There he is!" Mason said, reaching over the breadbasket to shake hands. "What's new?"

"Not much," Hoit said, scratching at his stubble. "Things went well out there, *really* well. Looks like we have agreements, and—"

"Now that you have claimed a few companies, our stock is on the rise," Mason said.

The waitress approached. Not wanting to interrupt, she stayed still at the edge of the table. "Did I tell you about the girl I'm seeing?" Mason said.

"May I take your order?" the waitress finally said.

"Ahi burger and a sparkling water for me," Mason said without even opening the menu.

"Same," Hoit said.

"Men who know what they want," she said.

Hoit always seemed to be attracted to waitresses. Something about the serviceable nature, the polite voice, the smile. Sure, it was all for fifteen percent—more like twenty these days—but it was nonetheless pleasing. The waitress sauntered away, her hips flowing from right to left in her tight black pants. Hoit spread his napkin over his lap and listened to Mason's story.

"So I met this woman at the Rainbow Room. Beautiful. Tanned skin. Big green eyes." There was always a new woman in Mason's life. Always beautiful. Always tanned. Always cliché. "So she's there, ordering some girly drink with one of those baby umbrellas, and I think she winks at me. I'm thinking the whole time . . . Did this girl just wink at me? Who the hell winks these days? But, at the same time, I'm thinking, I should wink back. I mean . . . wink back, you moron! She likes you! So I do. I wink back."

"Really?" Hoit took a sip of tea. There was relief in being interested in someone's story.

"Yup," Mason said, pausing. "And all of a sudden, she's like, 'Did you just wink at me?' And I'm like, 'You just winked at *me*.' And she shakes her head, bats her eyelashes. My heart's beating hard. I'm mean, this girl is something. I can feel the *bambambam* in my chest. Hard. Like the damn thing's gonna break my ribs. And she just starts to laugh. 'I've never heard that line before,' she says. I tell her that I swear on my life that I thought she winked. We get to talking. Turns out we're both from Rhode Island and both into cooking."

"Unreal. Don't you want to have someone to come home to? Don't you want the consistency?"

Mason laughed. "I'm thirty-three. I need to get this all out of my system now, I think."

"You remind me of that guy in the beer commercials," Hoit said. "You know, the silver-bearded man with the women and the velvet jacket."

"You're nuts," Mason said.

The waitress brought out the burgers, smiled, and asked them if they needed anything else. She had a slight dimple on her chin and dangly earrings that jingled as she spoke.

"We're perfect," Mason said.

She walked off, making her way to the little computer near the bar and stood, tapping the screen.

The chewing slowed the men's conversation, allowing Hoit a few seconds to reflect. "Let me ask you something," Hoit said. He scanned his surroundings. "Have you ever cheated on someone?" He thought the words were harsh, so he did his best to soften them with another query. "You know, with all the girls you have?"

Mason glanced up. "No," he said. "Not 'cause I'm some great guy I'm just not with women long enough for those things to happen. My dad cheated on my mom, and I know my mom knew about it, but I don't think she cared. I mean—I'm sure she cared, but she didn't show it. He was still a good dad in so many ways. He provided for us, put food on the table, let us live in a huge house and go to great schools. Bought me my first condo . . . Everyone loves the idea of family, but not everyone can be monogamous. I mean, I hope I can. I hope those things aren't genetic." He wiped his mouth. "What about you?" He tossed the tomato off his sandwich.

Hoit jammed his tongue into his bottom row of teeth, prodding a piece of fish that was wedged between his molars. "No, not really," he said.

"So yes?" Mason laughed.

Hoit saw the strip clubs, flashes of porn, felt the heat from Josie's touch, and heard the squeaking mattress with Biyu. "It's never meant anything to me. It's not like I've made love to them."

"You older guys and your 'making love,' but I understand."

"I just—I got married late. Stuck in my old ways. I miss that kind of excitement, I guess. When I was little, we were poor and powerless. Now, it's different," Hoit played with his straw, knocking it into pieces of ice.

"My friend went to a counselor a while back. Said it helped. I can get you the number?"

"No, that's okay."

"What about Searcy? Does she know?"

"No. No clue."

"What would she do?" Mason leaned in.

"Well, I know she'd hate me . . . I know that. But she wouldn't leave. She needs me. What's she gonna do? Go back to raising the kid on her own. She doesn't believe in divorce. I mean, shit, she married the first guy she slept with. That's why I love her, you know? Her purity. Her faithfulness. I married my conscience . . ."

"Just move on, man. Leave it behind you like a dirty towel in a hotel room."

Hoit's pulse clipped along. Mason continued to speak, offering advice and suggestions and generalities. The words floated his way, but didn't quite dive into his ears. He peeked over Mason's shoulder at their waitress, who was booths away, collecting the tab from another table. She straightened up bottles of ketchup and mustard, asked a busboy to collect dirty dishes and change the tablecloth. She fanned her hair over her shoulders and ran her tongue over her lips. Sarah, Hoit thought. She looked like a Sarah. Or a Rebecca. Maybe even an Ashley. And as she headed off, her eyes landed on Hoit's stare, and a smile played on her lips.

———————

"Hello? Madame Fournier?" Emerson said, knocking. The doors in the retirement home were almost double the dimensions of normal ones, probably for wheelchair access. In any case, their sheer volume made Emerson feel small. He heard the sound of the latch unfastening from its jamb and watched the knob turn.

She was just as he had seen in books and photos—her hair only a shade lighter, her skin more wrinkled.

"Madame Fournier," he said again. "I'm Emerson Toffler. The letter guy."

"Oh, mon Dieu," she said. "Monsieur Emerson. Thank you for coming." She had a classic French accent, almost musical. "It's nice to get a visit from a young man. I've forgotten what they look like." She invited him into her small space. Her "apartment" was nothing more than one large room, similar to Emerson's life on the boat but with a higher ceiling. He took a seat in a chair near a sliding glass door that let out on to a patio. She sat on the edge of her twin bed that looked institutional, with gears and levers, reminding him of his time at the hospital. It had been a little more than a year since Emerson had awakened from his coma after the accident.

"I imagine this is what it's like when normal people meet ball-players," he said.

"Emerson," she said—pronouncing it *Eh-mere-sun*—"I'm only five feet tall, much too small for sports. Maybe I could be a jockey."

He wanted to speak to her about art, but instead they just sat

there, like old friends. He scanned the room, noticing many cruci-
fixes—some in bronze, others in wood, a few in stone. No art hung
on the walls. "Are you still working?" he said. "Doing any painting?"
He crossed his legs.

"No more," she said. "My hands are . . . look at these things."
She held her hands out in front of her. "My knuckles are the Alps."

"Too painful?"

"Yes."

"You've done so much for painting, for art."

She stood. "You smell like cigarettes. Do you smoke?"

"Yes."

"I knew I liked you. May I?"

Emerson fished the pack from his coat pocket and Madame Fourn-
er slid open the glass door that led to the balcony. The two of them
headed outside and stood in the overcast weather, the small amount
of sun doing what it could to find cracks in the clouds.

"Ah, I've missed you," she said, taking the pack. "This was my
breakfast for so many years: just cigarettes and sweet nothings. What
are you painting, Emerson?" She lit up and passed him the pack.

Emerson told her about his eyedropper watercolor series.

"You're married?"

"No."

"Good," she said. "Love is the death of the artist. Too much sex
and happiness, and no work gets done. A painter needs to be on
edge, moody, one foot in dreamland, the other mired in loneliness
and anger. Picasso's blue period was his best, no? Certainly a choice
for you, no? Handsome and cool. You just don't want a girlfriend?
A wife?"

Emerson placed a Lucky Strike between his lips, lit up, and took
a long inhale, consuming nearly a quarter of the cigarette with one
pull. "I just want to be good at love," he said, thinking of his parents.
When he was a kid, his favorite place to be was in the hot tub, and
from there, through a window sliced by panes, he could see his parents
leaning into one another, watching sitcoms, their laughs warbling
through the glass. It was nice to see their love when things were mun-
dane and still—Mom in her blue nightgown, sipping white wine, and
Dad in his University of Vermont sweatshirt, eating pistachios. More
than a year had passed since the car accident, and Father Guffey had

been right: the tutoring, the routine, the becoming part of society had helped. His night terrors were now weekly instead of daily, and he hadn't been drinking in order to fall asleep. But the visions were alive: black night, yellow asphalt lines, snow whipping toward the windshield, and the thunderous sound that ripped apart the quiet.

"My husband was American, you know, and he told me about grades in this country. 'C is average,' he would say. 'Everyone is okay with average. But not me. I want an A or nothing at all.'"

"Something like that," Emerson added.

After Madame Fournier finished her cigarette, she flicked the butt off the balcony, trying to hit an old man below. She came close, only a foot wide. When the old man in the porkpie hat stared up at the balcony, Madame Fournier cupped her hands around her mouth and bellowed, "I almost had you!"

The man said, "What?" a few times but Madame Fournier didn't answer.

Emerson laughed, and Madame Fournier rested her hand on his shoulder. "I don't know much about love," she said. "People think, you know, I'm French . . . I'm an artist . . . I just wake up in love, singing Edith Piaf. But here's what I know to be true: If you love someone, stare at them for a moment. Really gaze at them, put all your energy into your pupils, like fire could fly from them. If the person doesn't love you back, she will say 'What?' But if she does love you back, she'll hold your eyes, too."

Emerson rubbed his cigarette butt on the balcony's railing, then dropped it into a bush. He loved the mercurial nature of Madame Fournier: one minute she was flinging cigarettes at the elderly, the next she was a sage. "You lived there, right?" From the high balcony, Emerson pointed to Catalina, a nearby island he had never visited, but only knew because of Natalie Wood.

"Yes, for a long time."

The sun finally bullied its way through the clouds, and Emerson felt the right side of his face begin to burn, but he knew this moment with Madame Fournier was special and that any indication of his discomfort might break the spell. "Cool," he said.

"You're strange, Emerson." She traced the outline of the island with her gnarled pointer finger. "I'm starting a foundation out there. Such an ideal place to paint. Acres of light, always a permeating trace of fennel, like pastis, in the air. There are bison and fox, and you feel *so* far away from L.A. Sometimes I forget about it entirely. I look out to the ocean, and think, When did that island get there? And sometimes, when I don't have my contacts in, I think, My goodness look at that oil tanker!" Madame Fournier shut her eyes and angled her face toward the sun.

They were silent for some time, and Emerson listened to the sounds below: cars rushing on the boulevard, the whir of a helicopter in the distance, mariachi music playing from some direction. "I wish I could be back there," she said. "It became hard. I thought it wasn't smart to be old on an island. It was the first time in my life I was logical."

"That was smart," Emerson said. His phone buzzed. It was probably Carly. She had called a few times today.

"I wouldn't recommend it—being smart."

"Would you like to get something to eat?"

"You have places to go, things to do. You should spend time with other young people."

"Do you like sandwiches?" Emerson asked.

"Of course."

"I know a spot," he said.

"Is it far?"

"No."

"I'd like to go somewhere far. And to a jewelry store. I need to get this watch fixed."

"I know spots like that, too."

Madame Fournier took a few moments to get her things together. She fetched her purse and put on a sweater that only buttoned at the top. After checking her pill organizer, she slid on her huge sunglasses that resembled a welder's helmet and made sure the door was locked. Here she was, Emerson thought, one of the greatest living artists, alone and in need of company. No matter how well a person planned, the ending was never desirable.

"Merci," she said as Emerson held the door open.

Emerson scoured his brain for *you're welcome* in French. Even after living so close to Montreal for all those years, nothing came to him. "My pleasure," he finally said.

November

THE BLACK LEATHER INSIDE Mr. Toffler's car was cold, especially where it hit Theo's bare legs. Maybe wearing shorts wasn't the best idea, but this morning had been relaxing, and Theo thought jeans seemed like too hard a material.

The car had a motorcycle sound to it, like the engine wasn't big enough to pull the two of them, but it did all right. Every few seconds, Mr. Toffler would pull this lever back, this little metal stick that poked out from the floor, and Theo fastened his eyes to the area, wondering what was happening. Mr. Toffler moved his feet a lot, too. Way more than his mom would when she drove the SUV. She usually just sipped coffee and listened to 91.5, a classical music station that didn't have commercials. But here there was a lot going on. The car was loud, the music—which was weird—was twangy, and the engine seemed right behind Theo's head, screaming. "Where are we headed?" Theo asked.

Mr. Toffler grabbed the metal stick and threw it back. "To a park. There's one I really like. Did you put on your seatbelt?"

"Yes," Theo said. Mr. Toffler had asked him that three times now.

"Good," Mr. Toffler said, looking at the buckle.

Theo kept his eye on the little round ball atop the metal stick in the center of the car. It had numbers and lines on it, even a letter: R, 1, 2, 3, 4.

Mr. Toffler wasn't chatty this morning, but there were two types of silence: the "I don't want to talk you" kind and the "words might ruin it" kind. Theo thought he and Mr. Toffler had the second one.

"What kind of music is this?" Theo said.

"Neil Young."

"It's cool."

"It is," Mr. Toffler said, rolling down the window, adding to the noise.

"What's this song called?"

"It's my favorite: 'Down by the River.'"

"That's sounds nice."

"It's about someone killing his girlfriend down by the river."

"Really?"

"Don't tell your mom."

They pulled up to a light. The car growled, almost angry sounding, wanting to continue to fly down the road. Theo thought Mr. Toffler was a good driver, always using his blinker and slowing down for curves. Theo hoped to be as good a driver when he turned sixteen. Maybe he could even get a Karmann Ghia. He wondered how expensive they were.

"I've never seen a car with this metal thing coming out of the floor. What are you doing?"

"You mean a manual transmission?"

"Is that what this is called?"

"Yeah."

"What are you doing to the car?"

"Changing gears." Mr. Toffler rolled up his window and scratched at his beard. He explained how a transmission worked. "Your mom's car, for example, has all these gears, but the car does the shifting automatically."

"Oh, that's why it's called an automatic," Theo said.

"Yup."

"She just slides the stick to *D*, and the car goes."

"Ha." Mr. Toffler sped up and yanked the shifter toward him. "You see . . . we're in second now."

"Is it hard?"

"Takes some getting used to. That's all. I've actually never owned an automatic." For the next few minutes, Mr. Toffler showed Theo how the engine pushed and red-lined at a certain point, how the gears begged to be changed. Mr. Toffler pointed toward his feet and demonstrated the process of taking his foot off the gas, pushing in the clutch, and tugging the stick.

"Can I try," Theo said.

"I don't think it's a good idea."

"Okay," Theo said. He folded his hands in his lap. He wished he hadn't asked. A banner that hung in the gym at school said, "You miss all the shots you don't take," but it sometimes seemed whenever he launched the ball, it never swished.

Mr. Toffler took a breath and then looked in his side mirror. Quickly, he U-turned and then swooped into an empty bank parking lot. "Maybe we can try it here," he said.

Theo bit his lip and dug his nails into his palms. "You sure?" he said.

"It'll be fine."

"I can't drive."

"Not drive," Mr. Toffler said. "Shift."

"Are you sure? I don't know."

"I'll tell you when, okay?"

"Okay," Theo said, his face burning. He focused, his eyes wide, not blinking. His hand hovered inches above the vibrating knob. He listened to the engine's beat.

"When I accelerate, the car will *really* want to go into second. First gear's a lot like childhood. It goes by really fast. So pull this sucker straight back when I point to you."

"Oh, God," Theo said. He thought Mr. Toffler looked more locked in than usual.

Mr. Toffler did exactly what he said he would, and when the Karmann Ghia pulled, he pressed the clutch and pointed at Theo. Theo grabbed hold of the stick, but didn't know he had to pull so hard.

"Yank it!" Mr. Toffler said. "Pull the bastard."

The noise got to Theo. His hands twitched. Sweat worked across his shoulder blades. He shut his eyes and pressed back into his seat, letting go of the knob.

Mr. Toffler changed gears. "Don't worry! You can try again. Don't be timid. You won't hurt the car. Remember: it *needs* you to help it out!"

Theo nodded. The once cold leather now stuck to his skin.

They lined up again and repeated the process.

"Now! Now! Now!" Mr. Toffler said. Theo took both hands this time, placing one atop the other, grabbing hold of the stick. He thrust the gear back, and the engine sighed.

"Yes!" Mr. Toffler shouted.

"I did it!" Theo's arms and legs tingled. He stared at himself in the tiny side mirror, checking out his smile. The air in the car swirled and messed up his hair.

Mr. Toffler let out a long breath and dried his forehead with his shirt sleeve. He reached for the corners of his eyes, too, and seemingly wiped hard at a couple of tears before they could really get started. Why? Theo thought, listening to the engine. He could detect it wanted a change, and Mr. Toffler was always there, in perfect time, hitting the clutch, pulling the stick back, making the car happy.

Emerson parked. He hadn't really seen the boy with this confidence before, and it was strange that all society did was tell children to have pride. Sure, people had to have some sort of innate belief in themselves, but more often than not, confidence came from accomplishments, and what undertakings did a young person have?

They got out of the car, stepping into the hot park. Emerson ran his eyes over Theo's clothes. "You should probably change your shirt. Should've said something earlier."

"I don't have anything to change into."

Emerson hurried back to the car. He reached behind the driver's seat and pulled out an old Harley-Davidson sweatshirt that was scarred with paint. "You might be hot in this, but we'll see."

Theo draped the hoodie over his head and lost himself in the mass of cotton.

"Your mom won't be mad at me for ruining your clothes," Emerson said.

"Do you know a way of memorizing the planets?" Theo asked.

Emerson unloaded the car. Brushes, canvases, easels. He backstroked through déjà vu, picturing his mom helping set up his supplies near the Winooski River. He could see her beauty mark above her lips, her grayish hair, and her small fingers. It amazed him that she thought he was skilled enough to paint a moving river, but he never questioned her decisions.

"Mr. Toffler?" Theo said.

"Sorry. Uh, when I was kid, my teacher taught me *Mrs. Vincent eats mint-jelly sandwiches under Nancy's porch.*"

Theo threw a bag over his shoulder. "That's weird."

"Now Pluto isn't even a planet, so the saying now just ends with 'under Nancy,' which seems kinda perverted."

Theo laughed. "Maybe Mrs. Vincent is *really* tiny."

"Maybe."

"I feel bad for Pluto. I mean, what did it do wrong?" Theo asked.

"It'll always be a planet in my mind," Emerson said. "I mean, it's still out there, orbiting the sun, right?"

They strolled to the middle of the field. The day was free and open, with little spurts of wind here and there. Trees surrounded them, and in the distance, Emerson could hear the thump of a basketball on the blacktop courts. He set up an easel for Theo and then one for himself. He showed Theo how to wipe his brushes clean and switch colors. "So this is it. Today I just want you to enjoy the process. Usually a painter sketches before, but today, I just want you to have fun. Get used to the way the watercolor feels, the way it smears on the canvas. We can both paint that tree over there, if you want." Emerson pointed in the direction, and stood behind Theo, showing him how to hold the brush and how to bend the bristles against the canvas. Then he backed off. He hated when teachers micromanaged, and he just wanted Theo to paint and discover. Theo, in time, found his own way with the brush, holding it almost like a chopstick, and Emerson told himself that astounding athletes often didn't grip a tennis racket or shoot a basketball correctly. There were certainly scientists and scholars that weren't good spellers and had poor penmanship. Sometimes it was good just to live. Good, just to do.

"I don't want to paint the tree," Theo said.

"Okay," Emerson said, setting up a palette for Theo.

"How about those birds over there? The crows on the wire?" Theo said.

"Perfect."

Time passed with purpose, and the outside world faded. Theo combined both real elements and fantastical ones into his work: his sky, painted a lemon color. His birds, instead of black, were blood red. "I'm hot," he said a couple of times, before tossing the sweatshirt to the ground, deciding to work bare chested.

When Emerson finally peeked at his watch, he realized that there were only ten minutes left in their session. He'd arrived at Theo's home to pick him up a few minutes early, and they still had to pack up the supplies, and he had to take Theo back home, but the boy was transfixed. It was strange how painting the world right there in front of you gave it deeper meaning.

"How's it coming?" Emerson said.

"What?" Theo said.

Emerson noticed Theo's shoulders had reddened. "You like how it's turning out?" He pulled out a cigarette and lit up, forgetting that Theo had never seen him smoke.

"I think it sucks."

"Welcome to art."

"Is that part of it?"

"Most of it, actually."

"My mom says if you want to be a butterfly, you have to spend some time as a moth."

"I think she means caterpillar, but we won't tell her." Mr. Toffler set his brush down on the easel's stand and took a drag of his cigarette. "Sorry," he said.

"It's okay. I can smell it on you sometimes." Theo licked his lips. "You shouldn't do that, though. Have you seen the pictures on TV, the one with the black lungs?"

"I have. The only thing that makes me feel better after I see them is smoking."

"Have you tried to quit?"

"I have." Emerson placed his hand on Theo's bare shoulder. The skin, when pressed, turned white, but as soon as Emerson removed his fingers, the burn reappeared. "Nice," Emerson said, glancing at Theo's work.

"Really?" Theo said.

"Better than this." Emerson pointed to his canvas.

"That's all you painted? Just one branch."

"Painting is patience. Plus, I was enjoying watching you." He flicked some ash into the air.

They washed their brushes in a little canister of water that Emerson had brought along. Then they took two trips to the Karmann Ghia, where they piled in the supplies.

"It's weird that the trunk of this car is in the front," Theo said. "It makes me think we're having engine trouble every time." Theo put his T-shirt back on.

"I know," Emerson said.

When they were about done, Theo scuffed his sneaker along the pavement, zig-zagging it in front of him. "Am I your favorite student?" he asked.

Emerson shut the trunk and walked Theo to the passenger-side of the car. The tag on his shirt poked out, and Emerson slid it back against his skin. "Without question."

The boy nodded and plopped inside the car, pulling the door shut.

Emerson strolled around the back of the car, grabbing his keys from his pocket. He took another pull of the cigarette before rubbing the butt out with his boot. His breathing came easy, and his usual impatience wasn't present. He waved at a woman who was walking her Doberman. "Such a pleasure to see a father and son painting on a day like today. It's all too rare," she said.

"Oh," Emerson said. "It's—"

"He looks at you with a lot of love," she said.

"Well, he's . . ." But Emerson stopped there. "That's nice to hear," he said, watching the tall woman saunter away with her dog, their bodies growing smaller and smaller as they headed across the field.

Hoit returned to the restaurant two more times before asking the waitress, whose name was Candace, if she would like to work for his company. Recently, an employee who did secretarial work had quit, and he'd told Candace that she'd been so kind and professional, and that the pay would be much better.

"I can't believe I've never stopped here. I've driven by time after time." Candace said, strolling along the cliffs of Abalone Cove, a little bay miles from Hoit's home. "Do you think we can go down to the water?" Her hair sheened.

People seldom frequented the beach because of its treacherous path, but Hoit agreed. And, after ten minutes of "be carefuls" and "watch your steps," they'd arrived at the seashore, where Candace removed her huarache sandals and tucked them into her purse. Her toenails were painted a bluish color, contrasting against her tanned feet. "I've never done an interview like this, at the beach," she said. "When I took the server job a while ago, I came in and we sat at one of the dining tables at eight in the morning."

Hoit scanned the shore. It was just the two of them and a few sandpipers that darted through the salty ebbs and flows. "I take my lunch break here often. Thought it was best to do it this way. I don't really have an office, and I hate meeting for coffee at two in the afternoon—then I'm up all night."

"I knew you were important," Candace said.

"What do you mean?" Hoit turned around, checking behind him, taking in the four footprints.

"Just had a feeling. There's a look to guys with power."

"I suppose the sword helps," Hoit said.

"True." Candace fanned out her hair, and a slight breeze unfurled her way, holding the strands up for a moment before allowing them to fall flush against her back.

"It's hard to meet friendly people, and I thought it was kismet that we met that day. It's not the first time I've poached someone from another company. If I see what I want, I go after it. Worst you can do is say no."

"Well, I could probably do worse than that." She grinned.

They made their way over to some tide pools, taking a seat on a piece of driftwood. As Candace tried to impress, speaking to Hoit about her degree (something to do with journalism), Hoit again thought of that word, *aphorism*. He'd decided that he enjoyed feeling desired more than being loved. Love was certainly a deeper, richer feeling, but being desired was more immediate.

"Do you think this kind of work would be something you'd be interested in?" he asked.

"The salary is much better, and I don't have to work nights. I love the idea of your company. The smallness, the one-on-one treatment."

"I'm glad you feel that way." Hoit crossed his legs. Despite the driftwood's lack of comfort, he enjoyed facing the same way as Candace, not having to partake in eye contact. "I was reading the other day that a person should change jobs every three years. We aren't built to do the same thing year after year. The whole system is set up to go to college, find a major, and work in that field until you're ready to hand in your gun and badge, and maybe it's wrong. Maybe we should sample more of what life has to offer. That's what allows us to grow and become richer."

"I can believe that. No one would think that being a server would help me so much, but I think everyone should have to spend a few years in some sort of service-based profession . . . have to wait on someone and offer customer service."

Hoit set his hands on his lap. When Candace spoke, he felt better about hiring her. She was savvy and interesting. There was a moment of quiet and, in its peace, Hoit forgot whose turn it was to talk. He thought he had just said something, so he remained still, taking in the water, which had a Caribbean-like hue to it today. Normally the sea was almost a navy color, but today, the sun found its way around algae and kelp and illuminated the Pacific in a tropical fashion. He had taken Searcy here early in their relationship and played hooky from work on a hot June day. They had eaten tacos at the far corner of the cove where an overhanging of rocks offered shade.

He studied a flock of pelicans, tracing along the water's surface. The image was freeing, relaxing, and induced reflection. No matter what a person did, however immoral, life continued to tick. There was beauty in that. Every day, every sunrise was a chance to be better, and he felt enlightened having arrived at that conclusion, but then disappointed that he couldn't actually see any of it through. Pressure built in his chest, gripping at his heart. He'd seemingly forgotten to breathe for a few moments. "So," Hoit said, "take some time to mull it over. The job's yours if you want it. I know you'll have to give two weeks' notice." He turned his head and smiled.

"Look!" she said.

A pelican careened downward, its wings tight against its body, its yellow beak reflecting the sun as it torpedoed. With no sound and an undetectable splash, the bird took to the water.

The two stood, waiting for the bird to emerge, the surface calm, but feet below, a warzone. It took longer than Hoit expected, maybe ten seconds, but eventually, the pelican buoyed to the surface with a silver fish snapping back and forth in its mouth.

"Look!" Candace said again.

"Wow," Hoit said.

The pelican rested on the water until the fish was gone.

"Did he eat it, or did he just store it in his . . . waddle?" Candace asked.

"Waddle?" Hoit laughed.

"You know what I mean."

The pelican wound up, working its large wings. When the sea was quiet, the feathers could be heard, pounding against the air, doing their best to gain traction. Finally, the pelican was up, feet from the surface, wings elongated and tilting.

"Must be nice," Candace said. "To just have a few things to do all day. Simplify it all: hunt, sleep, rinse, repeat."

"For sure."

Candace lost her balance in the sand and grabbed hold of Hoit's shoulder. She kept her hand wrapped around his arm while she worked her sandals over her feet. Her long nails pricked his skin, even through his T-shirt.

Then, Hoit kissed her. Candace resisted for a second, before giving way, her lips parting and her tongue gliding against his. After a few seconds, he pulled back. "I'm sorry," he said.

"It's—" she said. But she didn't finish.

"I'm sorry," Hoit said again.

They huffed as they climbed the steep incline to the parking lot. "The way down wasn't so bad," Hoit said, "but all that relaxation is now out the window." Candace didn't answer. When the path flattened out, they leaned against a tree to catch their breath. Hoit pulled the base of his T-shirt up and blotted his brow. "One more little push, and we'll be there," he said to fill the emptiness. They started up again. Their shoes grating at loose dirt, their mouths sighing. Once they were at the top, in the parking lot, they took in the view. Candace rested against the fence, and Hoit swung his head from right to left. Open on the right. A car on the left, at the far end.

A car he knew.

A car he'd seen before.

An orange Karmann Ghia with a black top.

He searched for Emerson but couldn't spot him. A compression took hold of his temples and his throat tightened. He walked Candace to her hatchback. *It's okay. You're with a friend. All is good. All is well.*

Candace offered a cold goodbye. "I'll call you," she said. But Hoit had a feeling she wouldn't.

———

The peaceful thoughts that Emerson enjoyed—the sun, the ocean, the sky, the book of poems he'd had with him—all vanished when he spotted Hoit at Abalone Cove. He'd been watching him this entire time, perched from the hill. He knew it was Hoit because of his gait—he'd noticed that right away—a certain gait, his toes always pointed at ten and two o'clock. And bouncy, like his shoes were built with springs. And Emerson had noticed his car, too.

What was Hoit doing here in the middle of the afternoon? Didn't he have a job? And who was this younger woman he was showing to her car? This twenty-something that he'd just kissed?

Hoit approached. Emerson gathered that Hoit had spotted him sitting atop the bench with his feet on the slab of wood usually reserved for posteriors. There wasn't much he could do now.

"Emerson!" Hoit said. "How are you?"

Emerson's body became one taut muscle. He closed the book of poems over his thumb so that he didn't lose his place. "Hoit," he said. "Nice to see you." For a moment he both lived inside his nervous system and somehow floated above himself, wondering how he looked. He wanted to appear causal, like he hadn't seen anything.

"Nice. Nice." Hoit stood in front of him, blocking the ocean. Sweat had stained the underarms of his white tee, and his face was burned. They shook hands. In a quick moment, Hoit threw his neck to the right and left, popping the vertebrae in perfect succession.

Emerson let his finger slip out from the poetry book. Hoit glanced at the cover.

"Never been one for poetry, myself," Hoit said. He joined Emerson on the tabletop. "Hate the subtlety. I mean, just come out and say it. All that mystery. It annoys me."

"Beautiful day, right?"

"You like doing the digging, huh? Trying to search for meaning . . ."

"I don't think about it much. Just like the way it makes me feel." A timely breeze pushed from the Pacific, cooling the sweat that formed along Emerson's hairline. "Like the idea that a poem can mean different things."

"I see. What's in front of you isn't always what's in front of you."

"Exactly."

"You're not from here, are you?" Hoit asked. "Where are you from originally?"

"Vermont."

"Yeah, you have a touch of an outsider thing going on."

"Really?"

"What's it like there? In Vermont? Just maple syrup and snow?" Hoit sucked his teeth.

"In Vermont I looked for noise, and here, in L.A., I search for quiet."

"You ever do any skiing?" Hoit asked. It was a frequent cause and effect. Emerson spoke about Vermont, and people mentioned skiing, and the horror replayed. A year earlier—more now—he and his mom and dad had visited Stowe. They'd spent a few days snowshoeing, sipping hot cocoa, and watching fires crackle—"real Norman Rockwell shit," as Emerson's dad always called it. The series unfolded, always in the same order: night, drive home, the yellow unfurling line on the road, music on the stereo, the parked snowplow, too little time, metal on metal, glass shattering—a long note that never faded.

"Did you?" Hoit said again. "Did you ever do any skiing?"

"Sure. Yeah."

"You any good?" Hoit asked.

Him, fading off at the wheel. Wanting to turn up the Marvin Gaye, but not wanting to wake his sleeping parents. Mom, in the backseat, no seatbelt. Dad up front, in the passenger side, his head against the window—the old Range Rover barreling through the night. Flurries like shooting stars, assailing the windshield. The wipers working across—a steady beat.

Emerson bit into his cheek. "Okay," he finally said.

Hoit and Emerson stayed seated. "It was a beautiful day for a walk on the beach," Hoit said. "A nice walk with a nice friend."

"For sure," Emerson said. "I bet."

"You married, Emerson?"

"No."

"Girlfriend?"

"Not really."

"So just the painting and the tutoring. A nice, little life."

"Something like that," Emerson placed his hands on his knees, rubbing them hard against his jeans.

Hoit's voice was steady, but underneath, he seemed tense, like a shaken can of beer. "Is Theo your best student? Your smartest?"

"Oh," Emerson said. "I—"

"Probably hard for you to say."

"Sure," Emerson said. "Hard to say."

"You probably have to keep all those types of things confidential, right?"

"Exactly."

"You seem like a trustworthy guy."

"Sure."

"Are you trustworthy, Emerson?"

"I think so."

"You are?" Hoit asked. "Yes or no?"

"Yes."

"It's an important quality—maybe the most important one."

"Nothing bigger than that," Emerson said.

Hoit exhaled. He jumped up and stood in front on the bench, leaning back, stretching his lower back. "I think there are whales out there right now, starting their migration from Alaska to Mexico. Hard to see 'em, though. They're close to the surface, but they never *really* pop out—all you see are their fins and the occasional spout of water."

"I've never seen one," Emerson said.

"If you keep staring, you might."

"Okay," Emerson said.

"It was nice chatting with you, Emerson." Hoit shoved his hands in his pockets and took to his car across the way, a green BMW sedan. He removed a dress shirt from the back seat and buttoned up, checking his reflection in the windows, dragging his fingers through his coarse hair. Emerson couldn't believe Hoit was doing this right here in Searcy's zip code. If Hoit had to run around, why not do so on the road? In China? In Japan? In wherever the hell? Sure, sure, a transgression was a transgression, but even so, there seemed to be a morality to cheating.

Emerson stayed on the bench, allowing the sun to soak into his pores. He lit a cigarette, took a pull, and stayed quiet. After a while, he opened the poetry collection and tried to read a few stanzas, but it was hard for him to concentrate on anything other than Hoit.

DECEMBER

"It'll be a long dinner in Malibu, but we should be home by midnight," Searcy said. "I'm trusting you, Theo."

It was the first time she'd left him alone for the evening, but she figured he was old enough now, and she didn't want Hoit to get on her about Theo being a mama's boy. She knew a few more "are you okays?" would trigger such a thing, and Hoit would start with the "don't baby hims" and she would say, "Don't you know mama's boys make wonderful husbands?"

"I'll be good," Theo said.

"Keep all the doors locked, okay? Oh, and I made you fried chicken"—she didn't tell him she'd baked it so it was healthier—"and mashed potatoes"—she didn't tell him that she'd whipped in some turnips. "Just hang out in the house and overdose on video games, okay?" She couldn't believe her words.

"Be good," Hoit said, patting Theo's shoulder. "Man, you been workin' out?" he said, laughing. "Almost hurt my hand."

"A lot of painting, I guess," Theo said.

"With a very heavy brush," Hoit added.

"I'll check in with you," Searcy said, strolling away from Theo.

Hoit held the car door open for Searcy, and she slinked in, smoothing her dress as she got situated. She wanted to see Theo go inside and shut the door behind him, but he stayed put until the car was down the driveway and in the road. "He'll be okay," she said, more to hear the words aloud than anything else.

Hoit drove fast, changing lanes and whipping between cars, and it wasn't long before they found themselves on Highway One. The ocean to her left, cliffs to her right. Sea breeze, salt, every which way. With a quick swipe of her hand, she brought down the vanity mirror and inspected what she could in the small rectangular glass. She'd bought a dress just for tonight—a strapless magenta gown. She'd even driven to a strip mall yesterday to get a spray tan so that her shoulders and collarbones wouldn't seem so pale. The dress was the type she would have loved to have designed for her own line, which, back then, she'd called "Assuage." Gravity pulled the folds down so they remained perfectly parallel, and there was a touch of an asymmetrical hemline that stood out to her.

"You look amazing," Hoit said. "Doesn't the mirror tell you that?"

She smiled. "I love this suit on you." She inspected his angular jaw. He hadn't shaved completely, leaving a small dusting of stubble.

It occurred to her to call Theo, but she resisted. She put her head back, but not too hard as to ruin her hair, and stared out the passenger-side window. The dunes of Malibu were something to behold. People from all across the world came to see them and dart up their quicksand-like bodies.

Soon enough, they entered a dim steakhouse with crisp tablecloths and flickering candles. One moment, she was daydreaming, and the next, she was in the restaurant, shaking hands with important people with long Japanese names that were hard to pronounce.

Before the conversation at the table was in full swing, Searcy's hand found its way atop Hoit's, and the two of them exchanged gentle strokes. She felt safe with him. He was strong and took care of her, and she felt guarded and important. He ordered a bottle of French wine and told a story about France: how he'd gone on this hike on a closed trail near Marseille, and when he was surrounded by police, he just continued to ramble on in English until he'd exhausted the gendarmes. He was a showman with clients, the life of the party, quick-witted and fast-paced.

In each woman, Searcy found a bit of herself. Quiet, polite, grinning, hair sprayed to perfection, jewelry glinting in soft light. There was something more, too: an old-fashioned quality, a tacit language that could only be spoken between kindred women. No one asked them questions. No one cared where they grew up or what their interests were. They filled seats, made their husbands more human, and complemented the meal (not unlike the breadbasket in the center of the table).

Two times, Searcy had excused herself to go to the restroom, and both times she had called Theo on the home phone. "Do not listen to music or play your games with your headphones on," she'd told him, but she knew he was. Why else would he not pick up?

No word.

She imagined, as only a mother could, the most brutal and horrible sights. Never did she believe herself to be all that creative, but when it came to tragic scenarios, her mind made *Dracula* seem like a fairy tale.

After one more call from the ladies' room, she decided that something had happened to Theo. He was a trustworthy boy. He had begged her a couple of times now to stay home alone, and the lock he always attached to his plea—his eyes big, his mouth tight—told her that he would adhere to any guidelines.

The idea of staying in the restroom embarrassed her. What would the people at the table think? Oh, who was she kidding? No one even noticed. In fact, just as she pondered this, a woman from the table came strolling in, a Japanese woman who wore a modern-cut dress fashioned from kimono-like material. Her dark hair reflected the light in large strands, making it appear white. Searcy explained her situation to the woman, who introduced herself as Reiko.

"Maybe the phone isn't working," Reiko said.

Searcy tried again.

The phone rang and rang.

Nothing.

Reiko reapplied some lipstick before blotting her lips on a piece of tissue paper. "Is there someone you can call? A neighbor?"

Searcy thought about Josie. But she didn't want to have to deal with her. Plus, Josie wouldn't pick up if she thought the call was from Searcy. She really only answered to Hoit. Sometimes Searcy would drive by Josie and offer a wave, and seldom was it returned. If Hoit was in the car, however, Josie turned into the Rose Parade, throwing her hand back and forth.

Emerson?

He wouldn't mind swinging by, would he?

She thought of children who always muttered, "My mom is going to kill me if she . . ." And part of her did want to kill Theo.

"Emerson?" she said. Her voice echoed across the tiled bathroom. "Hi, it's . . ."

"I know who you are." He laughed. "Haven't seen you in a while. You okay?"

"Sorry to bother you like this on a Friday night, but I left Theo home alone." The syllables popped from her mouth as if the sentence were just one long word.

"Oh."

She explained more of the situation. "Would you mind?" she then asked.

"No problem," he said. "That's fine."

"Do you have company? It seems noisy," Searcy asked. "I hate to do this to you."

"It's no big deal. I've had too much wine, so I'll have Carly drive me over there."

Reiko squeezed Searcy's hand as she got off the phone. "Is it wrong that I'm actually excited by this? I mean, if I have to hear one more of these stories . . ."

Searcy smiled. The two women returned to the table. In this world of uncertainty, it was pleasing to know that she could count on someone. Everyone had that one call—and she was surprised at how fast Emerson had become the go-to.

"I hope you're charging her for this," Carly said. "What kind of person calls and just expects something?" She pulled the car up the long driveway. The world was dark save for the headlights.

Emerson jogged the walkway, feeling dizzy. Through the windows, he could see that most of the home's lights were illuminated, their bright rays streaming through the glass, pouring onto various sections of the lawn. Even from the front door, he detected the flash of the TV. Emerson called for Theo, pounding on the front door. "Are you coming?" he said to Carly, turning around. Emerson faced the door once again. "Theo! It's me. It's Emerson. It's Mr. Toffler!" His senses sharpened. The fear of Theo having disappeared sobered him faster than black coffee paired with a cold shower, and he darted to a side gate, lifting the latch, sprinting to the back of the house. "Theo! It's me! You okay? Please! Theo!" His voice swirled around the yard, glancing off the tall trees and tile roofs. He balled his fists and let his heart strike at his ribs. "Goddamn it, Theo," he said.

Moments passed, and booze pushed to the peripheries of his brain.

"Mr. Toffler," a voice said out of the blackness of the backyard.

"Theo?"

"Yeah." Theo sniffled and coughed.

"You okay?" Emerson said.

The living room's light wasn't strong enough to do much else besides light the walkway surrounding the immediate perimeter of the home, so it startled Emerson when he felt the boy at his side. He ran his hand over Theo's hair the way he always did, and the two of them stood as one in the backyard, their bodies growing comfortable in the blackness. "I'm sorry," Theo said. "I went outside, to the garage, to get a drink from the other fridge, and the door shut behind me. I wasn't thinking. I've just been in the backyard. I could . . ." He stopped.

A trace of eucalyptus floated through the air, and the dewy grass worked through Emerson's canvas high-tops. He dialed Searcy, passing Theo the phone. Theo rattled off the same story, and he could hear Searcy, calm, on the other end of the line, telling him that she'd put four watermelon drinks in the kitchen fridge. "Here," Theo said, passing Emerson the phone. "She wants to thank you," he said.

"Hey," Emerson said to Searcy, "can I bring him back to my place, so we don't just have to wait in the backyard like two peeping Toms? You can just swing by on your way home and pick him up."

"All this because of a watermelon drink," Searcy said.

"It's always the drinks that get us into trouble," Emerson said.

Searcy laughed. "Okay," she said. "Text me your address."

The lights on the side of the property were activated as soon Emerson and Theo made their way toward them. When they reached the driveway, Emerson rubbed his wet shoes on the concrete, stamping off blades of grass, and introduced Theo to Carly. Carly rolled down her window and shook the boy's hand. "Emerson's told me a lot about you," she said.

"Really?" Theo said.

"He said you're a very talented painter."

"Cool."

"All right," Emerson said, wishing he had some gum. "You hungry, Theo?" he said.

"Yeah," Theo said. "My mom made me chicken, but I never got to eat it. It's there, on the kitchen counter, all cold and gross."

"I'll make you something when we get back to my place."

It might have been the booze. It might have been the cold air. It might have been the fact that it was a Friday night, but Emerson felt right, perfect. Every now and then, the world would swaddle. The feeling was rare, and no matter how much a person sought the sensation, it didn't come when expected. Sometimes all of the ingredients were there, but the results didn't follow. Sometimes none of the ingredients were present, and the feeling came along anyhow. Emerson turned up the stereo and whipped his head around to make sure Theo was okay.

"Is this Neil Young?" Theo asked.

"Nope," Emerson said. "No clue what this is."

"Not another Neil Young fan," Carly said. "Did you have him listen to 'Down by the River'?"

"It's good. And kinda scary," Theo said.

"You see?" Emerson said.

Emerson could tell that Carly was doing her best to adjust her mood. She'd probably taken in the scenario and realized that there was little he could have done better. But it did bother Emerson that she hadn't exited the car. Maybe she was just tired, he told himself.

Theo sat atop Mr. Toffler's boat and drank an Orangina. Every time Mr. Toffler opened up the latch and stepped down the ladder into the living area, Theo stretched his spine and shot his gaze at the opening. He wanted to see inside the boat. He wanted to walk around, run his hands over the furniture, and check out the sailboat. Usually the first thing adults did was give everyone a tour, like it was hard to figure out one house from another: bathroom, bedroom, kitchen, toilet. But now, he *needed* a tour.

"You like the Christmas lights?" Mr. Toffler said. "Carly and I put them up."

"How long have you lived on this boat?" Theo asked, staring at Carly, who descended the ladder into the boat. Her breasts moved as she worked her way down, and Theo tried hard not to look, and, at the same time, tried hard to remember what he'd seen. Why did her lips always seem wet? How did she keep them that way? Lots of licking? Chapstick? A special lipstick? Vaseline? Had anyone ever finished a tub of Vaseline?

"That soda treating you well?" Mr. Toffler said.

"Yes," Theo said. Mr. Toffler had gone on and on about how Orangina was the best soda around and how the bottle was the only one that had any character. "Rotund," he called it.

"Want to come inside? I'll make you a grilled cheese. My cooking won't compare to your mom's, but my parents always said, 'Hunger is the best sauce.'"

Theo followed Mr. Toffler inside the boat.

Theo had heard the word *claustrophobic* many times in his life (it was possibly the biggest word he knew besides *supercalifragilisticexpialidocious*, which didn't even really count, because he didn't know what it meant, and after a few times, it became annoying to say), but he actually liked the feeling of being trapped here in the boat. He didn't know if there was a word for that (he knew *phile* was good, so maybe *claustrophile?*). The ladder led him down into a kinda-big room, and in the far corner was a bedroom. He sat at a tiny table and looked out a window the size of a plate, watching the colors of the Christmas lights blend on the water like an oil stain.

A record player sat next to him. Next to it was a stack of records, glossy and shiny, some out of their covers. Theo ran his nails gently over the records, letting his fingers come into contact with the grooves. The difference in texture pleased him. All the covers smelled of dust, but one did stand out to him—one with a single figure on the cover, his head to the side, a cloud of cigarette smoke wrapping him. And around the man's face (which was impossible to really see) was a blue halo, almost turquoise, and the title was cool, too. *Bumpin'* it was called, by a man named Wes Montgomery. "Is this good?" Theo said.

"Do you know who that is?" Mr. Toffler stood at the smallest stove. There was only one burner, and Theo thought of his mom's stove—with six big gas flames.

"Not really. It just looked cool."

"Wes Montgomery is the coolest man to walk the earth. It's what we're all after—to have a sound. All you have to do is listen to this guy play one chord on his guitar and you know it's him. Just like all you have to do with Raphael is see the way he paints an angel or the way Seurat uses color. Go ahead, put it on."

"I don't want to hurt the record player."

"Here's how you do it." Mr. Toffler's breath was strong. "There you go," he said. "Lay it down flat. Nice." Theo was careful with the disc. It was lighter than he imagined. "Now flip the power on. Right there. Now bring that needle and drop it into the first groove. Good."

A pop. A crackle. Loud notes bounced across the tiny boat while

Theo stayed still in the corner, his hands together, his ears absorbing the sound. He tried to bottle the notes, the sweet guitar chords and the sharp bass beat. "This is 'Bumpin'?" he asked Mr. Toffler.

"Yes," Mr. Toffler said.

Theo took a seat on the tiny, built-in couch that was aligned with the right side of the boat, opposite the kitchen. He sucked on his empty Orangina, fishing at a few pieces of pulp that were wedged in the bottleneck. Carly wrapped her arms around Mr. Toffler's neck, and they swayed. Both of them seemed like good dancers, moving to the music, turning in a circle just like the record. Carly stared directly into Mr. Toffler's eyes, hard, like she was trying to pull something from him, but Mr. Toffler's gaze didn't rest just on her pupils. His bounced around. He took in the flames on the small burner, glancing at the spinning Wes Montgomery disc, even smiling at Theo. Carly leaned forward until her forehead was pressed against Mr. Toffler's. Her lips moved, and Mr. Toffler shook his head. She shrugged, and when the song ended a little while later, Mr. Toffler slipped out from her arms and returned to the stove. Carly was pretty and fun, but Theo thought Mr. Toffler could do better.

By the time Searcy reached the marina, it was almost midnight. Stars surrounded a crescent moon, and she could hear waves blasting the shore in the distance. The sounds aided in soothing her as she scoured the dock, searching for her boy. She had modified the story a bit, not telling Hoit that she'd called a bunch of times, but instead reporting that Theo had gone to a neighbor's home and called Emerson because "he didn't want to ruin our dinner." Hoit had been impressed, adding that it was "mature of him." Then he'd said, "This Emerson. He seems to be . . . *omnipresent*. Is that the word?"

"That's the word," she'd said. "I'll pick Theo up. Just drive home. I know you're tired." Hoit had wanted to take her to the marina, telling her they were both tired, but she'd told him she wanted some alone time after having to smile all evening.

Again, she texted Emerson, asking where his boat was located. But after a minute, she knew he probably wasn't going to respond. He'd mentioned dock ten in his text, but it was dark, and the pillars weren't lit. In between the ebbs and flows of the Pacific, the sounds of laughter rippled free from a nearby boat, one with Christmas lights wrapped around its masts. She tracked it down, removing her high heels that threatened to wedge between the worn slats of wood. After flinging her leg over the side of the hull and onto the boat, she took a deep breath and steadied herself. She grabbed hold of the captain's wheel while her other hand smoothed out her gown. "Hello," she said, peering down into something of a crawlspace.

"Mom!" Theo said.

"Searcy!" Emerson said.

Searcy clutched the ladder and lowered herself into a boat that was rich with yellow light, music, and a buttery smell. Once she turned around, she saw that Theo was safe, smiling, his legs crossed ankle-on-top-of-knee, and she was certain she'd never seen him in that position before. His forehead was sweaty, and his smile more than a third of his face. A young woman introduced herself as Carly. She wore chandelier earrings and fake eyelashes. Her teeth were white, even in this golden lighting. "I'm so sorry," Searcy said to her. "I ruined your night."

"Have a seat," Emerson said. He turned down the music.

"You look like Cinderella," Theo said.

"No shoes even," Emerson said.

She pointed to her purse, where her stilettos rested, and took a seat next to her boy, surprised at how firm the cushions were. Her first thought was that everything seemed old, from another era, as though a film crew could enter at any moment and set a scene in the 1970s. Near the bed rested a stack of self-help books, mostly on grief, and atop those stood a little skyline of orange prescription bottles.

Searcy then inspected Carly's button-down shirt, a take on a man's dress shirt but constructed of a more feminine material. She'd left the first three buttons undone, and a dark bra peeked through the lacy fabric. The bed was unmade, the sheets coiled and messy, and Searcy pictured Emerson and Carly together, wrapped in the blueish cotton, their bodies slick with sweat and excitement. She shook the image from her mind. "Is this Wes Montgomery?" she asked.

"It is!" Theo said. "Whoa, Mom."

Searcy rubbed her bare feet on the carpet and smiled. In this moment, she was the woman that knew exactly what was going, and it was as pleasant a sensation as expected. "My dad loved this record. 1963?"

"What's it say, Theo?" Emerson asked.

Theo crunched down on the bread. He inspected the back cover for a moment, then said, "1965."

"Sounds about right," Searcy said.

"Is that when your car was made?" Theo said.

"Close." Emerson laughed. "It's from '62."

"Maybe Wes had one," Theo said.

"Makes you think," Searcy said, crossing her legs. "When that car was new, Vietnam hadn't happened, Martin Luther King Jr. hadn't given his dream speech, and the Beatles were just four kids with bad teeth and floppy hair."

"And the moon was untouched," Emerson said.

"Yes, the moon." Searcy ran her fingers through her hair. She locked in on Carly's fingers intertwined with Emerson's, their bodies side by side, empty wine glasses on the counter. All the signs pointed to Searcy saying, "Goodnight," and taking Theo back home, but she wanted to stay. Energy buzzed about her being, and she felt invigorated. The strong yawns that had accompanied her on the car ride home with Hoit had vanished. Now, she felt caffeinated and alive, not focused on *how* to live, but just living.

"Mom," Theo said. "Do you know about this cheese? What's it called again, Mr. Toffler?"

"Jarlsberg," Emerson said, leaning against a table.

Theo reached over and grabbed a bite of his grilled cheese, pulling the bread away from his face. The gooey cheese didn't reach its breaking point until Theo's hand and his mouth were at least a foot apart.

"Theo," Emerson said. "Can I get you another soda? Searcy, a glass of wine?"

Carly unclasped her hand from Emerson's, picking one foot up off the ground and leaning forward toward his ear. "I'm pretty beat," she said. "I—" She fluttered her eyes and took a moment to search for her purse that was right on the floor by the ladder.

"Yeah," Emerson said. "It's late. Thanks for everything, Carly."

As much as Searcy railed against reality television, she enjoyed this. Either Emerson couldn't pick up the neon-lit context clues, or he simply didn't care that Carly wasn't too pleased to be bumped for a mom and a boy. She slipped into a shawl-collared cardigan and draped her bag over her shoulder, taking to the ladder, leaving the three of them all alone.

Emerson poured some wine into a "Kiss Me! I'm Irish" mug and passed it over to Searcy.

When the record stopped spinning, the needle lifted off the vinyl and swung back to its original position.

Searcy scanned the titles of a few books that were off to the side. "*Love in the Time of Cholera* is one of my favorites," she said.

"Oh yeah?" Emerson said.

"That ending. The yellow sail. The boat. Not being able to head back to shore. It makes me think about who I would want on my boat forever," Searcy said.

"It does make you do that," Emerson said.

Searcy was only four sips into her wine, but she'd been receiving texts from Hoit, so, after a few minutes, she patted Theo on the back and told him that they better get going.

"I knew it was coming," Theo said.

Searcy passed over her empty mug, and Emerson led the two of them to the deck and then out onto dock ten, making sure that they took their time and didn't end up in water. The mood felt right to Searcy—the laughter, the wine, the ocean's lilt in the background.

When they reached the parking lot, Searcy nodded in Emerson's direction and watched Emerson hug her boy. The light was soft on his face, and Emerson held out his forearm so Searcy could balance herself and slip on her heels. As their eyes held one another, a warmth dispersed through Searcy's spine.

Searcy and Theo hopped into the SUV, and it fired up. Emerson waved, and she watched him stand there, in the same spot, until she left the marina and turned out onto the main road.

———————

Hoit tapped a glass with a spoon, and Searcy's eyes worked open. He'd slathered some whole wheat toast with jam and made French press coffee. A glass of juice sat off to the side, and the *Los Angeles Times* was tucked under his elbow.

"What happened?" Searcy said.

"What?" Hoit said. "I need a reason to make my wife breakfast in bed?"

"I'm just surprised is all."

"I haven't been as good to you as I want," he said. He set the tray on her nightstand. "I'm gone. And sometimes when I'm home, I feel gone, too."

She brought the tray atop her lap and pushed down the French press's plunger. "I know what you mean," she said.

The night had been uneasy for Hoit, and he'd thought of Candace and the beach. Her toes, her freckles. Why had it taken him so long to hit his stride with women? Business had given him confidence. His marriage had given him confidence. Now, he felt, he had the tools to entice women, but no reason to do so. He told himself that he would try harder to be better. That he would do the right things until they felt like the *only* things. It was just like getting into shape. The first month was the hardest, right? But everyone—even Hoit himself—always felt better after a workout. "I was thinking that maybe we could do something as a family today. What do you think? Maybe whale watching? Or a movie? I know Theo's been talking about go-carts."

"I think Theo would love mini-golf."

Hoit laughed. "Mini-golf?"

"It's been a while since we've done that," Searcy said.

Hoit studied curls of hot coffee moving toward her chin. "How did everything go last night with Emerson?"

"Good," she said.

"I worried when I didn't hear from you."

"It was hard to find. He lives on a boat, so I had to find the right dock, and then I stayed to let Theo finish his sandwich."

"I get a strange vibe from him. Don't you?" Hoit adjusted the blinds, then took a seat at the edge of the bed. "Living on a boat? That car? His paints and stuff? I mean, really, the other day I think he wore suspenders."

"This coffee's good."

Hoit reached for her feet that were deep under the covers. "It's from the silver can."

"That's for special people, remember? Dinner parties and such."

"You're not special?" Hoit said.

"You know what I mean." Searcy smiled.

Hoit stroked Searcy's feet beneath the mound of covers. He hadn't lowered one of the window's blinds, and in the distance, he saw Josie, strolling along the edge of her yard. She plucked weeds in a light nightgown that seemed to lift whenever a wind worked through suburbia.

Searcy crunched on her toast and sipped her coffee. He thought about coming clean and telling her about the hotel room in Shanghai. About Candace. About Josie.

Mason had said something once, too, and Hoit had held the words in his mind: "Your life has been an unbroken boulevard of green lights. Whatever you want you get. Life's a big to-do list for you." Hoit thought maybe Mason was right. He checked boxes regularly: school, college, grad school, building the business, selling the business, starting a new one. Sure, there were failures along the way, but eventually, and quickly, things panned out, and when marriage became the mission, he'd found Searcy within months.

Searcy slipped into some yoga pants and running shoes.

"You going for a run?" Hoit asked.

"Want to come with me?"

"I did have enough cake and wine to kill a child last night." Hoit could sense that beyond her large pupils she was anticipating a no, so he said yes.

"Really?" she said.

"What about Theo?" he said.

"He sleeps until about nine. We'll only be gone a half hour."

"Half hour," Hoit said. "Jesus."

"This is gonna be fun," she said.

"Your definition of fun is so different than mine," Hoit said, heading down the stairs, wondering where he'd left his Nikes.

"The octopus is seductive, no?" Madame Fournier explained to Emerson. She pointed to the tank. "Look at the way the tentacles dance. I find it to be so . . . sexy."

"Bringing you to the aquarium was a bad idea," Emerson said, taking a pull of frozen lemonade. "You ever seen those Japanese paintings of octopi having sex with women?"

"They're delightful," she said. "I've been wanting to come to this aquarium forever, so thank you." She buttoned up her sweater and fished a tissue from her purse.

"If we're talking about sexy fish," Emerson said, taking notice of a small boy next to him, "I think I'd have to go with the jellyfish. Their tentacles—or whatever the hell they're called—are always beckoning."

The small boy whose family wasn't around smashed his hands against the glass.

"Be nice, you little monster!" Madame Fournier said. The boy scurried off.

Emerson and Madame Fournier headed through a hallway with an overarching glass roof, filled with sea creatures. There were schools of short, silver fish; and sea lions; and starfish, pressed against the glass. "All this ocean, and I don't have to swim," Madame Fournier said. "Look at us, here, on the bottom of the sea. We are two crabs." They stood still in the uncrowded museum, their heads rotating over the scene, oohing and aahing at different creatures.

"I've lived more with you during these little visits than I have in the last few years," Madame Fournier said. She stated her emotions with little regard for how she would come off, and Emerson admired her honesty. When he brought this up with Madame Fournier, they were outside, at the "petting zoo" portion of the aquarium, massaging the rough skin of small sharks and inspecting sea anemones. "You have to be old to say these types of things," she said. "At sixty, I stopped caring. I decided I was going to tell people what they meant to me. What good is all this quiet kindness doing us?" She leaned into his body, and Emerson peered down at her head. Her sawdust-blond hair was thin, and much of her scalp could be seen. Her perfume came to him in bursts, and he picked up the traces of rosewater. "Also," she said, taking hold of his hand. "This 'I've known so-and-so for thirty years' is a bullshit way to look at friendship. It's not a 401K. Friendship is a rocket. When things work, it's in the air in a flash."

Emerson agreed, leading her over to a sun-soaked bench that was in line with a few tanks. They now inspected the sea life from the outside. "After you've been under the water, this angle is crap."

"Can we smoke here?" she asked.

"I don't think so."

"No?"

"The fish, I guess," Emerson said.

"The fish don't give a shit. They don't breathe air."

"I think they do. They just don't get it like we do," Emerson said.

"Who are you? Jacques Cousteau?"

"My parents told me I took my first steps during his show. They were watching TV, and I just went for it." Emerson reflected on the way his parents always told the story: parts were reserved for his mom, others for his dad, and, at times, they spoke in unison.

"Is that right?"

"That's what I'm told."

"Everyone's loves first steps. These days, I sometimes think of my last ones." She reached into her purse for some lotion. She had trouble with the cap, so Emerson helped her.

Emerson didn't know how to transition. The sun worked into his forehead and cheeks, and a burning took hold of his nose, but he didn't mind. "You know that boy I work with?" he finally said.

"The one whose work you showed me?"

"Yes."

"Very impressive."

"Yeah, well," Emerson said, "I think his stepfather is cheating on his mother." It was the first time he'd said the words aloud, and even though they'd spent time eddying in his brain, the syllables seemed sharper when they hit the air.

The other night on his sailboat: Searcy, luminous, with tanned skin, far more tan than usual—due to a spray or a cream perhaps—with a hint of peek-a-boo cleavage, and her hair long and light, flirting with her collarbones. If he'd been any good at painting portraits, he would have started then. She had no idea about Hoit. And he felt the need—the desire, anyhow—to protect her.

"How do you know?" Madame Fournier asked.

Emerson told her about Abalone Cove: the woman, the giggling, the kiss, and the conversation on the bench with Hoit.

"Mon Dieu," she said. "Are you going to do something?"

"No. Maybe. Who knows? How would I? Go talk to her? Write her a letter? Ruin it all? She should have someone who is thrilled to be in her . . . orbit."

"Are you that person?" Madame Fournier asked.

A seal pushed through the water with ease, not only darting forward, but rotating its body as well. "No, no" he said.

"Be careful," Madame Fournier said.

He peered over the roofline of the aquarium at a Ferris wheel. He noticed that Madame Fournier's eyes were focused in the same direction. "You want to?" he asked.

The corners of her lips turned upwards. "What the hell."

––––––––––

Theo took inventory just like Mr. Toffler had instructed him, trying to find beauty where others saw none: a pigeon, graffiti, a broken bottle next to a dumpster. The shards of the glass sparkled on the concrete, and he wished he could paint the effect, though he wasn't sure it was even possible to capture something so pretty.

He headed to the computer lab, where Mr. McKendrick allowed the kids who didn't like recess to play games on the computer. He double-clicked and logged into his chess account. There were more fun games that people his age played, but he didn't care for them. Chess was a gentleman's game, a game of war. While the hourglass icon on the screen shifted, he thought about how Mr. Toffler had told him that as long as he could see the world's splendor, he'd never be lonely. "Don't tell anyone this," Mr. Toffler had said. "They'll think you're nuts."

Was Mr. Toffler painting at this moment? On his boat? With an Orangina and some Wes Montgomery? Theo wanted to be with him right now. He believed his mom did, too. Maybe his logic was stupid, but there was a photo in one of the albums in the living room, a red one filled with pictures of his real dad. And whenever Theo flipped through the heavy pages, he noticed his mother was always smiling, big and free, like she was starring in a toothpaste commercial. It was a happiness he had learned about through the album but never seen except for that night on the boat, when he saw the expression come to her, her head tilted to the right, her eyes the size of quarters. Theo didn't take it personally. It was a different kind of love. One that he couldn't give her. No matter what.

With sixteen more minutes of recess, Theo believed he could win at least two games of chess. He waited for the program to load—the internet at school was always crappy.

––––––––––

When Searcy flung open the front door to fetch the mail, she found a plate of cookies wrapped in heavy cellophane with a Post-it note deep underneath the plastic wrap. There was also a sealed envelope, closer to her, atop the welcome mat. Searcy brought her head up, scanning the street from her stoop. Nothing.

She picked up the envelope and then the plate of cookies, doing her best to read through the thick cellophane:

Made some extra cookies!!!! Hope you enjoy them!!!! –Josie

Her penmanship fit her well. The letters were huge, the sentences rife with exclamation points. The people of the twenty-first century had used more exclamation points than all the other centuries combined.

Searcy focused on the letter now. Why would Josie *also* give her an envelope? Searcy wedged her index finger under the flap and tore at the blank envelope. She pulled it free and smoothed the typewritten letter with her hands.

Dear Searcy,
Your husband is not who you think he is.
You deserve a better man.

She read it again and again, her body numbing. She combed over the words once more. With the letter memorized in moments, she turned and walked inside the house, shutting the door behind her. She waited for another feeling to make an appearance: heat, sweat, a sense of claustrophobia. But only a chill washed over her.

Finally, she took to the upstairs bathroom and locked the door. She sat on the edge of the tub. Had Josie written this note? And then brought cookies to soften the blow? Sure, she knew that Josie had always liked Hoit—a lot of women did—but why would she do this? What was the end game? She concentrated on her breathing, letting the air come and go, the inhales and exhales, the tightness of her lungs, the deflation.

The stationery didn't offer any clues. Everything was typed and plain, untraceable. Her brain overflowed. Didn't she have a solid enough relationship with Josie for her to come and speak with her—woman to woman? And what did it mean that Hoit wasn't who she thought he was? Was it Emerson? No, couldn't be. He wouldn't do this, would he?

In time, she left the bathroom and returned downstairs, stuffing the note and envelope into the garbage disposal and dumping the cookies in, too. She ran a stream of hot water and clicked on the blades. The whirring overtook the kitchen and home, pulverizing it all, except for her questions: Who? Why? What did it mean?

She dialed Hoit from her cell. Rings droned into the receiver, one after the other. Her throat constricted, her pulse pounded.

"Hun," he said. "Hun? Are you there?" He cleared his throat. "Searcy? Searcy?"

She hung up. How could a person live in the world for so long and have so few answers?

Hoit called back.

Searcy didn't pick up. She plodded up the stairs, opening the door to Theo's room. She lay down on his bed, staring at the tired glow-in-the-dark stars on the ceiling that were long past their prime, no longer lighting up the room like they had years ago. She dragged her finger from star to star, attempting to make something of a constellation.

———

The trip wasn't anticipated, but Hoit couldn't say no. He was scheduled to head to Japan sometime in late February, but the clients had other plans—wanting to speed up the process, and Mason thought it made sense to meet them now. After all, the two of them had decided to start a more personal PR firm, and that entailed more travel and face-to-face meetings.

When Hoit entered the house, he wanted to get the hard part out of the way, tell Searcy the news. "Sweetie," he said. "It will only be a couple weeks. Maybe three at the most."

Searcy turned the gas fireplace on, and the flames whirred. She then sat on the couch and opened a magazine.

Hoit stood with his back to the hearth, feeling the heat.

"So many places," she said, turning the page. "Do you ever forget about me when you're out there?" She closed the magazine and took to the kitchen. After she'd filled up the teakettle, she clicked on the burner and placed the blue pot atop the hard flames.

"Are you okay?" he asked. Hoit approached. "I don't like 'em either, but these trips are necessary for us to continue to live like this."

"Live like what?" she said.

"In comfort," he said.

Searcy wiped at her face. Hoit reached out with his fingertips, but she shooed him away. He dropped his hands to the counter, turned, and stared out the kitchen window. Some bougainvillea petals floated atop the pool's surface.

"When do you leave?" she said.

"End of the week. Friday morning. When I get back we'll go for more jogs, okay?" His fingers found the small of her back and eased into the heat of her body until he could no longer feel her clothes or skin.

"Do you love me?" she said.

"Why would you ask that?" Hoit asked, his mouth dry.

"Do you love me as much as you did when we met?"

"It's different now," Hoit said.

"How so?"

The teakettle screeched.

"We're a family," he said. "We have a life. It's not just wine lists and flirtation."

Searcy slipped her hand into an oven mitt. "Do you miss that?"

Hoit pulled two mugs from the cupboard, and Searcy plopped in tea bags and poured the scalding water. Steam rose in soft circles, and they dunked their bags in and out, letting the peppermint steep. He put his hand out on the granite countertop, his fingers splayed. He even stared in the direction of her hand, thinking that maybe his gaze would beckon her to reach his way, but she stayed still, bringing the tea bag up and down.

"I guess we're in a new place," she finally said. "As much as you think a relationship will steady out, it's a living being, right?"

"Something like that." Hoit tilted back his cup of tea, which burned his tongue instantly.

———————

Emerson took a sip of water. The discussion on *The Pearl* had left him parched.

"Hey," Theo said, "can I ask you a question *not* about the book?"

"I have a feeling you're going to anyway."

"That's true." Theo smiled.

Emerson leaned in and Theo lowered his voice, probably because he could hear his mother chopping up something in the kitchen, the rhythmic thump of the blade beating through the open home. "There's this new girl, Fallon, at school. And I think she's pretty. She just moved from Buffalo."

"Oh, yeah? That's good."

"Yeah, I guess." The boy's gaze roamed the room. "How does a person learn to kiss?"

"Whoa. You might want to say hi first."

"Not with Fallon. Just in general. I'm curious."

"I suppose it's the same way we learn to walk. It just sorta happens."

"Like, we're born with it?"

"Pretty much."

"Is there a way to know . . . like to test, if a girl wants to kiss you?"

"When I was a boy, not really a boy," Emerson said. He set *The Pearl* down on the glass table. "There was this movie theater on Main Street. And I came up with something that worked."

"What was it?"

"I would take a girl to the movies, and then, during the movie, about thirty, forty minutes in, I would reach for her hand. If she grabbed hold of mine, it was a good sign. After a little while, I'd rub her hand with my thumb, and if she rubbed back, I knew I could kiss her later."

"That's it?"

"It was a way of testing the waters."

"Weird," Theo said.

"Don't worry about all this stuff. It'll happen when it happens. Just be a kid right now. Can we get back to *The Pearl?*"

"Sure."

"One day you'll try my move, and you'll thank me. You'll say, 'Mr. Toffler, wherever you are, bless your heart.'"

"Whatever."

Emerson cleared his throat and retuned to Steinbeck. It saddened him that the pages were turning at paper-cutting speed: Kino and Juana needed to do something drastic to pay for their baby's treatment. And, in a stroke of luck, Kino had swum deep underwater to emerge with a perfect, snowball-sized pearl. The biggest pearl that he or Juana had ever seen.

There was always a cause and effect in life, and in this case, the stimulus was always the same: Theo reading. And Emerson's reaction was always consistent: happiness. It was one he hadn't felt in well over a year, ever since he'd fallen asleep at the wheel on snowy I-89 and crashed into a broken-down snowplow, killing his mom and dad. He'd never thought he'd find a duo again that could bring him that familiar warmth, but, during times like these, with Theo to his right, and Searcy cooking up a feast in the next room, he let himself believe, if only for a moment, that all this was his.

JANUARY

SEARCY JOGGED AWAY FROM the church, toward the house, with one conclusion: she didn't trust Hoit out on the road. She'd wanted to say something to him before he'd left, but she needed time.

Even though the note was long gone, she could remember the creases that lived on the page, the twelve-point font, the bright white, the almost-too-white paper, the content. And the more she replayed it, the more she believed it was true.

She placed her hands on her knees when she reached the top of her driveway and caught her wind. Far away, she spotted a plane, nothing bigger than a bird from this vantage point. It was hard to imagine all those humans inside, their seatbelts buckled, magazines on their laps, plastic cups of tomato juice on their tray tables.

At church, after she'd prayed, she'd stayed still in the pews, listening to the running water and the footsteps of Father Guffey. There were times, and she didn't say this to anybody—not even to Theo or Hoit—for fear that she'd sound ridiculous, but praying gave her a high, brought her to a place where her brain tingled. This didn't happen *every* time, but maybe twice a month, the occurrence presented itself. Searcy tried to push it aside, fearing that if she embraced the sensation, it would notice, and vanish. She'd received a message this past visit: this home, this road, this life, it was still all hers if she wanted it, and that was a powerful place to stand.

Inside, she drew a bath. As the water filled, she took to Theo's room to make his bed. He'd been good about it in recent weeks, but today his alarm had failed to sound—he'd actually failed to set it—and he'd had to rush. His desk was also messy, so Searcy sorted piles of paper and dropped pencils into drawers. There were more photos of Keith, too. Ones that he'd pulled from various albums, ones she'd snapped, one of him wearing a burgundy fedora that he'd purchased at a thrift shop, another of him preparing sushi with a tiny bamboo mat, and a third of him tucked under her old Volvo, changing the oil. Emerson's painting of the tree was also there, and a plethora of sketches from their painting trips. She was actually impressed with her son's artistic ability, and not in the customary maternal fashion. It was more than that. Her son was skilled. The line on which the crows sat was deliberate and fragile, and their talons were draped over the wire with detail.

Next to it all rested a notebook that read, *Weekend Journal*. She hoped Theo had left the notebook home on purpose, and that he didn't need it. She flipped through, combing over his inconsistent handwriting, then zeroing in on the content. Every entry seemed to be penned on a Monday and seemed to focus on an event that occurred over the weekend. She read the first few entries, her eyes absorbing as many words as possible. Lined page after lined page, she read about imaginary scenarios: trips with a boy named Maurice, a fishing expedition in Lake Tahoe, basketball with an older neighborhood kid, lemonade stands, surfing lessons. The teacher, Mrs. Stanton, scrawled in her perfect penmanship at the bottom of each one: *Wow, Theo! What a life you lead! 25/25!*

What pleased Searcy were the last few entries, however. They were truthful, mentioning Mr. Toffler and painting, calling him "a famous artist from Vermont." He mentioned the night he was locked out of the house and had to spend time with Mr. Toffler on the boat, and how he and Carly and Mr. Toffler had listened to music. "Then my mom showed up," Theo had written, "and she was in this long, red gown that didn't really go with the boat. She looked like a lost Cinderella." *Nice simile*, Mrs. Stanton had written. "It was nice to see her so happy and laughing. She smiled a lot and drank a glass of red wine. She knew the music was Wes Montgomery. Maybe one day, me and my mom and Mr. Toffler can hang out again. It was such a great day! I'm actually glad I locked myself out!"

Sounds like a fabulous night, Theo! Good food and good music! I've never heard of Wes Montgomery! I'll have to check him out!

"Shit," Searcy yelled, remembering the bath. She flung the notebook to the desk and tore to her room. Water teetered at the brim, and a few rivulets rolled over the porcelain edge. Searcy shut off the tap and ripped a towel from the rack to soak up the water.

Once in the bath, she regained her tranquility, brushing her arms with a loofa and running a razor over her calves. She grabbed her copy of *The Pearl* that she had recently checked out from the library. She wanted to be able to chat with Theo (and Emerson) about the novel, should the topic arise. The cover image grew on her. At first, she thought it was too plain: a beach scene, the figures dark and silhouetted, but now she found it intriguing—this husband, wife, and boy resting along the coast.

What if she and Theo and Emerson enjoyed a picnic at Abalone Cove this evening? She knew that would make Theo happy. She could purchase goodies for all of them, and maybe Emerson wouldn't mind grilling. On second thought, maybe she'd make it easy on herself and just pack up some sandwiches and fruit.

"Sure," Emerson said. His voice echoed in the boat's cabin, so he took to the deck.

"I know it gets dark early these days," Searcy said, "but I was thinking that we could get there at three-ish, right after Theo gets out from school, and have some sandwiches and fruit salad."

"What can I bring?" Emerson asked.

"Just yourself," Searcy said.

"What does Hoit like?"

"He's away on business," she said.

"Oh," Emerson said. "Okay. I'll see you soon."

He packed his overnight bag with the necessary toiletries and clothes, and hurried to the marina's clubhouse, where the shower pressure was significantly better than his boat's. In his stupor (it had been a morning of cigarettes and bullshit), he'd completely forgotten it was Friday and that he'd already made plans with Carly, so when he returned from the marina showers, Emerson picked up the phone and called her. He said he wasn't feeling well, that he was coming down with something, and even managed—by the grace of God—to *actually* sneeze while on the line with her (an effect of the dollar-store cologne he'd recently purchased).

"Poor thing," she said. "I feel bad. Don't worry about it, though. Rest up, okay?"

Her kindness made him feel guilty. He shut off the lights, plucked his keys from the hook near the entrance, and locked up. The plan was to head to the liquor store down the road and pick up a nice Bordeaux, and something for Theo, too.

———————

Searcy didn't think Emerson was dressed for the beach, in a white shirt, buttoned to the top—all the discomfort of formality, without the appeal of a tie. Clutched under his arm was a brown bag, and in his hand was a bouquet of flowers, the stems wrapped in butcher paper.

Searcy inspected the gardenias, their stamens delicate and pointed. She always told Hoit—and before that, Keith—that she didn't like flowers as a gift because they eventually died, but that was just an attempt at being realistic. "Come on in," she said.

"Hey, Theo!" Emerson said once he was in the foyer, his head tilted upwards to let his voice carry through the home.

"Hey, Mr. Toffler!" Theo said.

"Why don't you come downstairs, Theo?" Searcy said.

"Wrapping up a game!" he yelled. "Two minutes! I just took this guy's bishop!"

"Can I help you with anything?" Emerson asked.

"Let me get a vase for these flowers. Follow me."

Searcy led Emerson into the kitchen, where she flung open a few cabinet doors until she found the emerald vase she was looking for. Emerson ran his hand over the granite countertop. He often did that when he was in the kitchen, she'd noticed. Maybe he enjoyed the smoothness of the stone or the way it was always cold, even on the hottest of days. "Whatever you're cooking can be smelled from the driveway. They really need to make it a perfume," he said.

Searcy smiled. "Barbequed pork . . . by Calvin Klein." She remembered just days earlier, being in this same setting with Hoit, his fingers only inches from where Emerson's were now, and how that moment had been imbued with nerves and palpitations. Presently, however, the world was comfortable. Emerson had that effect. There was an ease to him, a soft confidence that didn't just seem to possess him, but that actually wandered from his being and wrapped whomever was in his company. "I'd been making pork anyway, and once I had the idea of heading to Abalone Cove, I dropped the roast in the slow cooker and poured in a ton of barbeque sauce. I thought we could put it on sandwiches." She shrugged. "No Carly tonight?"

"Not tonight, no."

"What do you have in there?" She pointed to the brown bag.

"A bottle of wine. And some apple cider for Theo."

"He'll like that." Searcy turned her attention to the flowers on the counter. She cut the paper with shears and let the stems fall into her hands.

Emerson strolled away, scanning the bookshelf near the fireplace, and she studied him as he combed over the books' spines. She dropped the flowers into the vase and fanned out the petals and took in the back of his hair. Normally, his locks were chestnut, but tonight, with a touch of product, they were darker, almost black. With her eyes steady on Emerson, the letter faded. The key was to cram her time with responsibilities: arrange flowers, organize the picnic basket, and eat dinner. "If you like anything, feel free to borrow it," she said. "Not that you want a bunch of books on fashion or cooking."

"Are you a Civil War buff?" he said. "Also, that's the first time in my life I've used the word *buff*, in that context, anyhow."

"Hoit's into it." She crumpled the butcher paper and tossed it to the trash.

"How did you fall in love with fashion and cooking?"

It was an easy enough question, but it took her a second to find an appropriate answer. "Cooking's the only artform that involves all five senses. And fashion, because I saw this teacher at school when I was a kid, and she was so perfect, and tall, and wore the loveliest clothes—and I learned she made them. It always stuck with me. Miss Wicker. I always enjoyed a good fantasy book, too. Loved the idea of getting lost in another world, one far different from ours."

"You don't like this world?" Emerson said, removing a Civil War book from the shelf, inspecting the cover, and sliding it back into place.

"Not always."

"Why not?" He turned and faced Searcy, taking a few steps her way.

"It can be predictable. And then what's unpredictable is often sad."

"I know exactly what you mean." Emerson dropped his hands into his pockets and closed the space between them. Ten feet, then five, then less than a single pace. "I can craft any fantasy I want on my sketch pad, build the perfect world with a smattering of shadows and crosshatches—and then take an eraser to all that seems unfit. But three-dimensional life is trickier."

"Wouldn't it be nice if you could use an eraser in life?"

"Just dig in and brush the dust to the floor with a quick swipe of your hand. Maybe, though . . . we have more control than we think."

"It's nice to think that," she said, pushing the vase into the center of the granite island, before swinging her eyes back to Emerson.

Then it happened. She felt skin and strength. One of Emerson's hands. She figured it was an accident, but no. There was purpose behind his touch, and instead of recoiling, she allowed his paint-stained fingers to melt into hers. She even brought her thumb up from underneath the pile to caress the joint on his pinky. While his hand was the same as others'—five fingers, tendons, bones—they were foreign. His palms were softer than Hoit's, and his fingers were thinner and longer, reaching far past her nails.

A cramp rippled in her abdomen. She started to pull away. But Emerson pressed her hand harder against the granite, and she stayed still, her eyes glued to the wicker of the picnic basket. Emerson had written the note. This was his way of telling her, right?

While she trusted her other four senses, sight was king, and she yearned to see the clustered formation of their hands. Her pupils soaked in the mass of knuckles and nails, her hand buried underneath his fingers that were splattered with flecks of burgundy paint. She noticed a black-and-blue nail on Emerson's pointer finger, and she wondered how it had happened, and how long it would take for the bruise to travel to the top. She let her mind breathe and enjoyed this, what Emerson would call, "3D moment."

The brittle scene ended when Theo blasted down the stairs.

Emerson dropped his hands to his sides, and Searcy did the same. The polished granite bore an imprint of their hands, and she watched as the blurs of heat evaporated.

"What are you doing here, Mr. Toffler?" Theo asked. "I won, by the way."

"We're going on a picnic," Emerson said.

"I was just kidding. I know what we're doing," Theo said.

Searcy ran her fingers against her brow and blotted her collarbones with a nearby dish towel. "Ready to go?" she asked.

"Yes," Theo said.

"Get a coat, sweetie. Once the sun drops, the chill can be strong," Searcy said.

"Okay," Theo said, darting to the stairs.

Emerson turned Searcy's way. "Do you want me to bring something to the car?"

"Sure," she said, passing him the basket.

Emerson clutched the wicker handle, which snapped lightly in his grip. He headed out of the kitchen, and Searcy leaned against the countertop, and drew a deep breath.

"We're the only ones at the beach," Theo said. "Look, Mom!" From atop the cliff, he peered over the railing at the vacant shoreline. "Are we even allowed to make a bonfire here?"

"I don't think so," Searcy said. "But no one's around."

Mr. Toffler looked like Santa, carrying everything that had been packed.

"What do you think, Mr. Toffler?" Theo said. "About the bonfire?"

"I say we do it. It's always easier to say *sorry* than it is to ask for permission." He started down the trail, and Theo strolled behind his mom and Mr. Toffler, breathing in clouds of dirt lifted by their footsteps. As they headed toward the shore, Theo's mind opened up. He figured daydreaming was natural, but sometimes he believed he was *too* skilled in this way. He could actually swim in imaginary ponds, taste salty steak, and feel the warmth of Fallon's lips even though he'd never touched a girl. Then, when reality overtook his made-up land, he was left feeling empty. He figured that life rested somewhere between what you thought of yourself and the movie you played to get yourself through it.

They fanned out blankets in the center of the beach, where the sand was soft and still warm, and dug through the picnic basket. Mr. Toffler sat close to Searcy, like Theo himself tried to sit with Fallon in history class when Ms. Roth let them study on the carpet.

Theo thought his mom was a rock, and rocks had to always be strong. Because of that, no one ever asked them how they were doing. But Mr. Toffler was a rock, too, so he knew what other rocks needed. And he asked her about herself, and for the first time in his life, Theo saw his mother not being strong, allowing herself to be soft and cracking. Theo chugged his sparkling apple cider, allowing the carbonation to bubble on his tongue and tingle down his throat.

When the reddish sun made its move for the horizon, Theo asked, "What color is that, Mr. Toffler? What's that red?" Mr. Toffler knew the names of strange colors, and often told him during painting lessons not to say blue or red, but to be more specific—that there were hundreds of hues within a single color.

Mr. Toffler took it in, as if the world itself was a painting. "Sanguine," he said, digging into a sandwich.

"Sanguine?" Theo said. "Cool."

"Summer gets all the credit here in California, but it's really all the other seasons I love."

"Plus no tourists and empty beaches," Searcy said.

"I like summer," Theo said. "No school. And the sun stays out longer. You know what this girl said today in class?"

"What?" Mr. Toffler said.

"It was kind of weird, but she said that sometimes she watches rated-R movies with her parents, and it annoys her that girls are always naked but never the guys."

"Dear Lord," Searcy said.

"We've got to work on your transitions, buddy," Mr. Toffler said.

"What do you think, Mr. Toffler?" Theo picked at the pulled pork. It was salty and fatty and sweet with barbeque sauce, and he was surprised his mom was allowing it.

"She's got a point, I guess."

Searcy smiled, then bit her bottom lip. She wrapped a blanket around her body and dug her feet into the sand, wiggling them until they were all the way under.

"Should we get the fire going?" Mr. Toffler asked.

"Yes, okay," Searcy said.

Mr. Toffler was quick to it, like he'd done this many times. Maybe he had. Theo knew Vermont was snowy, so building fires was probably taught to kids who lived up there. Mr. Toffler reached out in front of him, flinging dirt between his legs, like a dog. When he had a good-sized hole, he wrapped the perimeter with nearby stones.

"Why are you doing that?" Theo asked.

"To make sure the sparks have something to hit, other than us. No risk here, but you can't be too careful. Help me out."

Theo hopped up and placed the rocks around the hole. When the stones were in place, Mr. Toffler ripped open the bag of charcoal and poured it into the pit. "This is cheating," he explained, "but your mother brought it to make it easier on me, and I'm using it so I don't have to carry it back up the hill." When the briquettes filled the hole, Theo and Mr. Toffler scoured the beach together, searching for twigs, dead plants, and pieces of driftwood. The two of them found very little at first, but then, around one bend, just when Theo had begun thinking they wouldn't find any kindling, they encountered a thick hunk of wood that had been dried by the sun. Mr. Toffler said it was perfect.

While Searcy was certain of God's omnipresence, there were spots where it was even easier to believe in Him, and the ocean was one of them. As she dragged her tongue over her sauce-soaked lips, she studied the flames that, even in this chill, grew in strength and temperature.

They all sat in a line, facing the Pacific. Searcy on the left, Emerson to the right, and Theo tucked between them, drinking from his second bottle of cider. They all had a beverage, and waves, and a sunset before their eyes.

"Where's the sun headed now?" Theo asked.

"The sun's not going anywhere," Searcy said. "It's the Earth that moves."

"You know what I mean."

"Westward," she said. "Catalina, Hawaii, and so on."

"I feel bad for the sun," Theo said.

Searcy sipped some wine. She thought its acidity paired well with the pork's richness.

"Why?" Emerson said.

"It never gets any time to relax. We think it's relaxing when the moon comes out at night, but really it's just working somewhere we can't see."

"Do you feel bad for the moon?" Searcy said.

"Not really," Theo said. "It doesn't really do anything."

"It controls the tide, right?" Emerson said.

"I guess."

"I guess?" Searcy said.

"Whatever you're paying for that school is too much," Emerson said.

"It's the tutor that's the problem." She found it comforting that she didn't have to worry about eye contact, as the evening was upon them and their gazes were all pointed forward.

"Do you ever feel so happy that you actually get a little sad?" Emerson asked.

Searcy thought the question seemed more like one of Theo's queries, and she was right, as Theo seemed to pick up right where Emerson left off.

"Like right now," Theo said, "everything is so nice and perfect, and you know it won't be this way for long, so you get kind of depressed."

"Exactly," Emerson said. "I couldn't have said it better."

"How do you know it won't be this way for long?" Searcy asked.

"I don't know. Sometimes I can just feel it," Theo said.

Searcy couldn't find the words. She hoped that the thick silence would force Emerson to come up with a response, so she listened to the sea's roar and the fire's crackle, and waited, but the answer never came.

She adjusted her blanket, and the flickers from the fire brightened, the reds standing out harder against the dark. Usually when she strolled Abalone Cove, it was summer and the granules were sizzling, forcing her to hurry across the shoreline, but now, they were cold. "Do you guys want to make s'mores? There are some marshmallows in the bag. I forgot coat hangers, though."

"Theo and I will hunt for sticks," Emerson said. "Nothing's keeping me from having a s'more." Theo and Emerson rose from the striped blanket and began the hunt, and Searcy recalled *The Pearl*, which she had almost finished. This sight seemed like a Steinbeckian scene: Kino, Juana, and their boy, Coyotito. Sure, Theo wasn't an infant, but it seemed in this instant that they lived during a simpler time, an era of hunting and gathering. Here, on the same coast, it could have been 1822 or 1789 or 1675. She took to the basket, fetching marshmallows and graham crackers and squares of milk chocolate. Light cast by the fire extended only a few feet beyond the blanket; thus, Searcy could no longer see Emerson or Theo, but their voices and laughter weren't far and popped free like birds' coos every now and then. Was Theo right? Was perfection ephemeral? Or could it be sustained?

Emerson twisted his marshmallow carefully, and Searcy propped her feet up onto the stones that surrounded the fire. He hadn't pictured her as the toe-ring-wearing type, but she, like any woman worth pursuing, was a harmonious blend of contradictions.

"No more sun," Theo said. "But we kind of made our own, with all these coals, right?"

Emerson stayed focused, slipping his golden marshmallow between two graham crackers. After adding a slab of chocolate, he balanced his "sandwich" over the flames with two sticks.

"Wow," Theo said.

"That's enough of this," Searcy said, crafting her own s'more, using two marshmallows instead of one, three squares of chocolate, and then, something Emerson didn't see coming: sprinkling a little brown sugar (from a packet in her purse) for caramelization.

Minutes later, Theo devoured her creation, and Emerson scarfed down his. The coals blinked, and the wood burned through in the final stages of the fire.

Then a rumble. It wasn't the sea, though Emerson thought it was for a moment. It wasn't the whirring blades of a Coast Guard helicopter, but it *was* an engine. Emerson swung his head to the right, spotting a four-wheeler, its rectangular headlights illuminated, its motor cutting through the soft night. "Shit! A lifeguard!" Emerson said. He pointed as the vehicle gained speed, closing the distance at a quick rate.

Theo and Searcy sprung to their feet. It was a good thing that before the sun had disappeared, Searcy had gone ahead and packed up most of the supplies, stowing them away in the red-and-white-checkered picnic basket. Emerson clutched the blanket and rushed with Theo and Searcy to the trail's narrow opening, leaving behind the fire, marshmallows, and scraps of trash.

They churned up the hill. Emerson felt his legs burn and his back tingle. Wine sloshed in his belly, and his head seemed loose, like it was detached from his body. Searcy's hand wrapped his. Her fingers were soft, young-feeling, and even with the picnic basket swinging from his other hand and his heart pounding in his temples, all he could grasp was that she'd taken his hand in hers. He wished the trail were longer, harder, steeper, so that they would never reach the top and have to unclasp their fingers.

"Stop!" the man on the four-wheeler screamed, killing the engine and hopping off his vehicle. He stood steps from the fire, his frame barely illuminated. "Hey!" he said again, his voice sharp. "You three!

No bonfires! Hey, I'm serious. I can see you! Hey! I can see you!"

"We can see you, too!" Emerson said. "Hellooooo!"

"Shhh!" Searcy said, letting out spurts of restrained laughter.

Theo didn't hold back. He stopped climbing, placed his hands on his knees and snorted.

Paces from the finish, Emerson stared down at the angry lifeguard who didn't get the ending he wanted, who wasn't able to give a lecture, whose mood mimicked that of the flames—one minute, aggressive, the next, dull.

Finally, after a few more feet, they reached the peak, and Searcy dropped Emerson's hand before Theo could see. It would have actually been more practical to hold hands now, as they weren't scuttling up the cliff, but affection was never about convenience, was it?

In the parking lot, Emerson, Searcy, and Theo let out a rumble of laughter—a song of three—that Emerson stowed in his chest.

"You hear that? Shhh!" Theo said. "Someone's coming up the cliff."

They stopped.

They listened.

Emerson hurried and flung open Searcy's trunk and tossed the basket inside. They all piled in the SUV, slamming doors, huffing hard. Searcy scrambled for her keys, started the engine, and threw the car into gear.

Theo chuckled.

"What is it?" she said.

"I didn't hear anything." He laughed harder.

"You little . . ." Searcy shook her head as she ripped onto the main boulevard, switching lanes, and heading toward home. A ringing took hold of the cabin some miles later, and Hoit's name popped onto the dashboard monitor. "Incoming call from Hoit," the screen said. Emerson stared out the window. He touched the cold glass and scanned the homes that smeared by. Most were dark; some had lights on. "I can take this later," Searcy said. "It's late." She pressed a button and the ringing stopped.

―――――――

When they returned to the house it was half past nine o'clock at night. Hoit had left a message and, while Emerson and Theo unloaded the SUV, Searcy listened to her voicemail: "Hi, hun. Missing you. Not sure where you are, but I hope you're having fun. Not too much fun, though." He laughed. "Anyhow, I'm about to head into a meeting. Thinking of you." Thinking of you, she thought. What a banal phrase. Everyone could think of someone. It was *how* you thought of them. She hung up the phone and slid it back into her purse. "Theo," she said. "Get ready for bed. I'll come by in a bit, and we'll say our prayers together."

Theo's voice dropped. "It's still early, though."

"That gives you some time to get washed up."

"Come on!" he said, while at the same time listening to her instructions.

"Well," Emerson said. "What a night."

"The best evening I've had in a while," Searcy said. The words had exited her mouth without being filtered. "And, like Theo said, 'It's only nine.'" Her heart was percussive as she poured two glasses of Bordeaux, this time in real bulb-like glasses with thin stems. She carried them over the white carpeting to the couch, and perched the crystal stemware atop the coffee table. Then she headed to the wall and turned on the gas fireplace with the flick of a switch. The pilot lights clicked for a few seconds and, moments later, a rush of blue flames swallowed the fake logs.

Emerson sat on the far end of the couch, his legs crossed knee over knee. Searcy sat down next to him, her eyes in line with yet another fire. She reached and took the first sip of her wine; Emerson then reached over the table and did the same. He took a long pull and licked his lips after he set his glass back down.

Minutes later, Searcy stood, excused herself and headed upstairs to tend to Theo. After she tucked Theo into bed, they whispered the Lord's Prayer in a hurry and then she filed to the hallway and shut his door. "Mom," Theo said. "Can you leave the door open a little?" he asked. "I'll open it when I come back upstairs," she said, pulling the door closed.

When she reached the living room, Emerson was gone. His wine was still on the table, and his coat was still draped over the couch's armrest, but the door to the backyard was cracked and she could hear the shuffle of shoes.

"Emerson," she said.

"Busted," he said.

She saw that he was smoking a cigarette.

"I'm sorry. I didn't want to smoke around Theo or you, but I haven't had one in, like, six hours, and I'm starting to get jumpy. I thought I'd have more time, and that I could sneak back in and you wouldn't notice."

"Theo told me that he saw a pack of cigarettes in your car, and I've smelled it on you." Searcy watched him take a drag. "Do you know I've never had a cigarette in my life?"

"How is that even possible? I feel like even the Pope has had a few."

She asked if she could try his, and Emerson passed it over. For some reason she thought the cigarette would be heavier; instead, it was so light that she barely felt a thing. She held the filter, pretending she was Audrey Hepburn and pulled a bit of the smoke into her lungs. She didn't cough. She didn't feel a thing. She just let out a small puff of smoke and then passed it back to Emerson.

"You sure you haven't done this before?" he said.

"Do you feel better now?"

"Yes," he responded. "You have no idea how much I wanted one when we were down at the beach. The whole thing was like a commercial. The waves, the bonfire, and I could feel the soft pack in my pocket, calling me."

She thought he seemed more comfortable here, out in the backyard, with the pool in the distance, and a soft cool breeze washing through from time to time.

"I kinda feel bad. Your lungs were so pure."

"I don't know how pure they were. I mean I've lived in LA my entire life."

He smiled and put the cigarette out on the side of his leather boot. He then placed the butt inside the pack, and, in time, they had resumed their position on the couch.

"Were you ever close to getting married?" Searcy asked.

"Not really," Emerson said. His lips were stained purple from the inky wine. "You know that feeling you have when you first date someone in high school, when love is young and pure and you've never been hurt before. And you just want to get her name tattooed on your bicep and kiss her and hear her laugh on a loop in your head."

"I remember it," she said. "Like you were more in love with love than the person."

They were closer on the couch now. Only a long cushion apart, and Searcy repositioned herself, leaned in.

"In high school, I had a huge crush on this girl who was in all the plays, always the lead. Her acting was so-so, to be honest, but because she was pretty, she always secured the lead. She was playing Sandy in *Grease*, and we had spoken a little here and there, and I knew that if I could somehow get the Danny Zuko role, I would be able to spend time with her, so I stayed in my room, practicing the dance moves with my dad, singing the songs, styling my hair with Vaseline. All this for a chance, a shot."

"Did it work?"

"No."

"Young love. What a glorious mess."

"Like the Wright brothers' first plane: the intentions are pure, but it's just not quite ready for flight."

Searcy, light with wine and nicotine, let herself go, leaned forward, and met Emerson's lips. They were soft and drenched in Bordeaux. Her tongue tasted his mouth, and she picked up on traces of tobacco, and she wondered if she, too, had inhaled enough to have this bitter flavor on her palate. The world went quiet. She knew there were noises—the flames' roar, the crinkle of Emerson's shirt sleeves as he reached towards her hair, the heater's hiss—but her mind was clear, an open window on a high hill. And rather than think about the sounds, she let herself sink into Emerson's arms, where she felt safe. He rubbed between her shoulder blades, collecting strands of her hair every now and then.

Then, as she repositioned her legs, swinging them out from under her body, she toppled his glass of wine, and the long-stemmed crystal slammed against the table with a high-pitched ding and then, the few ounces of remaining red wine spilled onto the table, rushing into the spine of a coffee table book, and leaking over the sides of the polished wood. "Oh, God," Emerson said.

"It's my fault," she said. "It's all my fault. I'm sorry. I'm sorry," she said. Instead of rushing to the kitchen to fetch club soda and a rag, she sat up for a moment. Pressure pummeled her forehead.

"Can I help you clean?" he said. "Please, let me help."

"No! No! It's fine!" She kept her eyes in line with the stain. Droplets continued to patter onto the carpet. The wine wasn't red, but rather purple, almost black. "You should go." She shut her eyes. "You need to go. Yes, you need to go," she said again, breathing hard.

Moments later, when she finally opened her eyes, Emerson's spot on the couch was bare, and she heard the front door click shut.

At the hotel bar, Hoit called Searcy and left another message. A group of jet-lagged American tourists in New Balance shoes and baggy pants sat around a circular table: a mom and a dad with two girls that seemed close in age. He tried to disassociate, scan the bar's top-shelf bottles of whiskey, vodka, gin, and rum. He even took in the piano man, who pumped the golden pedals and dragged his hands up and down the keys, but his eyes wanted nothing more than to rest on the family of four. They were happily disorganized, equally involved, true partners, a real family.

Hoit did care for Theo and didn't mind gifting him a sweet life, but he knew that the paternal part wasn't really his. On his first date with Searcy, he'd taken her to the Ahmanson Theatre to see the musical *Flower Drum Song*, even though he hated musicals—any straight man who told a person otherwise was lying—but the things men pretended to care for when dating could fill the Grand Canyon. The two of them had tucked into the thick line, waiting for the theatre to opens its doors, when a man in a tuxedo and shiny shoes made his way to the middle of the crowd. He'd cleared his throat. "Ladies and gentlemen," he'd said. "The role of Mei Li will be played by the understudy today, a talented actress by the name of Pammy Chiu." The crowd had, almost as if rehearsed, puffed a heavy groan. "Too bad," Searcy had said in a soft voice. "Someone has to keep the show going," Hoit had remembered saying. "Without this actress, we'd all have wasted our time. We'd all have to get back in our cars and sit in traffic." But later, as Hoit had shuffled to his seat, he made the connection: he, too, was something of an understudy.

Eventually, the jet-lagged tourists paid their tab, stood from the table, and made their way to the elevators. With only an inch of whiskey left in his glass, Hoit twirled the amber liquid, allowing it to wash over the single ice cube, which was nothing more than a crescent-moon shape now. As he downed it all, a woman from today's meeting—he couldn't remember her name—entered the bar. Her name, he did recall, was incongruent to her looks—something like Beatrice or Bertha—and she approached him, her hair shiny and her lipstick a natural tone. "Hi," she said. "How are you?"

Hoit asked her if she wanted to have a seat, and she agreed. They spoke for a little while, exchanging pleasantries about the hotel, the city of Tokyo, the meeting from earlier in the day. She told him that this was her first real job out of college, and that she seemed to be getting the hang of it. "A gin and ginger, please," she said to the waiter, sliding off her high heels discreetly. "Do you mind?" she asked.

"Not at all," Hoit said. "I would do the same, but it's not as appropriate for guys."

"Are you sure?" she said. "I think you should."

"I'm not really sure what kind of socks I'm wearing, so I'll err on the side of caution. Don't want a toe poking out."

"No, certainly not." She smiled and adjusted the latch on her necklace. When her drink was brought out by the server, she ordered some fries and a small garden salad, and Hoit could tell that she wanted him to stick around, her eyebrows arched in expectation when the waiter asked him if he wanted another cocktail.

"Yes, sure," he said. "The same."

She went on, discussing the meeting, her boss, and the travel. She then transitioned to other subjects, like music, using the piano man as a springboard. "I wanted to do that when I was a kid," she said. "That was my dream job—playing piano in a bar, a big cognac glass sitting on top stuffed with money because I was that good."

"What happened?" Hoit asked. His drink had arrived and he'd already downed a good amount.

"Life. They tell us to dream when we're young; they tell us to get real when we're older. Did you have that?" she asked. "One of those little dreams as a kid."

Hoit reflected, picked the lemon wedge off the rim of his whiskey sour and gave it a squeeze. "To be honest, I didn't. I just didn't want to be poor." He took a sip. "We were so broke. My dad worked at a barbeque restaurant, and he always smelled of smoke, and his hands were always black. Money was always an issue. My parents fought about it all the time. All my clothes were so worn by the time they got to me. When I got to Wharton, I made some money working as a consultant for a few months, and I blew my entire check on a Hermes suit. It was the first time I'd ever owned anything brand new. And I wore that navy, double-breasted suit every day for a month, even when it was too hot."

The woman smiled. "I can relate. My mom always made us buy that cereal on the bottom row at the supermarket."

"Oh, the one in bags not boxes?"

She laughed. "Yes!"

It had been a long time since Hoit had thought about his folks, the Bayou, the tattered pants. Hell, even the love his folks gave him was a sort of hand-me-down. He drank some more, and the woman reached over and touched the top of his hand. "Well, you don't have to worry about those things anymore. Look at your suit now."

Hoit glanced down. She had a small, heart-shaped tattoo on the fleshy part of her hand, right between her thumb and her forefinger. "Thank you," he said. "Well, I better be off."

"Oh, so soon?" She dipped a fry into some ketchup.

"Yes," he said. "I'm beat from today. Looking forward to hitting the hay." He slapped down more than enough Yen to cover all the drinks and food, and pushed away from the table.

––––––

Even though a couple of days had passed, the recent events were still hazy, a gray Polaroid, with only the corners, at this point, coming into focus. Emerson remained confused, thinking that even David (of David and Goliath) would shake his head, buy him another beer, and tell him to sleep it off when it came to being part of Searcy and Theo's lives. When he'd discussed the situation with Madame Fournier, she'd offered some interesting advice: "Everyone is always talking about odds . . . but really," she'd said, "the chances to anything in life are fifty-fifty. Either it happens or it doesn't."

He opened his fridge and removed the hot-and-sour soup that Carly had purchased for him and brought to his boat the other night (when he was supposed to be sick, but was actually with Searcy and Theo). She'd written a message on the Styrofoam container:

Hope you feel better. Love, Carly

She'd also drawn a smiley face inside the *O* in *Love*. Emerson thought the face would've looked cuter without the carrot-like nose she'd drawn, but that was for another time. He'd smoothed things over by telling her that he must have been at the store buying meds when she'd come over.

Carly. Carly. Carly. She was ideal. She was single and fun. Warm and pretty. Her kisses were tender, her laugh contagious. After a recent date, she'd rushed across the street to give her leftovers to a homeless man, and he remembered thinking then that she was more than just attractive. She cared for him; she was easy and kind. More than anything else, her baggage was light, a designer carry-on that could be neatly stowed under the seat in front of her.

Searcy. Searcy. Searcy. Luminous, fragile. Religious and confused. She had Theo. Theo, Theo, Theo. There were shards of pain that glittered behind her bourbon eyes, jagged pieces of discomfort that he wanted to learn about and hopefully wash away. And every time he peeked at her heart, his own skipped a beat. But her baggage needed to be checked and hauled by a forklift. Needed to be tagged and labeled with a "Handle with Care" sticker. But that didn't dissuade him. Not in the slightest, because he believed that baggage bred depth, and that depth created womanhood. That was it maybe: Searcy was a woman. Not a girl. And by falling for her, Emerson felt himself become more of man and less of a boy.

He heated the soup on his single burner. When the temperature was right, he took to his bed and spooned the liquid from the pan to his mouth. He flipped through various art books, dog-earing pages that called to him. Lately, he'd been drawn to Toulouse-Lautrec. Madame Fournier had mentioned to Emerson multiple times that she thought their styles were simpatico. *The Kiss* was his favorite, two figures in bed, the covers messy and piled. The faces young, innocent, and one gathered that the scene was post-sex, though it could have just been a casual depiction of a French Monday—after all, Lautrec spent his days filling himself with absinthe, wandering Montmartre.

Emerson puffed on a cigarette. He wanted to know what Searcy was thinking, whether she'd liked the kiss from the other night. If ignorance was bliss, maybe consciousness was hell. A nice, little life where he could live with Searcy and Theo, maybe a small home, one level, with a fireplace and a studio in which he could paint and maybe teach students from time to time. Domestic visions of Christmas trees and tire swings and training wheels formed and evaporated, and in time, he saw the three of them, resting in the back of a Radio Flyer being towed by Norman Rockwell himself. They were in a kitchen—a kitchen that Emerson had never *actually* set foot in—one rife with light and red tiles. They prepared some sort of baked-pasta dish, taking turns sprinkling on shreds of mozzarella and ripping basil leaves.

"Hi," Theo said, introducing himself to the new kid at school. He could tell early on that Dylan was going to be popular. He was tall and draped in athletic wear: Adidas and Nike and even some brands Theo hadn't heard of. "Where are you from, Dylan?" Mr. Toffler had told Theo that the key to friendship was asking questions, but Theo thought that was maybe more for adults than kids.

"Cleveland," Dylan said.

Theo wished he knew about Cleveland, but he didn't know anything except that it was in Ohio, and that he'd missed a question on a quiz about President Cleveland. Another kid, Tyson, called from the field: "Hey, D! You wanna come play football with us?" Tyson was already calling him "D," and Theo was out of questions.

Dylan stared straight out on to the field before removing his hands from his pockets and jogging towards the mass of kids.

"Yeah, let's go," Theo said, following him.

"He didn't call you," Dylan said. "Just stay here. You can be a cheerleader. A fat one."

Theo stopped, feeling his shoes soak with morning dew and watching Dylan hurry across the field and join the other kids. Theo then made his way to the computer lab. He shuffled past his history classroom, where he peeked inside and spotted Ms. Roth—it was very important to call her "Ms."—filing papers and munching on some sort of bar. She offered a polite wave, and Theo did the same. Earlier in her class, they had been studying the Middle Ages and its societal structure: slaves, artisans, merchants, and royalty. While times were tougher back then, Theo believed there was a societal structure to middle school, too, and that his place rested somewhere between slave and artisan.

In the computer lab, he took a seat. For some reason, he had been holding his breath and his lungs were tight. While the computer fired up, he placed his fingers over the artery near his throat and felt the rhythm. The heart didn't do anything but beat. It had been beating before he had even been in the world, before his birthday even, and it would beat until it no longer could. It must be nice, he thought, to have such a simple job.

Normally after a situation like what had happened on the field with Dylan, Theo would have been more depressed, but he was surprised at how quickly the sadness passed. His brain had been able to change the channel; maybe because of the night at Abalone Cove he had collected enough good times to protect himself against a few bad ones. The same had occurred with algebra. He'd done well on the first and second quizzes and all the homework, so that when he scored a C on his test, his percentage had only dropped 2.7 points. Mr. Toffler had tried to make him feel better about the C grade, too, telling him that a C was only two dots short of a happy face. Theo thought it was corny, but he liked that Mr. Toffler made stuff up to try to make him smile.

Maybe the secret to being happy was to stuff enough joy into your body so that when the bad times came along, you kept your overall "joy index" high. Theo just wasn't sure how to do that. He wasn't sure how much longer Mr. Toffler would be in his life. After all, he was an amazing artist who lived on a boat. Life for Mr. Toffler seemed easy to move, and there were times when things were high and sweet, like they had been on the beach that night, and Theo couldn't help but wonder about the collapse, when he wouldn't see Mr. Toffler any longer.

With the house all to herself, Searcy headed up to her bedroom. It was after her jog, and she tossed her dirty clothes to the hamper before running the shower. She sliced her hand through the water's stream, found an agreeable temperature, then hopped inside. With all the outside doors locked, the bedroom and bathroom doors shut, even the shower's glass door closed, she let out a sigh. As steam took over the bathroom, she allowed images to leak from her thoughts: Emerson's hands and face and dark beard. The stubble on his neck. His paint-speckled fingers. His rich laugh.

She reached for the shower nozzle, holding it tight in her hands, then dragged the stream of water over her skin, letting the pressure sting her body. She tucked the nozzle between her legs, inducing quivers and stuttered exhales. She clenched her jaw and turned the pressure down a touch. She could have him this way. His skin was hers. She could taste his lips. Rip at his back. Nails over flesh. Trace his spine. Legs high. Pointed toes. Hair wet. Calves taut. Sighs swirling. Thrust. Push. Moan. Exhale. Exhale. Exhale. Her knees trembled. She leaned on the shower's wall, collecting herself, her chest rising and falling.

She drenched herself one last time, shutting her eyes and tilting her head back. Water beaded over her chest and stomach, reaching her thighs and knees before pooling around her pedicured feet and circling the drain.

FEBRUARY

THEO SHOOK HIS HEAD. "This Shakespeare stuff isn't even English!" He sighed. "It's worse than Spanish. At least I can sound out the words in Spanish. But this! I mean, what the heck is 'engilds the night'? Something is seriously wrong with this dude. And why do all these photos show him wearing an earring? I miss *The Pearl*." He put his head down on the glass table. "How am I going to memorize this? It's due Friday. And Fallon is my partner. I don't want to let her down." As Theo let the words go, he imagined the two of them: he and Fallon, in front of the class, putting on a show.

"Let's try it again," Mr. Toffler said.

"This time," Theo said, "I'll be Hermia, just so I can see what it's supposed to sound like, you know, with you being Lysander?"

"But I like being Hermia," Mr. Toffler said.

"Why?"

"It's nice to be wooed for once. I'm always the one on the ground, working hard, having to come up with anecdotes and compliments. Let someone else do the work for once." Mr. Toffler showed Theo how to enunciate properly. He demonstrated what syllables to stress.

"Okay," Theo said. "I think I got it."

"Just remember so much of love isn't what's being said. So much of acting isn't what's being said. It's about movement, your eyes—all that stuff, okay?"

Theo, as usual, took his cue from Mr. Toffler's high-pitched, "Nay, good Lysander; for my sake, my dear, Lie further off yet, do not lie so near."

Theo paused for a moment. "O, take the sense, sweet, of my innocence! Love takes the meaning in love's conference. I mean, that my heart unto yours is knit so that but one heart we can make of it;

two bosoms interchained with an oath; so then two bosoms and a single troth." He'd lost track of where he was, but pretended he was too overwhelmed to continue, and with his hesitation, a few of the words returned to him. Mr. Toffler stayed still, probably "enjoying the wooing," as he put it. "Then by your side no bed-room me deny; for lying so, Hermia, I do not lie."

Mr. Toffler clapped. "Nice!" he said. "I'm already falling in love with you."

"You think Fallon will like this?" Theo said.

"I can't understand why she wouldn't."

Theo closed the play and stared at Mr. Toffler. He thought his tutor looked tired. Small lines poked out from the corners of his eyes, especially when he smiled. "Is everything okay with you?" Theo asked.

"Haven't been sleeping all that well. Up late at night."

"It's weird, how when we go to bed, all this stuff seems to pop up, right?" Theo said.

"It is." Mr. Toffler kept speaking in a strange voice, half his, half Hermia's. He cleared his throat.

Theo thought back to the other day: chess, painting, the campfire on the beach, the s'mores, the angry lifeguard. That night, he'd tried to say his prayers, but whenever he started, he felt he was being too needy and treating God the same way he used to think of Santa—before he'd learned he wasn't real—asking for thing after thing. I want this. I want that. Could I have this? Could I have that? This and that would make me happy. Sometimes he thought God wouldn't help him if he just asked for things—so instead he just tried to think of all the "blessings," as his mother called them, in his life. "I worry that Fallon is just using me for schoolwork," Theo said. "That she doesn't like me in the way that I want her to like me, you know?"

"You think we'd have figured this out by now, right?" Mr. Toffler drank some water and let an ice cube plop into his mouth. He crunched down.

"What?"

"I mean, humanity has gotten a lot of it right in a short time. Made sense of galaxies, stars, planets. We've put man on the moon, torn apart the atom, conquered diseases and invented engines and computers." Mr. Toffler held up *A Midsummer Night's Dream*. "But we haven't come a long way with love. I mean for centuries we've been dealing with this emotion. People have written plays and songs, books and operas. People have put forth theory after theory, and we're still here, at square one. Billions have married, had kids, had a shot at understanding love, but Shakespeare could write this play today, and it would still be just as valid."

"How does that help with Fallon?" Theo asked.

"Oh, it doesn't."

"So, I'm screwed?"

"We're all screwed."

"Does this play end well?" Theo said.

"You'll see."

"*You'll see* is adult for *no*," Theo said.

Mr. Toffler picked up his copy of the play and ditched his normal voice: "Becomes a virtuous bachelor and a maid, so far be distant; and, good night, sweet friend: Thy love ne'er alter till thy sweet life end."

Theo answered: "Amen, amen, to that fair prayer, say I; and then end life when I end loyalty! Here is my bed: sleep give thee all his rest!" He set the book down. "I have no idea what I'm saying."

"There's no time for understanding right now," Mr. Toffler said. "We have thirty more minutes to get this down. At our next session, we can dive into meaning."

"Okay," Theo said.

Searcy entered the church, swinging open a tall glass door. The pews were vacant.

Instead of sitting in the front row, like usual, she opted to genuflect somewhere in the middle and then took a seat on the right side of the aisle. The votive candles that bookended the altar flickered in their red glass containers, and Searcy pondered what each flame represented: a divorce, a sick mother, an injured teen, a drug addict, a child in need of a transplant. The more she studied the flames' movements, the more her problems—if one could even label them as such—seemed to dwindle. She brought the kneeler to the floor and rested her knees on it. Still, she couldn't bring her eyes to the crucifix and the emaciated body of Christ. Most days, she traced the wooden curves of His body, from His toes, to His legs, to His ribs and arms and hands. *Forgive me*, she thought. Then, *Is this a test, God? Is this a test to see who I am? How strong I am? If it is, I think I'll fail*, she said. *Can You give me strength? Can You? Can You show me the path and give me the strength to walk it?* She brought her head downward, until her chin touched her chest. She listened to the lapping water in the baptism pool, and heard the bells outside strike noon. Even in this shroud of piety, she envisioned the two of them, together. A small place, maybe. Raising Theo, loving each other the way she and Keith did, but for longer, on the main stage. Then, once more, she begged God for forgiveness for even pondering such a scenario.

Her cell phone sounded, and even though there was no one to whom she could apologize, she hurried out of the church, forgetting to genuflect, darting past the holy water to get to the lobby. "Hi," she said, pressing the phone to her ear.

"Hey," Hoit said. He filled her in on his travels, explaining that he'd met with a few smaller, local business owners in Tokyo. "The strategy this trip is little different," he said. "Instead of focusing on bigger corporations, we're looking at little spots. We don't want to be known as just a corporate brand. Anyhow, it's all boring." Hoit changed gears, telling her about the views and smells of Tokyo. That he was being asked to attend a sumo-wrestling match later in the week, and that it was big ceremony. Searcy had just thought of it as two fat men slamming their cellulite into one another, but Hoit explained that the Japanese society viewed the wrestlers as gods, worshiping them with granules of rice and uttering hymns in their presence.

Streams of sunlight blasted her face, causing her to squint. She stared at the Stations of the Cross—they were outside at Saint John the Baptist—a few paces from the church. If Jesus had to do it again, would He? Would He sacrifice Himself for others? Or had humanity done such a poor job with His gift that He regretted the decision?

Hoit paused in the middle of his story. "You okay?" he asked.

"I haven't said anything," she said.

"I know. Everything okay?"

She walked over the bricks near the entrance. On some of them, Bible verses had been etched: "Love one another as I have loved you" and "God's voice is glorious in the thunder."

"Sleepy," Searcy finally said.

"Where are you?" he said.

"At church."

"Look at you," Hoit said. "I think that's what every man wants to hear when he's not around and he asks that question. 'I'm at church.' Hope you're not meeting too many men." He laughed.

"Just the one," she said.

"How's Theo?"

"He's good. There's a girl he likes. She calls him sometimes, and they Skype on the computer for a bit and go over their science homework. It's sweet. There's also this bully, Dylan, but he won't let me do anything."

"Good for him." Hoit coughed.

"Oh," Searcy said. She'd thought maybe it was best to wait for him to arrive home before bothering him with this, but it had been on her mind. "There've been a couple of burglaries in the area lately."

"Really?" he said. "Jesus."

"I know. Weird. I just thought I'd let you know. Nothing big or anything. They've preyed on people who leave their doors unlocked and their garage doors open. Makes me nervous."

"Anyone we know?"

"People a few streets over from us. I've seen them in passing."

"Are you scared?" he said.

"No," she said. "Well, maybe a little. I keep things locked anyway, but you never know."

"I'm sure the cops will get whoever is doing this."

"Yes," she said, stepping over a brick that read: "If you have faith, you will receive it."

"All right," Hoit said. He wrapped things up and told Searcy that he'd call soon. "Love you," he said.

"Bye," she said. She pressed her palms against the exterior of the building and jutted her legs out to loosen her calves. She then worked through the rest of her routine, swinging her body from side to side and then stretching her hamstrings and quads. The jog back home moved quickly, and she felt that her pace was snappy. Normally, about halfway home, her lungs would begin to burn, and this itching sensation would wash across her upper thighs, but not today.

When she arrived on Whiffletree Lane, she slowed her stride and walked the last fifty yards. She arrived at her mailbox and flipped through the contents right there on the street: *Boys' Life*, credit card bills, documents addressed to Hoit, and junk. She pinched the stack under her arm and headed up the driveway.

At the front door, she spotted another plain envelope on the welcome mat. She clenched her jaw and blinked fast.

She grabbed it. There were no markings on the exterior of the envelope. In fact, it looked and weighed the same as the first letter. Scanning her road, she begged for a hint, and just then, spotted Josie's closing garage door, the slats coming down one by one until they were flush with the driveway. She pressed her tongue hard against the roof of her mouth and listened to the hiss of her breath. She decided to open the letter inside, behind bolted doors. With her finger wedged underneath the flap, she tugged hard, in one swift motion, ripping the paper.

"Are you okay?" Carly asked Emerson. "You've been quiet tonight."

It had been a while since the two of them had been together on his boat, even longer since the two of them had fooled around. "Fine," Emerson said.

"Do you not like me? Do you not want me here?" She brought the covers up with one hand and pushed him away with the other. Then she flipped over and faced the opposite direction. "Is it her?" she asked.

"Who?"

"Searcy."

Emerson didn't want to say "what?" like so many men would have. He'd heard her, and, in fact, he was simultaneously shocked and impressed with her deduction.

"I mean, all you do is talk about her and her boy. About how good her house smells and how funny her son is, and blahblahblah. At first, I was happy for you, but you never ask me how I'm doing, and you never really treat me special. I doubt you're talking to Searcy and Theo about me . . . are you?"

"What?" Emerson said.

"I don't have a kid or a nice house. I'm not sad and weird like she is. I've worked hard to get my shit together. I don't have a rich husband. I don't have the time to sit around all day and make my house smell like tomato sauce, because I'm actually busy working and sending money to my dad and mom."

"Don't run your mouth about people you don't know."

"I think it's weird. I think you're weird. Here you are, a grown man, subbing in for her husband when he's gone. She has you take her boy out painting . . . maybe I need to be with a man who has a real job and who wants to come home to me and my normal-smelling apartment. I should be with a man whose hands don't always look like a kid's who just got picked up from daycare. Maybe with a guy who doesn't live on a fucking boat!"

He didn't think he'd been this transparent, but during the sex, he hadn't been totally present. It wasn't as bad as one of those Hollywood films, where the character called out the wrong name, but he had pictured the wrong person—that much was certain. He'd shut his eyes, and run his hands over Carly's bare shoulders, and imagined they were Searcy's. This was as close as he could get to her, and with that, he was thrilled that his imagination was as good as anyone's on the planet. "Sorry," he whispered, rolling over and facing the wall.

Carly sighed. Then she reached over and tugged on the lamp's cord.

In the darkness, Emerson found peace. He glued his eyes to a single spot on the wall where a splotch of moonlight had found its way into the cabin through a nearby porthole. He took in breath after breath, inspecting the light.

––––––––

Searcy was done calling for Theo. He had locked himself in his bathroom after borrowing her hair dryer and some mousse, and he would certainly be late for school. "My hair has to be big up in the front!" he said. (Fallon had certainly changed the way he used to go to school, always in cargo shorts and unlaced, much to her dismay, basketball sneakers.) Finally, he emerged, his steps hard on the stairs, so she would look his way. Instead, she kept her eyes on the *Times*.

"Mom," he said, clearing his throat. "What do you think of this outfit for Lysander?"

She laughed.

"What?" he said, placing his hands on his hips.

"You're not a superhero. You don't need to put your hands on your hips."

"Oh," he said.

He wore black pants, a much-too-large brown vest, and a white button-down shirt.

"Where did you get that vest?" Searcy asked.

"From Hoit's closet."

"*Really?*" she said. "Where did *he* get that?"

"So I look good?" he asked. "My hair is okay? I wanted it to swoop up more, but it won't work. . ."

"You're going to be a big hit."

Theo tore through the house. "I'm gonna be late."

Searcy took her mug in her hands and held the door open for Theo, passing him a toasted bagel as he hurried out the foyer, over the stoop, and down the driveway. His backpack bounced up and down, rattling with supplies, as he flew down the road. "Don't run so fast!" she said. "Be careful!" She watched him until he was just a dot in the distance.

Sipping coffee, she determined that consistency was paramount, and that life was about finding various situations that were sure to buoy you in times of discomfort. In California, about eighty percent of the time, she could count on the sun. She could depend on her coffee, her paper, and her toast. She could—for now—hinge her well-being on her boy hugging her. But so much was random.

The second letter had been as real as the first. There'd been times over the past few days when she'd looked at the newest letter, hoping she'd dreamed it all, missed something that would allow her to dismiss its content, but now she knew what she'd find when she walked up the stairs and made her way to her bedroom and opened her Bible's cover, the hefty book right there on the dresser. She remembered the first note, the one which she destroyed in the disposal:

Dear Searcy,

Your husband is not who you think he is.
You deserve a better man.

And now, upstairs, she read the new one, the second one:

Dear Searcy,

I saw him. Something was going on.

The second letter didn't seem to do much more than the first. From the first, she'd gathered that Hoit was cheating, so the more recent note seemed to just bolster that fact. This writer had a style: greeting her by name and then typing two quick sentences.

Searcy powered down the stairs, gaining confidence with each stride. She flung open the front door and left it that way. Still in her nightgown, she was determined to get an answer. So many times, she'd walked this driveway, crossed this street, and headed over to Josie's to thank her for a pie or ask her if she could recommend a handyman or a gardener, and those strolls felt like nothing, the physical equivalent of water. But this crossing was laborious. She never had trusted Josie: her all-the-time smile and happy, bouncing hair. Her wave, her tight jeans. Her "Love Thy Neighbor" bumper sticker—all of them added up in Searcy's mind, assembling themselves into a heavy premonition. She arrived on the welcome mat and pounded on the door.

Nothing. No sound. Just her exhales, her heart, and her muttered speech as she told herself how ridiculous she was. She peeped through a few windows, spotting Josie's perfect furniture and perfect layout: magazines stacked, a bar cart in the corner, and a bunch of her immaculate Meyer lemons in a bowl.

As she took back to the street and up her driveway, she tightened her lips. Thank God no one had been home. What would she have *actually* done? She had no proof. In life, if a person didn't see something happen, didn't have others to witness the event, then it was just hearsay.

———————

Emerson sketched at Java Bistro, his head inches from his pad, his hand windshield-wiping across the heavy paper. Displeased with his work, he filed into the line to grab a coffee and one of those chocolate muffins that were big as turtles. He returned to his seat with his goodies and got situated, changing gears and working on a series of portraits, something new for him that he'd discussed with Madame Fournier—drawings in which he never picked up the pen.

"So sorry," he heard a familiar voice say.

Emerson looked up. It was Searcy. Why was she here? He'd been coming here since forever, and not once had he ever seen her. "So sorry," she said again to the cashier. "I must have lost my money."

"Oh," the man behind the counter said.

Emerson rushed to the front of the line. He slapped down some money and told the cashier, with whom he was friendly, to "keep her order cooking." He wished he hadn't said those words, but nevertheless, he believed his gesture made up for the babbling stupidity.

"I usually keep some money in my sock," Searcy said. "Probably fell out." She shrugged.

"I'm gonna run to the restroom real quick. I'm by the window with all the supplies . . . if you have time to join me." Emerson smiled. Searcy wore little makeup and looked younger with just a natural rosiness from her workout. Emerson was happy he got to see her in this way, almost as if they'd been dating for a while or woken up together.

In the bathroom, he raked his hands through his hair, smoothing out his cowlick with some water, then rinsing his mouth out repeatedly with slugs from the faucet to eliminate any trace of coffee breath.

As he made his way back, he noticed Searcy at his corner table by the window, pencils and pens strewn about. She had angled a piece of paper her way and, with a fine-tip pen, was drawing. Heat scattered across his back and over his shoulders, and he stayed still, next to a big pile of newspapers, not wanting to disturb her. She'd told him that she hadn't sketched in years—or at least that's what he remembered—and here she was, connecting with an old version of herself. No matter how hard a person tried to be something else, the way of the world always seemed to push them back to their default setting. Emerson approached and took a seat. She looked up. "It's been a while, but wanted to see if I could still make something." She rotated the paper Emerson's way as he took a seat. The drawing was of a single figure, elongated, wearing an updo, and a long gown. The features on the woman's face were just there to signify that she was a woman—the focal point was clearly the clothes, the folds in the fabric, the large bow that rested on the woman's hip.

"So good," he said. "Do you mind if I keep it?"

"Sure," she said, crossing her legs.

"Why didn't you ever start your own line?"

She took a sip of her cappuccino. "Life got real, fast. I suppose I could have a boutique one day."

"What would you call it?"

"What I wanted to call my formal, ready-to-wear line—Assuage."

"I like that."

She scanned one of his don't-pick-up-the-pen sketches on the table. "This is stunning. Is this woman special to you?" she said, blowing across the surface of her drink, dispersing particles of foam.

"With most of my portraits, especially at the sketching stage, I just start with a line, a curve, and go from there. I have an idea of what I want something to look like, a picture in my mind, but it never matches up. Sometimes, I do wonder if there's actually a person out there who looks like my drawing." He erased a smudge on the side of the paper.

The way the sun floated through the windows in that moment made Searcy's eyes even lighter. "Does it ever make you sad to think about how quickly we experience art? Like, when I took Theo to the Louvre a couple of years ago, we hurried by so many paintings and sculptures. And the whole time, I was thinking, some artist spent months, years, perfecting this, and here we are, taking it all for granted."

"Masses pour into the Sistine Chapel, glance at the ceiling, and then turn to their families and say, 'Anyone up for gelato?' I always feel bad for the poor guy who built the floor at the Sistine Chapel. Supporting these fat tourists day after day, everyone staring in the opposite direction."

"We walk past so much beauty every day and never acknowledge it," Searcy said.

"I'm sorry about the other—" He stopped.

There it was.

This had happened once before in a supermarket long ago. The first few seconds of that smooth and rolling melody piped-in over the coffee shop speakers. Normally, he was able to tune it out, but this song would forever be part of his life. "Sorry," he said. "Sorry, Searcy." He pushed out his chair, the legs scraping against the tile. The cold, the snow, the yellow line, the sound—it all rushed back in a kaleidoscopic swirl. He rushed outside, far from the coffee shop and took deep breath after deep breath, allowing his chest to undulate, his eyes burning.

Searcy had wanted Emerson to finish his sentence about the other night, thinking that it could be the precursor to him telling her about the letters, but instead here she was—rushing out the door and chasing him down.

He sat on a bench, about a block from the cafe. A cigarette smoldered between his lips, and he wiped tears away before they encountered his unshaven cheeks. "What's wrong?" she asked, taking a seat

117

next to him. "The other night? The letters?"

"That song, that goddamned song."

"What song? In the coffee shop? Marvin Gaye?"

"Yeah," he said.

"What about it?"

He grabbed his cigarette from his mouth and tapped off some ash. "The song that was playing in the car that night. I hear it every now and then, and it's just the same feeling every time—the exact same fucking feeling. It had to be my dad's favorite song. He couldn't have liked something no one liked, so I wouldn't have to bump into it."

Searcy placed her hand on his knee. "I'm sorry."

Emerson told her about that night. He never minded talking, but these words were bombs. Each sentence laced with mines. "I crashed into a snowplow," he said. "I drifted off," he said. "I had turned the music down," he said, "enough to keep me awake, but still quiet enough for my mom and dad to get some sleep. I rarely drove on these trips, but my dad had hurt his foot skiing. My mom was exhausted and had to make some phone calls. I think about how perfect everything had to line up for there to be such a disaster. I think about that all the time. Why did I read that book that night, watch *Animal House* on TV. Why didn't I just go to bed? Why did my mom have to be a saint and always cover everyone's shifts? She was always too good for this world." Emerson's words came and came, faster and faster, unraveling, spinning.

"Shhh, shhh," Searcy said, rubbing his legs through his rough jeans.

"Marvin Gaye, singing, happy, not missing a beat, perfect trills and harmonies. The car bashed to shit. Just mangled. But his goddamn perfect voice still played perfectly. And I knew it then. I knew I killed them. Just like that. My two favorite people. Seven billion in this world, and I was given those two. And I killed them. I killed them. I fucking killed them! I did it all. And now, well, I'm all alone. No first phone call when good news comes in. When bad news comes in. I can't ever hear my mom say my name anymore, my dad's deep laugh. I can't ever see my mom's gapped smile, my dad's greasy hands from working on the Karmann Ghia. Just me, just me."

"That's not true." She leaned into his body as he finished off his cigarette and tossed the butt to the ground. "You have me. You have Theo."

There was a long silence, followed by some wind, and a skittering candy wrapper on the pavement.

"But do I?" he said.

"Yes," she said.

He blinked and swallowed hard. "I find myself dreaming about you and Theo in a way that I've only dreamed about things that have never happened."

Searcy stared at the cigarette on the ground. Tiny curls of smoke twirled from its body. "I know. Me, too. Maybe we can. Maybe we can do this. Pull it off, you know? I'm not sure anymore." Searcy stopped. In a way, she hated Emerson for making her doubt her steady ways. "I saw those books on grief on your boat. I saw the pills, too."

"I've been taking less of them since I've known you."

Searcy kissed Emerson, but this time, the usual bolt of guilt didn't accompany her affection. It felt right, almost. Then, however, she pulled back, not wanting to be this way in public. So what now? she wanted to ask, but she resisted. At times, she stood confident that it would work; other times, she was sure nothing would come of this. He was a boy still, living on a boat, a painter, a professional dreamer. Could he deliver? Could she? Had he ever been in a serious relationship? Would he treat her like Carly in a couple of years and move on to something more exciting?

There weren't any right answers, no path without its complications, and it seemed that the possible and the impossible occupied her mind as much as sin and virtue.

———

The man rattled Hoit awake. He was an older Japanese man, bald, with bushy eyebrows and glasses that distorted his eyes. "We're about to land," the man said.

Hoit couldn't believe how well the sleeping pill had worked. They had just taken off when he'd swallowed it with a glass of white wine. He'd remembered studying the patches of light from the city as they'd departed civilization, and he'd recalled the thought he'd had in his drowsy state, one that he'd thought was poetic and strange at the time: lights on Earth were just constellations of the land. He shook his head.

As soon as the plane's wheels touched down, he whipped off his seatbelt and plucked his phone from his pocket. He'd texted Searcy many times, but she hadn't responded. He was supposed to return next week, but a tragic situation had changed his schedule: the person for whom he was supposed to do PR, a businessman that had been caught sleeping with male prostitutes, had jumped off of the Kintai Bridge, a historical wooden bridge.

The old man clutched a brown box between his feet, and Hoit was confused as to why the man didn't simply store the box in the overhead bin. There was a tag on the box, and Hoit purposely dropped a pen so that he could get a closer look. The old man, startled by any movement toward the box, lurched forward and scooped the pen off the floor before Hoit had even shimmied to the edge of his seat.

"Thank you," Hoit said. Sometimes discretion was overrated, and maybe, too, Hoit still had some of the beta-blocker coursing through his veins, so he just came out with it. "What's in the box?" he said.

The man angled his eyebrows.

"My apologies," Hoit said. "I'm still sedated. That was rude." Hoit knew that the man would agree but would ultimately confess.

"My wife's ashes," the man said. His voice stayed steady.

"Oh, I'm sorry," Hoit said.

"You didn't know."

Hoit flipped up his window screen and checked out LAX as they taxied.

"Our last trip together," the man said, offering a broken smile.

Hoit nodded.

"She wanted her ashes scattered in Long Beach, believe it or not. We met there when I was in the service. I would go to the movies whenever I had a free moment, and I always had my eye on this girl who worked the concessions. I would make sure my uniform was crisp—crisper even than military regulations. I never liked popcorn, but asking for it allowed me more time with her than if I just ordered Raisinets, you know?"

"Smart," Hoit added.

"We call them ashes, but they're bigger than that. More like granules of sand."

"Really?" Hoit added.

"Yes," the man said. "And what I find so strange is that the ashes weigh about the same as a newborn—about six to ten pounds, somewhere in there."

"Full circle," Hoit said.

"I suppose there's beauty in that. I'm just not able to see it yet."

The man lifted the plain box onto his lap before reaching under his glasses with his thumb.

Hoit faced the other direction, scanning the parked aircrafts and blinking lights and traffic control center. How perfect it would be if humans could have something of a mission control center, someone on lookout, giving tips to navigate the mess. He didn't think he'd go on any more trips until the summer. Until at least June or July when Theo was out of school and on summer vacation. Even when Mason would insist, Hoit would push back. He needed to be there for Searcy, for Theo. He stiffened his arm, allowing the cuff of his sleeve to tug back and expose his wrist. Then, he pulled the knob from his watch and adjusted the time.

Emerson told Theo about the spot where they'd chosen to paint—a place suggested by Madame Fournier—only a half mile from Abalone Cove. It was called Portuguese Bend, a serpentine road that was built atop an active fault. Because of the constant seismic activity, plumbing pipes were exposed, above ground, and every couple of months, the city brought in construction crews to repair the torn asphalt.

What Emerson loved about the area was that no one bothered painting here due to the road's volatile nature. Clusters of fennel and mustard plants carpeted the hills, and whenever the wind worked eastward, a trace of anise hung in the air.

Emerson watched the boy's eyes widen with every tidbit of knowledge regarding a plant or a bird or the endemic Palos Verdes blue butterfly. "When you live somewhere, you know nothing about it. It's just home," Emerson said. "All the history just comes with it. Then someone comes to town and tells you everything about it, and you're there, just shrugging your shoulders, like 'Okay, yeah, whatever.' I know that's how it was for me in Vermont. People would tell me about maple trees and tapping for syrup, and I'd be like, 'Okay, cool. Pass it over. My waffles are getting cold.'"

"Were you a good kid?" Theo asked. He painted the curvy line of Portuguese Bend, paying attention to the shapes that jutted into the road.

"No," he said. "I got in trouble a lot."

"What's the worst thing you've ever done as a man?"

"There's a lot of time left for that one," Emerson said. "I'm only twenty-six." Emerson mixed white into blue, trying to pinpoint the sky's shade. "How about you?"

"I once stole a Snickers from the market down the road."

"Yeah?"

"My mom said I couldn't have it, so I just put it in my pocket. It was easy, but I felt bad about it, so I told my mom, and she made me take it back and apologize."

"Look at you."

"Yeah." Theo got back to it, working his brush in gentle strokes, staying steady in one portion of the canvas for a long time. He detailed what could later be filled in, and Emerson felt his limbs tingle as he took in the boy's work. It was the first time in his life that his passion had been caught by someone else—that he'd successfully passed his love on to another person. More often than not, he had to find a way to talk about painting that would make others feel included, comparing it to their passions—fantasy football or bowling. But painting was not fantasy football, nor was it bowling. "The light is prettier here than in any other spot we've painted," Theo said. "Is it always like this?"

"It's always interesting. Even when it's not sunny, even when it's not bright or warm." Since Emerson had many depictions from this location, he didn't paint the ocean or road, opting instead to draw Theo. He didn't tell him, because he thought it might distract Theo from his own work, so Emerson worked from memory most of the time, refreshing his imagination every now and then by stealing a peek, especially when he needed a specific detail, like how the boy was holding his brush, or how his hair was sitting on his ears, or how his shoelaces were moments from coming untied.

"I wonder why no one else paints here," Theo said.

"They're not as smart as us," Emerson said.

"Hey, have you ever been to Dominic's Steakhouse?"

"No. Nice?"

"It's good. Went there with Hoit and Mom the other day."

"I hear it's good."

"They have girlfriend dishes, so that might be good for you. You know, to bring Carly."

"What do you mean *girlfriend dishes*? Like oysters?"

"I don't know. Some of the things on the menu had *GF* written next to them. Things guys can order for their girlfriends, I guess."

Emerson set his brush down on his easel. "I think that stands for *gluten free*."

"Oh, God. That makes so much more sense. I thought it was weird. I mean girls love pasta, and it wasn't picked as a 'GF' item."

After their laughs settled, the only sound that could be detected was the sigh of wind, and Emerson turned toward Theo to see exactly how the boy's legs were bent. "Theo," Emerson said in a whisper. "I'm being really serious right now. Do not move. Okay?"

"What?"

"Do not move," Emerson said. "I need you to listen to me. I need you to trust me." Emerson stared hard at a spot a few feet behind Theo, coercing the boy to line his eyes with the dusty rattlesnake, whose split tongue licked the air. "Be still," he said again. He heeded his own advice, too: His mouth tightened. His molars adhered. Saliva pooled in the back of his throat.

The snake, however, disregarded the instructions, inching its way closer to Theo, its rattle now up and shaking, the sound of its heavy scales grating the dirt. Theo quivered. "Mr. Toffler," he said, his right Nike slipping loose. And just that, the sound of rubber against earth, startled the snake. It struck at once—a flash from the ground, its mouth wide, fangs plunging into Theo's calf.

"Shit!" Emerson yelled, as the snake slithered into a patch of tall grass, its taupe body blending into the weeds. The rattle stopped, but Emerson still heard the sound in his ears. Emerson knew panic wouldn't help, but his insides were knotted. Sure, he'd seen the sign warning of snakes in these parts, but he'd seen so many signs in his life and never actually spotted the thing they warned against. Task and then another task, he thought. He needed to view everything as step-by-step. Get Theo to the car. Take him to the hospital. Stay calm.

Lucky for Emerson, Theo was light, so Emerson flung the boy over his shoulder before tearing up the hillside to the car. His legs churned and prickled. Even though life was more important than usual, the tick of seconds, he found, possessed a slow-motion quality, and his actions were deliberate. "Keep talking to me!" Emerson said. "How are you feeling?" he said, dropping the boy into the passenger seat. Before he knew it, he whipped the car around, nearly taking out a fire hydrant, and peeled onto the main road. "The hospital isn't far," Emerson said.

"Not far at all. Just down here. Not far at all." He ripped the shifter back and the engine growled behind him as he zoomed past cars over double-yellow lines. "How's Fallon doing?" Emerson asked. His voice rushed. He took a turn hard enough to make the tires scream.

Theo held on. "Is this really the best time for this conversation?"

"She's good? That's good."

"Am I going to die?" Theo asked. "Is this the kinda thing that kills people or just deforms them forever?"

Emerson ground gears and downshifted into second around a tight bend. Color drained from the boy's face. "You're not going to die . . . so it went well with Lysander and Hermia?"

"What are they going to do to me at the hospital?"

"I don't know."

"It's getting really big. Look!"

"Does it hurt?"

"Yes. And it's numb, too."

"Shit."

Emerson pummeled his horn, then darted through a stop sign after scanning the traffic. "If anything, we're both going to die on this drive."

"Hey, Mr. Toffler," Theo said. "If I do die, can you tell my mom that I love her?"

Emerson honked again and flipped a guy off. "Sure, buddy."

"And," the boy added, his voice low, "can you tell yourself that I love you, too?"

Even with the Volkswagen's RPMs high, Emerson heard the boy's sniffles, so he reached over and cupped Theo's head, feeling his soft hair against his palm. He let the words hang in the cabin, careful not say something that would scare them away.

———————

Searcy and Hoit rushed into the bright hospital and squeaked across the shiny floor. There, in the corner of the waiting room, sat Emerson, his color-speckled hands bookending his pale face. "He's doing all right," Emerson said as the two of them approached.

"Where's he now?" Searcy asked.

"In the back. They gave him some sort of shot, an anti-venom thing, and now they're draining the wound."

"What the hell was he doing with rattlesnakes?" Hoit said.

Searcy reached over and touched Hoit's arm.

"Totally my fault," Emerson said.

Hoit spouted a puff of air. "I know *that*," he said. He dropped onto a chair next to Emerson, and Searcy sat across from them both. She made sure her eyes stayed away from Emerson's, staring at a heap of crinkled, waiting-room magazines.

"Just wanted him to paint something new," Emerson said.

"Can't you just paint at the house? It's gotta be some sort of god-damn safari just to draw some birds?"

"Can we see him?" Searcy pleaded.

"The nurse said she would come as soon as he's stable," Emerson said.

Searcy gripped the chair's arm. She was now paying the price for her sins and couldn't believe God had gone as far as to use a snake either . . . it seemed cliché, even for Him. What was next . . . a parting of the sea? An ark?

"Searcy," Emerson said. "I'm so sorry."

"I know," she whispered. Hoit rose and sat next to her, and she felt him curve his arm over her shoulders and work his fingernails across her skin, up and down, down and up, inches from her elbow. She had seen the signs around these parts for years—yellow signs that showcased rattlesnakes with their tails pointed upward, but in all her jogging miles, she'd never seen one.

When Emerson stared at the polished floor, Searcy inspected his features. She felt safer this way, knowing that he couldn't connect with her, even with the slightest brush of his pupils. He pulled hard breaths through his nose, pushing his nostrils out every so often. His hands were tightly bound, almost in prayer formation, and she wondered if he was, in fact, nudging his wishes northward. Hoit watched the TV in the corner. Dr. Phil's large face took up most of the screen, his Southern drawl pushing through the waiting room. "Everything's gonna be fine," Hoit said a couple of times. "Everything's gonna be totally and perfectly fine."

Finally, a nurse approached, wearing turquoise scrubs and a tight ponytail. "Yes," Searcy said, popping up.

"Your boy's doing great, responding very well to the medicine. You sir"—she pointed at Emerson—"did a good job of bringing him in right away."

Emerson didn't budge.

"Would you like to see him?" the nurse asked. "We can only take two people at time."

"Yes," Searcy said. She headed down the hall, feeling Emerson's eyes burn into her back as she walked the corridor and tucked out of sight. When she was no longer in his eyeshot, she relaxed and felt her body weaken.

The nurse pulled back the curtain in Room 148.

"Mom!" Theo said. "You're here! Look at my leg!" He shot his leg up, out of the covers, and the nurse placed it back, flush with the bed.

"I know it looks horrible," the nurse said to Searcy, "but everything is fine. It's best to let the wound breathe."

"How you doing, champ?" Hoit said.

"Okay, I guess," Theo said. "Where's Mr. Toffler?"

"He's here," Searcy said. "In the waiting room."

"Does he know I'm okay?"

"He does." She cupped her boy's face, pressing her lips hard to his forehead.

"Can you get him for me?"

"Not now, Theo," Hoit said.

"Why?"

"Be with us," Hoit said.

"Okay." Cartoons blasted on an overhead television, and the nurse reached for the remote control and muted the volume. Searcy pushed away a few strands of hair that were slick with sweat and stuck to Theo's forehead. "You should've seen him," Theo said. "He drove here fast." Searcy ran her fingers across the smooth skin of her boy's arm.

"He came in here," the nurse said, "with your boy over his shoulder, and it was a good thing he moved quickly. A bite of that size starts to affect the body in strange ways, hurting the lungs and lymph nodes within only fifteen minutes."

"Probably would've been best to stay away from a place with rattlesnakes to begin with," Hoit said.

"They're everywhere in SoCal now. You'd be surprised how many of these sorts of things we see. I'd say three or four a month. They're all over the beach, too." The nurse brushed her hand over her forehead as if she was sweating, but her face was flawless and matte.

Searcy returned her stare to a corner in the hospital room, running her pupils over a painting: a windmill in a bucolic setting, the blades rusty, matching the hues of the surrounding dry shrubs.

"We left all the paint and everything," Theo said. "I wonder if Mr. Toffler is mad about that," he said. "You think he's mad?"

"Who cares what he is?" Hoit said. "What matters is that you're okay. And what matters is that you don't do these sorts of things anymore. Look at how upset you've made your mother."

Theo reached for the thin hospital blanket and tugged it to his chest. "Are *you* mad, Hoit?"

"Of course, I'm upset. But you're okay." The nurse left the room, yanking the curtain across its metal tracks to shield them from passersby. "You're okay. You're okay. You're okay," Hoit said.

Each time he said the words, Searcy heard them in a different way. At first, she took them as intended, but as she replayed the sentences, she came to understand it as "You're all right . . . you're average . . ." And "okay" she thought was the worst thing a person could be. Bad prodded a person to change. Good made a person happy. Okay brought comfort, and comfort made a person complacent.

"I'll get Emerson," Searcy said. She made her way to the hall. Emerson's seat in the waiting room was empty, and Searcy hurried through the automatic doors into the parking lot, where she spotted him, sitting on the fender of his car. The sun ricocheted against the car's paint, causing her to narrow her gaze. "He's doing fine!" she said, closing the space between them, and softening her voice. "He's doing fine. Good even."

Emerson blinked his glassy eyes.

"Thanks for—"

"For what? For almost killing your boy? For almost destroying your life?"

"For bringing him here," she said. Pressure built in her chest until she was forced to exhale. "He wants to see you."

"You sure?"

"Yes," she said. "Room 148."

"I'm sorry," he said.

"Go."

Under gathering clouds, Emerson walked toward the hospital. His knees were rubber and a bright pain throbbed between his eyes. When he reached the front doors, he turned around. Searcy was staring at the ground, seemingly scrawling something with the tip of her canvas sneaker.

Emerson stayed still. "Mom, Dad: What the hell am I doing?" No one heard his declaration except for himself and an old woman who slid a walker fit with cut-up tennis balls on the legs. The old woman smiled.

The muscles in his back were taut from carrying Theo, but he worked through the open floorplan of the hospital, swinging his head back and forth, peeking into patients' rooms. Stethoscopes and charts and clipboards and drips and machines and beds with buttons. These people—most of them, anyhow—would get well, be cured with some pills or rest or both, and that had to be nice. Emerson's discomfort didn't come with a remedy. No codeine or Z-Pack here.

"Shhh," Hoit said as Emerson stepped into the room. "He's sleeping." Hoit sat in a red chair at the foot of the bed.

"Good." Emerson took a seat next to Theo. The heart monitor let anyone who cared to know that his pulse was eighty-eight, and Emerson studied the peaks and valleys of the green lines on the screen. That's all life was—just a jagged mountain range of green streaks.

"I still can't believe you would take him somewhere like that," Hoit said. His voice, even in a whisper, was sharp. "You know you could be liable."

"It was an accident, Hoit." Emerson spoke at a normal volume.

"This could've been *so* bad. This never would have happened on my watch."

Emerson twisted his neck, hoping to loosen the muscles. He leaned forward and set his forearms on his knees. "That's because your watch is in another time zone, Hoit. You need to be around for shit to go wrong." The boy's heartbeat entered the low nineties; the beeps came harder and faster before settling at ninety-four.

"Some of us actually have to be men," Hoit said. He swiveled in his chair.

"Listen, with me, he'll always be happy. He'll always be appreciated. He'll always be cared for . . . maybe that's what I think a man is—taking care of someone." Emerson took one last look at Theo and took to the hallway.

Theo had reacted well to the medicine and treatment, so the staff at the hospital permitted him to leave at nine o'clock at night instead of having him stay overnight. Theo smiled wide, and Hoit and Searcy did, too. "Keep an eye on him," the doctor said. "Anything strange. Anything at all, please come on back, okay? You were a trooper," the doctor said to Theo.

Theo thanked the doctor. He thought it was good that the doctor was smart and rich, because otherwise he was very strange looking, with rough skin and a thin mustache that guarded his top lip like a fence.

After Theo crossed the parking lot, using his mom as support, he got into the back of the SUV and leaned his head against the cold window. He had a story now, one for Fallon, and he had a wound to show to her and the other kids. It wasn't a broken arm. It wasn't a few stitches from skateboarding or surfing. No, this was a rattlesnake bite, the fang marks still totally visible.

When the car shook to life and Hoit put it in gear, Theo cracked the window and felt the coolness on his forehead. This past morning—eating oatmeal in the kitchen and taking a shower—seemed as though it had happened months ago, when he was a different person, and as he pictured the brown sugar and golden raisins, Theo peered out the window at the dark parking lot. Cars, of course, were everywhere, but Mr. Toffler's Karmann Ghia stood out, a few rows over, under a tall streetlight. He didn't see Mr. Toffler in the car, or even around the car, but Theo was certain it was his car. "Mom, did Mr. Toffler come and visit me?" he asked.

"He did. You were sleeping, though, and he didn't want to wake you."

"Oh," Theo said. Theo kept his eyes glued to Mr. Toffler's car for as long as he could. As they rolled by strip malls and laundromats and butcher shops and cigarette stores that Theo had passed a million times, he kept telling himself that life was different. The last time I passed these stores, the last time I sat in this car, the last time I was on this street, I hadn't been close to death. I hadn't been as cool as I am now. I hadn't slipped away from the monster. He liked the word "slipped" whenever he had this conversation with himself.

When would Mr. Toffler collect all the supplies in the hills of Portuguese Bend? How long would these items take to completely decay and become one with the earth? Wood, paper, canvases, horse hair— the materials all seemed biodegradable. With his thoughts swirling, the drive ended, and Hoit pulled the vehicle into the driveway. He helped Theo out of the SUV, and into the home, and up into his bed.

Theo slid between the sheets. His mom didn't sit on the edge of his bed like usual, saying that she didn't want to accidentally hit his leg. She pulled up a chair and Hoit sat on the floor, next to her. "Is he dead now?" Theo asked.

"Who?" Hoit said.

"The snake."

"Why is 'it' a 'he'?" Hoit said.

"Hard to picture a girl being so mean," Theo said.

"No, no," Searcy said. "They're not like bees. He's still out there, slithering around, probably telling his friends that for the first time in his life he bit something that didn't die."

"I'm happy you're okay, Theo. You don't know how scared your mother and I were."

The words seemed strange when Hoit spoke them, like when he spouted out business stuff on the phone. Sure, Theo knew Hoit was speaking English, just like he knew it was Hoit saying kind words, but it didn't seem to *really* be him.

"We're all together again. We're all a family again," Hoit said. He stood and walked over to the foot of the bed. "There's something to that, right? Maybe this was just a way for us to get closer. Remind us of what's really important."

Searcy agreed.

"Goodnight, Hoit," Theo said.

"Goodnight, you two," Hoit said, exiting the room. His steps too soft on the plush carpeting to be heard.

"Is he okay?" Theo asked.

"Just scared. You frightened us all, you know?"

"Not Hoit," Theo said. "Mr. Toffler . . . was he okay when you saw him?"

"He was relieved. He feels very guilty."

"I saw his face on the drive over. He was all red and, I think, ready to cry. I could tell he was close, like he was holding it all back and trying to be brave. He kept saying, 'It should've been me. It should've been me.'"

"It's hard to see someone you love going through pain."

"I wasn't sad for myself. I feel like death could only be sad if you could watch yourself die from outside your own body and see everyone being sad. So, when Mr. Toffler was driving fast, all I could think about was how sad you'd be. How sad Mr. Toffler would be. How maybe the two of you would no longer speak because you'd think it was all his fault."

"Shhh. That's enough." She carefully took a seat on the bed.

Theo dropped his head to his pillow, feeling the down crinkle around his ears, and the world go quiet. His mom dragged her fingers up and down his forearm, and he felt sleep come his way, especially with the drugs still pumping through his body.

MARCH

EMERSON CALLED SEARCY. "I think it's the flu," he told her. "I've been in bed. I can't move. Can't do anything. I'll let you know if anything changes, but my guess is that it's going to take a few days, maybe a week, to get my strength back." His voice sounded like Joe Cocker's.

Searcy was polite, a touch distant, not offering warmth, but cliché after cliché: "get well soon" and "drink lots of fluids." In case, without her advice, he was going to take to the beach and attempt to cross the Pacific using only a hearty breaststroke.

"How's Theo?" he managed to get out before a sneeze overpowered his body.

Searcy told him he was recovering. That he was at school and seemingly happy. "He'll be sad that he won't see you, but he'll understand."

"I'll miss him," Emerson said.

"Emerson . . ." she said.

"Yes."

A few seconds of quiet ticked off the clock. Her breath was strong. Inhale, exhale. "Nothing," she said.

"No, please. Go ahead." Emerson thought he could hear Hoit in the background.

"I've forgotten. It was right there on the tip of my tongue."

"All right. Talk soon, Searcy," he said.

"Yes," she said.

If Emerson was being totally truthful, no, he wasn't feeling well. His stomach turned, and his body ached in places he didn't know it could ache: the soles of his feet, his triceps, even his hands. But that wasn't it. There was more to his call.

He was exhausted from emotion, from care. It was too much to see Theo and Searcy on a daily basis and not *totally* have them. As progressive as he was—a Greenpeace guy, a millennial man—he always envisioned a fantastical scene from the 1950s: him, pulling into the driveway in a T-Bird, flinging the door open, scooping up Theo, and heading to the kitchen where he'd plant one on Searcy. To modernize it some, he'd help in the kitchen. He'd set the table, cook, do the dishes, bring Searcy a glass of wine as the evening reached its finale. But in this world, the real one, he was nothing more than a window shopper. So close. The jewelry glinting in the store window behind a thick pane of glass. And he wasn't sure what good waiting near the storefront did him, other than allow the gems to pull him, beckon him, tease him. So for now, he would do his best to avoid the street where the jewelry store was located.

He spooned some dark coffee grounds into his machine and added the perfect amount of water before flicking the switch, hearing the gurgles, and studying the droplets that, one by one, filled the pot

---

I should have, Hoit repeated in his mind as he fixed the pantry's jammed pocket door. Searcy had invited him to the mall to go shopping with her and Theo. She needed jeans and Theo wanted some new sneakers. Hoit wanted to be more involved, and yet, every time a situation was gifted to him, he passed. Being one of seven children, he was accustomed to the noise of family, the background murmur, the hum that accompanied all tasks, but he wasn't used to the closeness. Not far from a restaurant he took clients, there was a marriage and family counselor, in a small office with a Dutch door, and Hoit had popped in the other day to see if the therapist could see him, but there was no availability. Discussing this with an MD, he thought, might be the way to go, allow him a safe place to open up.

"Your funeral," Searcy had said to Hoit before she'd left with Theo, and even though she'd paired her words with a coy smile, he knew there was some truth to it.

Because of his guilt for not heading to the mall with Searcy and Theo, he checked off items that had been scribbled on his to-do list for months. The pantry door was now fixed. The latch on the stove was greased, and the doorbell had just sounded, meaning that the security camera installation folks were here.

Hoit hoped they'd be quick, so that he could show Searcy when she returned, play it off as though he'd *wanted* to go to the mall but had planned this from the start as a surprise. Every night—well, not every night—but most, she'd discussed that it was startling to see so many robberies in the area. No matter how many times Hoit told her that the suspects were only stealing out of people's open garages, it didn't do a thing. "But what if they decide they want more?" Searcy would say. "What if this is just the beginning?" she'd ask. "No human is content doing the same thing every day."

So, here they were. Two men on the doorstep. One fat, one skinny, like a comedic team. The tall one was fat, the short one, thin. They said "sir" constantly; even after Hoit told them to call him "Hoit," they said, "Okay, sir."

The men were quick to work, strolling the perimeter of the home with Hoit, pointing to places where it would be wise to place cameras: at the corners of the eaves, along the walkways, one at the front door, another along the roofline of the garage door. "You just don't want any blind spots," the skinny one said.

Hoit stared at the man's goatee. "So six cameras all in all, right?"

The men nodded. They told Hoit that it wouldn't take long, but that installation wouldn't happen today. That this was just the evaluation portion.

"Really?" Hoit said, shoving his hands in his pockets. "Was hoping to score some points with my wife."

"Maybe next week," the man said. "We're busy. Lots of calls because of these burglars."

Hoit nodded. "Give me a ring. In case we get robbed before then . . . then, you know, I'm not sure we'll go through with it."

The men strolled to the driveway and opened their van's doors.

Hoit returned into the home and up to his bedroom, where he organized the contents of his garment bag. Sometimes he took so long to unpack that he figured he'd just stayed packed for the next trip, but Searcy had put it on the list, so he figured he'd check off all the tasks.

"Damn!" he said. "Come on!" The zipper stuck. He clutched the bag with one hand and yanked with the other. When the zipper finally gave way, he lost his balance and tumbled into Searcy's dresser, knocking a watch, some earrings, and her Bible to the carpet. He made quick work of the dangly earrings and watch, returning them to the silver plate they called home, then reached for the Bible that had landed page-side down. Lifting the thin pages from the carpet, his eyes lined up with a verse from Isaiah. "Come now, let us settle the matter," says the Lord. "Though your sins are like scarlet, they shall be white as snow." He placed the book back on the dresser with care, directly to the left of the silver plate, where it always rested, then he stood. A folded piece of paper remained on the floor, its white hue blending into the carpet. Had it fallen from the Bible? His garment bag?

The paper was creased, so it took him a few seconds to open. He lay it flat against the dresser and smoothed the sheet with his palm, holding it in place. He read its content, took in the words again and again, trying to make sense of them.

Dear Searcy,

I saw him with a woman.
It seemed like something was going on.

His knees softened, and the muscles in his back contracted hard enough for him to have to shift his posture to escape pain. Heat rushed to his temples, and he drew a rasping breath. *Saw. Him. Woman. Going on.* That was all that stood out. The other words popped in and out. But those five assailed him.

Who would do this?

Type this?

Send this?

It could only be two people, he thought.

Josie. The neighbor whom he had kissed once in her garage. He'd helped her move some furniture, had drunk two potent whiskey sours, and had eaten too little of her homemade bread. She was lonely. He was weak. But he could sense that she had feelings for him, always being *too* friendly and *too* warm when she saw him in the street.

Or it was that other one, that fucking Mr. Toffler. Hoit knew he had seen him and Candace that day. Hoit chomped down on his bottom lip hard enough to draw blood. The pain was sharp but also soothing, and he knew that hours from now, the area would swell and irritate him, but presently, it was enjoyable to suck on his blood that carried a hint of sweetness. He returned the sheet to the Bible and dropped the cover and pages atop it. Staring out the window, a wind swept through the neighborhood, shimmying dead leaves, twirling them in something of a tornado.

————————

Damn was the only word that mattered to Theo. He'd heard it so many times in his life, mostly after some sort of pain: a toe-stubbing, a banging of a knee on the coffee table, an inability to find the remote control. But these past few days, he'd just heard it in good ways, as in, *Damn, Theo! Is it true that you got attacked by a snake?*

For the first time this week, he had some alone time with Fallon. She'd had to get braces one day; then the next, her science class took off on a field trip; and yesterday, some sixth grader pulled the fire alarm and ruined their quiet moment. But now, he sat across from her on the blue picnic tables, where the sun had spent the morning warming the slats. Heat oozed through his pants and underwear, making the outside of his body feel the same way his insides felt.

"Let me see it," Fallon said. She squinted her eyes. "Can I see it? Please, let me see it! I hear it's big." A few of the teachers that were on lunch duty looked their way, and Theo thought they seemed relieved when Theo reached for the bottom of his pant leg. He rolled up his khakis and pushed his sock down.

Fallon bit into a strawberry as she inspected his leg, bringing her fingers close to his skin, centimeters—millimeters, maybe, Theo thought—from his leg hairs. Her index finger grazed the wound, and she yanked it back. "Oh, my God. I'm sorry," she said. "Did that hurt?" She licked the strawberry's juices from her lips.

Her touch hadn't hurt at all, but Theo played into it. "No, no," he said, sucking in his cheeks.

Fallon continued her inspection of Theo's leg. And Theo continued his inspection of Fallon's face. Could people develop more freckles? Because it seemed to Theo that a few had sprouted in a new location, a touch south of a cluster near her cheek. That constellation—Theo liked to think of them as stars—had always possessed seven. And now there were nine. He called the constellation "The Queen" because it looked a little like a tiara. There were days, like now, when he thought of telling her that, but he wasn't sure how it would be received. Was that what affection was—just keeping things to yourself until you got to a place where it was safe to release them? Or did you have to release these private thoughts in order to gain affection? Theo wasn't sure. And the more days he lived, the more he suspected that nobody else was either.

His eyes hopped from freckle to freckle. The two new ones didn't quite fit in "The Queen," but he made room for them, telling his imagination to turn them into jewels that had fallen off the tiara.

"Were you scared?" Fallon asked.

"No," Theo said. "I mean, a little. Dying, or thinking you're gonna die, is surprisingly peaceful, you know?"

"No," she said. "I don't."

"I mean, if I had died that way, everyone would have been sad, but death by rattlesnake bite wouldn't be that bad. It would hurt, and then you'd die."

"You're weird." She smiled.

"I know."

"You're also lying."

"I am," Theo said. "It really hurt. And I was really scared."

Fallon finished off the strawberries and tilted back the Tupperware container that held a little juice. "I saw one when I first moved here," she said. "I was mountain biking with my dad. We were on a trail, and my dad slammed the brakes on his bike. He shouted for me to stop, too. We just sat there and watched one slither across the trail."

"Did it rattle?"

"No, but I saw the rattle."

Theo gathered Fallon had had enough of his leg being propped up on the bench, so he yanked his sock up and unrolled his pant leg. "Mr. Toffler said there's lots by the beach."

"Mr. Toffler sounds nice."

"He is. I haven't had the chance to talk to him about it. I was asleep when he visited me in the hospital, and now he's sick. So we're not working together right now."

Fallon peeked inside of her lunch box. She pulled out an individually wrapped string cheese and split it with Theo. Earlier, she'd offered him some of her strawberries, but he'd declined—not because he didn't want any, but because they were messy and he didn't want to get juice all over his hands and face. "Do you think that maybe one day I could come and paint with you and Mr. Toffler?"

"Sure," Theo said, thinking that maybe—just maybe—she had

invited herself on a strange date with him. "His car only fits two people, but we could probably figure something out." Had he just talked about the capacity of the car? Why hadn't he just let out an exuberant *yes*? He gathered Mr. Toffler and Shakespeare would have been disappointed by his reaction.

"Is that the car he let you drive?"

"Yes, the stick shift."

"My cousin from Iowa let me drive his tractor last year when we visited him. I wasn't very good. And that wasn't even stick shift."

"It was hard to pull the shifter back at first. But Mr. Toffler's car is old."

"My cousin's tractor looked old, too. But all tractors look old."

Theo ripped his piece of cheese into tiny ribbons while Fallon just chomped on hers like a banana. He wanted to ask her about Iowa and her cousin, but he didn't. Instead he just stared at the tabletop and pretended to shoo away an insect. "I'm excited for our scene tomorrow."

"When you practice with Mr. Toffler, does he play my part?"

"He said he likes being Hermia."

She giggled. "Why?"

"He said it was nice to be wooed for once."

"*Wooed*. My grandma says that word."

"I'd never heard it before." Theo glanced up at the outdoor clock. Everyone alive had heard the line, "Time flies when you're having fun," but it didn't feel that way when he was with Fallon. It didn't fly. It danced a complicated dance. Everything mattered, and there was a rhythm to it. Theo didn't want to twirl Fallon too fast; he didn't want to step on her toes or have sweaty hands. He just wanted to be with her, closed off from the world, and stay on this blue bench for hours, until his back hurt, and it was nighttime, and it was cold. He thought that maybe he was in love. Though even the thought embarrassed him. That would stay forever in his brain, in a metal box, along with his love of black licorice and his imaginary friend (from years ago), Lionel.

Mr. Toffler had mentioned something like this—this light sensation. He'd told Theo that there would be a moment when he'd be with Fallon, and the world would go silent, and everything would make sense, and the weather would be right—even if it was cold or hot—and he'd feel this calmness . . . that the earth—all of its trees and rivers and mountains—would transform into an *arcadia*. Mr. Toffler had said that word. *Arcadia*. Theo hadn't asked him what the word meant, because he could tell that Mr. Toffler had been speaking with passion, and he hadn't wanted to ruin the moment. Theo gathered from the context clues that it meant a harmonious place, but he wasn't totally sure.

For the first time in his life, Hoit wished he'd listened to Theo and bought a dog. Not for cuddling or petting or posting cute photos, but for the escape. He needed an excuse to take a stroll, and he wished right now, while the three of them watched *Wheel of Fortune*, that he could spring off the couch and say, "All right, guys. Be back soon. Gonna go take Vinny to do his business!"

Sure, Hoit saw his face every day in some capacity, but he'd noticed something about it recently, and other people had, too, including Searcy. "Nice tan," a gas-station attendant with whom he was friendly had said. "You look sunburned," Theo had said. "Are you okay? You're really red," Searcy had said. And he was. No matter how much water he splashed on his face or how strong the A/C blew on his skin during his drives around town, he couldn't shake the hue. His body reminded him of something he begged to forget. But he knew the letter and its sentences would stay with him until they were addressed.

In time, everyone turned in, and Hoit tossed in bed, letting himself come up with a plan. If he was smart enough to start a business, he could come up with a way to address this problem. In fact, in a few days, he'd already taken care of one suspect: Josie. She'd been filling a watering can from a spigot in her front yard, and he'd bounded out of his house and asked her directly if she'd written the note. She'd stammered at first. "What?" she had said, her pupils stretched to the rims of her irises. "The cookies?" she'd said. "The note that came with the cookies? Yes, I wrote a little note. Did you get them? Did you enjoy them?"

"Oh," Hoit said. "The cookies, yes." He didn't remember a thing about them, but, feeling bad, he told her how delicious they were, how he'd savored them all and had eaten so many one evening that Theo had taken to calling him "The Cookie Monster." Sure, she was lonely, Hoit had thought. Everyone was. The more the world's population grew, the harder it was to foster a connection. But she wouldn't sabotage a marriage.

"Are you all right?" she'd asked. "You seem stressed." She'd touched his arm. "Would you like to come in?"

Once he'd entered, they'd stood in the kitchen. Munching on a lemon bar, he'd told her about the note. "Oh, my," she'd said, not asking if it was true. "It's probably that man who comes to your house in the orange car." Hoit let the rest of the lemon bar crumble in his hand. "He's always over there, and he looks to be very enthralled with your family, your boy, your wife. Sometimes I see him. He parks right along the curb by my mailbox. He gets here early, and I study him."

Now, as Hoit lay in bed, staring at the ceiling, he wondered whether he'd even said goodbye to Josie, or whether he'd even thanked her. He swung his feet out of the bed and placed them on the carpet, rubbing them back and forth across the plush fabric. Tiptoeing, he made his way to Searcy's nightstand, where he disconnected her cell phone from its charger, slipped it into his pocket, and made his way to the bathroom, sliding the lock into place before flipping on the light.

"Tutor" was right there in her recent contacts and he sent him a message. *Where's your boat dock again? What marina?* It was only half past nine o'clock at night, but Emerson put off an "I don't sleep before midnight" vibe, so Hoit waited there, sitting on the edge of the bathtub, staring at the phone.

Maybe this wouldn't work. Maybe he'd have to go to bed and not hear back from Emerson. He could picture the scene: sometime tomorrow, Searcy's phone would chime and she'd answer, tell Emerson that she never texted him.

His heart seized him—two rhythmic thumps in his ears, in his chest, in his wrists.

Minutes passed before the phone buzzed in his hands.

Dock 10, the text read.

Hoit wrote back. *Would it be all right if I came over right now? You're not busy are you?* He tried his best to sound like Searcy, even via text. She was always asking the main question, then asking another that apologized.

Sure. Come on over, Emerson wrote back. Then a few seconds later in another message: *Are you bringing Theo?*

No, just me, Hoit wrote, pairing his words with a smiley face.

Cool, Emerson answered.

Hoit collected himself, listening to the heat leak out from a vent in the corner. Its stream strong enough to flutter a single square of toilet paper that hung over the tight roll. Before shuffling over to the sink to splash some water on his face, he deleted the recent messages and slipped the phone back into the pocket of his pajama pants. He washed his hands, finding the rose scent of the bar soothing. Mr. Toffler's word, *cool*, irked him. It wasn't cool that a married woman was coming over at nearly ten p.m. It wasn't cool how casual it all was. None of this was cool.

His brain burst with questions: Had Searcy slept with him? Was she falling for him? Were *I love yous* exchanged? No, no. He didn't know everything that swam through her gray matter, but he knew she hadn't been intimate with him. But there had to be a connection. And for some reason, this emotional link nettled him more than the idea of their bodies coiled between sweaty sheets.

Hoit killed the bathroom light and let the water air dry on his face. He stepped across the dark bedroom, around the strewn pillows, atop a patch of moonlight that split the curtains, and plugged her phone back in, just as she'd had it. He then took to the door, the hall. He didn't slow down at Theo's room, nor at the top of the stairs. If he stopped, even for a second, he might do so permanently, and he knew he just needed to concentrate on small tasks: donning his coat by the front door, slipping into his loafers, grabbing his keys.

With five days off, Emerson felt revived. His cold had subsided, and he'd been sleeping fifteen hours a night due to a combination of cold medicine and cheap wine. And, he had to admit, a life without Searcy or Theo possessed less complication. Carly was just what he needed at this point in his life. When he wasn't spending time with Carly, paintings occupied Emerson's days, and when he wasn't painting, he was thinking about painting, even discussing art with Madame Fournier, who had written him a couple of letters of recommendation for fellowships in both Paris and Sydney, despite her failing health.

Emerson figured Searcy would be arriving soon, so he made sure the scene was tidy, running his hands over his bedspread, lighting citrus-scented candles, and organizing stacks of records and books. He left out a couple of his most recent paintings, ones he was proud of, hoping that she'd take a look and be impressed.

Clean glasses rested atop the counter, along with a bottle of wine, and he took to the deck, his ears blocking out the sea and concentrating on the nearby parking lot. He swallowed more than normal. He paced and breathed. *Should I run out to the lot,* he thought. *No, no,* he told himself. *Too desperate.* He sat back on the deck of the boat but then decided to make the whole scenario more casual. He dropped the needle of the record player to a Tony Bennett LP, *Summer of '42,* and then lolled out on his couch, flipping through an art book, taking in the same paragraph over and over.

He turned down the music, feeling the reverberation on the deck. "Searcy?" he said. "That you?"

There was no answer.

Moments later, a foot dropped down onto the wooden ladder that led into the cabin. Thunk. A loafer. A leather one, with a tassel that bopped atop the expensive shoe. The legs of the person's pants were striped. "Excuse me," Emerson said. "I think . . ."

"Emerson," Hoit said as he stepped onto the carpet, releasing his hands from the ladder.

Even with the chilly air wending through the open windows, Emerson's scalp burned. "Hoit," he said. Closing the book.

"Surprised?" Hoit stayed standing, right below the entrance. He scanned the surroundings with a quick swoop of his eyes, seemingly taking in the record player and the candles and the paintings.

"A little," Emerson said. The silky sound of Bennett's voice oozed about the square footage as the crooner held on to a note from "It Was Me."

"A little different than you imagined."

Emerson reached over and shut off the record player. The quiet felt louder than the love song. "Can I get you something to drink?" Emerson asked. "A beer?"

"Sure," Hoit said.

Emerson found strength and stood. He reached inside the small fridge for two bottles of beer and popped off the tops with a quick yank of the bottle opener. He found solace in the fact that he hadn't done anything *really* wrong. Yes, he'd fantasized. Yes, they'd kissed; they'd held hands. Yes, he wanted to be with a woman who wasn't available. But if these vices were punishable, prisons would be

Siberia-sized.

Hoit shoved the paintings aside and took a seat on the table, directly in front of Emerson, who had returned to the small couch. With the table so high, Hoit's feet didn't quite reach the ground. "So," he said, taking a slug of beer and setting the bottle next to him.

Emerson let the cold Budweiser coat his throat and combat the burning that had taken hold of his body.

"I'll be frank," Hoit said. "I'm not loving getting up in the middle of the night and coming to some shithole little boat, but I know it's you." Hoit wrung his hands. "I'm not the best man myself, so I'm just going to be honest with you, and then I need you to follow my instructions—take my directions, okay? Can you do that?"

Emerson took a pull of beer that was mostly foam. Had Searcy put Hoit up to this? Had she told him about the bonfire? About kissing?

Hoit kept on. "I know it's you. You're the only one that saw me that day at Abalone Cove. I didn't think you'd do anything about it, though."

Emerson's heart steadied at a high rate, and he stood.

"Sit down," Hoit said, rushing toward Emerson. "Your fucking letter! Be a man!" He lunged, wrapping his hands around Emerson's throat, and they both staggered around the cabin, before hitting the ground in one quick motion. A perfect arc. Ending in a thud.

In the chaos, Hoit's beer tumbled to the carpet. The liquid rushed against Emerson's bare feet. Hoit returned his hands to Emerson's neck, and Emerson felt as though Hoit's fingers were lengthening, hardening, covering his entire neck. His palms choked Emerson's Adam's apple, and when Emerson tried to gasp, it only gave way for Hoit to push that much harder, ridding the throat of any air. Emerson focused on his breath, pulling a single one through his nostrils, which helped for a second, but it wasn't enough. He flailed his arms, punched Hoit in the ribs, but the process only exhausted him further. Finally, Emerson's fingers came into contact with Hoit's bottle of beer, and he grabbed the neck of the bottle and swung it as hard as he could over Hoit's back. The Bud shattered in one blow, exploding into shards that sprinkled Emerson's face and chest. Hoit, dazed, loosened and pushed himself up. Emerson coughed violently, over and over, as if his body were trying to pull in thirty breaths at once. He then got up, and turned on the faucet to drink some water.

"If anyone is going to stand, it's me," Hoit said. "You sit back down. Right there. You're going to sit. You're going to listen." Hoit dropped his head into the palms of his hands and scratched hard at his face, leaving three red traces on his cheek. "Listen."

"Shit, you don't have to keep telling me to do something I'm already doing."

Hoit snatched Emerson's beer bottle from the floor and wrapped his right hand around the glass. "You've reminded me. It's not all for nothing. I mean, the way you've done it—going behind my back, sending your little bullshit, letting her know I'm not a good man, that she deserves better—well, that's horrible. But how else can it be done? It has to be secretive? The intent was bad. The words were devastating, but you've awakened me." He stood and paced back to the ladder. There, he downed the rest of the Emerson's Budweiser—what hadn't spilled out—in one, hard gulp, his Adam's apple moving up and down.

"Don't you think she has a say?" Emerson asked.

He tossed the bottle into the metal sink from a foot away. The bottle didn't break, but it clamored off the sides and rolled around the base before steadying. "Sure," he said, taking a seat next to Emerson. "But as the husband, as the father, I deserve a chance to make things right."

"I made you want to be better?"

"The way you're willing to sabotage me and my family . . . it's gross. But maybe that's all I would've responded to."

Emerson thought Hoit's voice had more of a Southern twang than usual. Through the spaces between button holes, Emerson got a peek at Hoit's chest, thick with black hair. He looked at Hoit in his silly striped pants, his sunburned face and specks of beard. All this power and respect, all this money and clout, and here he was on a boat, just like Emerson himself.

Family was touted as steel, but its construction was nothing more than papier-mâché: flaps of wet fabric sealing other flaps of soaked cloth, finding its strength in hardening over time. But Hoit's creation hadn't dried well.

Everything had lined up exactly how Emerson had wanted it. He'd worked himself into their family, so much so that Hoit was sneaking away in the dead of night. Had Searcy just come out and told him her feelings?

Hoit's face began to contort, the muscles stiffening around his cheeks and mouth. Up and down, he ran his hands over his skin, digging his thumbs into his eye sockets. When he finally spoke up, his voice was no longer smooth, cracking at times. "On my way here, I wanted nothing more than to kill you. That you would sneak around, put things in my wife's head. But the drive calmed me, and after some time, I thought you just sensed an opening, saw a rift, and just. . ." Hoit stopped there. His chest moved up and down, hard and fast. "Can you do something for me?" Hoit asked, bubbling with emotion.

"What?" Emerson said. He rose.

"Call Searcy in the morning and end the sessions altogether?"

Emerson folded his hands in front of his chest. "What about Theo?"

"All he talks about is how you're going to be a famous painter." Hoit lifted his head out of his hands. His eyes wet, his skin red. "Tell him something that's too good for you to pass up. A job or something. He'll be sad, but he'll understand. He's a good kid that way."

They had swapped spots: Hoit now sat, Emerson stood at the table. "He's the best." Emerson studied the flame of the citrus-scented candle. What a different life he'd envisioned for its flicker.

Hoit spouted a hard laugh, one that startled Emerson. "I don't know about that," Hoit said. "He's a kid. And he's sweet. Nice. Too nice."

"What is it with people always telling others that they're too nice? Maybe people who say that are just trying to justify their own shitty behavior."

"People say that to you or something?"

"No one's ever said that to me, but here we are telling people to be good—and when they actually are, we say, 'Take it down a notch.' He's your son. Be fucking proud." Emerson glowered at Hoit.

"Stepson," Hoit said.

"His real dad is dead. You're what he has. He doesn't get to see his real dad every other weekend or some shit."

"Just tell me you'll go away, Emerson. This past week, with you gone . . . it's been calmer."

"You're going to be better to her? Better to Theo?"

"I'm sure you not being around will help. You don't really have to put in any of the heavy lifting. It's a wedding for you—you just swoop in, all dressed up, not a care in the world, hit on all the pretty girls. No arguments. No mortgage. No chores. No tooth brushing and dishwashing." Hoit wiped his mouth on the sleeve of his shirt. "You don't actually have to be there for her, for Theo. You don't have to support them. You really think a woman like that is going to be with you? Going to live on this crappy boat? Sleep near a life-preserver? No wonder little kids like you—you are one. Let's face it, you're a valet driver, and eventually you're going to have to bring my Ferrari back around."

"Is that what she is to you? A Ferrari?"

Hoit stood and walked across the small cabin, cocking his head to the right to keep it from bumping into the ceiling. A vertebrae in his neck cracked. "I never should've been worried," he added.

Emerson could hear his own his breath.

"I should've come here long ago," Hoit said. "It's made me feel better, seeing you, with your little records, your little candles." Hoit reached for the ladder and took hold of the railings.

Emerson listened to Hoit's steps head up the ladder and onto the deck. Just as quickly as the noises had come, they left, and now Emerson was still with the silence, collecting the Budweiser bottle's shards that glittered on the carpeting.

He could've been more careful, but what good would it have done? His affection for Theo and Searcy was palpable. Love was heat, and people could feel a furnace blow no matter how disconnected they were from their own temperature. Glass sliced his thumb, and Emerson stuck his finger into his mouth and sucked on the skin. He got up and took to each candle, drawing in air, and snuffing out the flames with big breaths.

A haze surrounded Searcy, because hours earlier, when she'd tried to treat her headache, she'd plucked the wrong pills off the shelf in her medicine cabinet, accidentally swallowing two Tylenol PMs instead of regular Tylenol. So, now, at 10:23 in the morning, they had kicked in, and she felt drunk.

Through the living room window, she watched Hoit pay two men who had just finished installing security cameras. (The thieves had actually been apprehended a few days prior—nothing more than three high-school seniors having stupid fun.) "A deal's a deal, though," Hoit had said. "Not bad to have some extra security, right?"

Searcy set her coffee down and reached for her phone that vibrated against the granite countertop. "Yes," she said, answering without having checked who was on the other end.

"Searcy, hey. It's Emerson."

"Hi." It warmed her to hear his voice. "You feeling better?" she asked.

"Somewhat," he said.

"Will we see you this week?" she asked, knowing the response would be a formality. He had been ill, sure, but he was now good enough to tutor and paint and spend time with Theo. He coughed three times and excused himself once before launching into a speech. He told her about painting and passion and getting it right. He told her about dreams and determination and seeing things through. He discussed Theo and, in a soft voice, let her know that he was bright and kind and full of charm. He used the word "winsome." He discussed a fellowship in Madrid that he'd applied for in the fall, just before he'd met Theo. "A long shot," he kept saying. "A total longshot. Such a long shot," he said. "Not sure why I applied. I asked myself many times why I was even putting the application together, you know. Feeling like I was just in the mood to pay the post office a visit and see how expensive international shipping could be."

Such a speech was a precursor to sadness. Bad news was delivered in minutes, good news in seconds. "So?" she said. "You won?" She kept her responses short as to not allow her voice time to weaken.

Emerson paused.

She heard him take a gulp over the receiver. She asked again.

"Yes," he said in a whisper.

Hoit and the men on the driveway laughed, and she watched all their heads cock back in unison. One of the men dropped both hands to his stomach. The other one clapped.

"You must be happy," she said.

"I'm totally thrilled."

"You don't sound it."

"In shock, I guess—the whole thing. Moving to Madrid. For a year."

Searcy reached for her coffee. The brew was bitter, and she figured she'd added too little cream. "I'm sure," she said. She took another sip. "What does that mean for us?"

"I have to be there soon, so I have to get my things in order. Sell the boat, my car, and get to Spain."

"So you won't be coming this week?"

"Not sure it would make any sense."

"Sense," she said. Hoit handed over a check to one of the workers and opened the front door. "I'm not sure it would either. Maybe you can stop by before you leave and say goodbye to Theo."

"Okay," he said.

Pressure built in her chest as she plodded up the stairs. With the nighttime medicine coursing through her system, each step required attention, and she labored to get down the hall to her bedroom. "We'll miss you," she said. "I'll miss you."

"I'll miss you," he said.

"You'll be so far away."

"I know." He let out a breath. "You hang up first, Searcy. I just can't hang up on you."

"But you can leave . . . that you have no problem doing," she said, hanging up. She dropped onto her bed, the duvets and mattress supporting her as she curled up and pressed her face into a pillow. No more after-school arrivals, no more Karmann Ghia sounds, no more head rubs for Theo, or blue-eyed gazes that told her she'd be okay.

Hoit entered. Searcy welcomed the diversion. "All set," he said. "Good to go." He twisted his neck from side to side. "Everything good?"

"Emerson has to leave us. He won some sort of fellowship, and he has to head to Madrid pretty soon. Shocking, right? Just out of the blue like that."

Hoit sat next to her, sliding his arm around her body. "Oh, no. How strange."

"He didn't think he was going to win."

Hoit wrapped Searcy, brushing long strands of hair away from her face. When Hoit kissed her, her mind traveled. She shut her eyes and felt her hands find their way to Hoit's waist. He kissed her more, warm lips parting hers. Heat flooded her chest. She felt force in Hoit, confidence. His back was taut as he lay atop her, and he removed her clothes with purpose. When cooler air met her skin, goosebumps came to life on her stomach. She kept her eyes tight, not just closed, but firm. No light could enter, not a sliver. Stubble grated her inner thighs. Her heart pumped. Her fingers balled.

Hoit's shirt hit the floor in a soft hush. Then the metal jangle of his belt. Then two thunks, his shoes, knocking against the carpet.

He moved fast, pushing her hands above her head and holding them together tightly. He spread her legs, and she adjusted her hips for his. The thrusts came over and over. Hard. The mattress screamed. The headboard beat.

Droplets pushed from her eyes, leaking to the corners, where they eventually evaporated. "Searcy," he said in a rush. "I love you," he said, reaching for her face. "I love you," he said again, his breath moist, smelling of coffee. She kept her lids down, and once again, the burn in her ducts returned, starting as an itch. She tried to pull one of her hands down to relieve the sensation, just a flick, but Hoit gripped her arms tighter, so that her palms touched one another as if they were handcuffed. "Searcy," he said. "Searcy," he said again. "SearcySearcySearcy."

Wind tore at Theo's face as the muscles in his thighs and calves fired. Down the boulevard, he bombed. It had been years since he'd ridden his bike, but he just wanted to be alone.

His memory wasn't good. He had the grades to make that argument. Whenever he needed to recall a math formula or how to conjugate a Spanish verb, his mind went blank, but in this instance, as he savored the descent, the Pacific and Catalina in the distance, he thought about his mom and what she'd said. He could remember every piece. Mr. Toffler was leaving. Mr. Toffler had won a fellowship in Madrid. He was moving soon; he wouldn't be back. How? How had this happened? Why? Why did this happen? It wasn't fair. Theo blamed his mother for not paying him enough. He blamed himself for not being cool enough to make the decision harder. And he even found himself blaming God. How could He do this to him? God had already taken his father. Wasn't that enough? God had to take his favorite man, too?

As his bike worked over some of the sidewalk's cracks, the chain jangled against the bike's frame. *He pretended to care for me, but he was just like everyone else. Not even coming by the house to say goodbye. Hoit wasn't perfect, but at least he'd stayed around.* Maybe it was hard for Mr. Toffler to say goodbye. He'd seen a movie once where the main character couldn't bear the idea of the word *goodbye*, so he would only say *see you later*, but what did it matter what a person said? If they had to take a plane, and change money and time zones, they were gone.

Theo dropped his bike into a bush and plopped down on a bench. He'd seen the bench many times but had never actually sat on it. He figured it was mostly for tourists wanting a good photo of the ocean to filter and post on Instagram, but here he was, breathing in the world, trying to make sense of his sadness while staring at beauty. Pillows of marine layer rolled in across the sea, filling the space between Catalina Island and the coast. The clouds were thick, spongy, and he watched the process unfold, until the clouds seemed dense enough to walk across. He had never been to the island. He wasn't sure what the distance between home and Catalina was—he thought it was something like fifty miles, but it seemed closer today. The shape of the island seemed odd to him, too—high on the ends and low in the middle, like a slept-on pillow. All islands seemed weird, broken off from the rest of society. Ms. Roth, Theo's history teacher, always talked about Pangaea, and how it was basically the only continent long ago with all the countries of the world mushed together in one mass: Brazil and the Congo and the U.S. and the Philippines. And there was only one ocean, too, that wrapped the whole thing, but Theo had forgotten what it was called.

After some time, the ocean no longer made sense. Nothing did. He pushed his bike up the hill, rethinking his decision to have ever barreled down it in the first place. Five dollars had been in his pocket since the early part of the week, and so he took to a nearby supermarket where he scanned a bin of DVDs. He hadn't heard of the titles; he hadn't heard of the actors, and maybe that was why they were all in a heap, selling for $2.99. He strolled the perimeter of the store, feeling the mist of the tiny sprinklers in the produce department.

A crying baby, a price check on diapers, a spill on aisle nine, and then a voice. "Theo!" a voice said. "Theo!" There, in the cereal aisle, stood Fallon, holding a box of Froot Loops in her hands. Her two braids dangled, and Theo thought of that word that he'd heard Mr. Toffler use once. *Besotted.* It meant an infatuation. But he wasn't sure how to use it. *I besot you?* That didn't sound good. Or pretty. "Hi," he said.

"You here alone?" she said.

"Yeah." He shoved his hands in his pockets. "Came to get a snack.

Rode my bike."

"I knew you either rode your bike or walked. It's not like you have a motorcycle."

"What about the bus? I could have taken the bus, right?"

"For, like, a mile?"

"Maybe." He went through the drill: be cool, stand up straight, suck in your gut. "Are you here alone?"

"My mom's over there." She pointed to a woman down the aisle who wore purple tights. Lots of women wore tights these days, Theo thought. "What are you up to today? Do you want to come with us?"

Theo took a breath. He wished he could breeze over to the produce aisle again and get sprinkled with water. "Um . . ."

"We're going whale watching. Have you ever been?"

"I've never actually been on a boat. Well, I have, but it never left the harbor."

Fallon cocked her head to the side. "That's weird. Anyway, my dad says that most of the whales are long gone, that the prime season is past us, and that we're just throwing money away, but you never know. We might get lucky and catch a slow one that left late. I don't know how it works."

"Sounds really cool. I love whales. Let me call my mom." Theo couldn't believe he'd just said *I love whales.*

"Here." Fallon handed him her phone. It was blue, and the case had all these little fake diamonds on it that made it look like a disco ball.

APRIL

EMERSON TORE HIS HANDS through Carly's hair and pushed her up against a wall in her apartment. She kicked off her high heels, and he carried her over to the bed, spending time kissing every inch of her body, working his way from her ankles (that seemed to bear cuts from a recent shave) to her flat, pierced-belly-button stomach. She quivered. Her toes stiffened. Her breath stammered. She clawed for his neck, the back of his shirt, the top of his head. "What's gotten into you?" she said twice, but Emerson didn't answer.

While he wasn't the brightest man, he wasn't stupid enough to scream Searcy's name. He was, however, able to imagine that every centimeter of Carly's salty skin was Searcy's milky flesh. Why couldn't he just love Carly? She had so much of what Searcy had: long hair, a quick laugh, bones and tissue, chromosomes, DNA, cells, nuclei. He ground his hips against Carly's repeatedly, hearing her moans and exhales, kissing her collarbones that were slick with sweat.

Then he rolled over and felt his heart decelerate.

"That was something," she said. "My knees are . . . Jell-O."

Emerson didn't like the image. He pictured green, shaking food and weird commercials starring Bill Cosby. He wondered if he should just commit to this Madrid lie. Tell everyone the same story, fly to Spain, drink sangria, run from bulls, and hurl tomatoes. Maybe he should just quit. There was always this talk about quitting like it was the worst thing a person could do, but Emerson didn't see it that way. It took strength. Maybe that was exactly what was needed. Quit. Move away. Get on with it.

The rays from a lamp lit the ceiling, producing something of a Rorschach blot. Mountains? The ocean's surf? A bassinet? Carly rolled towards Emerson, propping her head up with her left hand. "You know what might be fun?" she said.

Emerson had a feeling that whatever she was about to mention wouldn't connect with him as fun. In fact, in all his years frolicking the earth, never once had he agreed with someone who uttered the words "You know what might be fun?" But he played along, hoping she'd say something like, "It'd be cool if we both stopped seeing each other and just went after exactly what we desired, you know?"

"I was thinking," she said, "since you're always telling me about Vermont and Montpelier, maybe we could go this summer, for a week or two?" Emerson opened his mouth to stop her, but her sentences flew. "You could show me where you grew up, the graveyard you talk about, and that river, too, where you swam. What's it called?"

"The Winooski."

"Ah, yes, the Winooski. I was going to say Whip-poor-will. Isn't that a bird? Do they have that maple candy you told me about in the summer? Or is it winter?"

"They have it all year. I think the shelf life on those packages reads *George Burns*."

"Don't you think that'd be fun?" She bit her lip.

"It would." He fluffed his pillow. Was this what it was like to be Searcy? To feign emotion both between the sheets and out of them? "Carly," he said. "I didn't tell you something a while back."

She rolled over and her breasts smashed into his shoulder.

He faced her, then got out of the bed and began searching for his underwear. His blue boxers decorated with smiley lobsters were balled up in the corner, and he realized he was about to have a serious conversation while donning crustacean-covered shorts.

"What didn't you tell me?" She yanked the blanket over her chest and fanned her hair out.

Spain. Madrid. Fellowship. At this point, the story had become a sort-of truth. The details sharp, the story coherent. He began, starting with the art, the painting, the email he had received informing him of the opportunity. He painted the mood, the scene, telling her he had nothing to do that summer day, and that the application made him feel purposeful, so he sat on the deck of his boat, hammering out a cover letter—one that wasn't rife with "dream come true" shit, but one that was honest, and the more he spoke, the more his heartfelt lies seemed to appease her.

"Spit it out, would you?" she finally said.

"I have to move. The fellowship is there."

"When?"

"Soon," he said.

"Can I visit? Can I come out there? I've never been to Spain. We could be like that book, you know the one with the bulls and Hemingway?"

"I know it." He remembered the book from high school, though he didn't recall much of anything from the text except for all the alcohol—Pernod, wine, whiskey, champagne—and that his English teacher had had to brief the class on impotence. He remembered chuckling and being kicked out. He remembered telling his dad about it later, and his dad laughing hard, too.

"You got this," Hoit said. Theo swung the putter hard—too hard, Hoit thought—and the dimpled ball careened off the windmill and bounced into a patch of agapanthus.

"So close," Searcy said.

"I'm still leading by a stroke, right?" Theo said.

"Nope," Hoit added. "Down by one now. I just knocked in a hole-in-one."

"Oh," Theo said.

Hoit leaned against a tree and watched Searcy set up. She was six strokes back but blamed the putter most of the time, saying that all these games were "designed for right-handed folks." She dropped the putter back, and her yellow ball traced along the synthetic grass, missing the blades of the windmill, nearing the cup, then circling around the rim of the hole before spinning to the side. "Ahhh," Searcy said. "Every time! Every single time!"

"That was close," Theo said.

"I'm always close," she said.

"Your turn, Theo," Hoit said, instructing Theo to use his hips more, and not so much of his arms, and, to Hoit's surprise, Theo followed his guidelines. His ball rolled with gusto, stopping within inches of the hole. Hoit cheered.

"Thanks, Hoit," Theo said.

The rush of cars on the main road was a consistent hum. Only a few clouds were out, and the sun had settled behind one, leaving the temperature high, but diminishing the need for sunglasses. Hoit was happy he had agreed to mini-golf. Ever since Searcy and Theo had learned that Emerson wouldn't be returning, they'd seemed down, so he was here, hoping that miniature golf would lead to full-sized emotions, and that those emotions would carry over to the next hour and day.

Hoit had made love to Searcy twice yesterday, and even though she'd cried the second time, he'd figured it was a side effect of her intense orgasm. She'd shuddered and clawed at his back, and he couldn't recall her reactions ever being that intense, and he hoped she hadn't faked her excitement in the past. He knew women who did—who had—and he always suspected that if a woman could be that convincing fooling a man during intimacy, than how simple would it be for them to simulate more typical emotions?

Searcy putted her ball into the cup, holding her follow-through. As she headed over to the hole and bent down to fetch her ball, her dress tightened around her body, showcasing the outline of her underwear. Between the lingerie and the thought that Emerson and his paints and his orange car and his little beard were long gone, Hoit felt powerful, like Los Angeles was a small town, and he'd won over the prom queen. She was his. All his.

They strolled the path to the next hole and repeated the process. Putt, putt, putt. Groan, groan, groan. Laugh, laugh, laugh.

Eventually, they made it to the snack shack and wolfed down some hotdogs. Without the distraction of the radio, like on the car ride here, or of the game of miniature golf just moments ago, conversation didn't come to Hoit no matter how hard he racked the corners of his brain. "That was fun," he said. Then said it again. Both Searcy and Theo agreed. "We should do that again, don't you think?" he said, but Searcy and Theo took the rhetorical route with that query, even though Hoit wanted a response. "Harder than it looks, right?" he added, but not much came of that sentence either.

Quiet sat in the air, and Hoit scanned the rest of the picnic area: men and women laughed with their kids, some parents disciplined their children, held their toddlers. Action, movement, people delirious with conversation and Saturday fun. Searcy passed Theo some napkins, and Theo slid a packet of ketchup his mother's way.

"How are the dogs?" Hoit said. "Mine's perfect."

"Delicious," Theo said.

"Juicy," Searcy said.

Hoit couldn't get the conversation to pick up. It was like trying to fly a kite on a windless day.

Emerson had never been the subject of a painting before. Sure, he'd done the occasional self-portrait (the original "selfie"), but never had he been a vehicle for someone else's brush. He hadn't wanted to dissuade Madame Fournier, however. She hadn't painted in three and half years, and she'd been taken like this, while on his boat, something about the "cones of the light." She'd repeated that phrase twice before asking Emerson for his supplies.

He stood behind the captain's wheel, his hands draped over the metal bar, his head turned to the left. "It's going to be shit," she said. "But, not to be maudlin"—she gave the word some French flair, pronouncing it *mau-de-len*—"it just feels nice to wrap my ugly fingers around a brush." By her own admission, she hadn't been well. "I'm in a horror movie," she'd said. "I can sense the beast is around the corner. Oh, hell, maybe I'm dramatic. Maybe it's not a beast. Maybe it's an angel. Maybe it's my sweet husband. But you know, no matter how much we have of life, we get greedy. A day. A week. It all matters," she said.

Between an ebb and flow, when the sea was still for a moment, Emerson could hear the scratch of the charcoal pencil on the canvas. The scribble much faster and noisier than his method. He wished he hadn't selected a pose where he was turned from her, so that he would be able to see her process.

"No need to act," she said.

"What?" The sun beamed off of a neighboring yacht, causing Emerson to squint.

"No need to put it on," she said.

"Put what on?" he asked.

"Be natural. You don't need to act sad."

Emerson hadn't been pretending, but now that he'd been alerted, he supposed his lips had been resting in a downward curve, so he pulled them straight.

"Better," she said.

Emerson felt the sun burn his nose and cheeks. But after a while, his body adjusted, and he felt as though the sun's rays were holding him, swathing him tight in a cocoon of luminescence. He was thrilled that he'd sold four paintings at a recent art festival, so that he could pay the docking fee and gas up the Volkswagen. But he didn't like that his days were aimless, held together by chunks of free time and longing. The feeling—the one that seized him every day around three in the afternoon—was akin to hunger, presenting itself with regularity. Sometimes, he even forgot about Spain and the lie, and made sure his face and hair were presentable and patted his pockets to make sure he had his car keys. He'd reach for his briefcase, then stop. One day, this aching in the pit of his stomach would soften, and he'd look back on these months with a touch of humor, maybe regret. Remember Theo and Searcy from in a different place, far from here. Maybe in Spain? Who knew? Maybe he'd find a Penelope Cruz look-alike, and they'd stroll the cobblestone streets of Sevilla, searching for a café, not really because they were thirsty or in need of caffeine, but just because sometimes romance needed people to sit and stare at each other. He wondered when that day would be. Far in the future, he guessed. Certainly not this year.

"You're moving," Madame Fournier said. "Like a toddler getting his hair cut. Stay still, or I'll make you ugly." She laughed.

Emerson straightened out. Direction of any sort had never been his thing. Rules, guidelines, instructions . . . he'd always been one who obeyed as long as no one directed him to do so. As soon as someone blew a whistle, or used an imperative, he sought the opposite. Even now, close to the marina, stood a sign that grated him: Please Don't Climb Over Railing. But that wasn't it. This in and of itself didn't bother him. It was short. To the point. The word *please* tucked in there. The following sentence, underneath it, though. DON'T EVEN THINK ABOUT IT! Loud. All capitals. An exclamation point. And, because of it, Emerson had climbed over the fence twice for no other reason than to piss off the sign.

The fight with Hoit reminded Emerson of that very sign. Some portions were similar to the first part: sincere, sensible. Other sentences were demanding: all caps, exclamatory. And when he thought of those bits, his body tensed, and he wanted nothing more than to hop the fence, take a drag of his cigarette, put the butt out on the sign.

Madame Fournier's thoughts on the matter were direct. "The good news for you, Emerson," she'd said some time ago, "is that assholes never stop being assholes."

But Emerson had never been sure whether Hoit was an asshole, or whether he was just a married man that probably shouldn't have gotten married. Everyone had good qualities. Even Mussolini probably had a hidden kindness about him: a good tipper perhaps, a churchgoer, a polite houseguest—one that always made his bed in the morning before leaving his quarters for breakfast.

Last week, Emerson had been running errands not far from Searcy and Theo's home and had decided to drive by. He'd told Searcy that he'd be leaving soon, so, at worst, he thought, if she did spot him, he could tell her his flight had been delayed.

It had been noon when he'd made the turn onto Whiffletree Lane. A line of cars were parked along her side of the street, and Emerson had wondered what could have brought all these vehicles to the street—a PTA meeting? Neighborhood Watch? Tupperware party?

He'd killed the engine and glided up the road in neutral, so that his air-cooled four cylinder wouldn't give him away. He'd waited. He'd waited more. He'd waited the entire length of a Coltrane album. He'd waited so long that he came up with some stupid correlation for B.C. and A.D.—his world before Searcy had been B.C.—Before Complication—and now life, upon falling for Searcy, had transitioned into the A.D. half—After Delusion.

At 1:05, after having sat in silence for about an hour, Searcy had emerged: barefoot, a wicker basket dangling from the crux of her elbow. Emerson inspected her as she walked her front yard, plucking lemons from her trees and piling them into a mound in her basket. When she'd collected enough, she returned inside, and then reemerged moments later with an empty basket. This went on for twenty minutes, and Emerson watched with care, detecting changes in her appearance from one moment to the next: strappy shoes, hair tied back, a different basket.

"Too much!" Madame Fournier said. "Mon Dieu!"

"What?" He turned his head to the left for the first time in at least thirty minutes, and his neck popped.

"Your eyes are moving, your lids are shaking, and you're smiling like an ass."

"Like an ass?" Emerson laughed. He thought of Theo and *A Midsummer Night's Dream* and the donkey character, Bottom. One time,

Emerson had referred to him—Bottom, that is—as an ass, and Theo had howled with laughter, as though it were the first time he'd ever heard a curse word.

"Just focus. Be still. The light, the sun, it's making your marsh-mallow go soft."

Emerson shook his head, forgetting that Madame Fournier liked to use the word *marshmallow* as a pseudonym for *brain*. He smiled her way, happy to see the light in her straw-colored hair and the rays working on her arms. Today she would overdose on Vitamin D, and for that he was glad to be an enabler.

"Parfait," Madame Fournier said. "Now cement your body."

Searcy and Hoit exited Mrs. Liotta's Spanish class. The whole school year, Theo had complained about her. ("She's boring," Theo had said. "She has pit stains big as pancakes," Theo had said. "When she talks, this little line of spit sticks between her lips and stretches up and down.") And though Searcy had always steered Theo clear of such talk, she did feel—even after only a fourteen-minute confer-ence—that she'd drunk a bottle of NyQuil. (She had also noticed the rubber band of saliva.)

"How much time do we have before our next one?" Hoit asked.

"A few minutes," Searcy said.

Hoit scurried down the hall to the boys' restroom.

A cramp knotted in Searcy's stomach, pinching at her lungs. She leaned against the lockers and drew a breath. Ever since she'd started pushing herself farther on her morning runs, these pains rushed her way at random moments, ones far from the actual exercise. She hadn't admitted it yet, because it was far too early, but she was hoping to compete in next year's L.A. Marathon. Year after year, she told herself she would do it, and just a few weeks ago, when the newspaper had arrived, Theo had seen the sports page and asked, "When are you ever going to do that?" She had smiled and said, "Someday." But the next morning, when she'd started her slog toward Saint John the Baptist, she'd heard her boy's words, and she pictured him at the finish line of the race, hopping up and down, his arms over his head.

Hoit exited the restroom, and they knocked on the open door of Mrs. Stanton's classroom, Theo's English teacher. Her classroom was different. Instead of the overhead lights, floor lamps were scattered about the room, and she had throw rugs in various places, too. No posters lined the walls. Just bookcases and windows and framed paintings. She was an older lady—Searcy guessed seventy—and she wore a buttoned-up cardigan and a pair of turquoise flats.

Mrs. Stanton took a seat behind her desk, and Hoit and Searcy sat on two chairs, facing her. "It's like we're in trouble," Hoit said.

"Maybe you are," Mrs. Stanton said. A fuzzy kiwi rested near some papers, still wearing the bar-code sticker.

"Theo raves about you and your class," Searcy said.

"He's such a doll." Mrs. Stanton smiled, causing her large cheeks to lift. "To be honest, this is my last conference of the day, and it's a lovely way to close out the conferences." She riffled through some papers. "Theo's a wonderful student. Inquisitive, kind, generous, innocent. He's an old soul. My husband came by one afternoon and met him, and later said to me, 'That Theo boy. He reminds me of Horace from the Elks.' It's nice to see a child be so aware of himself and others."

"He loves the play," Hoit added.

"He's been great. It seems the best actors are always the most timid."

"Is that so?" Searcy said.

Mrs. Stanton peered at her notes. "I was sorry to hear about Mr. Toffler having to leave so suddenly."

"Oh?" Searcy said. It felt surreal to hear someone other than she or Hoit or Theo utter his name. "You know about him?"

"Theo speaks of him often, and he would share tidbits from their sessions. I credit him for Theo's love of this class."

"He would have loved it without him," Hoit said, crossing his legs.

"Enthusiasm is contagious," Mrs. Stanton said. "It was also nice to see him happier."

"Was he not happy before?" Searcy asked.

"Not as much," Mrs. Stanton said.

The pain in Searcy's stomach rippled across her abdomen. "How could you tell?"

"I've been in this field my whole life. More than English, I know children. No matter the instruction, it's very difficult, near impossible, to teach a sad student. Here," she said, "you can take a look at his work, if you like." Mrs. Stanton passed over an accordion folder.

"These are the highlights. His portfolio . . . it'll go home with him at the end of the year. Much to be proud of."

Searcy sorted through grammar quizzes and reading checks; she landed on essays and tests, too. Then she spotted the spiral journal and leafed through its pages, finding the essay where Theo had detailed the Abalone Cove night. As she read her boy's words, she noticed that a few times he'd slipped up and had used Wite-Out to cover up his mistakes. Two blobs sat on one page, the liquid hardened and raised.

Searcy picked at the Wite-Out, and bits of the hard gunk gathered beneath her nails. Underneath the paint, the words were also crossed out.

> *The funniest part was when ~~Emer~~ Mr. Toffler kept pronouncing the word "smores" like there was an "H" in them. He would say "shh-mores."*

> *Then ~~Eme~~ Mr. Toffler screamed, "Run! Run! Run!"*

Searcy turned the crinkly page and, seconds later, shut the spiral notebook, sliding it inside the accordion folder. She balled her fists and listened to Mrs. Stanton's words, unable to gather much. "I hope you'll be at the play," Mrs. Stanton said.

"Of course," Hoit said. "It's in late May, correct?"

"That's right. The sixteenth."

"I may be out of town," Hoit said.

"You're gone often, aren't you?" Mrs. Stanton asked.

Searcy turned her head in Hoit's direction and folded her hands on her lap, picking bits of Wite-Out from under her nails. She wondered whether her emotional symptoms—the heat in her cheeks, the sweat on her scalp, the tightness of her back—could be detected in any way.

"I am," Hoit said.

"My son travels a lot for work. He likes so much about it, but he told me recently he feels like he no longer knows where home is."

"I can relate."

"There's a Welsh word that I love." Mrs. Stanton pressed her fingers to her chin. "*Hiraeth*. It's a gorgeous word that I told the students about earlier in the year. It means homesickness for a place that doesn't even exist. A yearning for a place that never was."

"It sounds like an illness," Hoit said.

"It kind of is," Mrs. Stanton said. She rubbed her palms together.

Searcy stood up, smoothed out her long skirt, and draped her purse over her shoulder. Her decorum saved her: she looked Mrs. Stanton in the eye and thanked her for the wonderful year and for being Theo's favorite teacher.

The hallway's lights burned after her pupils had gotten used to the warmer hues of Mrs. Stanton's floor lamps, and she narrowed her gaze as she headed toward the parking lot. Hoit walked beside her, his leather-soled dress shoes beating in rhythm with her heels. Eight minutes, Searcy thought, before she would be home and upstairs and able to change into her nightgown, then twenty-six minutes to wash up, and then, hopefully, only a few to drift off to sleep.

"Fallon doesn't actually like you. You know that, right?" Dylan said, his face only inches from Theo's. The blue of Dylan's eyes was concentrated, dark, especially around the pupils, and lighter toward the rims, a grayish, steel color. "You know that, right?" Dylan said again. He shoved Theo, and Theo slammed into the lockers, clanging against the metal. "You're just some nerd that helps her get good grades." A few of Dylan's friends stood behind him, laughing.

Theo had been rehearsing *A Midsummer Night's Dream*, and it seemed that Dylan and his friends had been playing basketball on the courts. They were sweaty and wearing high-top sneakers and more basketball gear than the Lakers: headbands, sweatbands, arm sleeves.

Theo quickly flung his bag over his back and started down the hall. He had an inkling that Dylan liked Fallon—always teasing her and poking her and stealing her lunch from her and having her chase him. Teenager shit. Dylan had tried out for the play but then had backed out. According to Raul—the kid who was playing Bottom—the audition didn't go well.

All Theo had to do was throw the hallway door open, cross the basketball courts, and head down the hill to the trail. Then, some one hundred steps later, he'd be home. But the squeaks of Dylan's new basketball shoes continued to sound on the clean tile behind him. "She doesn't fucking like you!" Dylan screamed.

Theo smashed into the swinging doors, pressing the metal bar in the center.

"Hey," Dylan said again. His voice was sharp. "Did you hear me?"

Theo told himself Dylan wasn't getting invited on whale-watching trips, that he wasn't the one sharing sour cherry gummies with her during break.

"Hey!" Dylan said again.

Heat, tightness, a stinging in his head. It didn't help that Ms. Cheng had told Theo to start wearing his tights, so that he would feel comfortable in them for the performance. *You're doing the right thing. Walk away. One foot in front of the other.*

Dylan grabbed the base of Theo's backpack and swung it, thereby spinning Theo around until he faced him. "She's ugly anyway," Dylan said. "And so are you."

"Who's ugly?" Theo said.

"Fallon. You know she is."

"Fuck you," Theo said. He had *thought* the F-word many times, even uttered it to himself or said the word in his head, but never had the word been formed by his mouth.

Dylan raked his hand though his hair. Then he turned towards his friends.

More out of wonder than anything else, Theo balled his fist. He placed one foot behind the other and jutted his hand back. Even though his arm was short, the journey from behind his head to Dylan's jaw was long. The fist arced through the air, passing over Theo's shoulder and by Theo's ear, and Theo caught a glimpse of his own fist traveling hard and purposefully. Sure, his tight hand was attached to his own body, but it seemed disconnected, like the F-word. He knew he could use it, but it wasn't until now that he had seen his own body morph into something that he'd tried so hard, for so long, to push away.

Dylan turned his face back toward Theo.

Just like in the cartoons, as soon as Theo's fist connected with Dylan's left cheek, it whipped his head back, and a *BOOM!* cartoon bubble seemingly popped into the air.

"Shit!" Dylan screamed. His friends didn't offer any words, just the sound, *Ooooooh*.

A welling developed in Theo's chest, expansive and lasting. He didn't know what to do with himself. He stood tall and stared at Dylan. Then, Dylan staggered up, ran his tongue hard over his lips. His eyebrows formed a *V*, and Theo crisscrossed his arms in front of his face as Dylan neared.

"What the hell are you boys doing?" A voice shouted from behind Theo. Theo crouched, snapped his head back: the janitor, emerging from the corner, wheeling a mop bucket behind him. "Get the hell home! Quit dicking around, you hear?"

Theo sprinted, feeling the wind on his tights, and his backpack bouncing hard, up and down. He swallowed, felt a lightness in his head, and when he was sure no one could see, he smiled.

Tranquility didn't find her, even in the pews, even at Saint John the Baptist. Her forehead remained balmy, and despite her recent trips to the ladies' room to blot her skin, the clamminess returned by the time she reentered the church.

She leafed through the missal guide and turned pages in the song-book. Finally, she fetched her cell phone out of her pocket. The Wi-Fi needed a password, and, on a whim, she thumb-typed "Jesus Christ," and to her surprise was connected. Turning her head to the right and left, she scanned for any parishioners. It didn't feel right to surf the Web inside the church, but she would ask for forgiveness in a bit.

She searched for "Emerson Toffler" along with the words "Fellow-ship" and "Madrid." By now, he had most likely arrived and forgotten them. He had never called or sent a note or visited Theo. A couple of times when she and Theo had been saying their prayers together, Theo had wished happiness to Mr. Toffler, and she hadn't been able to respond. She had kept her mouth closed, fearing that if she gave her emotions the tiniest opening, they would make her pay. "I hope he keeps winning prizes," Theo had said. "I hope he is eating good Spanish food."

Theo had asked her why Mr. Toffler hadn't called or stopped by, and Searcy had told him that he had—twice—"but you were at school."

There was probably another woman in Emerson's life now: one that wore a beanie when it was seventy degrees out, one with a tiny nose ring, one that pronounced his name with an accent. And they were arm in arm in bright air, near old, clanging church bells and flaking shutters, strolling through cobblestone roads.

Nothing came up on her search.

Maybe since applications were closed, they had decided to shut down the site, or maybe it was run by a bunch of flighty artists.

Photos of him did pop up, however. Mostly ones in which he was clean-shaven, looking like a boy, a touch heavier without the contour of his facial hair. She placed her fingers on the screen and pulled them apart to enlarge the pictures. A knot formed in Searcy's throat, blocking her ability to swallow.

When the church regained its quiet, she turned off her phone and slid it back into her pocket. She flipped through the hymnal and landed on the serenity prayer. "God grant me the serenity to accept the things I cannot change; courage to change the things I can; and wisdom to know the difference." This prayer had been tattooed in her mind since she was a girl, when she'd had to hear her father scream and hit her mother. Many times, Searcy had hidden under her bed, listening to an oldies station on her Walkman, repeating the words over and over, until they became more than words, almost companions. Twice, she had picked up the phone and wanted to dial 9-1-1, even gotten as far as pressing nine, but she didn't know what would happen if she dialed all three digits.

In time, she left the church. Wind swirled about the peninsula today, leaving flower petals strewn about the sidewalk, and bringing scents from surrounding jasmine. With her arms swinging and feet plodding, she tightened her abs and corrected her posture. Her new running shoes offered softer landings, and the flash of pain in her knees wasn't noticeable for the first time in weeks. With these shoes, she could continue to train and push toward her goal. She stopped in the middle of her trek and took in the view. Catalina was clear: deep mountainous ridges, clusters of green, and spiny formations.

As she regained her rhythm: breath, stride, breath, stride, lifting her legs high and strong, her chest out, her head forward, the serenity prayer returned. "God grant me the serenity to accept the things I cannot change; courage to change the things I can; and wisdom to know the difference." Down Crest Road, Searcy ran, the words playing on a loop. What bothered her most were the last two parts. She wasn't sure she had the courage. Yet she knew she had the wisdom to know the difference. The courage to change was just a statement, but Searcy wanted specifics. She needed God to hand her signs and point her to the path. If there was only a way not to hurt everyone, a way to ensure Theo's safety. Courage—at this point, anyway—needed to be something of a road map.

Before showering, she hurried to the back yard and watered the plants. This task had been on her to-do list for days, so she ventured into the yard and turned on the spigot. The water swelled through the hose, and she placed her thumb over the opening, aiming the fanned stream in the direction of lavender and forsythia. A purple patch of yesterday, today, and tomorrows seemed happy and bouncy, and while she knew their petals were fleeting, she believed, this year, they had flourished more than ever.

Light broke through the clouds now and sliced through the stream, making something of a rainbow, and she remembered the mnemonic device from school, Roy G. Biv, and picked out as many colors as she could.

"You know that scene in the movies?" Hoit said to Mason as they sipped iced tea at the golf course bar. "You know the one where the good guy is somewhere in a warehouse, kicking ass, beating up a bunch of men." Hoit swung his hands around and pretended to do some karate. "Punch a guy here, kick a guy there. Then, all of a sudden, he knows the building's gonna blow. He sees some car leaking gas and a fire in the background, and so he starts for the door. The director zooms in. His face. Arms swinging. Legs up and down. He's going, going, going. Sweat pouring on his dirty face." Mason shook his head and smiled. Hoit continued: "He gets to the door and doesn't just keep running. No. He takes a few gigantic steps, and leaps! He flies, his body completely parallel to the ground. Then boom! As he's arcing through the air—a blast! Fire! Explosion! Even some of the fire comes with him, but not enough. He pats out a bit of flame on his jeans, and that's a wrap. He's saved the day." Hoit took a swig of iced tea and cooled his throat.

Mason called the waiter over and ordered another gin and ginger. "I'm glad. I'm glad."

"Just in the nick of time," Hoit said.

"So, he's out of the picture completely?"

"I just decided one night to go over and let him know who was in charge. Can't have a man spending all that time in your house, cozying up to your stepson and your wife. Just weird, you know?"

Hoit had edited his story, too, leaving out details about the letter, just telling Mason that enough was enough.

Hoit paid the tab while Mason worked on his cocktail.

"Makes sense," Mason said. "You see it happen, people getting too close, with nannies and men, right? All the time, every year, some guy gets caught. I'm always shaking my head like, uh, maybe don't hire the twenty-year-old sorority girl to be your nanny . . . but then the more I think about it, the more it makes sense. There's a bond there. The nanny is caring for your child, in your home, there's probably something primal at work that can't be controlled."

"True," Hoit said.

"Come here," Mason said.

Hoit leaned forward.

"You see that woman? The one at the bar?"

"Yes," Hoit said.

"I was in here a couple of weeks ago with a potential client, and he had to leave, so I stuck around. Me and that girl got to talking and ended up . . . you know . . . in her car." Mason intertwined his fingers and splayed them, popping his knuckles. "She was something else."

Hoit stared at Mason. For the first time, his boasting—his description of her moans and dirty talk and tattoos and nipples—came and went with little effect. They occupied the time, but Hoit's mind stayed stuck on Searcy.

Mason rambled on.

There was a French brasserie in Beverly Hills that Searcy had been talking about, and when Hoit returned home, he would look it up and make reservations for two, maybe three, and when the host asked whether "he was celebrating anything special," he would say, "Yes," and come up with something.

Mason finished the last inch of his gin and ginger. He pushed out his chair and stood. "Well, I hate to ruin a perfectly nice day," he said, "but I got some news for you. You have to make a trip out to San Francisco around the Fourth of July."

"Shit," Hoit said.

They both stood and made their way to the exit.

"I know, I know," Mason said, holding the door open for Hoit.

Hoit walked carefully, not wanting to ruin the cleats of his golf shoes. (He'd forgotten his regular shoes in his car.) "I have everything where I want it," Hoit said. "I can't travel right now. Can't we postpone this until the fall?"

The two men entered a little tunnel. Overhead was the twelfth hole's green. Hoit believed he could hear footsteps of men putting atop them. "Trust me," Mason said. "I tried. But it's a new app developer, and they need representation. If we get in with them, we could be in with a lot of tech companies. I swear on my life, this will be it until September."

"How long?"

"Five . . . ten days max."

"You swear?"

"That's it. Trust me, I've gotten you out of a lot of obligations. I can't make up any more dental issues. They're gonna think you wash down Pop Tarts with root beer. Implants. Bridges. Crowns. Gum surgery. One guy even said, 'Christ, get that man some fluoride.'"

Hoit untucked his polo shirt.

"I just don't want to lose this account, especially because it's pretty local. It sucks that you'll miss the Fourth of July, but if it works out . . ."

Hoit remembered then that Theo's birthday was on the fourth. "It just seems like every time I'm out of town, things take a step backward. Being in the house is important. Even if I never do a thing. If I just stay in bed. I'm like tonsils—not really needed, but at least I'm part of the body, you know?"

They emerged from the tunnel into the parking lot, said their goodbyes, and took to their cars. Once seated, Hoit reclined his cushy seat. He clicked on the ignition just enough to activate the radio and allow classical music to seep from the speakers. The crescendos were severe, and for the softer parts of the movements, he actually leaned forward and turned up the volume; then, when the sound came rushing, he lessened the sound. Pine needles from surrounding trees fell to his windshield without a sound—then slid into the wiper area. He took in the practice putting green. There were families and older folks and pros giving lessons to teenage boys and girls.

MAY

EMERSON'S CELL PHONE BUZZED atop his bedspread, and he swatted his hand around the comforter until he made contact with the device. "Yes," he said, wedging the phone between his pillows and his ear.

"Mr. Toffler?" the woman on the other end said.

A bolt of pain worked through his frontal lobe. Too much cheap whiskey. "Yes," he said.

"This is Cecilia at the Belmont."

"Yes," he said.

"I'm sorry to call you this early, but I wanted to let you know that Mrs. Fournier has moved on."

"Oh," he said, dropping his phone back into the thick duvet and rolling over onto his back. This phone call was imminent, but he hadn't thought that it would arrive *tonight*. It was too cliché: three a.m., Madame Fournier telling him she loved him earlier in the day, the doctors saying her kidneys were responding well to the treatment . . . that she could go on living like this for some time, even a year.

Emerson hoped it wasn't the cigarette. No, it wasn't the cigarette. Oh, God, had it been the cigarette? Hours earlier, while in his care at the Belmont, it had been only the two of them. She hadn't been eating much, desiring only cold, liquid items, so Emerson had gone to a nearby shop and had picked her up a smoothie. After she'd finished her strawberry-banana drink, she'd told Emerson to close the door. "Lock it, too." He had followed her instructions. "Let's have a smoke together," she'd said. "I need one." Emerson had said no, and Madame Fournier had told him "not to be a little shit."

"I don't think it's a good idea." Emerson had stood by the front door. Outside, in the hall, nurses' and doctors' footsteps squeaked.

"Who cares if I die next week or next month? If anything, you're the only one giving me what I want."

He'd reached for his pack of smokes. "Here," he'd said, tapping the pack against his palm, emitting a single cigarette.

"You better have one, too," she'd said. "Now open the window, and push this goddamned bed over there so that I can see the ocean. And put on some music."

He had followed her guidelines. After finding a jazz station and lighting both their cigarettes, he'd clicked on a fan in the corner of the room. The oscillation reminded him that he was breaking the rules. Even the fan shook its head from side to side, the oscillation saying, "No, no, no."

With the glass door all the way open, he blew his smoke hard, so that it drifted near the threshold of the glass door, away from the hall. Madame Fournier did not care. She tilted her head back, pushing her exhales to the ceiling where the thin bands of smoke dissipated in time. Along with smoke, jazz swirled, too. Horace Silver, Emerson had thought it was, yet he'd had trouble placing the name of the song.

He'd made sure his inhales were small, hoping to keep the cigarette burning forever.

"Mr. Toffler!" someone said on the other side of the door. It was one of the nurses. Emerson had asked for her name so many times and still couldn't place it. "Could you open the door, please? Mr. Toffler? Are you there? Can you open the door?"

"No," Madame Fournier had said. "I want to be left alone," she'd whispered to Emerson.

"Please," the nurse had said again.

Emerson had gotten up and blasted the radio. An explosion of sound had taken hold of the small room: piano and drums and bursts of mellifluous saxophone.

He hadn't been able to hear Madame Fournier's laugh due to the club-like atmosphere, but he knew she had. Her head had rocked back and forth. Her eyes had narrowed, and her lips had pulled back to expose her smile. Every now and then, when Horace Silver slowed his rhythm, he could hear the pounding of the nurse's fist on the wooden door. *Bam, bam, bam. Bam, bam, bam.* But it did nothing other than complement the four-four rhythm.

They stayed that way for another twenty minutes, long after the cigarettes had burned to their filters, and the butts were dropped into an empty container of Metamucil.

Even now at three o'clock in the morning, he got out of bed, exited the cabin, and strolled the wobbly docks, inspecting what he could of other people's ships, searching for something—anything—that would bring sense. The moon, stars, and sea. All this ceaseless natural beauty. The world didn't dole out moments of silence.

He took to his car sometime later and drove the seaside streets. Diners were closed, laundromats, too. Metal armor blockaded newspaper stands, and bars were mopping up. Eventually, he worked his way toward the Belmont. He sat in the lobby before accruing the courage to take the elevator to the third floor.

When the elevator doors dinged and opened, he strolled into her room. Her furniture still there, her clothes on hangers, and the container of Metamucil on the nightstand.

If there were such a thing as angels, people who did, in fact, "look over us" from high above, he knew she would take her duty seriously. What also made him happy was that when it came to Madame Fournier, he'd gone for it. He'd wanted to speak to her and let her know how big a fan he was, and he had. He'd learned more about painting from her than anyone else, and he would never let her wisdom fade. Just like the ceiling of the Sistine Chapel, whenever the hues would lessen and lose their patina, he'd repair each and every line to make sure she'd live on forever.

He left the Belmont and drove again without purpose, visiting streets his car had never driven, taking in views his eyes had never scanned. The Point Fermin Lighthouse. Sunken City. He felt that only two people could make him feel better, and they were no longer around. Well, actually, they were, but he was in Madrid, doing the goddamned tango. Was that dance even Spanish? What did it matter? He parked and made his way to the edge of a cliff, where he sat down and let his feet dangle, watching the sky blue with the coming dawn.

Theo sat on the toilet in the bathroom stall, his pants at his ankles, running through his lines as Lysander. The air vent hummed, and he thought about how cute Fallon looked, dressed up as Hermia. *It's only dress rehearsal*, he told himself, but his nerves didn't listen.

Suddenly, the door shot open.

Theo picked his feet up off the floor, holding them high, so that no one would be able to tell he was in the stall. His abs twitched as he strained. He wanted to lower his head to inspect the person's footwear. From that angle, he thought, he would be able to tell a great deal: athletic or casual shoes, grade level, height, age, adult, kid. But to lower his head, he would have to set his feet on the ground.

He stayed frozen. In an attempt to distract himself from his surroundings, he thought of Lysander and his scene with Fallon/Hermia.

Fair love, you faint with wandering in the wood;
And to speak troth, I have forgot our way:
We'll rest us, Hermia, if you think it good,
And tarry for the comfort of the day.
One turf shall serve as pillow for us both;
One heart, one bed, two bosoms and one troth.
O, take the sense, sweet, of my innocence!
Love takes the meaning in love's conference.
I mean, that my heart unto yours is knit
So that but one heart we can make of it;
Two bosoms interchained with an oath;
So then two bosoms and a single troth.
Then by your side no bed-room me deny;
For lying so, Hermia, I do not lie.

Theo swallowed. He glanced at his watch. Six minutes till curtains up.

As the sound of a flush took over the bathroom, the door opened again, and a new person entered. "Anything?" this new person asked.

"Nope," a familiar voice said.

Theo rested one of his legs atop the toilet-paper dispenser. He knew that voice. He would be able to detect its rough sound for the rest of his life. Dylan. It was definitely Dylan.

"I saw him come in here," the new person said. This person didn't use the bathroom, just stood next to Dylan at the sink.

"Yeah, well. He left," Dylan said, running his hands under the faucet.

Theo didn't think Dylan would be the type to wash his hands, but he could hear the soap dispenser being pumped.

"What do you want to do?"

"I'll see him soon. It's not that big of a school," Dylan said.

Dryness overtook Theo's mouth. He wished he could bring emotion like this to the play—*actually* have his body react to words.

"He walks home, right?" the friend said. Theo thought the guy's name was Mike, but he wasn't sure.

"I've seen him a few times, waddling across the street in his tights." Dylan laughed, then reached for some paper towels and wiped his hands.

Theo's legs no longer shook. His muscles had given up, found comfort in discomfort.

"Let's go," the friend said.

Theo held his breath, hearing the four footsteps head toward the door, savoring the squeak of the hinge. Theo counted to ten. He didn't want to get up and have one of them pop back in for some reason. He took his time, pulled up his pants and didn't flush. He felt bad for the janitor, especially after how the guy had pretty much saved his life, but he would understand if he knew the details.

Theo darted from the bathroom and took the long way to the auditorium.

And run through fire I will for thy sweet sake.
Transparent Helena! Nature shows art,
That through thy bosom makes me see thy heart.
Where is Demetrius? O, how fit a word
Is that vile name to perish on my sword!

Theo didn't know when Shakespeare had lived. He thought it was sometime during the 1500s, but any time before 1900 seemed about the same to him. No TV, no Internet, no cars, or Hot Pockets. But what he did think was interesting was that Shakespeare had made a career on love. Mr. Toffler was right. It seemed no one could comprehend love, yet it was all people wanted to know.

Theo tucked into the backroom of the auditorium. "Where have you been?" a woman said. She was the mom of some kid playing a tree and took her job seriously. "Time for makeup." She ran a rag over his forehead and cheeks. "Why are you so sweaty?"

"These tights make me hot."

"Stop sweating, okay?"

"Okay," Theo said. What could've occurred in her life to make her so miserable? If only people wore patches on their backs indicating why they were the way they were. Something like bumper stickers for adults. *Mean mother. Never made dad proud. Overweight as a kid. Did time in jail.* That way when some guy was being an ass, you could just wait to see the back of their shirt and then say, "Oh, Kyle had tuberculosis as a child." He wondered what Dylan's would say. What would his own read? He thought of Mr. Toffler's, too. *I don't say goodbye to people.* That's what Theo thought Mr. Toffler's would say.

Someone tapped on his shoulder. Theo turned.

"Hey," Fallon said. Her hair was parted down the middle, and each half of her hair bookended her face. Her skin was smooth with makeup, but Theo liked her better without all the gunk, so he could see her freckles and detect the "The Queen."

"Hi," Theo said.

"Even though it's only dress rehearsal, I'm nervous," Fallon said.

"Me too," he said, making his way toward the side of the stage with her.

Fallon cleared her throat:

Help me, Lysander, help me! Do thy best
to pluck this crawling serpent from my breast!
Ay me, for pity! What a dream was here!

Theo stared at Fallon's lips that opened and closed, each syllable prettier than the last. In her presence, it was as though all his flaws and fears were being swiped and covered with makeup, too. They hurried to their marks at stage left.

"Good luck, Theo," she said.

"Good luck, Fallon," he said.

The two of them stood in the dark, behind the thick velvet curtain. Theo shut his eyes. He sent a quick prayer to God. Actually, it was more of a thank-you note.

———

Madame Fournier's will detailed that she wanted to be cremated, but a small service was still held at Green Hills Mortuary on a bright, sunny day. Birds clutched at high branches as Emerson slumped through the parking lot, his body blending with a cluster of people who wore dark clothes and heavy expressions. In time, he worked his way into the chapel and shuffled into the pews.

She'd told him months ago that there wouldn't be many friends at her funeral. "You could all take a van. Save some gas," she'd said. "The longer I've lived, the less I've needed people. Except for you. You're not people."

Emerson had understood then, and understood now. He'd left his friends behind, too. The more time he'd spent with them, the more he'd become like them. Their words and mannerisms seeped into his pores. Sometimes their interests, too. And if he wanted to know who he was, he'd have to take a challenge not many could, and be alone.

The priest delivered a generic speech, eerily reminiscent of the one given at his parents' service, and Emerson wondered if this sermon was a prerequisite in the priesthood. He didn't remember much from that day. He'd brushed his teeth, spilled coffee on his dress shirt, slept in the guest room. There were all these people, too, shaking his hand, nodding, crying. Tissues, bad lighting, hard kisses. He recalled being numb. Going home later and throwing out his clothes, never wanting to open that front door again, or see the worn banister, or turn on the coffee pot, or feel snow.

Madame Fournier's lawyer, Jeffery, whom Emerson had once delivered papers to, told a story about how she'd come into his office and told him that if he wanted to be taken seriously in life, "He would take down those stupid motivational-quote posters." His speech wasn't sentimental, but honest, and Emerson appreciated that. The lawyer discussed her paintings, her ways, and her philanthropy. He said that after her husband passed away, she passed in a sense, too, and that she'd told him as much. "I never wanted to go until he did," she'd told him one day. "Maybe heaven isn't a different life at all, but this one on Earth—perfected. A second draft."

Speeches came and went, and eventually the priest uttered something in Latin that sounded like a disease, before adding, "Please join us in the reception hall where coffee and light refreshments will be served."

Emerson obliged. He could be sad here. It was expected, and in a world where everyone was trying to sweep emotion out the front door with a hefty stoke, he didn't mind being truthful. After placing some pieces of shortbread on a paper plate and helping himself to some tepid coffee, Emerson took a seat at the back of the reception hall and loosened his tie. Outside, a white-haired man in a gray suit tended to a grave. Even from this distance—fifteen or so feet—Emerson thought he could detect the man mouthing words. By the time

Emerson had finished one piece of shortbread and most of his coffee, the man stood and headed off. The bouquet rested atop the polished stone, and when the wind picked up, it dislodged many of the flowers' petals, causing them to flit over the surrounding headstones.

"Mind if I sit down?" the lawyer asked.

"Please," Emerson said.

The two men shook hands from the seated position.

The lawyer wore a navy suit, a white shirt, and a dark tie with little fish on it. The fish were small enough to resemble polka dots, but at proximity, it was clear they were bass or trout. "So, I hate to do this here, but I figured I'd save you a trip to my office. Can we take a walk?"

"I don't feel like walking," Emerson said. "You can tell me here."

"All right," Jeffery said. He scooted his chair closer. His eyebrows were curly, and his nose was long. "Well, Madame Fournier told me she would like you to scatter her ashes."

"She mentioned that to me at one point. Even said something about using them in a painting. I told her I wouldn't do that."

"That sounded odd to me, too."

Emerson finished his coffee but wished he had more in his cup, so he could break eye contact with Jeffery. Even though he was far from trouble, anything lawyer-related made him sweat. "Do you have any idea where she'd prefer her ashes to be . . . sprinkled, scattered? Not sure what the right word is."

"She mentioned Mount Orizaba."

"Looks like I'm getting on a plane, huh?"

"No, no. It's on Catalina Island. The highest peak."

"Really?"

Jeffery laughed. "Yup."

"I guess we'll be in touch then."

"Yes," Jeffery said.

"Take care, Jeffery." Emerson pushed out his chair and tossed his cup and paper plate into a nearby trashcan. He waved to the priest and headed out into the parking lot. Sun seeped into his black suit, and he let the rays loosen his tight neck and shoulders.

"Emerson!" Jeffery called. He hurried down the small steps.

"Yes?"

"One more thing. I was hoping to take a walk with you or

something to discuss this, but I might as well come out with it. I just don't want to bother you right now, but you should know. It's nice news. I promise."

"Okay?"

"Madame Fournier made you the director of her art program that will start on the island in the coming months."

Emerson narrowed his gaze. "You sure?"

"She did so months ago."

Emerson grinned. "She would probably say that I'm smiling like an asshole."

"She said this would finally make you a man. That you could finally dock your boat. Get a little house, have some solid income, and live easy."

Emerson hadn't received this kind of news in years, maybe in all his life, and he kept waiting for Jeffery to add fine print in a hushed voice, but it never came. "Thank you, Jeffery."

"You made this last chapter a good one for her." Jeffery nodded.

Emerson slid into his car and buckled his seatbelt. His emotions began to spar. Sadness from the funeral, the loss of a dear friend. Then, happiness. He could live away from it all, yet close to it all. Her essence would stay with him, like a strong perfume.

When he arrived home, he disrobed and lay down. No one except Theo knew of Madame Fournier's connection to the island, because Emerson had mentioned it to him many times. "Oh, man," Theo had said one day. "I've never been. I hear it's cool. One time, in fifth grade, my class went over there for a field trip, but I had the flu."

"We should go there one day, together," Emerson had said.

"I hear there's a fox that only lives there. And these bright orange fish."

Emerson checked the calendar on his wall. *A Midsummer Night's Dream* wasn't that far away. And he needed to be there.

In hours, Searcy would have to be at the show, so she preened her hair in something of an updo and slid into a blue dress that cinched at her waist and fanned out to the floor in small pleats. Hoit, too, had decided to wear something worthy of the theatre, selecting a charcoal suit. After Searcy made eye contact with him in the mirror, he slipped his hand behind her neck and pulled her toward him.

She thought that his force would mess up her hair. She'd primped the strands for minutes before clipping them into place using only three bobby pins, but she told herself to stop, to let go, to shove her neuroses aside, and she allowed his tongue into her mouth, hot and wet. She kept her eyes open throughout the kiss, inspecting his shiny nose and a few broken capillaries on his left nostril. Then she swung her eyes to the bathroom mirror, where she focused on the two of them as if somehow detached from herself. Two figures, the blending of their beings. This was it. Her life. This home on Whiffletree Lane. Hoit was the only man she'd ever kiss and know until her passing. How much longer did she have? Forty years, at least. Maybe longer. Women had a higher life expectancy than men, right? And she was in great shape. At her last physical, her EKG came back, and, as her doctor put it, "Gorgeous, Searcy."

Hoit's kisses moved to the side of her neck, just below her ear, and he muttered, "I love you." He balled the excess fabric in her dress and yanked her closer. The woodiness of his aftershave lifted into her nose, and she wondered whether it would overpower the light scent of the Chanel she'd applied minutes ago.

She drifted to an island in her mind, where only she could be, and it gave her comfort that she could travel there as much as desired, and no one would be able to tell. She took a deep breath and let Hoit suck on her earlobe. Another deep breath.

"Hey!" Theo called, followed by a slamming of the back door. At first she thought she was imagining the scenario. Why would Theo be home now? He was supposed to be preparing, getting dressed and ready for the big night. "Mom!" Theo called out again. Hoit sighed and rubbed his eyes hard.

"Yes!" Searcy cleared her throat. She smoothed out her dress, peering over her shoulder at the fabric. She readjusted her hair and left the bathroom. "What are you doing home?"

Theo was below, in his tights, his hair matted with product. He looked more like Robin Hood than anything Shakespearean, but she knew better than to say so. "We had a little break, so I thought I'd get a snack."

She descended and prepared him something—a piece of leftover barbequed chicken and some carrots. Carefully, she touched his hair. "A lot of stuff in there, right?"

"I know," Theo said. He was reddish and short with his words.

"You okay?"

"I've peed, like, twenty times today."

"You're going to be good."

"I don't even like talking to one person. How am I going to talk to five hundred? Why did I do this?"

There wouldn't be any more than a hundred people, maybe a hundred and twenty, but nevertheless she understood the sentiment. Love was simple; she felt what her boy felt: The emotions were transferred as if their two bodies weren't distant at all, but one pair of lungs, one assemblage of limbs and blood, and she herself became nervous, too. Theo had only tried out for the play because of the confidence that Mr. Toffler had given him, and now, her boy was on his own.

"What do you think of my dress?" she asked, hoping the change of subject would aid him.

"It's fancy. You know this thing's in the cafeteria, right? The same place they serve pizza?"

"You do know my boy is Lysander, right?" she added.

He smiled. "I can't help but think of where I'll be in three hours. I'll look back on this moment, running over here, and scarfing down this food, like it was a dream. Tonight, I'll sleep good, I bet. Or maybe I won't because I'll be all excited."

Whenever he spoke like this, Searcy thought of her mother. She was always a believer in anticipation. Saying that happiness was ephemeral, but anticipation lingered for days. She used to say that about the movies. I don't actually care for films, she'd say, I just like the concept of going to the movies. Thinking about it all day. Wondering where we'll sit. Whether I'll buy licorice or Milk Duds.

"Bye, Mom," Theo said. He hurried to the bathroom. She heard a flush a few seconds later.

"Your teeth," she called out. "Be sure to brush your teeth."

Theo tore up to his room. Within thirty seconds, he'd apparently completed the task and had returned downstairs. He held his hand high above his head, waving, as he exited the back door and scampered to the trail.

"Break a leg!" Searcy called out.

Theo had five minutes until he had to be back in the cafeteria. If he walked normally, he could get there within four and half, maybe five, but he wanted to get there with a couple of minutes to spare, so he jogged.

Just as his brow became moist and he could feel sweat leak from his underarms (whatever this costume was made out of didn't breathe), a breeze whispered through, cooling his face. And, even though it was just wind, Theo thought it was a sign that things were going to work out for him. He left the trail and slowed his stride. The main road was deserted tonight. *Everything's good*, he told himself. *I'm not hungry anymore. I'm on time. I'm going to do an all right job.*

"There he is," a voice from behind him said.

The tone was rough, and Theo knew it was Dylan. He knew he would be back, but he just didn't think it would be now. Theo didn't turn around. He kept walking. With each pace, he wondered about what to do.

"You think you can just outwalk us, you Peter Pan fucker," Dylan said.

Theo prayed for Los Angeles to do what Los Angeles always did: produce traffic—so that someone could help him. But nothing came. The seaside streets were only active a few hours per day, and they'd long since passed. Theo counted down from three. When he landed on zero, he sprang forward. Air rushed over his forehead and blew past his ears. All he had to do was arrive at school. There, they wouldn't be able to touch him. He hurried. Felt his legs and arms and body fling forward. Never had he run so hard, so fast, and he was simultaneously amazed and scared. The *boomboomboom* of his heart paired with the *slamslamslam* of his legs. But it wasn't quick enough.

A hand ripped at his neck, reaching for the collar of his tight shirt. The fingers worked under the fabric and tugged. Theo choked, slowed down. His throat closed.

One by one, the boys surrounded him. Theo didn't have time to even assess the situation. He wasn't sure who was who. All he knew was that a fist had struck his eye, and that those stars in cartoons, the ones that circled a person's head after a punch, were real. Bits and flashes and pops of light orbited his face. Down in a heap, he pulled his knees to his chest and covered his face with both hands. The cartoon stars faded moments later, bringing darkness. Theo could feel loose pieces of asphalt dig into his skin. "You want some more?" Dylan said. "You thought you could sucker punch me and get away with it."

He was alive. He was okay. Sure, he'd been punched, once, hard in the eye, but he was fine. He wouldn't die. It was just another snakebite, some story to tell, this one just not as awesome. After two quick kicks to his back, Dylan and his guys darted off. Theo cracked open his eyes and watched the six legs rush away. He breathed. He rubbed his hands together, and then brought his fingers to his face, scared of what he would encounter. There was a little blood, but not much else; it took time for injuries to show. He stood, wobbly at first, but capable, and he limped and hobbled, with his muscles fighting their way through the pain.

A high-whirling engine, a sound he'd memorized, cut the quiet. Theo knew Volkswagen had made more than just the one car, so it was possible it wasn't him or his. Very possible. But it was orange and perfect and unmissable. And, moments later, it cranked to a halt, the engine still running. The driver's door flew open. "Hey!" Mr. Toffler said. "You okay? Why are you hobbling?"

Theo didn't know what to say. It was so good to see Mr. Toffler. It was as good to see Mr. Toffler as it was bad to see Dylan, and he couldn't believe that the two moments had been positioned so close in time.

"You okay?" Mr. Toffler asked again. He had shaved his beard, and his face now looked soft, even with the dark shadows beneath the smoothness. He approached until he stood at Theo's side.

"I guess," Theo said.

Mr. Toffler's arm wrapped around him. It was strong, and he felt okay in this moment, even though his left eye stung.

"Dylan?" Mr. Toffler said.

"You remember?" Theo rested his head on Mr. Toffler's chest. "Getting punched hurts a lot more than I thought it would. I mean, I've seen it in movies and they just jump back up, but my head feels huge, like I'm wearing a helmet."

"I bet."

"Where have you been?"

"Around," he said.

"You never went to Spain?"

"No," Mr. Toffler said.

"You lied?" Theo stared at the ground. A line of ants worked toward the street.

Mr. Toffler waited a long time before answering. "I did."

"What do you mean?" he asked.

"I was getting too close to you and your mom, and thought it was best to move on before someone got hurt."

"Who would get hurt?" Theo asked.

"Hard to say," Mr. Toffler said.

Theo coughed and spit blood onto the sidewalk. He'd always thought something weird had happened. It was unlike Mr. Toffler never to mention Madrid.

Even after getting the crap knocked out of him, Theo felt perfect being next to Mr. Toffler. It was like when he slept in and the covers were hot and the sheets were soft, and he flipped the pillow over and found the cool side.

Leaves scraped the ground when a breeze kicked in, and Theo let Mr. Toffler wrap his arms around him harder, almost in a hug, protecting him from even the wind. Theo thought that if someone shielded you from air, then they would probably try to keep you safe from everything else, too.

"I liked you being close with us," Theo said.

"Me too. But you guys are already a unit, a family. I had one of those once upon a time."

"But then the accident?"

"You know about it?"

"My mom told me."

"Oh."

"Does anything help?"

Mr. Toffler shut his eyes for longer than a blink, then opened them. "Being with you," he said finally.

Theo felt Mr. Toffler's hand dig into his shoulder. "Did my mom say something to you? About going away?"

"No."

"Hoit then?"

Mr. Toffler paused. "Take my coat. It's chilly."

Theo wrapped the jean jacket over his shoulders. "Why are you here? I mean, how did you find me?"

"I was going to the play, but as I got closer, I thought it wasn't a good idea, so I started to drive off."

"Everything you think is a bad idea, I think is a good one."

Mr. Toffler smiled.

"Is it starting to swell?"

"Yeah."

"You been punched before?" Theo asked.

"Been on both sides."

"I'm so late," Theo said.

"How much?"

"Like ten minutes."

"Let's go!"

"You think I can perform like this?"

"You can't let Fallon down!"

It had been a while since Theo had sat in this car, and the gasoline scent was comforting. He wrapped the jacket hard around himself and took in the world with one eye, hearing the gears rush by: first, and second, then third. In no time, they were on campus, and Theo directed Mr. Toffler where to go. "Right there, go for it. Drive straight to that door. Just drive across the field."

Mr. Toffler did as he was told, and Theo dropped the jean jacket to the floor and popped out of the car. He sprinted for the back door of the cafeteria and pounded on it with both fists.

Fallon opened the back door. "Where have you been?" she said, pulling him inside. We've been waiting!"

Then she saw his face.

His left eye had sealed. "I got my"—he started to say "ass kicked" but didn't want her to think he was weak. "I got in a fight on the way over here."

"Oh, my God," she said, hugging him. The top of her hair aligned with the bottom of his nose, and he savored her coconut-scented shampoo. "You okay?"

"I'm not nervous anymore."

"Dylan?" she said.

"Yeah," he said. "But I hit him, too." He wasn't lying. He had. Just not during this fight.

"I'll tell everyone you're here!"

Theo took a few steps and stood behind the thick curtain. With his finger, he parted the opening just a touch and scanned the audience. Thousands, he thought. No, maybe hundreds. Maybe dozens. But still. Their voices blended, their laughs echoed, their rustling vibrated.

He swung his one good eye from side to side, searching for his mom and Mr. Toffler. He didn't spot her, but there, leaning against the left wall underneath the Exit sign, stood Mr. Toffler, nice and tall.

———————

A man who wore his hair in some Elvis-style sat directly in front of Hoit, so Hoit kept having to shift his weight from side to side to catch a glimpse of the stage.

"Oh, dear," he heard Searcy say. "Look!"

"What?"

Searcy stood and sat back down, then stood once more. "His face," she said. "Look at his face!"

Hoit leaned forward. He couldn't tell with the bright lights. "It's makeup, right?" he said.

"I just saw him. He was fine. That's why they started late. He must have fallen backstage."

"What's important is that he's here. He's okay. He's doing great."

A pronounced shush came from behind them.

Hoit turned around, trying to locate the sound. "Asshole," Hoit muttered. As he turned his head back toward the stage and started to cross his legs, he spotted a figure resting against the wall of the cafeteria. The red glow of the Exit sign spilled onto his face and body, and for a second, he believed it was Emerson.

What was he doing here? Why did he think this was okay? Who did this fucking guy think he was?

No, no, Hoit thought. It wasn't him. This man, from what he could gather, was clean-shaven and taller. There was no way Emerson would come to the performance. He'd understood Hoit's orders, and he'd moved on. A perfect transaction: Hoit had learned from his mistakes, and Emerson had stopped seeing Theo. Once more, Hoit swung his head in the direction of the Exit sign, but the man was now obscured by an old woman who stood. *Man, I'm really out of it.* He massaged the firm muscle above Searcy's knee, puffed his chest, and straightened his back.

"You think he's okay?" Searcy said.

"Just a hard fall," Hoit said. "He's doing great."

"He is," she said.

Hoit felt her hand atop his, savoring the feel of her long fingers.

On one of their earlier dates, they'd gone to some charity event, and there had been a palm reader. Searcy had asked Hoit if he wanted to "give it a shot," and it had surprised him that she'd wanted to, so he had obliged. He'd learned there how practical she was, how dedicated and selfless she was, how she possessed long, slender fingers that were called "water hands," while his were thicker, "heartier," and known as "earth hands."

Laughter erupted from the crowd. Hoit had no clue what was so funny, and he wondered whether Theo himself knew what he was saying. A donkey came into the fray, coaxing another chuckle from the audience, and this time Hoit joined in, overcompensating.

"He's a natural," she whispered. "And he's doing something with his voice."

"Is that what's-her-face?" Hoit asked.

"That's Fallon playing Hermia. They actually have kind of a weird relationship in the play, but in real life it's going well." Searcy shrugged. "Kind of makes me wonder if maybe he's too good an actor."

Theo launched into a soliloquy. The boy's mannerisms were strong, and he ran his eyes over the crowd from right to left, pausing and taking his time with his words. Hoit did agree with Searcy: he was a talented actor. And with this, he wondered why Theo just didn't *pretend* more. He often wondered that about actors in general. If they were having trouble being something, why didn't they just fake it until it became a sort of truth? Wasn't it Humphrey Bogart who'd said, "I just imagined I was Humphrey Bogart until I actually was." Why couldn't Theo sink into a day-to-day character that was cool and popular and funny? It had to be easier than playing Lysander.

Searcy tucked Theo into bed. She wasn't sure he'd be able to sleep.

"So I did good?" he asked, flopping his hands over the covers.

"There were times, and I swear it, that I forgot you were my boy, and I thought I was watching Shakespeare in the Park, in New York."

"Fallon was great, too. I wasn't that nervous. I mean, just for a second, and then it kinda went away. It helped that the lights were bright, so I couldn't see the crowd. Sometimes I felt like I was alone up there, like in rehearsal." Searcy adjusted the eye mask she had given Theo. It was a beauty mask that was to be kept in the fridge and applied in the morning to rid the skin of dark circles and heavy bags, but the cold gel inside the mask was effective for a black eye, too.

"You feel better?" she asked.

"It would probably hurt if I had a math test tomorrow, but knowing that I did a nice job and that tomorrow's Saturday. . . that makes it feel better."

Searcy motioned to the Advil and the glass of water she'd left on his nightstand. "If you have any pain, just take this, okay?" She made her way to the door. "I'm proud of you."

"Mom," Theo said, his voice timid. "Can you close the door?"

"Of course," she said.

He removed the mask. "No, can you close it all the way and come here?"

"I'm tired, sweetie."

"I lied to you before," he said.

Searcy shut the door. The cold of the mask had lessened the swelling. "What?" she said.

"I didn't fall like I said."

She took a seat on the edge of the bed. "Oh, what happened then?"

"I got beat up."

"By Dylan?"

Theo nodded.

She reached for his eye, hovering a centimeter above it. Both lids, the bottom and top one, were fat, and it seemed many of his eyelashes, usually dense and long, had fallen out due to the trauma. Last time he'd told her about Dylan, she'd offered to call the principal, but Theo hadn't wanted to be a baby, and she'd respected that, but this time, regardless of what he was about to say, she was going to let the administration know.

"Sorry," he said.

"What *exactly* happened? Tell me everything."

"Okay," Theo said. His forehead was scarlet, and she wondered whether it was due to the cold compress somehow burning his skin, or whether he had a fever induced by Dylan's punches. She felt his brow. It didn't feel hot, but it was clammy, and she took a tissue from a nearby box and blotted his skin. He told the story, slow and with suspense. But, as with all stories, only a few words mattered. And she'd heard them: Karmann Ghia. Mr. Toffler.

There was a reeling, a falling sensation, even while on the bed.

After a considerable silence, she said, "He's here?"

"He never left."

"What did he say about that? Did you ask him that? Did you ask him that?"

"Said he was getting too close to us. I asked him more, but that's all he really said."

A thudding seized her ears. "Are you sure that's what he said?"

"I'm good at memorizing lines."

"So there's no Spain," Searcy said.

"Nope. No Spain. Well, there's a Spain, but he's not in it."

Routine saved Searcy. Because of so much practice, she was able to navigate the motions: tucking the sheets around Theo's body, making sure the window was a touch ajar, and planting a kiss atop his forehead. She said goodnight and headed downstairs.

Every time Emerson drifted into her thoughts, she'd done whatever possible to erase him, but now he reclaimed her brain, the ridges, the squiggles, and what she found fascinating was that she'd been wrong (everyone had been) about passion. Sure, feelings were conjured when the person was present, but they were really allowed to breathe when the person was absent. She trembled and sat down on the first step of the staircase. She held air in her lungs for a few moments before setting it free. He was around. Had he not wanted to ruin her life? Was he that selfless? Why had he come to Theo's play?

When the pinching at the base of Searcy's stomach lessened, she made her way to the living room and clicked on the television. An infomercial boasted about knives, and the chef on the screen rambled on about chopping. He diced a scallion, then held the blade knife side up and dropped a plump tomato directly to the blade, splitting it into two perfect halves.

JUNE

EMERSON MET WITH MADAME Fournier's lawyer, and squared away the details.

"Have you thought about where you'll live?" Jeffery asked. "There are some little homes for sale right now. Do you think you'd have enough for a down payment?"

"My parents left me all their money," Emerson said, his eyes wandering about the walls, inspecting all of Jeffery's diplomas. "I just never knew what to do with it. Maybe you could help me?"

"Of course. Do you see yourself moving there?"

Emerson never imagined that a man who'd grown up drawing nudes would one day be a homeowner.

"Emerson?" Jeffery said again. "What do you see?"

"I see myself working hard to satisfy Madame Fournier's vision, then working on some paintings, and having a lovely woman there with me. Maybe she has a job in town, something she's passionate about. When we're done working for the day, me and her and her boy, we go for a hike, tour the island, maybe snorkel. Try our best to search for this gray fox that I hear is native to the island. We'll have a hell of a time, too. One of us will see it and point to it, but we'll never all get to see it at the same time. 'Look!' one of us will say, but the then the other two will just be standing there, the wind whipping up hard against them, going, 'Where? Where?' We'll always keep at it, though. No matter how hard it is. No matter how hard this fox is to find."

Jeffery nodded. "Are you familiar with the island at all?"

"Are there schools?"

"All the way through twelfth grade. There are some restaurants. Many of them close in slower months, however. There's a grocery store, a bookstore, a hair salon. I'm mean, it's no Vegas."

"I miss her," Emerson said. "I drove by the Belmont the other day, and out of habit, clicked on my turn signal."

"I know." Jeffery rose, and the two men shook hands in the oak-paneled office.

Emerson took to his car. He'd left his cell in his Karmann Ghia and when he checked his phone, he noticed a missed call from Searcy. He stared at his screen, those six letters, the curve of the S and the C and the long tail of the Y. *Should I return the call? What does she want? Did Theo tell her the story? Did she see me at the play? Does she want me to leave her alone?* It was good news that she didn't leave a message. If she'd wanted him gone, it would have been easy to leave a message. That's probably what she would have wanted—the beautiful beep and then all that time to tell him how she felt.

He called back, right then and there without much thought. Her voice on the message was light, free, and he felt his pulse in his throat as the beep approached. "Hi, Searcy," he said. "Saw you called. So, I never did leave the country. I'm still very much here—in all ways." He pressed End and leaned back in the driver's seat. Words were so easy to spout, but now he replayed his message, having a hard time believing that he'd dialed without a plan. Thank God she hadn't answered.

He drove fast, too fast, rushing though yellow lights and weaving through slow traffic. The streets were crammed, but the top was down, and he zagged and zigged, letting all that California air blow hard over his body.

———

"Hello, Searcy," Father Guffey said as he genuflected and opened the tabernacle.

Searcy always wondered about Communion hosts and who made them. Were they made on-site, or were they relegated to a baker who kneaded dough for all the churches in the area? Did this baker slide the hosts into the oven with an assortment of other goodies— cakes and pies and sugar cookies? Or just alone? Searcy stood and approached the altar.

Father Guffey turned. His glasses were smudged, and his long beard was poorly trimmed, as if it had been done with scissors. "Can I help you, dear?"

"Could I speak with you for a moment? When you're done, of course."

"Sure, he said. "Let's go to my office."

Searcy hadn't expected him to agree and move forward with this process right away, but she appreciated the service. In his office, little occupied the room except for a cactus in the corner and a Newton's cradle on the desk. Father Guffey removed his glasses and smiled. She figured he wore dentures, because his teeth were so white and perfectly shaped, and he had to be about eighty. "What can I do for you, dear?"

Now that she was in this room, she had to speak. The scene reminded her of being reprimanded as an elementary school student and having to sit in the principal's office. "I have feelings for another man," she said. "I haven't done anything horrible, just small sins, but I do think about him often." There was a pause, and Searcy braced herself for judgment, clasping her hands together. "I want him. And I don't know how to proceed. I called him and wanted to talk, but I got scared. I drove over to his place, but the same thing happened—I just got scared and took off." She could feel her mouth moving fast, and when she stopped talking, she was out of breath.

"You aren't happy?" Father Guffey said.

"What a childish word, *happy*? I don't need to be *happy*. I care for both men. My husband works hard, takes care of me."

"All the essentials," Father Guffey said.

"Yes," she said. "All the stability I wanted as a girl."

"All the essentials except happiness, perhaps." A deep cough bellowed from Father Guffey's lungs. "I know it seems strange to ask a man who can't marry for marriage advice, but the constant observation of it all Sunday after Sunday, the vows and rice grains. All these sacraments and all these by-the-power-vested-in-me's . . . maybe this combination of constant proximity and perfect distance has honed my outlook."

"The word *happy*, though. It seems as out of place as—oh, I don't know—fireworks at a funeral."

"You don't see God that way?"

Her hands moistened against one another. "God likes rigor and discipline."

"He does. Sure. But He also loves mercy. He also gave Himself to us."

"Mercy?"

"Yes, mercy," Father Guffey said. He leaned back in his office chair that creaked under his weight.

"I love the idea of a plan," she said. "That we walk the path He chooses for us."

"I don't," Father Guffey said. "That wouldn't have been worth dying for us. He's given you free will, my dear. He has a heart the size of the solar system."

Searcy exhaled in something of a flat chord. "I like the comfort of the railroad-track life. The path. The plan."

"But what about all those divorces, abandoned children, murders, the jetsam of battle? Maybe God wants us to be free—free in *all* ways. He knew there'd be masses of mistakes, but He also knew there'd be plenty of miracles."

There were more questions, but Searcy didn't have the energy to flip through them. She glanced to her right, her eyes steadying through the small window. A group of students from the church's preschool waddled across the parking lot. Their teacher seemed to be positioned in the middle, tall among the tiny children, holding a container. The students fanned out and formed a circle around the instructor, and in a matter of moments, the students clapped, and an explosion of what had to be butterflies flitted across the parking lot. Even from this distance, Searcy made out the smallest details, these little flecks and flickers of orange light.

"I never tire of the kids' caterpillar-to-butterfly project," Father Guffey said.

Searcy scratched at her knee. "Why can't you just tell me to stop this?" she asked. "Why can't you just be firm with me? Implore me to stay away. Tell me I'm evil."

"Because that's easy, Searcy." Father Guffey's voice stayed even. Searcy couldn't remember a time when it had wavered. "I'm starting to think you and I believe in different gods," he said. "How is your boy? Is he happy? How does he factor in all this? Let me ask you this—if your boy was going through something similar, would you tell him to follow his heart, or would you tell him to slog it out?"

As much as Searcy liked Father Guffey, she wished it had been Father Dyer whom she'd bumped into—he was much more of an Old Testament priest.

"I've come around on divorce," he said. "Those marriages . . . decades ago that lasted forty, fifty, sixty years, they're not as lovely as they sound. I hear people's hearts, Searcy. Every week they whisper through the confessional screen that they've stayed for nothing more than staying. They have as long a relationship with regret as they do with their spouses."

The church bells sounded. Searcy imagined a man yanking cables high in a tower, but remembered that everything now was automated. Even the sound was piped in. So much of life had progressed, had been made easier, yet all the difficult tasks remained. "Thank you, Father," she said, nodding. She tightened her forearms and pushed herself out of her chair. With her head light, she left the office and church, heading back across the parking lot to her SUV. She noticed a missed call from Emerson and listened to his voicemail over and over. Her cheeks warmed, and she cranked on the air conditioning, lining the vents with her face.

I'm still very much here—in all ways.

At home, she headed up the brick walkway and spotted a white trace against the welcome mat. She knew instantly. Another letter. The same stimulus. The same effect. She hurried over and scooped it up. Another sealed rectangular envelope of identical weight had reappeared just as Emerson had.

She ripped open the letter. Just a single sentence this time:

Dear Searcy,
I know we would be great together.
—E.

Searcy placed the paper flush against her chest, feeling the world around her: the gentle stir of a wind chime, sparrows chirping on telephone wires, and the reticent rays of sun on her skin. She then read the note one last time and tore both the letter and the envelope into strips, letting the scraps scatter around her. It wasn't long before a delicious wind swept the bits into the front yard and twirled them. She kept her eyes on the confetti for as long as she could—until the scraps were no more, and the grass was nothing but unobstructed green once again. Her stomach stayed tight, pitted, and she placed her hands on her abdomen and pushed down to alleviate the pain, but the pang persisted and strengthened until she had to lower to a knee and eventually take a seat, right there on the stoop.

She knew it. She'd known it. Her heart lifted and stayed high and happy. Then flashes of sense returned. Wasn't he scared to be so bold? So brazen? Wasn't he worried that Hoit might find the note or spot him at the door? Pondering this worry led her to think of the recent burglaries, and her robbery-laced visions gave way to the security cameras. Hoit had told her that they canvassed the perimeter of the home and front door, so she decided to play God and see what exactly had happened.

She logged on to the site, and typed in her password, *TheoTheo07042005*. Within seconds, all the technology, for once, worked, and she was watching a live shot of her home's surroundings. Eight boxes filled the screen: four on top, four on bottom. The top row showcased the back of the home while the bottom ones recorded the action at the front.

Searcy ran the cursor over her computer screen, selecting different drop boxes and settings, until she bumped into a feature that allowed her to rewind. She double-clicked and watched the world spin backward—the welcome mat and stoop and carnation-filled pots staying perfect in the frame, untouched, unmoved. 12:15, 12:14, 12:13 flew by in a blur. At 11:22, she saw a rush, a figure, but the rewind feature moved too fast for her to get a glimpse. She ground her teeth and locked in on the screen. Eventually she had gone back so far that she witnessed herself, leaving the home.

Then she fast-forwarded too quickly, missing the moment yet again.

This tug-of-war persisted for ten minutes before she was able to find a speed that wasn't lightning-quick.

She expected Emerson to be there, his confident walk, his beard, his squinty gaze. She slowed the footage, getting it just right, so each second was lengthy. The black-and-white film gave way to this figure. For a moment. And even after she'd seen it, she inspected the tight shot over and over.

The date on the screen was correct, right?

As was the time?

She paused. Let her eyes trace the edges of the figure—around his head and hair and arms and legs. Then, her pupils swirled around the face. In the multitude of images, one beamed: The tossing of the envelope and then the glancing back, as if to make sure the note had landed perfectly.

Searcy blinked, feeling her eyeballs dry out under the glare of the computer. When she shut her lids, she could still see the outline of the screen, a perfect white box that wiggled in the blackness. The computer hummed. She knew what would be waiting for her when her eyes reopened.

Recess at Theo's school equaled 11:22 in the morning. For years parents had written group emails, which she'd disregarded, about the lack of supervision during break. The parents always cited the occasional fight or broken arm, but Searcy believed those moments were just the collateral damage of letting two hundred students have fifteen minutes of free time. Never did she think that Theo could actually break out from the school, rush home, and make it back. Then again, he did so for lunch every now and then, and for the occasional rehearsal break.

Theo's face glimmered on the computer. She dragged the little arrow over his skin and around his ears, tracing the shape of his head. In black-and-white, he seemed old-fashioned, like a star in an old movie. She recalled those moments when she was pregnant, heading to the OBGYN's office with Keith, having the cold gel smeared over her stomach, and the ultrasound wand dragged over her belly. The heartbeat—more of a rushing sound—warbled through the machine. Then the sonogram photo, which she'd showed to her family and friends, trying to remember where *exactly* young Theodore was located. An arm here, a head there. And now, here she was, looking at another screen, studying his face, developed and clear, but still pining to make sense of it all. So Hoit hadn't done those things, right? Theo didn't have a feather of proof, did he? Was it just a hunch, or a lie to push her toward Emerson?

After studying the video three more times, she moved on, shutting down the program. "Would you like to erase this footage? Doing so will permanently remove it". She clicked *Yes* and then confirmed her answer. She thought of Father Guffey and his speech about signs. She'd always sought them, figured they needed to be hunted. But this wasn't a sign. This was a road map: the highways detailed and measured, distances to scale, with a compass tucked in the far corner.

———————

After dinner, Theo arranged a bowl of fruit in the living room: lemons, pomegranates, and clementines, piling pieces atop one another in a mound of orange, yellow, and red. Theo tried to remember what Mr. Toffler had said about still life paintings—that it was about details: the oranges' skin rough, the lemons' smoother, the pomegranates' almost polished. "Hi, Mom," he said. She wasn't wearing any makeup, and for a second, he thought she looked sick.

"What are you doing?"

"Wanted to paint something for Fallon." Theo wondered if his mom had gotten the letter. He'd checked the front stoop and had seen it was empty, so he gathered it had been snatched, but wind was also a factor.

After recess, he'd settled into his seat in math class and had peered out the window. A gust had attacked the school, whipping the American and the California flag on the pole outside. He'd cringed, hoping the wind just sailed over the letter. "Is everything okay?" Theo asked.

"Why wouldn't it be?"

Theo shrugged.

"Hi, guys," Hoit said. "I'll be upstairs. Gotta make a call."

Theo nodded. His mom did the same.

The room sat still and Theo reorganized some of the fruits.

"Why don't you come sit with me?" She patted the cushion next to her.

"Okay," Theo answered, placing his materials to the side and joining his mom. It took him a moment to get comfortable, working his weight right and left, adjusting his underwear.

She wrapped her arm around him and settled her fingers around his shoulder. Theo stared forward, out the window crisscrossed by panes, at the tall tree with purple flowers in the front yard. He didn't know the name, but around this time of year the tree rained purple petals that stuck between the grooves on the soles of his sneakers. "Did you have a nice day?" she asked.

"Pretty good."

"Anything eventful?"

"Not really."

"I thought you didn't like still-life paintings," she said. "You called them boring."

"Mr. Toffler told me they're the best to practice details. He said it wasn't really about the objects either, but the fire behind them . . ."

She smiled. "Even the quiet has secrets."

"I guess," Theo said.

"Even a little lemon, a perfect little lemon, sitting in a bowl. You do have to wonder, right?" she said. "What's going on in the house where the lemon sits? Who are the people to whom the lemon belongs? What are the things the lemon overhears? Happy things? Sad things? Just quiet?" She brought her hands to her lap.

"I don't know about that," Theo said. "I just hope Fallon likes it. I can't sit on this couch. It's too soft." Theo grabbed hold of the armrest and yanked himself up. He walked across the carpeting and grabbed hold of the canvas and began drawing, seeing every part of every shape, just like Mr. Toffler had said. Whenever he thought of Mr. Toffler, he could hear him, the low voice rolling through his brain. He could hear his chuckle and smell his black-licorice scent. The tutoring had stayed with him, and he couldn't work without his words—"round it out more," "take your time," "be patient," "the difference between good and great artists isn't in what they draw but what they choose to erase." He turned his head back toward his mom.

Darkness fell upon the room, but neither of them made a move to turn on a light. Theo finally yanked a lamp's cord, and a yellow glow flooded the space. His mom looked healthier in the warm hues, but her eyes still seemed heavy and tired, and Theo gathered there was no way she would be that sad if she'd read the letter. It was what she wanted, right? A happy life with Mr. Toffler? It was what they both wanted. And needed. Theo knew many people at school whose parents had divorced, and they had moved on quickly. He figured his mom was too nice to make that move on her own.

All he knew—however stupid it seemed—was that his mom smiled and laughed and seemed peaceful when Mr. Toffler was around. Theo felt the same. Like Mrs. Stanton said, "Maybe tragedy wasn't watching someone you love pass away, but letting them pass away before you could love them." He didn't think Hoit was a bad man, and he didn't have proof of what he'd written, but Hoit didn't look at his mom the way Emerson did, and his mom, he thought, deserved those eyes, those gazes. "What?" he finally said. She had been staring at him.

"Can't a mom watch her boy paint?"

"Do you want some paper? So you can draw."

"No."

"Aren't you gonna be bored?" Theo asked.

"I'm thinking."

"Praying?" Theo asked. "Or thinking?"

"Both."

Theo picked at a scab on his elbow. Everything else on his body had healed fast, including the black eye, but this crust on his elbow was thick. "Every time I start painting or working on some piece of art, I have this idea of what it's going to look like in my head. I have it all perfect. All the shapes and colors. I mean, in my mind, it couldn't be more beautiful. Then I start, and after the first few lines, I realize that it's not going to look like that at all."

"Visions are always different than what actually happens," she said.

"But it's a good idea to try to go after that perfect image, don't you think?" Theo said, scratching at his neck. "And you know what's cool?"

"What's that?" she said.

"No one ever gets to see the first draft, the one in our brains. It just stays there forever and never tells on you."

Hoit's voice thundered as he approached. "All right. Perfect. Take care." He ended his phone call, chasing out the leftover conversation, then dropped onto the couch where Theo had been sitting minutes earlier. "Dark in here, isn't it?" Hoit said. "Want me to click on a few more lights?"

"It's okay," Theo said.

"You gonna paint me and your mother, Theo?" Hoit laughed. "Look at how beautiful we can be!" He sat up straight and wrapped his arm around Searcy. "Gorgeous, right? Better than that ugly painting of that farmer and his wife, you know the one that's so famous?" Hoit laughed again.

"I know the one," Theo said, turning back to his canvas.

Even though it was June, a chill seemed to come from all angles. Emerson wore a gray sweatshirt and sweatpants, two pairs of socks, and he'd piled every blanket he had atop his body. A space heater had been churning, but he worried if he fell asleep, the slight rocking motion would knock it over, setting the boat ablaze. He stayed tight, not moving his limbs, listening to water lap against the hull and the ropes squeak.

Footsteps pattered across the deck, and he thought he heard a voice. He sat up. "Emerson," he heard.

"Searcy?" Emerson said. He jumped out of his bed and worked up the ladder, opening the latch and shoving open the tiny door.

"Did I wake you?" she said.

"No." Emerson helped her down the ladder and flipped on a couple of lights. She took a seat on the edge of his bed, and he joined her. "Sorry it's so cold in here."

"You shaved your beard," she said.

"Yeah, not sure how I feel about it."

"Me neither." She smiled.

"Where do Theo and Hoit think you are?" Emerson asked.

"They are both in bed, sleeping."

The glows of the lamps worked through the cabin, its hues akin to candlelight, orange and soft. "You cold?"

"Yes," she said.

He cranked the space heater to max, angling it toward the bed and tossed Searcy a topcoat that he'd bought at a garage sale, long ago. She slipped into the fabric, losing herself in the largeness of the garment, and eventually the two of them settled into the moment. Had Emerson been aware of her impending arrival, his day would have been a series of panics and flop sweats, but her surprise meant his emotions were startled, too, and he did his best to deal with the instances as they came. For now, they were quiet—the world, the sea, rocking beneath them. The red coils of the space heater put off a gentle amount of light, and Emerson felt the same amount of warmth and wattage within himself. He had pictured Searcy here, in this boat, many times, and now, with her present, he wished he'd thought it through a touch more, maybe hadn't been dressed like Rocky Balboa. As he searched for words to match the situation, Searcy kissed him. Her head tilting suddenly. Her arms that were lost in the overcoat worked around his neck, pulling him toward her. Her lips were firm, digging into his, and he, for once, didn't picture himself from afar; rather, he allowed all the blood in his being to focus on her.

The room was quiet. The water had steadied, the only sound now, the buzz of the space heater.

"I know what I want," she said, pulling away a touch.

"Same here," he said.

She skirted her eyes away from him, then brought them back. "Do you think we could actually have this?"

"Better," Emerson said. "I have a good job in Catalina now. I'm looking at houses with the money from my folks. Things are falling into place. For once."

"This isn't another Madrid story is it?"

"I'll never Madrid you again," he said.

She reached for his hand. "I know at some point, I'm going to head home, but I really don't know how I'm going to move my body. I'm well here."

"I know."

"So Catalina?" she said. "Twenty-six miles away, right?"

"That's right," he said.

"Just like a marathon," she said.

Emerson kissed her. Her lips were salty, thin, and he savored each second. A ripping sensation came over him, as though the skin on his chest wasn't the right fit and was tearing at the seams. With his hand still atop hers, he gripped her fingers hard. His imagination was in better shape than anyone else's: he could imagine a frosty tree in the Green Mountains, a white Tahitian beach strewn with kelp, the cold-cracked face of a Confederate soldier. All of these images were available to him within seconds, ripe with detail, but when it came to Searcy, he struggled to envision the exact hue of her naked body, the texture of her shoulders, and the sensation that would transpire when he ran his hands over the relief map of her figure.

Searcy helped him, tearing at his clothes, and in time, they were together, as one, in a swath of cotton and down, their bodies warming and sweating and contorting and moaning. He said he loved her with his lips pressed against her earlobe, and she returned the three words while scratching at the base of his head.

As invariably disappointing as anything overhyped could be, he wasn't let down. She took control, straddling him, and placing her hands strongly on his chest. Her hair bounced inches from the boat's ceiling, and Emerson didn't thrust as hard as he wanted for fear that he might cause her to strike her head. In fact, much of the sex with Searcy felt foreign; sure, it consisted of the same movement and rhythm, but the intimacy stood worlds apart from anything he'd ever done. He figured it was the way you had sex with someone when you were certain you wanted to see them again—and he concentrated on details, brushing her flesh, stroking her calves, dragging his nails over her goosebump-dotted stomach. She gazed at him, and he gazed back, their eyes holding each other as strongly, it seemed, as their bodies.

Emerson then sat up, yanked her body against his, and dug his hands into her shoulder blades as she tightened her thighs around his waist. He finished this way, hoping he'd lasted long enough, but after almost ten months of foreplay, he was proud that he'd at least felt her legs stiffen and body shudder once.

They lay next to each other, and Emerson touched her alabaster face. Her head tucked against his shoulder, and they stayed silent, in a cocoon of warmth powered by their bodies, the heater, and earlier sentiment. He hoped that this post-sex high would stay with her—the goodness, the skin on skin, the love—and that it wouldn't give way, like it sometimes did, to regret, even rationale.

"I have this picture in my mind," he whispered, treating the ambiance like a bare lightbulb, careful not to crack its shell. "I sometimes think about us all, in a little place. It's October and a light rain is falling, but it's still warm enough to leave the window open, just an inch. We all huddle and listen to the droplets on the pavement, and inhale that perfect smell. Do you have anything like that?" he said. "Any visions that are real enough to almost touch?"

"I do," she said, fanning out her hair.

"It's nice not to be stupid for once," he said.

"It's nice to be stupid together," she said.

Emerson turned and faced the wooden ceiling. It all seemed too good to be true, as perfect as it did with his folks on the skiing trip in Stowe.

––––––––––

The plan had made contact with the world, and Searcy played through the events in her brain. It was her time to pack up the car, something her mother never could do, and while Hoit wasn't abusive, a breakup, even one on good terms, wasn't exactly peaceful. "You guys want another egg?" she asked Hoit and Theo.

"I'm good," Hoit said.

"Yeah," Theo said.

She clicked on the burner and dropped a pad of butter into the skillet. She cracked an egg into the pan and tossed the shell to the sink. Was it worth confronting Hoit? Telling him the truth? Or could she just float off with Theo and Emerson on the sailboat, head twenty-six miles west, and stay in the bungalow forever? She took a breath, watched the egg bubble, and pictured Theo flinging the note—his feet close to the stoop, his hair in his face, his tongue between his teeth, as if urging the letter to land atop the mat.

The scene of the three of them—she and Emerson and Theo on the Catalina shore—recalled *The Pearl*. Coyotito, Juana, Kino. For them, the gigantic pearl had ruined their lives, caused envy and instability. But they weren't ready for it. Too much too soon. But Emerson wasn't Kino; she wasn't Juana; and Theo was no infant. Steinbeck's characters had moved from a zero to a ten in one day. They weren't doing that: they were moving from a six to a ten.

Searcy transferred the egg from skillet to plate. The smell of butter and egg wafted about the kitchen. Hoit folded the newspaper in half, then helped himself to another glass of grapefruit juice.

"Here you are, sweetie," she said, sliding the plate in front of Theo. When the toast popped up, she ping-ponged it between her hands, reaching the table in a hurry. "Hot! Hot!"

Theo laughed.

"Searcy!" Hoit pointed to the burner. "It's still on!"

She hurried over, turning off the flames with a quick turn of the knob. "Got it just in—" The smoke alarm shrieked. "Never mind," she said. The pulse of the alarm was fast and shrill, firing again and again. She and Theo and Hoit tore through the house, flinging open doors and windows, fanning and waving their arms.

Her phone rang. She pulled it from her jean pocket. She hurried outside, far from the screaming alarm. "Hi," she said. "It's not a good time."

"Do you want to meet for coffee?"

"Maybe later."

"Want to run over some details with you. I'm going to head over there to make sure the place is nice . . . and maybe you and Theo can take the ferry. I checked online, and there are a few of them a day. I'm trying to sell my car in the next week, so we'll have a little chunk of change to get things rolling."

"Okay," she said. "I'll talk to you later." She hung up.

The fire alarm stopped, and her ears took a moment to remember what quiet felt like. Theo returned to his cold egg, and she worked her way to the sink and ran the tap until the water was warm enough to rinse the pan and dishes. She watched Hoit and Theo finish up their breakfast. They smiled, and Hoit made a joke about a golfer needing a new pair of pants because "he got a hole in one."

She glanced toward the pool. The sun refracted through the liquid in white, web-like patterns. She wondered when exactly her life would begin again. A person was always one decision away from a different life. She heard Emerson's words, felt his hands and breath and back. She was still surprised at how timid he'd been in bed, almost as if he didn't want to hurt her.

———————

"Let's get our own pizza," Fallon said.

"Sounds good," Theo said. He passed his eyes over Hoit and his mom and then to the back of the restaurant where men shoveled wood into a pizza oven. Fallon was still in her dress from "moving up" (it wasn't graduation until eighth grade, but the seventh graders still had a ceremony). Theo had removed his blazer and tie but still wore his white shirt that he was sure to stain with tomato sauce. "Do you see the guys keeping the fire hot?" he asked Fallon.

"Yeah," she said.

Theo had imagined bringing Fallon out to dinner for a long time, and here he was now. He'd also dreamed about asking her to be his girlfriend. Just the other day he'd Googled "How to ask a girl out" and had landed on some good advice, but now that he was here, he didn't know if he could do it. There was a better than decent chance that she liked the way things were, and if he asked her to be his girlfriend, it would be like taking a gigantic leap over a lava pit. The reward would be breathtaking, but he knew he wasn't that athletic and that he might plop into the hot goo and die. So instead, he got to sit next to her and smell her and laugh with her and wonder with her. He knew about the "friend zone"—he'd seen movies and heard about it from people at school—and by now he was probably its mayor.

Again, he studied the burning wood in the oven. The embers not just red, but incandescent. How hard was it to get a job back there? He jotted down a mental note to tell himself to apply here when he was in high school.

When a quiet moment presented itself, Hoit told a story about almost hitting a man with his car. Lately he'd been telling a lot of stories, and Theo thought that the endings changed a little every time he told them.

Fallon nodded and reached for the Parmesan shaker, rolling it between her hands. Then she turned back toward Theo. "Your face is healing up good," she said.

"Right?" Searcy said. "I wanted to put a little makeup around the side of his eye—just a little foundation, but he didn't want it."

Fallon laughed. "Why not? You already wore some for the play.'

"I like the way it looks," Theo said.

Fallon dropped a lemon wedge into her glass of water and took a sip. "You were lucky Mr. Toffler showed up, you know?" she said. "I mean, who knows if Dylan would've come back or something. . .'

Theo hadn't mentioned this to anyone but his mom and Fallon, and Hoit immediately brought his eyebrows together and scratched at his face with his index finger.

Sweat pooled at the base of Theo's back.

"I thought he was in Madrid." His voice was serious—different from the happy red-checkered tablecloths and Italian music that crackled overhead. "Did you know this?" Hoit whipped his head toward Searcy.

Searcy reached for a breadstick and tore in in half. "Theo mentioned something," she said.

"Why am I always the last to know?" Hoit raised his voice. "Fallon knows, and here I am again."

Theo leaned forward. Heat on his head, his legs, and feet. "It wasn't that big a deal, Hoit. He was driving by. I was limping, so he pulled over."

"Just driving by? I never trusted that guy. Who says they're leaving for Madrid and doesn't even leave the city? What a—"

"Maybe he just wanted to move on and not hurt your guys' feelings," Fallon said. "I know I make up stories to protect people. I mean, he saved Theo, that's for sure. So who really cares, right?"

Hoit loosened his blue tie and exited the booth. "Gonna go wash my hands before the pizzas get here."

When Hoit was a few paces away, Searcy smiled at Fallon. "I'm glad you could be here with us."

"Me too," she said.

The balminess on Theo's body began to evaporate, and his mom moved the conversation along with quick sentences here and there. Theo hadn't wanted to tell Hoit about Mr. Toffler because he'd wanted to see if his mom would tell him. The fact that she hadn't—that and the fact that she seemed happier lately—made him believe Mr. Toffler was not only on her mind, but in her life. The glow, the softness to her skin, it was back, just like when Mr. Toffler would ring the doorbell and exchange "how are you's" on the front stoop. Sometimes he'd offer a joke, and she would offer a laugh, and then at the end of the tutoring session, she'd watch him get into his Volkswagen, and Theo would see her, still inside the home, bring her hand up and wave.

"It's cool the way they keep the ovens going, you know?" Fallon said.

"The way they stoke the fire," Searcy said.

"Yeah," Fallon said.

Theo lined his straw with his mouth and took a pull of cola. He stared at the three men with shovels, feeding the fire, making sure the temperature stayed hot. He knew who stoked the fire of his heart. And he knew about his mother's, too. He was just lucky that he had a fire, because he wasn't so sure everyone did.

Hoit made it back to the table. His face was wet, and he carried a wad of paper towels in his hand, running them over his forehead every couple of minutes. "I'm hungry," he said. "How 'bout you guys?"

"Yes," Fallon said.

And just like that, the waiter rammed his way through the swinging kitchen doors, carrying two pizzas: one sausage and peppers, and one cheese for Theo and Fallon. He placed them on the table and brought out a metal wheel, cutting the pizza into perfect slices.

"I feel bad for you," Hoit said.

"I feel bad for me, too," Searcy said.

"You sure we can't take two cars? You can spend a little time at the auction and then take off if you're not feeling better." Mason had invited him to an ALS charity event—Mason's grandmother had died from the disease—and Hoit didn't want to go alone.

"I want to stay here, in bed. Maybe take a little walk if I feel better."

Hoit kissed her on her hand and took to his car, backed down the driveway, and parked on a side street. Classical music steadied his mood. He rolled down his window and waited. His phone buzzed a couple of times, and he responded to the texts, letting Mason know that he was tending to Searcy. Mason answered politely and told Hoit to take his time.

When patience wore thin, he reached for the ignition. *This is stupid. Searcy's sick. That's not uncommon. Theo's always bringing home germs.* But then he stopped. *Give it a few more minutes. Stay put. She erased all the security-camera footage from the past few days. Emerson must have come over.* Every time he became antsy, he told himself to wait until the end of a song, or ballad, or whatever the finish to a classical piece was called. This went on for thirty-four minutes, and he was glad he'd listened to his premonition, for just as Debussy came to a close, he spotted the flash of Searcy's champagne-colored SUV. He clicked the ignition when she was down the road and shadowed her, doing his best to tail her car, yet simultaneously keep his distance.

He knew it. She was always "playing" sick, like a grown-woman Ferris Bueller. Even her coughs and sneezes sounded cartoonish, and it always bothered him the way the illness didn't come on slowly, like it did with most people, but rather arrived in a fury: she would go to bed healthy one night and awaken the following morning, her housecoat tightened and her forehead "burning up." She didn't like Mason. She didn't like fundraisers. Why couldn't she just tell him that? Why couldn't they just *talk* to each other?

As he drove by parks and restaurants and pedestrians both with and without dogs, he realized that he, too, suffered from the same "stuffing" condition. Both of them crammed their issues in an attempt to snuff them out, leave them to die, but in effect, all they did was fester.

Searcy drove fast but did so in the slow lane. Hoit removed his foot from the gas, letting her put some space between them. As they neared a main boulevard, Searcy tucked into the turning lane and waited for the green arrow. The few cars that provided a buffer between Hoit and Searcy flew through the intersection, heading straight, and Hoit was forced to pull up behind Searcy. He still left a car length between them. He slouched down in his seat, swung his eyes from right to left, and pleaded for the light to change. *Come on, come on, come on! Did she see me? Come on!* Hoit finally swallowed a lump of saliva as the light clicked green.

She continued to sail up Hawthorne, pushing fifty miles per hour, weaving between confused drivers, splitting her time between the two lanes. Hoit pushed along, too, doing forty-three, watching the dashed median line blend into one long yellow strand.

They caught all the green lights. Hoit let a pedestrian with a stroller cross the street, doing his best to keep track of Searcy's SUV. Hoit then hit the gas. She had slowed down and passed the church, working her way down to the mall. She clicked on her blinker and, with no traffic behind him, Hoit dropped his speed to eleven so that he wouldn't wind up close to her. His plan worked. As soon as the arrow pointed green, she turned, and he smashed the gas, sneaking through as the light glowed yellow. Doing so, however, brought him within feet of her bumper, and he thought that he spotted her sunglass-wearing eyes flash up in the rearview mirror. He tapped the brakes, letting space grow between their vehicles. After turning some corners, she puttered outside Java Bistro, working the roundabout, seemingly searching for a parking space. She waited in the middle of the road and U-turned across a double-yellow line. She came at Hoit from the opposite direction, and he propped his head on his left hand and stared out the right window. When the space was open, he made a three-point turn and worked back along the road, passing the Java Bistro, and hurrying to catch up to Searcy. In a minute, she'd driven past the mall and art center and had taken the long road up to Saint John the Baptist.

Hoit parked down below, a block away, and rushed toward the church, holding Searcy in his gaze. She walked across the parking lot and sneezed loud enough to startle him. He dropped down behind an outdoor bronze statue of Mary, before scampering along the side of the church. Most of the windows were stained glass, and many of them were red, not too opaque, and provided a look at Searcy. She made the sign of the cross and prayed. And Hoit, while watching and wondering about her words, dropped his head into his hands. His thoughts came in short bursts: *I want to be a part of this family. I know You still believe in me. Don't You?*

He took a seat on the ground. Heat from the warm bricks transferred into his body, erasing some of the aches that lived in his lower back. He said *thank you* and *please* and *sorry*—what he believed to be the real holy trinity.

"Hoit?" Searcy said.

Hoit jumped to his feet and swallowed. "Yes," he said. "Hi."

"What are you doing here?"

"Oh, I—"

"You followed me?"

Hoit scratched at his neck. He'd shaven about an hour ago, and the razor burn had intensified with the contact of his dress shirt. "I did."

"Why?" she asked.

"I always saw my life a certain way, Searcy. I had an image of perfection in my mind. And we're close. But I haven't been good. I've always been able to make images work, you know? And I possibly failed the biggest one."

"We're not supposed to be an image," she said. "This isn't a PR campaign."

"I know. But everything's an image in a way. All the choices we make."

"So you've been unfaithful?" she said matter-of-factly.

"No, no" he said, lowering his gaze. A petal of a marigold stuck against his polished wingtip. "Yes," he finally said. "I haven't been faithful."

Searcy wrung her hands. "For how long?"

"A while."

Words climbed up her throat. "Could you ever be who I need you to be?"

"I hope so."

"That's not good enough," she said.

Hoit was impressed that she hadn't cried. Hadn't even changed her expression. A passerby would think they were talking about nothing more than weather. "You, though?" he said. "Have *you* been perfect?"

Searcy didn't answer. She walked back into the church and slid into a pew near the altar.

"Do we work?" he shouted. "Or do we just let it crumble?" Hoit stood with his hands in his pockets for a while longer, studying a hummingbird that settled onto a granite statue of Saint John the Baptist. He'd never seen one in repose, and the moment didn't last long before the bird started up again, its wings whirring, and its body vanishing in a blur.

July

Emerson set sail for Catalina Island on a postcard kind of day, but early on, he found the task more difficult than he remembered as a boy on Lake Champlain or on the Fourth of July with his folks, when his father would grow a beard and buy a pipe just to look the part of an old-timey captain. And, about seven miles in, he lost his way and radioed the Coastguard. He explained his situation, and the men were more understanding than he would have been. (It helped that one of the younger guys was also from the Northeast.)

About thirty minutes later, Emerson's boat headed toward the island, roped to a large, powerful Coastguard ship that bred an enormous wake. He looked back at the coastline as if he were leaving it all behind. The word *mainland* summed it up perfectly. It was the *main* land, and his new destination was the *extraland*. Islands were perfect—almost forgotten by the earth, these bits of floating mass.

He hadn't spoken to Searcy in a few days, since they'd shaped the plan: Hoit was to leave on the morning of the third for San Francisco, and she and Theo were to take the 11:00 a.m. ferry into Catalina. She'd been nervous, jittery, but he had faith that she'd come through. He was going "down the slide" to quote his mother. She always said that as a boy, he was overly cautious, and that she would take him to a nearby park and tell him to "go down the slide," but he never would. He'd cried. He'd resisted. Then, two weeks later, when she didn't ask him to, he just climbed the ladder and glided down the polished steel. "When you're ready, you'll go down the slide," she'd always said. "You don't do anything until you feel it," and, for sure, he felt it right now. He'd gripped the bars; he'd tugged himself up to the last slat on the ladder.

The city of Redondo gleamed in the slanted rays. Its large pier stood strong, wearing mussel-clad pillars and rusted beams. People darted along the sand, and he thought of how quiet and tranquil it all seemed, a scene from a Seurat painting—everything and everyone a combination of atoms instead of dots.

Madame Fournier's wish was to be sprinkled atop Catalina's tallest peak, and Emerson whispered a prayer. Let her know he missed her, and told her that if she was doing that "looking down on you" stuff, then she wasn't getting the most out of heaven.

Emerson whipped his head around and took in the shrinking coastline. He tried to pinpoint exactly where Searcy and Theo's home was located. They didn't have an ocean view, but their home wasn't far from the coast, so he matched the surroundings while shielding the sun from his eyes. He made out the area right around Portuguese Bend. Just in case Searcy or Theo was around, or anyone for that matter, he offered a wave. The wave was like "aloha." He was saying hello; he was saying goodbye.

"I'll just take the car service," Hoit said. "I can deduct it."

Lately, Hoit had been narrating his life in the hopes, Searcy thought, that his little words would give way to actual conversation, but it hadn't worked. She hadn't wanted to speak to him because, like he'd mentioned at the church, she hadn't been perfect either. She, too, had failed, but it did comfort her that she actually loved her sin, whereas Hoit had simply sinned while having love at home. What good would conversation bring at this point? Reheated food never tasted the same.

"It's raining pretty badly in San Francisco, so I'm gonna bring this guy." He held out a navy trench coat that she'd purchased for him at Neiman Marcus two years ago for Christmas because he'd mentioned how his cold-weather gear wasn't becoming. Searcy had an older gentleman at the store try on the garment. Even though she'd bought it in early November, the store had already been filled with Christmas trees and Frank Sinatra's holiday album had bounded through the open space. She'd inspected the older man from all angles, brushing his shoulders, feeling the water-resistant fabric with her palms. Hoit had liked the coat so much that he'd donned it over his red pajamas and had worn it all Christmas day.

209

Searcy took a sip of club soda to ease her nausea. The effervescence prickled.

"Can you believe it?" Hoit said. "Rain in July? What's that Twain quote? 'The coldest winter I ever experienced was a summer in San Francisco.' Something like that." Searcy took notice of Theo's laughter, even from all the way downstairs. He'd discovered the *Caddyshack* series yesterday and couldn't be moved from the TV. "So yeah," Hoit said, "just a few days in San Francisco and then two more in Seattle. What about you? What are you and Theo up to this weekend?"

"Not sure," she said. "I may take Theo somewhere for his birthday."

"Really?" Hoit smiled. "Where?" He patted his pockets. "Do you have any mints?"

"In my purse." She cringed as he reached into her bag, his hand sliding past the sealed letter in which she'd explained that she was moving on, that he deserved better, and that she didn't want it to be a "big deal." She'd hated the term "big deal," and she'd hated writing a letter, but for now it was best. She didn't have to send it. She could call him once she'd arrived and settled in, but it had done her good to sit down and articulate her thoughts. She didn't want a thing of Hoit's. No money. No house. She wanted nothing more than what she'd arrived with: clothes, books, and Theo. For now, she told herself she would stay for July and August, see how she liked it, see how Theo liked it.

As Hoit gnashed on the mints, he headed into the bathroom. In the mirror's reflection, Searcy inspected him as he rubbed some mousse through his coarse hair. His phone buzzed. "Yes," he said, pressing the phone to his ear. He took one last look in the mirror and nodded, as if telling himself he looked good. He hung up. "I'm off. Car's in the driveway."

She rose from the bed and followed him down the hall, where his loafers left prints in the carpeting. They walked down the stairs together. When he reached the front door, he hugged her hard, his fingers digging into her bathrobe. "I'll miss you," he said.

She stared into his eyes, those little green discs.

Hoit called out goodbye to Theo.

"Bye, Hoit!" Theo said. "Have a great trip!"

Hoit picked up his suitcase and opened the door. The tapping of his shoes and the wheeling of his carry-on softened as he moved away, reaching the driver, who stood behind the open trunk. "So long," Hoit said, lifting his hand.

Searcy, too, brought her hand high above her head, leaving it there until the car backed down the driveway. A stitch knotted her stomach. She leaned against the doorframe, then grated her bare feet on the straw of the welcome mat.

When she reentered the home, Theo howled with laughter. "Mom, you gotta see this!" This was her last full day in this house. The shower, the bathroom, the packing. Soon, it would seem as if she was checking out of a hotel.

She took a seat next to Theo. Rodney Dangerfield appeared on the screen and before the man even said a thing, Theo giggled. "This guy's face," he said.

An image of Hoit in the back seat of the car flashed in her mind. She could see him in that black sedan. She wondered if he'd finally doffed his coat. He'd put it on too early in the trip, and it was cumbersome and heavy, but probably easier to wear than carry.

"Headed upstairs," Searcy said.

"Okay," Theo said. Then he laughed.

In her room, she pulled a leather duffel from her closet, folded a few pairs of flattering jeans, some blouses, and her favorite pair of dream-catcher earrings. High heels made the cut, though she was certain she wouldn't wear them. Before stashing her perfume in the side compartment of the bag, she opened the bottle and sprinkled a few drops atop her clothes, so that twenty-four hours later, the contents would smell like Chanel rather than leather. Strength came with each fold of each garment, a confidence that *she* was acting rather than being acted upon. She packed a bag for Theo, too, in an old-fashioned suitcase smattered with stickers from trips across the world. For Theo, she rolled up some shorts and T-shirts, a bathing suit with stars on it, and his favorite Lakers sweatshirt. For good measure, too, she packed jackets, sunscreen, and hats. Before long, she'd put together three bags that befitted a vacation more than a sojourn. Her mom had packed many times—Searcy remembered peeking through the pocket door one night to see her mom plop clothes into a huge suitcase and bring it out to the car—but always, the luggage was hauled in and plopped on the bed and unpacked, usually within a twenty-four-hour window. Then, a couple of days later, her father would bring her mother flowers, and Searcy would watch her mom drop the tulips into a vase and tend to them each morning. Sometimes, too, after realizing that running away was off the table, Searcy would add a little note, trying her best to duplicate her father's handwriting, saying how sorry he was, and how much he loved her.

The zip code for Catalina Island was 90704, but Emerson thought "Heaven" would have been more appropriate. Sounds of sea echoed across the land, wildflowers blanketed hills, and the main street was simple, like the little fake town families wrapped around the base of a Christmas tree: a bank, a diner, a bookstore.

Emerson filed down a small street flanked by cozy homes. He'd rented a 1,400 square-foot, furnished place that he'd found online. The real estate woman had been helpful and exuberant, and had told him that she'd place the key under the mat at 16 Lilac Circle.

This was it. The soft yellow place with navy shutters. Lavender wrapped the property, some of the shutters flaked paint, and a brick chimney poked out from the right side.

Emerson opened the small wrought-iron gate and walked to the stoop. He located the key and worked the lock before the door gave way. Everything had a worn-quality to it: old and tired. The brick now pink, the floors needing varnish, the moldings chipped. But it was clean. Bedrooms were bare. Just the essentials: beds, dressers, mirrors. The stove needed to be lit with a match, and Emerson could feel wrinkles of heat from the pilot lights as he explored the kitchen. He entered the larger of the bedrooms and sat on the mattress. In the corner sat a record player with a Perry Como LP already in place. Emerson clicked it on, and the notes cooed and brought a warmth that made the home feel lived in. Even though it was warm outside, the house possessed a hard chill, and he made a fire to rid the house of any coldness.

The house, with a few adjustments—maybe more than adjustments—had potential to be a home. Cleaning and decorating wasn't his forte, but he didn't allow himself to settle in until the place looked good.

A musty smell gave way to a lemony oil that Emerson worked across the floorboards. Dust and time vanished, giving way to bright, fresh panels of hardwood. With each improvement, it became easier to clean, and he gained momentum. Sweeping and tidying up, erasing odors with fresh air and fire.

Emerson leaned on his broom. This quiet wooden enclave would soon light up with stories and laughter, milk spills and Christmas stockings. Prayers and advice would cram the harmonious space, as well as homework and housework, bouquets and books, bedtime stories and dating advice. Emerson ran his eyes over the walls and ceilings, seeing his life unfold in an instant.

He piled some blankets near the couch, where he guessed he would sleep once Theo and Searcy arrived. The process had to be gentle. A steady take-off from an expert pilot—smooth and calm—so that the passengers barely felt the progression from ground to 30,000.

At 9:23 a.m. on July third, Hoit checked in from San Francisco, saying the meetings had gone well and that he'd be headed to the airport in a bit to catch his plane to Seattle. Searcy thumb-typed "glad all is well" and forewent the usual happy-face emoji. With energy buzzing about her body, she took to the kitchen and whirred through the motions: whipped up some eggs and a couple discs of Canadian bacon for Theo.

He ate and told her about how he'd finally beaten the computer in chess. "It's taken me all year," he said. "I got lucky. Made some moves I didn't know would work so well." She hadn't told Theo about the adventure yet, but had mentioned to him yesterday that they were going to have some fun today and certainly tomorrow, for his birthday. "Like what?" he'd said.

"It's a surprise," she'd said.

"Will I like it?" he'd asked.

"How are the eggs?" she asked.

"Everything tastes better when school's out. I never think the end is coming, you know? Like in September, I can never imagine that Christmas break will come, and then it does. And when it's February, June seems miles away, and I think summer will never arrive, but it does."

"Time is undefeated." She inspected the home next door. It looked as the owners were putting in new grass. Within weeks, maybe sooner, the sod's roots would find their way into the dark soil, and the lines between each patch of grass would fade until it always looked as though the grass had been one large, unobstructed lawn.

Theo was right. No matter what, a person couldn't slow time, and in hours she'd be in Catalina. She didn't know much about the island, except for the common stuff: that Mr. Wrigley used to have his Cubs come out for spring training, and the melee with Natalie Wood. "I have to get moving," she said. "Think I drank too much coffee, so I'm going for a run." Already her heart thumped, and her blood beat through her arteries like she was a mile into her jog. "I'll be back in an hour."

"Okay," Theo said.

After swapping her nightgown for a matching tracksuit, she took to the road. She pushed along, her arms swinging, calves pounding. Air cut over her face, and she relished the contact.

When she reached Saint John the Baptist, she didn't press up the hill, instead offering a quick sign of the cross. *I hope I'm following the signs You laid out for me. I think I am. Continue to show me the path, and I will continue to navigate it.*

Her cell rang. It was Hoit. He didn't leave a message, but minutes later he wrote, "Do you think we can chat?"

Searcy began to type back, but deleted her words. Hoit was forming a plan. He was an artisan with words and tact. Sports franchises and Fortune 500s had used his services to recraft images of their stars, and he had once told her that the secret to rebuilding was admission, a sincere apology, and a few obvious steps in the right direction. She knew he was on to the second step.

From here, she descended the hill, letting loose, gliding, her gait covering three feet with each stride. She'd read about how running downhill could be harmful to a person's knees unless embraced, so she allowed herself to be pulled by gravity, gaining speed with each bound.

Catalina rested on the horizon, and sailboats dotted the sea in a broken string of pearls, with white flashes here and there. And in this moment, with the sun at her back, she stopped near the edge of the road and exhaled, letting her body return to form. Her lungs swelled and flattened. She could make Theo happy. She could be happy, too.

Once again, her phone rang. It was Hoit. She hit Ignore and returned the phone to her pocket.

Emerson puttered around the only grocery store in town. One of the cart's wheels never touched the ground, and whenever he turned right, the cart pulled left. Already he'd run over three patrons' toes and had apologized to each of them, motioning to the faulty wheels.

Up and down the aisles he headed, tossing breads and pastas and veggies into the cart. He knew Searcy loved tea and coffee, so he sought ones with fancy packaging and hard-to-pronounce names. Many items were sold out, and when Emerson asked a salesperson why, the woman said, "Tomorrow's the Fourth of July, silly. People bought every last burger and hotdog. Still got the expensive stuff, though. Steaks and the like." Emerson nodded and approached the butcher, asking for three filets. He then took to the produce area and bagged some green beans and potatoes.

As he neared the checkout line, he saw some cartons of cigarettes behind the cashier. He was down to his last pack but decided to forego the usual order. It was time to give his lungs a break.

Two hours to go. That would give him time to pay for the groceries, organize them, fix himself a strong drink, and then make his way to the harbor, where he'd watch the ferry come powering in, its wake formed by two parallel lines of stirred ocean.

Hoit paced in front of Gate 18. He munched on raw almonds and sipped coconut water, trying his hardest to heed Searcy's "eat healthy" advice.

He checked his phone compulsively, hoping for a reply from Searcy, and once, it slipped. A young woman, presumably of college age, reached to the carpet and took a glance at the screen. "All good," she said. She sat back up and passed the phone over to Hoit, readjusting her loose braid. "Is that your family?" she asked. "On the screen?"

"No," he said. "Just some random folks." He smiled.

"Thought you were serious for a second." She crossed her legs.

Hoit glanced at his phone: the image of the three of them huddled around a table at a sushi restaurant had become familiar, just a smattering of colors and faces on which he searched for numbers and contact information. He remembered Searcy had accidentally set the image to his phone in an attempt to send it to her email, and he had just kept it there. A sake bottle rested in the center of the table, half-drunk, and to the side, near an icon for the Internet, Theo held up a Coke.

"Are they with you?" the woman asked.

"No, business trip."

"Must be hard."

"It can be," Hoit said.

"I know how that goes. My boyfriend's in Fallujah right now, on his third tour. I've gotten so used to being apart that even when he's in the next room, I still feel like he's wearing camouflage." The woman stroked her braid. "I'm Avery," she said.

"Hoit."

The two of them shook hands.

She stole another peek at the photo. "How do you get there?"

Hoit downed some coconut water. Through the large-paneled windows to his right, a jet taxied down the runway, lights on its wings flashing. "I don't know," he said, taking a peek at his messages, hoping for a little "1" to pop up.

"Don't want to part with your secrets, huh?" Avery smiled. She reached her hand into her backpack and pulled out a pack of M&Ms. "Want one?" she said.

Hoit's hand started to make the journey, but he stopped mid-arc. He pulled back and rested his palm flat on his jeans. "Trying to cut back," he said.

Avery nodded and tossed a couple into her mouth. A blue one nicked her front tooth before falling to her tongue.

The P.A. system crackled and beeped. An airline employee spouted some news regarding his trip: "Those passengers traveling with us today on Flight 447 to Seattle, I'm sorry to report that one of the wings has a ding, a dimple they call it. We are having inspectors check it out. Thank you in advance for your patience. It should be resolved quickly."

"Resolved quickly . . ." Avery said.

"That's code for two hours. Resolved in no time means three."

"A *dimple*," Avery said. "I've got two of them, and I don't need to be checked out."

Hoit uncrossed his legs and leaned forward, resting his forearms on his knees. He gnawed on more almonds. In the distance, a Boeing 777 launched forward until the nose lifted, and the rest of the body followed. How something that massive could take flight was beyond his comprehension. "We've gotten so used to it all, right?" he said.

Avery turned her head. "What?"

"The way everything just works. Nothing impresses us anymore. I mean, we're just sitting here, waiting to fly through the sky at five hundred miles per hour, while reading our favorite books, drinking, doing a crossword, and everyone's pretty much, like, 'Yeah, okay. What else you got?'"

"It doesn't take long before we get complacent."

Hoit reached into his briefcase and pulled out the newspaper. He tried not to watch Avery eating the M&Ms. He kept his eyes straight, glued to the headlines and articles. He checked his phone again, and studied the picture some more, moving banking icons out of the way to better see Searcy's face.

Searcy stared at the bags. She scanned the boarding passes on her phone. She checked the time and realized that she and Theo needed to leave right now if they wanted to make it. Again, she took a breath and tried to steady her shaking hands by plunging them into her tight jean pockets, but the worry just manifested itself in other ways: a dry mouth, taut shoulders.

"Mom!" Theo called out from downstairs. "Mom! It happened again! A bird!"

Searcy hurried.

A hummingbird had flown into the house through an open window and couldn't find an exit. It fluttered in the corner, panicked, its wings beating, its pointed beak tapping against the wall. "Mom! Get the brooms!"

Every time this happened, about three times per year, she fetched two brooms from the garage and, like chopsticks, tucked the bird safely between the bristles before leading the bird to an opening. As soon as she pulled the brooms apart, the bird would shoot off in a perfect beam. "It's good luck," she'd always say.

"Mom!" Theo called. "It's slamming into the wall!"

Searcy threw open some doors, but the bird stayed high. Feathers small as blades of grass fluttered to the carpet. She told Theo to stay put and hurried to the garage to where she kept the brooms. "Go, go!" Theo screamed. But Searcy knew the bird wasn't going to find its way—they never did. They became scared and flew up and up, into the most difficult position, but only once had Searcy let one die, about a year ago. She remembered that little bird, knocking against the glass, the strokes of its beak hard, almost like a knock. Then, suddenly, it dropped to the carpet, barely making a sound as it landed, and she picked it up her hands. It was hard to imagine that a heart and lungs and blood could pump through such a tiny body.

She grabbed a step stool and two brooms and darted back to the den.

Emerson watched the first ferry navigate the harbor and dock. Elation took over, and in the time it took to tie down the ship, his legs and body numbed. He hoped Searcy and Theo were on this boat. He'd been careful not to text her, and she hadn't texted him. All she'd detailed was that she was arriving on the afternoon of the third, but there were three ferries that were to arrive after midday: a one o'clock, a two-thirty, and a five. The scenario that had haunted him—Hoit's flight getting canceled and him having to return home.

Every passenger that debarked from the Catalina Express was subject to Emerson's assessment. He traced the shape and height and weight and hair color, doing his best to pick up on Theo's wide gait and Searcy's perfect posture. No, no, no. Not them, not them, not them. Old man, young woman. Old woman, young man. Two young men. Two weird-looking men. A fat lady and her fit dog. A thin woman and her fat feline.

Emerson scanned the marina, taking in the masses, making sure no one was looking for him. "Searcy! Theo!" he called. No answer.

The temptation to call and text pulled at Emerson, but he attempted to portray a certain casualness—sipping beer. Searcy had a life to tie up, and he didn't want to pressure her. She would show when she showed. It was that simple.

Imagining them aboard the Catalina Express was as real an image as the sea in front of him. He could see Theo and Searcy gripping the railing on the top deck, their hair tousled by the wind, their faces cool from the air. He took a jaunt around the marina and waited for the two-thirty boat. Sure, he had about an hour and a half before its arrival, but he didn't stray far from the unloading area. A person couldn't be too careful, especially with travel. Sometimes two-thirty meant two-fifteen. Maybe the sea would be glass, and a breeze would aid. Who knew?

A thin layer of fog wrapped the island now, decreasing visibility to the mainland, and Emerson sat on a formation of rocks and studied the way bits of the island gleamed and stretched in the water's reflection. Hills, roofs, birds, and masts—all splayed and distorted in the Pacific.

At quarter after two, a horn bellowed across the sea, and Emerson rushed over to the dock, studying the Catalina Express as it parted tendrils of mist and pushed toward the shore, its speed low, its growl heavy. It honked again, startling a cluster of gulls and pelicans atop a nearby fence. Emerson stood with his hands in his pockets. *Be cool,* he told himself. *Act like you've been here before.* This time he stood right next to the little bridge the crew tacked to the island. He nodded and smiled and said *hello* and *welcome* to some forty people, all seemingly wearing hats and sunglasses and blobs of sunscreen. A crewmember in a white dress shirt with blue epaulettes came out some time later and lifted the small bridge with a crank. "That's it?" Emerson said. "No one else aboard?"

"If there are, they're hiding." He smiled. "Maybe they got one look at you and decided it wasn't worth it." The man kept cranking the pulley. "I'm just joking," he said.

"The five o'clock still on schedule?"

"Yeah, one more today."

Emerson sat back down on a bench and stared at the sea. It seemed gorgeous from this vantage point, but in actuality, it was probably a cesspool, rife with chemicals and plastic, Styrofoam and abandoned fishing nets. He pulled out his cell and flipped through old photos, finding one of him and Theo, minutes before the snakebite. Theo's eyes were closed, and Emerson's smile was open. He then returned to the home screen of the phone and typed a text to Searcy. "Everything okay?" he wrote. Then he backspaced and watched each letter vanish.

Theo walked into his Mom's room. It had taken almost half an hour to free the bird, but she'd done it. She sat at the edge of her perfectly made bed—he didn't understand how she managed to get the covers so creaseless—and he knew by sitting down with her, he'd add some wrinkles, but he did so anyway. "You okay?" he asked.

She put her hand on his knee. "Of course I am. You?"

He kicked off his shoes and brought his feet up onto the bed, then he turned and faced her. "I know you're planning something," he said.

"What do you mean?" she asked.

Theo thought her voice was weak, like it could break if she spoke longer. "I see the bags."

She paused. "Are you happy?" she said.

Theo gazed at his mom. He couldn't tell if she'd put on a lot of makeup or if her cheeks were just naturally red today. He grabbed her wrist. Here, without Hoit or society, he didn't have to worry about being perceived as a mama's boy, and that was a relief. "I just feel bad for you, Mom."

"Why?" she said.

"Because *you* could be happy, and all you do is worry about me being happy."

"But are you?" She lifted her chin.

Theo didn't think happiness was that easy. He thought it was like hunger, that you needed to fill yourself with enough calories each day. "I'd be happier if you were happy," he finally said.

She smiled with her lips. "I thought we could take a little vacation. Stay in Catalina with Emerson," she said. "See what it's like. Maybe stick around if we like it."

"I think that sounds perfect."

"You won't miss this life? Things are going to change, Theo. It's not as easy as you think."

"What's so great about this?" he said. "I see the way you are when you're with Emerson. It's the same face you have in the photos with Dad. I never saw it before." Rays of sun found the white bedspread, forcing Theo to squint.

"Sometimes I just think with your dad . . . well, it was so nice, but maybe it's been made perfect by his passing, you know? Who knows if it would have stayed like that?"

"We don't know anything, Mom."

"What about Fallon? Won't you miss her."

"Her house is like ten miles away, so it's almost the same. She loves boats. She can visit." He paused. "Remember when I was little, and you were working a lot, and you always said, 'We're in this together'? Do you remember that?"

She placed her hand on top of his, and Theo let the heat transfer to his knuckles and fingers. Then he hopped off the bed.

Once again, the airline pushed the flight back another thirty minutes. Hoit texted Searcy, venting his frustration, thinking that maybe some sort of causal subject might be worthy of a reply, but it didn't go as anticipated. He wondered about his wife and Emerson. She'd said she was going to do something with Theo; however, the kid wouldn't object to an afternoon with his beloved "artiste."

Hoit checked his e-mail, then his texts, and after that, he scanned his banking account. There was some new activity from Searcy, from hours before, and it was there that he spotted that she'd purchased two, first-class tickets for the Catalina Express. Hoit's pulse climbed, and it seemed that his heart was too large for rib cage, the organ seemingly pushing and prodding at the bones underneath his flesh. What was she going to do in Catalina? Sure, she'd mentioned a little something for Theo's birthday, but this was unlike her, and as with all things unlike her, he detected the impressions of Emerson's paint-stained fingerprints.

Hoit shot up.

Avery said something, but the world had become one cacophonous note, and all the noises and sounds swirled: beeps, rolling bags, coughs, conversations, PA announcements, sneezes, shuffling, zippers, newspapers.

Hoit started running. He hadn't moved at this speed since he was a kid, back in the Bayou, in his worn-out saddle shoes and backwards LSU cap. His body and momentum worked across the shiny airport floor, wending his way through duffels and suitcases, screaming at folks to *movemovemove!* His bag, his limbs, his heavy coat—it all dragged forward toward the ticket counter. As an employee hammered on the keyboard, a scenario opened in Hoit's mind: a spark he tried to snuff before it found kindling. A cold life without Searcy. *How would his world change? How wouldn't it? Would he ever find someone else like her?* Hoit balled his fists and slammed his garment bag atop the counter. "It's an emergency," he said. His voice sharp. "I need to get back to LA." The ticket person lifted her hands off the keyboard, looked at the woman she was assisting, as if asking for permission, and then proceeded to help Hoit. Hoit breathed hard through his nose and felt his face and limbs heat at a rapid rate.

The woman continued to type and search and scroll, and Hoit's eyes worked over to a TV. A news ticker dragged along the bottom: the rain wouldn't relent this week, a man in Oakland had set fire to his home with homemade sparklers, the DOW had fallen 104 points and wasn't done.

The five o'clock ferry arrived precisely at one minute after five.

This ship was smaller than the other two, and instead of being white with blue trim, its paint was red with yellow accents. Emerson knew the drill by now: the deep horn would sound twice, a crew-member would hurry to the exit ramp, lower the small drawbridge, and people would debark.

It played out just as Emerson believed. The horn, crew member, bridge. The passengers smiled and laughed and took in the island. All thirty-nine of them. He counted. "That's it for today?" Emerson said to a crewmember, mostly to confirm what he already knew.

"Yes," the mustachioed man said. "Tomorrow we take the day off for the Fourth." He nodded and unhooked the drawbridge.

"Back at it on the fifth, though, right?" Emerson said. He pictured the steaks he'd left out on his kitchen counter, so that they'd be room temperature when they hit the grill. He saw the table he'd set, and the wine he'd opened and let breathe.

"You bet," the man said.

Then Emerson heard a voice. He wasn't sure if his imagination willed the sound—the high-pitched laugh of Theo, and the light, mellow voice of Searcy talking about how she'd left her sunglasses behind—but he *did* hear it. And it lingered between his ears long enough for him to believe it was real. "What's that?" Emerson asked.

"Oh," the man said, leaning his head into the ship. "Oh," he said. "Two more!"

"Really?" Emerson said.

"A woman and a little kid. I must've miscounted."

Emerson rushed across the loading bridge and whipped his head around the ship's opening to see for himself. There they were. Exactly as he'd imagined. They didn't see him yet, and he took in these moments, as they approached: Searcy in a white blouse tucked into tight black jeans, sunglasses atop her head, and Theo wearing a red, long-sleeved shirt paired with cargo shorts. Emerson took a few steps back and waited, their sounds and beings nearing with each tic of the clock.

The rest of the world melted away—sounds, sights, even the sensation of being alive. All his energy poured from his pupils, and he remembered how Madame Fournier had once said that you could tell someone you loved them through a single gaze. Searcy then saw Emerson, too, before Theo, and picked up the pace. Her eyes shared the same focus. When she reached him on the loading bridge, he dug his hands into her silky blouse and wrapped his thumbs through her belt loops. He shut his eyes. He exhaled.

There were significant times in life where one needn't be retrospective—where one knew the beauty in the now, and this was one Emerson would hold close to him, as close as he held Searcy in these very seconds.

———

Theo cut into his steak and ran his eyes over his mom and Emerson. He liked the table in this house better than the one back on Whiffletree Lane, because it was small and circular, and it seemed like everyone was together and that no seat was more important than another.

A fire blazed behind them, and even though it was chilly, Emerson opened a nearby window, because the chimney didn't do a good job of swallowing the smoke.

Theo could see himself in this house, in this town, too. It was a lot like him: small, simple, and as contained as a snow globe.

He thought Emerson seemed nervous, fidgety, the way a person could act when they got what they wanted but now had to see it through. He did seem to relax, though, when he told a funny story about how his mom thought he wanted to be an architect when he was a kid because he'd bought a nude photo of a woman from a kid at school and taped her in a coffee-table book on architecture. His mom hadn't known, and Emerson spent a lot his time studying the photo after school, and his mom thought he was super interested in the book itself, so she'd started buying all sorts of books on architecture and architects from all over the world.

Emerson talked about his family with a lot of love, and seemed sad when the story ended, taking a big gulp of wine. Twice, Theo saw his mom touch Emerson's hand, and it didn't feel strange, not even for a second, mostly because he had never seen her do that with Hoit, so he had nothing to compare it to.

After dinner, they all did the dishes together. Emerson's place didn't have a dishwasher—it didn't even have a TV yet—so they set up something of an assembly line: Emerson washed, Theo dried, and his mom returned the glasses, cutlery, and plates to cabinets and drawers.

Emerson then filled them in on the new job. That he had access to his own golf cart, and that he was in charge or four painting residencies. He said the pay was solid, and that they were in good shape. Searcy smiled and touched him between the shoulder blades as she reached to set down a serving platter on the counter behind him.

"I saw a store that was for lease in town," she said. "The last one as you exit the harbor. Thought it might be nice for a little clothing boutique. A bunch of ready-to-wear fashion."

"I love that," Emerson said, rinsing some suds from his hands. "What would you call it?"

"Theo and Me," she said.

Emerson smiled. "Got a nice ring to it."

"I don't want to be part of a woman's clothing store," Theo said.

"Just dry the plates," Searcy said.

"Yeah, just dry," Emerson joked. "You ingrate."

After about ten minutes of cleaning up, they sat on the couch by the fireplace and talked about what they would do in the morning.

"What does the birthday boy want?" Emerson asked.

"A hike maybe?" Searcy said. "Didn't you say something about scattering Madame Fournier's ashes?"

"Yes," Emerson said, "but that doesn't sound like a birthday celebration."

"We could do that," Searcy said.

"Yeah, that would be cool," Theo said.

"I think it's long way, though. Maybe too much for tomorrow, don't you think?"

"Spoken like someone with smoker's lungs," Searcy said.

"Let's do it!" Theo said.

"Okay," Emerson said. "There's a fox that we should be on the lookout for, a gray one, that's native only to Catalina. Not sure if we'll ever see it, but we should keep our eyes peeled."

"I packed my binoculars," Theo said.

"There's plenty to see besides that, though, even if we don't get lucky," Emerson added.

Searcy smiled.

The fire popped and fizzled, and eventually went out.

Emerson said something about damp logs, and returned to the fireplace to rebuild it from scratch. Theo thought that they, too, were something of a fire, and right now, they were at the same stage as the one Emerson constructed: newspaper and twigs, but eventually the big pieces would catch, and then it would be easy to throw on any log and watch the flames conquer the wood.

Searcy let Theo hike ahead of them. Her logic was twofold: one, she liked that her boy was enjoying himself, away from the computer, and taking in nature, and two, she wanted to kiss Emerson. She wasn't quite sure how to balance her affection last night in front of her son.

When the distance was great enough, she turned and wrapped her hands around Emerson's back and pulled his head hard to meet hers. This time, he was far less timid than he'd been in his bed, putting pressure on her lips and clutching her loose hair in a tight fist. "I know this is awkward," she said. "But it won't be soon."

He nodded.

After that, they carried on, and she thought that maybe later tonight she would send Theo to the store with a long list.

The hike was screensaver perfect: swaths of orange poppies, saline smells, and a three-hundred-sixty-degree view of the Pacific (with the occasional dolphin pod). After the first couple of miles, they were done running into people on the trail who'd opted for a casual Fourth of July hike. When three solid hours passed, the trail narrowed into a thin strip, and they arrived at Mount Orizaba's peak. Emerson sat on a stone, closed his eyes, and muttered a few words to himself before bringing the collar of his shirt up to his face and wiping his eyes. Then he stood, took the urn from his backpack, and reached inside, tossing handfuls of granules into the hot sky, where most of the ashes mixed with the thin air, and some fell to the ground in a soft hush. "So long," Emerson said. They all sat in silence.

Searcy had ignored the last few calls from Hoit, but this time, he texted, and she stepped away from Theo and Emerson to take in his words: "How's Catalina?"

Her stomach pinched. She read the text again to make sure. She wouldn't put the call off. She would do it now. Enough positive energy surrounded her; she could take the hit. "Be right back," she said, noticing that Emerson and Theo had honed in on a hawk in the distance. Emerson's hand was outstretched, pointing, and Theo did his best to pick up what Emerson had spotted. "There," Emerson said. "Right there." The two of them laughed and Searcy enjoyed the sound.

She hurried down the trail a quarter mile. Half the time, she couldn't get service on Hollywood and Vine, but here, not an issue. She leaned against a boulder and told herself to be strong. Hoit picked up after half a ring. "I knew that would get you," he said.

"I need some time away from you. Okay?"

"Running away, all your secretive shit. You're such a coward."

"I don't want to fight with you, Hoit. I don't want anything. I just want to be alone with my boy right now."

There was a long pause. Searcy could hear Hoit breathe.

"And him. To be alone with him," Hoit said.

"Emerson, you mean?"

"Yeah," he said.

Searcy rubbed her foot on the path, zigging and zagging. Just as she was about to answer, Emerson and Theo turned the corner, bounding down the trail, with Emerson singing "Happy Birthday" in an operatic-style voice.

"That's him isn't it?" Hoit asked.

"It is," she said, scanning the two of them as they approached.

"How could you do this?" Hoit said.

Searcy had many words—some about how *they* did this, how *he* did this; some about how maybe they didn't do a thing because there never was something to break in the first place—and she was sure quips would come her way in future days, and that she'd want this moment back to deliver the perfect sentence, but she didn't care. She had her two guys on the same trail, paces behind, and all this Pacific, all this air, all this freedom. "Goodbye, Hoit," she said calmly, bringing her finger to the End button.

A buzz. A lightness. She turned, facing Theo and Emerson and decided to have some fun, pushing ahead and jogging quickly down the hillside. Within thirty seconds, her muscles fired perfectly, and she could feel the backs of her heels nearly striking her hamstrings. She laughed, and heard the guys behind her, trying to catch up.

Hoit miles away, all that ocean between them. Her little house on Lilac Circle. Her possible clothing store. Dinner at the round table every night.

She laughed harder.

Ran faster.

Took a turn.

Leaned hard right.

She churned, undid a few bobby pins in her hair and let the strands unravel. The trail thinned. Her feet struck in blows akin to her heart's pulse—solid thuds of new Nikes on loose dirt. Then, her back foot slipped, her ankle gave way, and she lost her balance. She stumbled for a few paces, her body doing what it could to right itself, but her momentum was too great, and she began to fall: seeing the ground in slow-motion, the red dirt coming into focus, and her body whooshing across its surface. She extended her hands, felt a snap in her wrists, and tumbled to the edge, swinging her arms to clutch anything that would aid her—a plant, an exposed root, a sturdy rock. But her fingers whiffed, missed, and she rolled over the trail's edge, digging her nails into soft dirt. Emerson and Theo shouted. She saw them dive towards the cliff's edge, but it was too late. Her body lost contact with all surfaces. Air swallowed her limbs and blasted over her ears.

Theo sat in the waiting room at the hospital, hearing the beeps, voices, and footsteps that played around him. He couldn't process much of anything. He was numb. Every now and then, though, he'd pick up on something—come to his senses—and feel Emerson's hand on his back or hear Emerson answer to or introduce himself as "Hoit," which he had been doing since entering the hospital—since the accident, actually. Theo thought he was doing this so no one would contact Hoit, and they would be able to get back to Catalina without seeing him, and it seemed to be working.

Theo couldn't stop replaying the day: the early morning, tearing the wrapping paper, opening up the chess set from Emerson, the hike, his mom, in her turquoise T-shirt, looking over at him, then slipping. Then falling, men and women with equipment, shouting. A helicopter. Long Beach Memorial. It was the most real image his brain had ever held. How could his mom have been so stupid? Why couldn't she have waited for them? Why did she sprint on a tiny trail?

"Do you think she's going to—" Theo started to say.

"No," Emerson said with authority.

"Okay," Theo said. He remembered to breathe. There was a clawing at his heart, and he tried to say more but found little breath.

Finally, after two hours, a doctor approached. "Come with me," she said. The doctor walked fast enough for the tail of her lab coat to lift. Her face was plain and her dark blue eyes seemed more pronounced because of her pulled-back hair. "I'm Dr. Retchy," she said when they reached a small office.

"How's my mom?" Theo yelled.

"How is she?" Emerson said.

"She's okay," Dr. Retchy said. "She regained her consciousness. She's incredibly lucky. A fall like that, and she could have had severe brain damage or paralysis, or both."

"What is it?" Theo said.

"She has badly broken both her legs. She will need immediate surgery. We don't know how her legs will heal. She's young and healthy, so that's good. But she will need lots of care."

"Will she walk again?" Theo asked, his voice weak.

"We don't know exactly how her legs will rebuild, but I'm optimistic," Dr. Retchy said with restraint. "I'm astounded that she doesn't have any spinal issues. My first thought was that at the very least, she'd have fractured her spine with a fall like that. It's a miracle." One of Dr. Retchy's eyelashes fell to her cheek, and Theo stared at the tiny curve.

"Can we see her?" Emerson asked.

"Not right now," Dr. Retchy said. "She's being prepared for surgery. She'll be done with it all in about six hours. I would . . ."

A shrill sound seized Theo's ears, a flat line that pushed away the world as Dr. Retchy kept speaking. The sound overpowered her words, stretched and bent, and Theo remained frozen while the doctor's mouth continued to flap, the stethoscope around her neck, swaying as she moved her arms.

Emerson nodded and the lines on his forehead hardened.

The doctor kept speaking to him, and Theo zoomed in on a photo in Dr. Retchy's office. It was a boring one—a tropical beach, white sand, turquoise water, a single palm tree. The photo was all about perfection, but sometimes perfect was too much. And Theo didn't even think it existed. Somewhere on this beach, maybe even just a few feet to the right of the palm tree, lived sadness. Maybe a mom who'd lost her daughter to cancer, a father who couldn't stop drinking, a kid who'd just seen his mom break both her legs. The heartache was always there, as present as the sand, as present as the salt water.

Eventually, Emerson led Theo out of the office and waiting room. The two of them sat on a bench in the dim parking lot, staring out across the cars and nothingness. Almost on cue, in the distance, the first few fireworks shot up and thundered, their colors fanning over the roofs of nearby homes. Theo turned and watched the reds and blues glow in Emerson's dark pupils. There was a seriousness to Emerson's face—this look presented itself every now and then, mostly when Theo was sad and Emerson tried to help, but it was always quick to lighten with a smile or an expression, and Theo hoped all of this wasn't too much for him, that he wasn't regretting leaving an easier life on the boat with his paints and all the pretty girls. "Are you still happy about this?" Theo thought of saying, even kind of did, but Emerson didn't hear it. Sometime later, Theo brought his head against Emerson's shoulder and shut his eyes. There were intermittent pops and rips of fireworks, even the occasional passerby who said, "Wow," but Theo kept his lids down through all of it and felt Emerson's strong hand work across the back of his neck.

"Searcy," Emerson said from the kitchen. "What do you feel like for lunch?"

Theo popped into the room, leaning against the door. "We have tuna salad or some rice and chicken," he said.

"I'll have the tuna salad," she said loudly.

"Got it," Emerson said.

Dishes clanged and cabinet doors slammed.

"Your skin is so white, Mom," Theo said. "Your lips are still red and pretty, but your face is like a ghost's."

"Probably the meds."

"Just never do that to me again, okay?" he said.

It had been two days since Searcy had left the hospital; she'd even been cleared to return to Catalina. She rested now, on her bed, her cast-covered legs atop a bolster pillow that Emerson had borrowed from a neighbor. All this time in bed, but her mind was anything but idle. "I'll try not to," she said.

"Are you happy?" Theo whispered.

She smiled. "Not really. Not right now." Her Vicodin-laced dreams were a re-run: Hoit, in the empty house, her running, her falling. Her sin punished quickly. Sometimes karma took the backroads; other times it took a shortcut. Almost twice a day, Emerson would shake her from a nightmare, and she would gasp for air so hard that it would manifest itself in a coughing fit. She told him it was the fall, and he would lay next to her, stroking her arms until she returned to sleep.

"But you're alive," Theo said.

"I know," she said. "Are you happy?"

"I think I will be."

"That's good," she whispered.

"You're going to heal," he said. "Bones heal good. And the doctors all said it went perfectly."

Searcy imagined her bones, deep below her tissues and tendons, the metal and screws fastened, the fractures repairing, the calcium and collagen lining up with one another. They were healing currently, at an imperceptible rate, but nevertheless, she was getting stronger minute by minute, and it made her smile that her body could possibly bounce back in a matter of months.

Emerson entered with a tray of food: a plate of tuna salad, a couple pieces of whole wheat toast, and a glass of juice. There was even a little marigold off near the fork and napkin that Emerson had snipped and placed directly above the dish.

There was a thick silence for few moments and Searcy filled the void by offering sounds, letting Emerson know the food was good.

She'd never seen Emerson look so tired. There were dark circles under his eyes, almost purple in color, and he had been cooking and cleaning round the clock. His beard had grown back quickly, but it was unkempt, especially around his neck and cheeks, and whenever he sat down, he emitted a long breath.

The pang of sadness in her chest eventually worked its way to her eyes. She didn't move. She angled her head towards her plate and kept it there, so that if a tear did escape, it would be unnoticeable.

"Theo, why don't you get the chess set?" Emerson said. "We can play right here and keep your mom company."

"Sounds good," Theo said. "You got so lucky last time."

"You were too good a teacher," Emerson said.

In time, the board was out, and they moved pieces, and her ache left her body. She popped another pill after her lunch and found some peace with her head on the pillow and Theo and Emerson chatting about strategy. Theo said Emerson's defense was weak—he actually used the word "porous"—which made her happy.

"Maybe I'm baiting you," Emerson said.

"Maybe you just stink." Theo laughed.

Searcy's body softened and sleep came her way. Emerson and Theo's voices faded through her subconscious and into her dream, and she imagined herself doing everything as the doctors said—the rest, the pills, the therapy, the walking, and so on.

It was late evening, after dinner, and, like usual, Emerson and Theo did the dishes. They played some music on Searcy's phone, a song called "Baby Workout" by Jackie Wilson, and when the singing would stop and instruments would take over, especially the louder brass ones, Theo would saunter out to the living room, where Searcy rested in her wheelchair, and dance in a silly, old-white-man twisting motion. Her smile, like her health, Emerson thought, was improving. Her grin was nowhere near as large as it had been the day she'd stepped off the ferry, nor was it as full as it had been at the top of Mount Orizaba.

As Emerson adjusted the volume on Searcy's phone, he noticed a new text message on her screen. "Hoit," it said. He scanned the room, and seeing that her eyes were firmly fixed on Theo, he read the message. "I miss you," it said. "I love you. I think we can work whatever it is out."

"Let me turn this up a little bit," Emerson said. He lowered his head to the phone and pressed Delete. His pulse clipped and his index finger trembled as he squished it against the screen to confirm his command. Then *poof*, it vanished. He took a deep breath and re-inspected the room.

Afterward, they watched TV (Emerson had finally purchased one) in front of a weak fire: the news first, then a couple of game shows. Searcy asked Emerson if he could wash her, and he agreed, wheeling her to the bathroom, careful not to bump her casts into any of the furniture. Theo continued flipping between a show on Canadian wolves and a sitcom with piped-in laughter.

Emerson flipped on the lights, closed the bathroom door, and ran the water. He sliced his hand through the stream until he felt Searcy's perfect temperature, a place between hot and scalding. He lifted her from the wheelchair to the edge of the bathtub, and she placed her feet on the floor, while Emerson rolled his pants up before stepping inside the tub. Then they worked through the usual sponge-bath routine.

She unbuttoned her jean shirt, removed her black bra, and Emerson soaked the washcloth under the spigot and ran the fabric over her skin. The heat always turned her flesh rosy, and he savored the hue. She sighed, and Emerson worked the cloth across her back, over the ridges of her spine, and along the sharp outlines of her shoulder blades.

Eventually, he poured a few droplets of body wash onto his palm and massaged the suds into her skin. When she exhaled, Emerson shut off the water to better hear her. He knew everything he needed to know was in her face at this very moment. Her expression wore her mood, her outlook—did she have buyer's remorse? Or was she happy?

He turned his head as he rinsed her back and brought some water to his forehead to soothe himself. In the reflection of the medicine cabinet's mirror, he spotted her face. A silhouette. Her eyes closed. Her lips outstretched, bent in a smile. She was soft, peaceful, and he erased the remaining soapy suds on the nape of her neck in a quick swipe before bending down and kissing her below her ear. This section of skin was still hot from the water, and he allowed his lips to linger.

She twisted her head to meet his lips. They kissed in the warm bathroom, steam curling off the hot cloth and playing near their faces. Afterwards, when they were inches apart, Emerson looked at her. And she stared back. He sat on the edge of the tub with her, and they piled their hands together. "You survived," he wanted to say. He'd wanted to say that so many times, but he kept the words to himself.

"Guys," Theo yelled. "There's a funny movie on!" He waited a few seconds. Then he laughed loud enough to silence the TV's volume. "Guys! Want to come watch it with me?" His voice worked through the closed bathroom door.

"That sounds nice," she said. "Don't you think?"

"It does," Emerson said.

The bathtub faucet dripped behind him.

"Maybe some popcorn! Do we have popcorn?" Theo shouted.

"I can get some," Emerson yelled back, his voice ricocheting off the bathroom tiles, then falling still.

Emerson returned to rinsing Searcy, and minutes later, her skin was shiny and a trace of lemon swirled about the air. Emerson rose and pulled a large towel off the hook on the back of the door and wrapped her in its mass, wicking away the beads of moisture. Some flecks of water had settled onto Searcy's cheeks, and he brought the corner of the towel to her face to wipe them away. As he worked the towel gently across her nose, he noticed that she didn't possess smile lines, and he wondered if that was due to an expensive cream or just years of unhappiness. There was some permanent tension in her forehead and jaw, however, in which Emerson could detect the inner her—the struggle, the loss. He thought of her as an M.C. Escher work—there would always be something new to savor, and he would never tire of mapping her features or discovering her secrets.

Eventually, he wheeled Searcy back to the living room, next to Theo, and they watched TV together. "Gonna run to the store real quick and pick up some popcorn. Be back in a jiffy." He thought it was dad-like using the word "jiffy," and it made him smile.

"Hurry back," Searcy said.

"Hard to stray far on an island," Emerson said, grabbing his flannel and rushing outside. When he reached the end of the walkway, he turned, thinking he'd left the door open. But he hadn't. It was shut and sealed.

With only nine minutes until the store closed, he permitted himself a few seconds to gaze back at his place, right through the main window that was crisscrossed by panes. There they were: the two of them, sitting with their backs towards him, their heads rocking, soft laughter popping free.

Emerson stayed put, firmly on Lilac Circle, soaking it in—the warmth of the fire, the yellow lights, his family—all spilling from the window and onto the street.

ACKNOWLEDGMENTS

LIKE MOST BOOKS, THERE is only one author, but truth is every published work is a team effort, and I would like to thank these people that help, inspire, and keep my overall "happiness index" strong: Racquel Henry, Maggie Morris, my VCFA crew, Tim Antonides, Kali VanBaale, Courtney Ford, Donald Quist, Jennifer Cohen, Sophfronia Scott, Susan Solomon, Shirley Omori, Christine Donlon, Lyndsay Hall, Margaret Evans, Christina Gustin, Christiana Ward, Cheryl Wright-Watkins, Kevin Grosher, Adam Walch, Charles Maceo, the Surfwriters, Little Lou, the Los Angeles Lakers, my students and their amazing families, Chaz Cipolla, Kim Holdsworth, Cris Boggiano, my South Carolina family, my French family, Tim Johnston, Cassie Ciopryna, Elizabeth Schmuhl, Laurie Alberts, and Niles Reddick.

Huge gratitude to Kelly Huddleston, David Ross, and Open Books for seeing the value of this novel—and the value of fiction, storytelling, and art. I cannot thank you enough.

And, of course, thanks to you, dear reader. You are the only reason I am in this gorgeous position, and I do not take that for granted.

www.ingramcontent.com/pod-product-compliance
Lightning Source LLC
Chambersburg PA
CBHW031945010726
47493CB00007B/2083